LITTLE, BROWN

LB

LARGE PRINT

For a complete list of books by James Patterson, as well as previews of upcoming books and more information about the author, visit JamesPatterson.com or find him on Facebook.

BLOWBACK

JAMES PATTERSON
AND BRENDAN DuBOIS

LITTLE, BROWN AND COMPANY

LARGE PRINT EDITION

Little, Brown and Company
Hachette Book Group
1290 Avenue of the Americas, New York, NY 10104
littlebrown.com

First edition: September 2022

Little, Brown and Company is a division of Hachette Book Group, Inc. The Little, Brown name and logo are trademarks of Hachette Book Group, Inc.

The publisher is not responsible for websites (or their content) that are not owned by the publisher.

The Hachette Speakers Bureau provides a wide range of authors for speaking events. To find out more, go to hachettespeakersbureau.com or call (866) 376-6591.

ISBN 9780316499637 (hc) / 9780316473439 (large print)

LCCN 2022941568

Printing 1, 2022

LSC-C

Printed in the United States of America

"If you want to test a man's character, give him power."

—traditionally attributed to
President Abraham Lincoln

BLOWBACK

CHAPTER 1

JOHANNESBURG, SOUTH AFRICA

IT'S A BRISK autumn day in June in one of South Africa's largest cities, and thirty-year-old Benjamin Lucas is enjoying an off day from his South African Diamond Tour. He stands just under six feet, with close-trimmed dark-brown hair, and has a muscular physique from hours in the gym he likes to keep hidden by wearing baggy clothes. On the all-inclusive, ten-day excursion package, he and the other eleven members of his group had walked Pretoria, visited Soweto, the famed site of the decades-long simmer, eruption, and fight against apartheid, and spent a day and night up north at the Madikwe Game Reserve, *oooh*ing and *aah*ing at the sight of elephants, hippopotamuses, and zebras from the comfort of their air-conditioned Land Rovers.

Alone now in Johannesburg, Benjamin keeps up his appearance as a travel writer on an off day, while knowing deep down that if this day ends in failure, the best outcome would be an arrest and expulsion after some torturous days in the custody of South Africa's State Security Agency, and the worst outcome would be a slit throat in some back alley.

Yet Benjamin keeps an open and happy look on his face as he saunters into the popular section of Johannesburg known as Cyrildene, the city's Chinatown. At the entrance to the neighborhood on Friedland Avenue, he stops and takes a photo of an impressive arch ornately styled to resemble a pagoda.

There are close to a half million Chinese living in South Africa, most of them in and around Johannesburg. A few blocks in, he feels like he's in his hometown of San Francisco. The Chinatown residents, the tourists, the outdoor stalls, the blinking neon signs in Chinese characters marking shops and bookstores, restaurants, and tearooms, the scents of all the cooking bringing him back to his childhood, before he went to Stanford, before he got his master's degree in Asian Studies at Boston University, and before he joined the Central Intelligence Agency.

Benjamin makes it a point not to check the time because he doesn't want any watchers out there to think he's heading for a meeting, which happens to be the truth. But his legend as a freelance writer is airtight, with real articles written under his cover name searchable on the internet, and because everything he's carrying in his shoulder bag marks him as what he pretends to be: a travel writer.

His wallet contains his identification in his cover name of Benjamin Litchfield: California driver's license, a San Francisco Public Library card, credit cards from MasterCard, Visa, and American Express, as well as loyalty cards for Walgreens and Chevron, and other bits and pieces of what's known as wallet litter.

He's wearing white sneakers, tan jacket, plain khaki pants, and a bright-yellow baseball cap from South Africa's football team, nicknamed "Bafana Bafana."

If examined, his Olympus OM-D E-M5 Mark III digital camera would reveal lots of photos of his tourist activities. There are only a few pieces of technical equipment in his possession, including a tracer in the camera's electronics, so the CIA station at the Johannesburg consulate knows his location.

And then there are his Apple earbuds. If they were taken from his ears without his approval, they would continue to play tunes from his iPhone, contained in his travel bag.

But now, securely in place, they are playing a double role: thanks to overhead, highly classified Agency HUMMINGBIRD drones, the bud on the left will send out a high-pitched tone if it detects surveillance radio frequencies used by officers of the State Security Service, and the one on the right would send out a low-pitched tone if it detects surveillance radio frequencies used by officers of his real opponent today, China's Ministry of State Security.

Benjamin casually checks a clock in the window of a store selling medicinal herbs and powders.

It's 10:45 a.m., and in fifteen minutes, he's to meet an officer from the Ministry of State Security—their equivalent of the CIA—who wants to defect to the United States, and both earbuds are silent, meaning everything seems to be going well. A countersurveillance team from the Agency ghosted his route earlier, and if they had spotted anything amiss, he would have been instantly contacted through the same enhanced earbuds.

So far, the earbuds have been quiet.

But it's not going well.

He can't spot them, but he feels he's under surveillance.

Being undercover overseas is always one delicate balancing act, constantly evaluating the people and scenery around you, juggling the external legend of who you are and what you've done, while keeping the training and discipline of being a clandestine operative inside.

Studious Dr. Jekyll and murderous Mr. Hyde, their sharpest instincts combined and enhanced with state-of-the-art technology.

The exterior Benjamin is still happily wandering—apparently aimlessly—through these Chinese markets, while the interior Benjamin becomes more assured that he's been spotted.

He feels like his balancing act is one fatal step away from collapsing this vital op, potentially the most important he's ever been on, into a bloody failure.

CHAPTER 2

BUT THE HALF smile of a curious tourist remains as he continues his job.

It's hard to explain but after years of doing overseas operations, you develop a sixth sense that you're being watched, nothing you could learn in class or during field training while at the famed CIA Farm. The old-time lecturers would tell amusing tales of how their predecessors stationed in Moscow during the height of the Cold War had a hell of a time meeting up with agents. The KGB had everything wired in Moscow, from taxicab drivers to spa attendants, but one funny way of determining that the KGB was after you was taking a few seconds to look at the surrounding cars and their windshield wipers.

Cars without windshield wipers, innocent. Because every driver in that worker's paradise Moscow knew that windshield wipers were kept in the car and were taken out only when it rained or snowed. Parking a car with the windshield wipers attached meant they would be stolen within seconds.

But cars with windshield wipers, they belonged to the KGB, as well as cars with the best tires. No Moscow thieves would dare go after those vehicles.

Smart tradecraft, back in the good old days when the intelligence world was black and white.

Here, in the Chinatown section of Johannesburg, it was all shades of cold grays and blood red.

Benjamin keeps on walking, not breaking stride, looking at the reflections in shop windows and car windshields, and he can sense it. There is a rhythm in the movement and swirls of crowds, but in running surveillance, sometimes you have to stop and see what you are following, and in doing so, risk standing out like barely hidden rocks in a smooth-flowing stream.

Up ahead are a series of food stalls with bright large umbrellas shading them from the June sun. A thought comes to him. Benjamin stops and smiles, chats to the shopkeepers in English, takes photos, and then buys a skewer of disgusting-looking fried food.

He takes it in hand, starts munching on it, and, approaching a municipal wastebasket, suddenly stops and spits out whatever spicy piece of meat was in his mouth, doing his best to upchuck what was left in his stomach from breakfast, and in doing so, sweeps the area around him with his sunglasses-hidden eyes.

There. Young Chinese man suddenly stopping while crossing the street.

There. Young Chinese woman, smartly dressed, carrying a briefcase and talking on her phone, taking just a few seconds to turn her head away from the phone to look at him.

Benjamin has been made.

He's being surveilled by Chinese intelligence.

Depending on what orders his Ministry of State Security counterparts have received from Beijing, he might not be alive by the time noon arrives.

CHAPTER 3

BENJAMIN DROPS THE skewer into the trash and resumes his walk, wiping at his face with a paper napkin that he drops onto the street.

There's a brief temptation to cancel this highly dangerous op, but he won't do that because of all that is at stake for Langley.

More than a decade ago, in a horrific series of still highly classified events, nearly every CIA agent and asset in China was identified, rolled up, and disappeared, most likely executed with a bullet to the back of the head. To Langley, it was like being comfortable at home, with a worldwide internet connection, and having it suddenly go dark, with calls to customer service going unanswered, the constant unplugging and plugging of the modem leading to a black screen.

No news, no knowledge, nothing.

Which is a dangerous way of living in today's

world, no hint of what your leading global rival is thinking, planning, and preparing to do.

Then there's something else about this mission, something deeply personal hidden away for years, but that has surprised him by coming back so raw and open.

A cherished memory of a beautiful woman sitting next to him in a college class, a decade ago, and—

All right, he thinks. *Put that away.* He's sure he's been made but there's always a chance that those two Chinese pedestrians are truly innocent, just reacting in shock at seeing a tourist vomit in the street.

Is he overreacting?

Time for evasion, Benjamin thinks, as he again resists the urge to check his watch.

Benjamin comes to a busy street, and then slips through a narrow space left by two dull-green taxicabs that have abruptly stopped. Here the crowds are just a bit more thick, and he increases his pace and ducks into the lobby of the Fong De restaurant, whose layout he memorized a month ago.

Just moving, seconds in play, he goes into the men's room, luckily finding an empty stall.

Move, move, move.

The bright-yellow baseball cap is gone, and he takes a small squeeze tube and sprays the edges of his dark-brown hair, making it instantly gray. A floppy tan rain hat goes on his head. The white plastic earbuds are tossed. The tan jacket, turned inside out, is now blue. A wet wad of toilet paper is swept across his white sneakers, turning them black. The sunglasses join the baseball cap into an overflowing trash bin and are replaced by clear reading glasses. From his travel bag he takes out a black flashlight and after some pulling and twisting, it becomes a black cane.

After some folding and zippering, his shoulder bag is now a fanny pack, fastened around his waist. He flushes the toilet and starts limping out of the bathroom, through the crowded lobby, and now outside.

Time elapsed, about sixty seconds.

CHAPTER 4

HARD TO EXPLAIN again, but Benjamin knows that his change-up back there has thrown off his surveillance, as he takes his time, limping along, the map of this part of Chinatown still vivid in his mind, and now he's close.

Down a narrow alley, overflowing trash bins on both sides. A dog barking somewhere, a car with a bad muffler rattling nearby.

The alley comes out to a narrow road lined with low-slung brick and stone shops and apartment buildings, lengths of clothesline hung with clothes drying in the breeze.

At the corner he comes to a front door bracketed by a pair of fat, smiling tiger sculptures, their stone faces chipped, the bright paint nearly faded away. Breathing hard, Benjamin leans his cane against the doorway, bends down to tie his right shoe, his fingers slipping for a moment to the rear of the two-foot-tall tiger, pulling away a key fastened by a drop of putty.

Key concealed in his hand, he retrieves the cane and enters the ill-lit apartment building.

He trots up the three flights of stairs to the top floor. The place smells of old diapers and cooking oil. There are two doors at the top landing, 3-A and 3-B.

He unlocks the door to apartment 3-B, steps in, closes the door behind him.

The dark apartment seems small and cluttered, and a shape erupts from behind the couch, coming at him hard.

CHAPTER 5

HE TAKES THE cane, thrusts it between the person's legs, causing a trip and tumble, and then he's on top, twisting arms behind, breathing hard. He says, "Hell of a day, don't you think."

"You go to hell, right now," comes the woman's voice.

"Dante won't approve," he replies, and he gets up, the recognition phrase he used, and the reply, and his reply to the reply, all checking out.

He gets up, puts a hand against the wall near the door, fumbles for a second, turns on the light.

A slim and attractive Chinese woman gets off the floor, wearing black shoes, gray slacks, a light-yellow blouse, and black leather jacket. Her hair is long and ink black.

She stands staring at him, and he stares right back.

"You nearly broke my leg," she says, her English perfect.

Ben says, "Had to do it. You came after me in the dark."

Another stare, and then she shakes her head.

"Damn, Ben," she whispers. "It's good to see you!"

"You too, Lin," he says, stepping forward, giving her a good hard hug and kiss on the cheek. She is Chin Lin, a fellow student back at Stanford, one-time girlfriend of his and now an operative of the Chinese Ministry of State Security.

He looks around the cluttered and dirty apartment, checks his watch, sees he has five minutes before he signals for the exfiltration.

Good.

In exactly three hundred seconds after his signal, a black delivery van is going to pull up in front of this apartment building and spirit him and Chin Lin away. By this time tomorrow she should be in a safe house somewhere in Europe.

"How was your morning?" he asks.

She smiles. Damn, that smile...

How long before she gets back to the States? How long from then can he have the opportunity to be with her, one on one, with no Agency handlers or interrogators nearby?

"Fine," she says. "Managed to slip away from my minders back in Pretoria and got here about ten minutes ago."

Lin reaches over, gently fluffs the edge of his

newly grayed-out hair. "Damn, Ben, you're letting yourself go."

He smiles. "You . . . you look great."

Again, that sweet look and dark eyes that gripped him, the moment she sat down next to him at a Writing and World Literature English class at Stanford, and the class after that, and the one after that, when he had finally worked up the nerve to ask her out for coffee.

Those were definitely the days.

Stop it, he thinks. Stop thinking of those wonderful, sweet days at Stanford, studying and traveling and learning together, him telling her his story of being a lonely adoptee, her telling her story of being part of a large Beijing family, involved in both business and government in China.

After graduation she had returned to China, and he had stayed home in California, still alone. In a series of weird twists that could probably end up as an internet meme, they had both found employment with their own nations' intelligence agencies.

"Long way from Tresidder," she says, mentioning a student hangout back at Stanford.

"Six years' worth of a long way," he says, which is true—that's how long it's been since he last saw her.

He spares a thought: she wanted to defect, and she chose *him.*

Checks his watch.

Time for the signal, and after that, five minutes to the exfil.

He goes to the near window, overlooking the main avenue. He lowers and raises a window shade halfway.

Signal sent.

He and the defector are ready for pickup.

Just five minutes and this op would be on its way to conclusion, months in planning, from when word came to him at Langley, *Chin Lin wants to come back to the States and have a tequila with you.*

What a stunner that had been, her making a private joke about the first time she drank tequila and threw up on his shoes back at school. His and everyone else's first response was that this was a trap somehow, something to embarrass the Agency and the country, but after slow negotiations and an agreement to make it happen in a neutral country like South Africa, the slow wheels of planning commenced, the communications going through a complicated email cutout process using systems in the internet cloud.

He looks at Chin Lin and thinks, she's the one who got away, and the Stanford student in him thinks—*Do we have a chance to make it work this time?*—but no, back to the job at hand. *Stop thinking about the past, stop wondering what she's been doing these last six years, get your focus back, buddy.*

"You have luggage?" he asks. "A carry-on?"

With disappointment in her voice, she says, "Benjamin . . . what kind of tradecraft did they teach you in Virginia? You think I could leave my apartment in Pretoria with a bit of luggage in hand? My minders would have picked me up in seconds."

She pats the hem of her jacket.

"Thumb drives sewn in," she says. "With enough photos and documents to keep your analysts busy for months."

In the old building, a floorboard creaks.

Why, is what he wants to ask, for he knows from his briefings back at Langley that Chin Lin's father is a senior official at the Chinese Ministry of State Security. What is driving her to make this ultimate betrayal, not only against her country, but her father?

With her defection, her father will bear the brunt of Beijing's anger, and will probably end his days in a miserable prison cell after months of severe torture and interrogation.

Benjamin looks one last time at his watch and there's a sudden loud *crash* as a large Chinese man leads with his shoulder to break through the thin wooden door. Another Chinese man rushes in through the broken door, carrying a pistol, aiming it straight at Benjamin.

CHAPTER 6

BENJAMIN'S TRAINING KICKS in and he lifts his arms up in surrender, saying, "Hey, hey, hey, what the hell is going on?," desperately trying to exit his CIA persona and get back to Benjamin the innocent travel writer.

One armed Chinese man pushes Chin Lin against a cracked plaster wall, and the closer man says, "You! Don't move!"

Benjamin puts a tremble in his legs and fear in his voice. "I mean it, what is this?"

The man who told him to stop puts a pistol to Benjamin's forehead—a 9mm QSZ-92, he coolly observes—and roughly searches him, pulling his fanny pack off and tossing it to the floor. When he is done, he speaks rapidly in Chinese to a third man who has come in.

The third man is older, better dressed, and he gingerly closes the broken door into place. He turns to look at Benjamin, but ignores Chin Lin, who is standing quiet and still against the wall.

"Who are you?" he asks, in precise, barely accented English.

His training kicks in again, as hard and logical as it must be. In situations like this one, you have one responsibility: you.

Your asset, agent, defector...they are to be cut loose. Get yourself away, best you can.

But thinking about Chin Lin...he's both angry and sad.

It's clear now.

She's betrayed him.

But why? For what purpose? To capture a regular field operative in a neutral nation? Doesn't make sense.

He says, "Benjamin Litchfield. I'm from San Francisco, in California. I'm a travel writer...who the hell are you?"

The older man stares at Benjamin. "And this... woman?"

Benjamin tries an embarrassed laugh. "Jeez, I don't know. I was here, walking around, checking out these hot Chinese babes...and I was getting... Well, you know. A hankering for one of those famous Chinese massages you hear about. I never dared to get one back home. Always was concerned I might see someone I know, either going in or coming out. Know what I mean?"

Another embarrassed laugh, though part of his soul is dying at seeing the look on Chin Lin's face. Even in this moment of great betrayal, there is still an old love there that won't be extinguished.

But he remembers his training at the Farm: get off the X, meaning, if you're trapped or in an ambush, don't freeze, don't hesitate, make a move to get off the X.

Right now he's in the middle of the X, and save for trying to dive through that window—only doable in TV shows and movies with their special effects—the only way out is through that door. Benjamin isn't armed, because he's not in downtown Lahore but Johannesburg—not particularly dangerous—and because these men are pros. A three-to-one gunfight tends to end quickly with victory for those with the best odds.

"I do know what you mean," the older Chinese man says.

"Here, I'll show you," Benjamin says. "Just . . . hey, relax, okay?"

From his left pants pocket he removes a folded-over newspaper clipping from a local weekly alternative newspaper, passes it over the near gunman, who gives it a glance. Benjamin says, "See? *Lotus Blossom Massage Parlour*. I made a call and I was told to come here and—"

The older Chinese man drops the clipping to the floor. "Your name is Benjamin Lucas. You were adopted by the Lucas family of San Francisco when you were eleven months old. You went to Stanford and Boston University, and for the past six years, you have been an operative for the Central Intelligence Agency of the United States."

Benjamin refuses to let his emotions come to the surface. He is no longer in control, no longer in charge. He is in survival mode.

That is all.

The older man turns and speaks rapidly in Chinese to Chin Lin, who is standing quietly and bravely against the far wall. He goes back to Benjamin and says, "In order to be polite among professionals, I will tell you what I've just told Chin Lin."

With horror growing now, Benjamin says, "No, please, it was my fault. I—"

The man says, "I told her, Chin Lin, you are a traitor to your Party and your country, and you must pay the price."

He quickly removes a pistol from a waist holster and fires off three shots into Chin Lin's chest. The sounds of the gunfire are ear-splittingly loud in the small apartment. Chin Lin cries out, the front of her blouse torn and bloody, and she collapses and slides down the wall.

So many memories of their time together—their first lovemaking, the strolls along El Palo Alto Park and her gentle and laughing critiques of Chinese food at Stanford flash through him as he sees a woman he's loved for years slowly die before his eyes.

The near man slugs him, he staggers back, and the third man comes to him. A hood is placed over Benjamin's head, as the punches and kicks continue.

Before he slides into unconsciousness, he thinks, *Chin Lin*...

CHAPTER 7

THE WHITE HOUSE

Two Months Earlier

ON THE SECOND floor of the White House, where the private family quarters are located, thirty-three-year-old Liam Grey of the Central Intelligence Agency is sitting on an antique couch waiting to see the president. It's nearly seven a.m. as he looks around at the priceless furniture and framed paintings and feels the quiet of the place. These walls have seen the romping and playing of presidential children from Theodore Roosevelt's to JFK's, Jimmy Carter's, and Bill Clinton's, as well as the attentions of numerous first ladies, but not now. This president is the first bachelor chief executive to assume office since James Buchanan—more than a century and a half ago.

As he waits, Liam spends a few moments reflecting on the odd circumstances of his life that led him here. He knows DC well, having grown up in the Southwest & The Wharf neighborhood of the district, and definitely not in the tony Georgetown part. He barely made it through the lousy local schools and luckily caught a track scholarship to BU, where he thrived and joined the Army ROTC, following in the sad footsteps of his older brother, Brian, a captain in the famed 10th Mountain Division who had been killed during his second tour of Afghanistan.

The Army had triggered something in Liam, leading him to military intelligence and a master's degree in foreign service at Georgetown, where he easily slipped into being recruited into the CIA and, from there, its Directorate of Operations. He's bounced back and forth from overseas assignments to Langley, and now he—a kid who used to fish off the wharves in his old DC neighborhood, getting into lots of fights and committing petty thefts after school—is moments away from giving the commander in chief the President's Daily Brief.

The thin black leather binder in his lap contains the morning report—known as the PDB—and he's still surprised that he's the only one here to pass it along to the president. The PDB can run anywhere from ten to fifteen pages and is one of the most closely guarded secrets in Washington, containing a morning overview of the world that is assembled through reports from the CIA, the NSA, the Department of Defense, and lots of other three-letter agencies.

Traditionally it's presented to the president by a high-level administrator in the Agency, accompanied by two or three aides. Three months ago, Liam had been called away from his office to join the director of national intelligence and the acting director of the CIA to accompany them when they presented the PDB. Several weeks later, it had been Liam and his boss, the acting director, and now, he's here alone.

Very strange, off the books, and not the typical way it is done, but President Keegan Barrett is known to like being atypical and off the books. As a former director of the CIA, the president still has friends and allies at the Agency and is known to keep a close eye on the operators that catch his notice.

Like one Liam Grey, apparently.

A door opens to a small office next to this empty living room, and one of President Barrett's aides, a young Black male wearing a lanyard displaying the required White House ID, says, "Mr. Grey? The president will see you now."

"Thank you," he says, and he gets up and takes the half dozen steps that will change everything.

CHAPTER 8

LIKE SOME OTHER presidents before him—Nixon and Trump, for example—President Barrett doesn't like to work from the downstairs Oval Office. The day after his inauguration last year, in a sit-down with editors and reporters from the Washington bureau of the *New York Times,* he had said, "Too much history in that place. It feels like you're in the middle of a museum exhibit. I want to be able to kick back, put my feet on the furniture, and get work done without being interrupted all the goddamn time."

President Barrett is sitting behind an old wooden desk that was supposedly used by President Harding. He gets up from the neatly piled folders and telephone bank and briskly walks over to Liam.

That's when the CIA officer notes he and the president aren't alone in the small, wood-paneled room.

On one of two small blue couches arranged around a wooden coffee table is a woman about Liam's age, sitting still and looking smart. She's wearing a two-piece black suit—slacks and jacket—with an ivory blouse. Her light-olive complexion is framed by black hair that is cut and styled close.

She stares at him with dark-brown eyes, and President Barrett says, "I believe you know each other."

Liam nods, smiles. "Noa Himel. We were in the same training class."

She gets up, offers a hand, and says, "Glad you remembered me. My hair was longer back then."

He takes her grip, firm and warm, and says, "I remembered you outrunning my ass on the obstacle course."

She smiles, sits down. "It's not called that anymore. It's the confidence enhancement course."

With his trademark perfect smile, President Barrett says, "I hate to interrupt this company reunion, but we've got work to do. Liam, take a seat next to Noa."

Liam goes over and does so, catching a slight whiff of her perfume. It's nice. The office is small, with bookcases, a couple of framed Frederic Remington western prints, and not much else. The PDB feels heavy in his lap, and the president says, "Liam, you can put that aside for now. We've got more important things to discuss."

"Yes, sir," he says, now confused, as he puts the leather-bound volume down on the coffee table. The PDB has been nearly sacred since the era of President John F. Kennedy, when it was known as the President's Intelligence Checklist. Since then it has expanded and grown in importance, and it's now considered the most highly classified and important piece of intelligence the president receives on a regular basis. Some presidents wanted the briefings daily, others weekly, and during the last several administrations, it was prepared on a secure computer tablet, but this president—sitting across from him and Noa, wearing dark-gray slacks and a blue Oxford shirt with the collar undone and sleeves rolled up, his skin tanned and thick brown hair carefully trimmed—demanded it go back to paper.

And now he's ignoring it.

Liam thinks maybe he should say something, but...

Liam is CIA but also former Army, and he's in the presence of the commander in chief, so he keeps his mouth shut.

The president says, "Quick question for you both, and one answer apiece. Who are the most dangerous non-state actors we face as a nation? Noa, you're up."

Noa crisply says, "Cyber."

"Go on."

She says, "We've gone beyond the point where hackers and bots can go out and influence an election or steal bank accounts or hold a city's software ransom. They can turn off the power, switch off the internet, and incite people in a country to rise up against a supposed enemy. You can be a First World nation in the morning, but after the cyberattack you can be a Third World nation come sundown."

The president nods. "Exactly. Liam?"

With Noa going before him, he has a few seconds to think it through and says, "Freelance terrorist cells and organizations. They'll preach their ideology or twisted view of their religion while they're killing people and blowing up things, but secretly they're for sale to the highest bidder. They preach a good sermon, but in reality they're nihilists. They'll strike anywhere and anybody for the right price."

"Good answers," the president says. "Which is why I've called you both in here today."

"Sir?" Liam asks. He's not sure where the hell this is going, but his initial impression of his good-looking couch mate, Noa, is positive. She gave a neat, thorough answer to the president's threat question. He has the odd hope that Noa has a similar feeling about his own reply.

The president clasps his hands together and leans over the coffee table.

"After decades of our being the world's punching

bag, I've decided this administration isn't going to be reactive anymore," he says. "We're going to be proactive, go after our enemies before they strike. We're no longer going to be the victim. I'm going to set up two CIA teams, one domestic, the other foreign, and you two are going to run them. I'm going to give you the authorization to break things, kill bad guys, and bring back our enemies' heads in a cooler."

CHAPTER 9

NOA HIMEL LETS the president's words sink in for a moment before replying, still wondering what odd circumstances of life have brought her here, her first time meeting the president.

She's originally from Tel Aviv, moving at age five with her family to New York City when her corporate banker mother got a great job offer. Dad is a graphic artist, and she's their only child. After she graduated with a master's degree in international relations from Columbia, her uncle Benny flew in from Israel to congratulate her and recommend that she talk to an old friend of his in Virginia about a job.

That led to two developments: getting employed by the CIA, and confirming the family rumors that Uncle Benny worked for Mossad.

The Agency was still "old boy" in that a lot of managers thought women recruits should go to desk and analysis jobs, but at the time Noa thought, *Screw that shit*—she wasn't spending the rest of her life in a cubicle. She went for the Directorate of Operations and got in, not afraid to ask tough questions along the way.

Like right now.

"Sir . . . with all due respect, you know we can't operate in the United States," Noa says. "It's against the CIA's charter. Congress and their oversight . . . they would never allow it."

His eyes flash for a hot second. "You think I don't know that, Noa?"

Noa knows he's quite aware of that, given his background as a former Army general, the secretary of defense, the CIA director, and a two-term congressman from California before he won the White House.

"Sir," she says, "that's what I meant by 'all due respect.' You have the authority to have the Agency conduct overseas operations and missions, but inside the United States . . . it can't be done."

"Nice observation, Noa, but it *will* be done," he replies. "I've issued a presidential finding regarding the temporary deployment of CIA assets within the United States, and my attorney general has signed off on it. You and Liam have no worries about doing anything illegal. It'll be on the books . . . though I'll be the one keeping the books, of course."

Noa waits for Liam to speak, but he's keeping his

mouth shut and his opinions to himself, usually a wise career move at the CIA. He's dressed well and has a nice-looking face and light-brown hair, but he sits oddly, like he'd rather be standing armed in a desert somewhere. *Besides,* she thinks, *he's former Army, meaning in most circumstances, when receiving an oddball order like this, his instinct will be to salute first and ask no questions.*

But Noa sees things differently. Working in the Agency means both competing in the field and dealing with the bureaucratic infighting that comes with every large organization, but she feels like President Barrett is the proverbial bull in a china shop, asking her to come along for the ride.

A thrill for sure, but to what end? she thinks.

"Sir," she says—thinking if she's going to commit career suicide, why not do it in style?—"don't you think the respective intelligence committees in Congress are going to raise hell over your finding?"

His smile seems to be made of steel. "The Intelligence Authorization Act allows the president to proceed without official notification to Congress if I inform them in a 'timely manner.' That's up for me to define, isn't it? 'Timely manner'?"

Next to her Liam bestirs himself and says, "Absolutely, sir."

Damn Army vet, she thinks.

Barrett seems happy that Liam has spoken and

says, "The time of nations and organized terrorist groups fighting other nations in the open is long gone. Now they conceal themselves, depending on our adherence to the rule of law and due process not to respond. Our enemies are activists, now more than ever. We have to be activists in return. Now I want to tell you why I selected you, what I expect of you, and why I decided to brief the two of you together."

He stares at Noa, and she feels uneasy. The president has never married, has borne himself like a "warrior monk," similar to famed Marine general James Mattis. He's totally dedicated to the United States and its defense, yet he has that "thing" that some former presidents had, including JFK, Johnson, and Clinton. When one is in their presence, one takes notice.

Noa also takes notice of an edge to the president's look, like he is sizing her up, and she isn't sure if it's her experience or appearance he is evaluating.

The president says, "In my time at the CIA, I knew where the deadwood was located and that there were open cases involving possible Agency traitors that dragged on for years. But I couldn't do anything about it, due to politics. The director serves at the pleasure of the president, and back then, the president didn't have the nerve to do what had to be done, no matter how many times I briefed her. That stops now. Noa, you're going to have my full authority to clean house at the Agency. I'm going to chop up all the deadwood into very small pieces that will never be found again."

Noa says, "But Director Fenway—"

He snaps, "*Acting* Director Milton Fenway, if you please. No disrespect to your boss, but I've told him what I've planned and he's on board. Don't worry about him."

She thinks she sees Liam give a slight nod to the president. Poor Acting Director Fenway. A few months ago, the president had nominated a smart hard-charger—Hannah Abrams, a former deputy director—who was known at the Agency as a top-notch street woman operating in what was called the "night soil circuit," meaning she took every overseas assignment available, even the worst of the worst. Most in the Directorate of Operations are looking forward to Abrams taking command of the Agency, but her nomination is still being held up in the Senate for some obscure political reason.

Until that logjam is broken, Milton Fenway is the acting director, and he comes from the CIA's Directorate of Science and Technology, meaning he is experienced in various aspects of those technical means of gathering intelligence—SIGINT and ELINT—but not HUMINT, human intelligence. The men and women who work undercover around the world, rightly or wrongly, think they are the tip of the spear for the Agency and have no respect for the man.

The president adds, "There are also safe houses for the Chinese and Russians located across the country. We know where most of them are located. We leave them alone because we don't want to cause a stir or embarrass the Chinese or Russians, or because we don't have the evidence to prosecute them. To hell with that. Those houses are going to be taken out, and the foreign agents within are going to disappear."

Noa is silent for a few seconds.

What did the president just say?

"Disappear"?

CHAPTER 10

NOA THINKS THAT if she doesn't get a good answer right now, she's getting up and leaving.

"'Disappear'?" she asks. "Sir?"

He smiles. "I don't mean like the Argentine Army did back in their 'Dirty War,' tossing arrestees out of helicopters over the South Atlantic. No, 'disappear' to a facility where they won't have access to the Constitution and American lawyers. They're here illegally, they're conducting war against the United States, and they will be treated accordingly."

He shifts his attention to Liam, and Noa feels a sense of relief, that the force of the man's personality—like the beam of a high-powered searchlight—is now pointed at someone else. She's still processing what's been assigned to her by the president.

Domestic work, she thinks. The legal and institutional handcuffs put on by Barrett's predecessors and Congress have just been slipped off.

One hell of an opportunity.

Sure, she thinks, *an opportunity to really hit hard at some bad actors out there, or an opportunity to be humiliated, arrested, and stripped of my pension if this turns into another Iran–Contra disaster.*

Noa wants to make a difference in the world by being in the Agency, and the president has just given her a golden ticket to do so.

President Barrett is talking a good talk, but will that be enough once the bodies start piling up?

"There are terrorist cells, hackers, and bot farms controlled by the Iranians, Chinese, and Russians, and there are hackers-for-hire across the globe," the president says. "They attack us day and night via cyberspace or in the real world. We don't retaliate appropriately because we don't want to escalate the situation, or because we're not one hundred percent sure of a target, or because we don't want to stoop to their level. That stops today. You're going to get a team together of people from the intelligence and military communities. From there, overseas you'll go. These farms, cells, and other structures...you know what Rome did to Carthage?"

"Yes, sir," Liam says. "Once Rome finally conquered Carthage, they destroyed every building and salted the earth around the ruins so nothing would ever grow there again. And that's exactly what happened."

The president nods. "I want them gone. Gone so hard that whoever survives won't go back to a computer keyboard or an AK-47 ever again."

Liam says, "If I may, it sounds risky, sir."

"Of course it's risky," he says. "Fortune favors the bold, correct? And it's time for us to be bold. I'll give you both twenty-four hours to pick your teams and then come back here tomorrow. We'll go over your candidates, and then we'll discuss logistics and support. And when it comes to support, you'll have everything you need, with just one phone call or text. As commander in chief, I can get any branch of the military to assist you under any circumstances."

The president leans back into the couch. "I've followed both of your careers over the years. You have the intelligence, toughness, experience, and . . . well, the perfect background and history of heartbreak to do what must be done. Any questions?"

Dozens of them, Noa thinks, but she doesn't want to speak first.

She feels she's spoken enough, and even though she has misgivings about what's being offered to her, she is also relishing the thought of taking the fight to enemies who have set up camp within the nation's borders.

Let Liam take the lead.

But Liam refuses to do so.

"No, sir," he says. "I'm good."

Noa says, "I'm good as well."

President Barrett nods with satisfaction.

"Get out, get to work, and I'll see you tomorrow. I'll be supplying you both with an initial set of targets, complete with locations and defenses." He adds a chilly smile. "I'll also supply the salt."

CHAPTER 11

A FEW MINUTES after Liam Grey and Noa Himel depart, President Keegan Barrett reviews his schedule for the day when the door to his office opens and Carlton Pope walks in. On the official White House organization chart, he's listed as a "special assistant to the president," which covers a lot of ground, water, and sky—exactly what Barrett wants.

Pope is stocky, heavyset, with a type of blocky body that makes Savile Row tailors toss up their respective hands in despair while trying to tailor a suit to fit. His prematurely gray hair is trimmed short, and his nose is round and misshapen, from a long-ago break that never properly healed.

He takes a seat in front of Barrett. Except for the Secret Service, Pope is the only one allowed to come into Barrett's office without knocking first. Even Barrett's chief of staff, Quinn Lawrence, isn't allowed here without a warning phone call.

Pope says, "Well?"

Barrett says, "I think they'll work out. They're young, experienced, and dedicated."

Pope smirks, and Barrett allows him that one look. Years ago, when Barrett was in the Army and on a still-classified mission to Serbia, Barrett had saved this man's career and life, and in the ensuing years, Pope has diligently worked to pay back that debt.

Barrett always relies on the loyalty of others and is glad to pay it back.

He says, "All right, you ignorant peasant, pack that smirk away. Because of bad movies and past history, most people don't realize that the CIA attracts the best and brightest, who'll go to the extremes to perform their mission. It's not the pay that drives them, and it's sure as hell not the publicity. They do it because they're dedicated to the Agency and this country."

Pope says, "All right, I'll take back the smirk. They both seem experienced...and that Noa." He smiles. "A real looker."

"Glad you noticed."

"But sir...this is one hell of a risky venture."

"One that's worth it," he says, feeling reflective. "In my years at the Pentagon, at Langley, and in Congress, I had this…understanding of what threats our nation faces. But to get the right people to listen to you and act…it never could happen. Politics, inertia, bureaucracy. Now that I'm here, that's going to change. I'm finally in a position to make it happen."

"But…"

Barrett glances down at his schedule. If this keeps up, he's going to be late for a coffee-and-Danish visit with the Senate majority leader and his staff downstairs in his private dining room. He needs to keep his relationship with that fool steady for as long as possible, before the hammer falls.

The president says, "I think you're about to ask me, 'But what if they don't work out? Have a change of heart? Decide to go confess all to the *Washington Post*?'"

"That's what I was thinking, yes, sir."

One of the many attributes that Barrett likes about his special assistant is his blunt way of talking and getting things done, and all without any attendant publicity. He's never had his photo in the *Post* or on the various news sites and blogs and prefers to work in the shadows.

Which is part of Pope's unofficial job description.

Barrett says, "If that happens, they'll be replaced. There are twenty-two thousand employees of the

CIA. I'm sure we can find two other dedicated individuals."

Pope gets up from his chair. "Replaced or disappeared?"

Barrett says, "Whichever works."

CHAPTER 12

CARLTON POPE, SPECIAL assistant to the president, smiles with satisfaction as he walks downstairs back to his office, on the first floor and next to the Oval Office, its proximity marking his real power behind the throne here in the White House.

He's come a long way from his nearly deserted hometown back in Oregon, where the forest industry had collapsed due to imports from China, and new rules and regulations issued by distant, faceless bureaucrats who cared more about some stupid owl than real people with real problems. The economy in that crappy town was empty for guys like him and his classmates, high school graduates who weren't going to college.

Selling meth, OD'ing on opioids, and getting busted for petty crime was the most popular path.

Pope had picked another one.

The Army.

He almost deserted a few times but he found a home in the military police—what a joke!—and things had been going okay some years back until he got caught up in a mess in Kosovo. Other times and places it wouldn't have been a big deal, just tuning up a prisoner who wouldn't talk about the ratlines up in the mountains that were protecting Serb paramilitaries.

But his luck being his luck, the prisoner checked out, and Pope was facing serious prison time at Leavenworth, until a colonel he barely knew visited him in the brig.

The colonel didn't waste time. "I'm going places, and I need a guy with a hard mind and hard heart at my side. Are you that guy, Sergeant Pope? No time for questions or debate. Say 'yes' and your charges get broomed."

Of course he had said yes, the first time he had spoken to Keegan Barrett, and Barrett had kept his promise. Pope had followed him all the way to here, 1600 Pennsylvania Avenue, working with him and for him as a consultant during his time at the Pentagon, Langley, and Capitol Hill.

And here he is, number two guy in America— forget the veep, he has real power and authority in this White House, especially for the important weeks ahead—and only one thing troubles him as he nods in satisfaction at the administrative staff sitting outside of his office.

He goes in, shuts the door, sits in his comfortable chair, admires his fine office with all the power and authority contained within. Not bad for a near high-school dropout, most of whose class members are either serving time or lying in cold graves up in the Northwest.

But that's not what bothers him.

It's the president.

Lately, he's been . . .

Stop, he tells himself.

He won't allow himself to go down that path.

There's a lot to be done between now and that day Barrett has planned for the world, and he will not—and cannot—be distracted.

He picks up his phone, gets to work.

CHAPTER 13

IT'S NEARLY ELEVEN p.m. and Liam Grey is at the Tuckerman Roadhouse outside of Langley, Virginia, finishing up a hot roast beef sandwich, homemade fries, and a draft Sam Adams beer, when he spots a familiar face at the other end of the bar. Nearly sixteen hours have passed since this morning's meeting with the president but he still feels wired and alert. He drops three ten-dollar bills on the mahogany bar and picks up his beer, to see if the woman down there feels the same.

Noa Himel sees him approaching and lifts a glass of clear liquid in salute, and he returns the gesture. She has on blue jeans and a plain gray sweatshirt, and as he gets near, he leans in and over the noise of the customers, says, "Want to find someplace private?"

"Sure, if there is such a place."

Noa picks up her drink and he maneuvers her

to the rear of the tavern. This roadhouse is off the beaten path for most tourists and is a popular after-hours destination for military and civilian workers from the Pentagon, as well as those working for the Agency. One of the old-timers who had mentored Liam at the Farm told tales of how decades ago, off-duty workers would go to bars wearing Company lanyards around their necks, badges hidden in their shirt pockets. A way of concealing your true employment but quietly demonstrating your importance.

That was probably a cool thing to do during the Cold War, but ever since 1993—when a terrorist shot up a line of cars waiting on Route 123 to turn into CIA headquarters and killing two CIA employees and wounding three others—the rules had changed.

Noa finds a corner table that is cluttered with half-empty glasses and crumpled napkins. She sits down, back to the wall, and he does the same.

He sits quietly with her for a long few seconds and says, "Well?"

"Well, what?" she says sharply. "You were so damn chatty this morning, I thought I'd let you go first. You suddenly shy all the time?"

Liam takes a swallow of his beer. "What to say?" He checks the crowd, knowing from training and instinct how to converse out in public, without letting classified details slip out. "The boss made good points. I liked what he had to say. You...you sounded like he was about to set up reeducation camps or something like that."

Noa frowns, runs a finger around the edge of the glass. "Remember your first real day at work? In the Bubble? We took an oath about defending the Constitution. Not the president of the United States."

"He's making it legal. That's good enough for me."

"He's stretching it, and you know it."

Liam says, "There's an opportunity here for both of us to make an impact, to really hit some bad guys where it counts."

"So pretend we're in the Army, just salute smartly, and go up that hill?"

"No, as Agency employees, we say 'yes, sir,' and follow his instructions. The Agency works for the president. I don't have a problem with that."

Noa stays quiet. Liam takes in the faces of the government employees and contractors, crowded around the tavern's square bar and tables, talking in small groups, seeing lots of smiles and laughter, but also seeing the quiet ones. They were the ones with haunted eyes, either just home from abroad with fresh, bloody memories, or just left their offices, the burden of looming deadly threats still fresh in their minds.

Liam says, "Last year I was in the Middle East. Country in the middle of a civil war. Keeping watch on things. A couple of folks of interest wandered into this house we were observing. Checked them using our facial recognition software...two solid hits on...guys of interest. With long histories, you know? We sent word up the line, and the word came back. Leave them alone. Negotiations were in a delicate stage. They left later, and they were responsible for...some stuff. Deadly and horrific stuff."

He finishes his beer. "You know what? Negotiations are always in a delicate stage. Screw it. And if you don't want to take the job, Noa, don't. I plan to do it, and with great professionalism and enthusiasm."

She picks up her drink and lowers it. "Don't get ahead of yourself, Liam."

"Didn't think I was."

"Six or seven months ago, I was in Cambridge," Noa says.

"The one here or the one over there?"

"The one here," she says. A loud burst of laughter pauses Noa for a second, and when it quiets down, she continues, "I was assigned liaison to an FBI task force, running surveillance on a foreign intelligence cell working out of Cambridge."

Liam says, "Were they on the city council?"

For a moment it looks like Noa is considering a smile. "No, it was a husband-and-wife team, and their neighbors were another husband-and-wife team. They all had jobs in various defense firms out on Route 128. I was getting briefed by the lead FBI agent and I asked how long they had been here. Three years...can you believe it? Three goddamn years...I asked, well, when are you planning to take them out? The FBI guy just laughed at me. 'Never,' he said. 'They're money in the bank. We keep them happy, let them do their work, and if there ever comes a time when one of you folks gets captured overseas, we use them for an exchange.'"

Liam stays quiet, sensing she wants to say more. She does.

"Get that?" she says. "We were letting those four spies steal our most advanced military technological developments, just because one day, someday, they could be used as poker chips. Meanwhile, our enemies get advanced targeting technology, software, and weapons systems schematics without being bothered. We weren't thinking about the now, about damage they're doing every damn day, week, and month. Once again, we were being played for suckers for some possible future goal."

Noa finishes off her drink, holds up the glass like she's examining it. "Me, turning this down? Not a chance in the world. I just want to go into it with clear eyes and an understanding of the rewards and the possible risks. Truth be told, I like being picked out by Barrett."

Liam picks up his empty tavern mug, clinks it against Noa's empty glass. "Me, too. We just got our hunting license from the boss. Let's go hunting."

Noa clinks it in return, puts her glass down. "Yes, let's go hunting. But remember this, Liam."

"What's that?"

Noa says, "One of these days, the game wardens are going to find out what we're doing, and there'll be hell to pay."

CHAPTER 14

SAINT PETERSBURG, RUSSIA

TWO WEEKS AFTER that late-night meeting at Tuckerman Roadhouse outside of Langley, Virginia, Liam Grey is sitting in the front passenger seat of an orange-and-white van parked a few short meters away from a one-story concrete building with armored doors and narrow windows in an office park just outside of Saint Petersburg.

The building's flat roof holds a number of satellite dishes and from a small substation heavy power cables run to its west side. Similar concrete buildings are scattered around this office park, the pavement cracked and bumpy, but the vehicles parked in front of the target building are sleek and new, reflecting the status of their owners.

Sitting next to him in the driver's seat is Boyd Morris, an operator from the CIA's Special Activities Division and a former member of the Army's Delta Force. He's slim, with blond hair and a charming smile, who looks like he would fall over in a stiff wind, but Liam knows from experience in the field just how hard he is behind that skinny body and sweet smile.

"Well?" Boyd asks, holding a clipboard up to his face, like he's checking directions or a business order.

"Looks okay from here," Liam says.

"Yeah."

It's a sweet sunny day in April, and traffic roars along the near E-20 highway. The landscape is flat, with lots of brush and pine trees surrounding this quiet-looking office park. Hard to believe that more than eighty years ago, German Army units came racing along these same roads on their way to nearby Saint Petersburg—then known as Leningrad—in their task to conquer or starve the city and kill millions.

History, Liam thinks. This nation is bloody with it.

He also thinks of how utterly alone they are. In the Army you had communications, contingency plans, and Air Force and other airborne assets one radio message away to save your ass if you got in trouble. That all changed when he joined the Agency, of course, but most times, there was an out. You were under some form of diplomatic protection or you were someplace where, if captured, you'd eventually be traded in some future spy swap.

But not now.

They were alone, in enemy territory, going in heavy, with no cavalry over the horizon, ready to ride in to rescue them.

Liam shifts in his seat. The president ordered him here, and that is good enough.

Boyd says, "Funny how something so important is stuck out in the middle of the sticks, no razor wire, no guard towers."

"Hiding in plain sight," Liam says.

Boyd grins. "Gee, you Company fellas know all of the tricks of the trade, don't you?"

"You'd think," he says.

Liam waits, looks at his watch.

Sixty seconds to go.

In that unimpressive concrete structure before them, adjacent to a scrapyard, a gas station, three other warehouses, and a line of old green-and-white *Avtobus* vehicles—their tires missing—from the Saint Petersburg transit system, is a facility operated by the GRU, Russian Military Intelligence.

The military personnel inside that building belong to the GRU's Twelfth Directorate, responsible for Information Warfare and more than a decade of cyberattacks and news bots spreading lies and disinformation without consequence.

Until today.

Liam recalls what he told his crew last night, in an Agency safe house in Imatra, Finland, less than ten miles from the Russian border and just over a two-hour drive away from Saint Petersburg.

The military personnel in that building all have blood on their hands, Liam said. *They've been responsible for disrupting elections, taking down governments, and stealing millions of dollars. They've taken the lead crippling the internet whenever they feel like it, and their internet postings have fostered tribal and ethnic cleansing resulting in the deaths of tens of thousands of innocent people, all to fulfill their government's strategic goals.*

He checks his watch.

Time.

He calls behind him, "Tommy, do your work!"

"Roger that," comes a male voice from the rear, the cargo space back there hidden by a taut black curtain.

A handful of seconds passes.

"Done," Tommy says. "No phone service going in and out of that building, electronic door locks disabled, as well as their surveillance equipment."

Liam says, "It's a go, Boyd."

"Roger that," he says, starting up the van's engine, shifting it into Drive, and then speeds a hundred yards or so to the front parking lot of the GRU installation. Boyd parks the van as close as he can to the front door. He gets out, and so does Liam.

Working calmly yet efficiently, they go to the rear of the van, which Boyd unlocks. He takes out a two-wheeled dolly, and with Liam's help, loads up three black, hard plastic containers, ignoring what else is in the rear of the van. Boyd pushes the loaded dolly up the narrow concrete path and Liam joins him, holding a clipboard with some shipping documents fastened to it.

He and Boyd are both wearing, among other items, black trousers and short jackets with black hems and orange shoulders, marking the work uniforms of TNT Express, the largest domestic shipper in Russia. Black baseball caps with the orange-and-white TNT logo are on their heads, the van also painted with the same TNT logo.

Underneath the jackets are ballistic vests, not a typical part of the TNT dress code.

Boyd stops and Liam goes up, clipboard in hand, and rings the doorbell, ignoring the signs in Cyrillic lettering saying NO ADMITTANCE, KEEP OUT, and PROPERTY UNDER SURVEILLANCE.

Once more.

And once more.

Boyd says, "I bet they're distracted in there."

"I bet you're right," Liam says, pounding the metal door with his fist, calling out in Russian, *"Hey, anybody in there?"*

He turns the doorknob.

It freely moves.

He looks to Boyd, raises an eyebrow, and then the door abruptly opens, with a young man, wearing jeans and a black turtleneck shirt, with shoulder holster, pistol, and one pissed-off look on his face.

In Russian he says, *"You clowns, you've got the wrong address."*

"Sorry, sir," Liam replies. *"We're here to make a delivery of twenty keyboards to Popov Associates."*

A curse from the GRU man, who says, *"Morons, that building is over there."*

He breaks his concentration for a moment, pointing over Liam's shoulders to another squat building in the distance, and Liam takes out a 9mm Beretta pistol from a concealed waist holster and shoots him in the forehead.

CHAPTER 15

ONCE LIAM DRAGS the body of the dead GRU man aside, Boyd pushes the dolly in, and the rear of the van reopens. Four other men—also wearing TNT Express gear—run up the entranceway, unlimbering their weapons. Each has been assigned a quadrant of the building, and thanks to a host of three-letter agencies that are part of the American intelligence apparatus, they have a perfect layout of the building's interior.

The four highly experienced operators race by Boyd and Liam as the two of them get to work, opening the hard plastic storage containers on the tiled floor. From the building's interior they hear muffled shots, a few shouts and cries, and within two minutes, one operator—Ferris Walton—comes out into the lobby and says, "All targets down and accounted for. You two are good to go."

From each plastic container, Liam and Boyd pick

up a black satchel with a carrying strap, make their way down a narrow corridor. Open doors reveal desks and computer terminals and dead GRU men. Liam doesn't spare them a glance.

He's got a job to do, with little time to get it done.

Another operator—Mike Cooper—waves them through the heavy metal door he's holding open. "All clear in here, guys."

He and Boyd enter a dark, cool, air-conditioned room. In banked rows on metal shelves, computer equipment blinks with red-and-blue indicator lights. The rows go on as far as the eye can see. In a desk chair before a computer terminal, an older GRU man with a closely trimmed black beard sits calmly, eyes open, a bloody, round hole in his forehead.

He and Boyd unzip the black satchels, start removing timed thermite charges—black plastic cases about the size of a paperback book—and go down the line of computer servers, placing each charge in a strategic location. When the timers later click to zero, the temperature in this large concrete room will approach that of the surface of the sun, and Liam wants to be as far away as possible when that happens.

"Looks good," Boyd says.

"Got that."

He takes the lead up the corridor, thinking through the next steps and he abruptly holds up his hand.

Boyd stops.

Doesn't say anything but raises an eyebrow.

In a soft voice, Liam says, "Heard something. From that door."

Boyd steps forward, pistol in hand.

The door has a sign in blue, showing a stick figure of a woman and the English letters WC. *Water closet.*

And the Cyrillic letters for *toilet.*

Boyd nods to Liam and he nods back.

Liam grabs the door, spins the knob, hurls it open.

A cry from inside.

A young blond woman, wearing a dark-green uniform shirt and black skirt, sitting on the dirty tan tile floor, hunched up against a toilet, weeping, hands held up.

"Shit," Liam says.

CHAPTER 16

BOYD SAYS, "WHAT the hell are we going to do, Liam?"

Liam doesn't reply.

Running out of time.

Take her prisoner?

Take her out of the building and release her later?

Or...

"Liam?" Boyd again says, urgently.

The young woman moves quickly, dropping her right arm, going behind her back, emerging with a small pistol.

Liam shoots her twice in the chest.

"Damn," Boyd whispers.

"Back to work," Liam says.

He closes the bathroom door.

Resumes his fast walk to the lobby, where

the other four team members are placing hard drives, thumb drives, and collected documents into the hard plastic storage containers, snapping the covers shut.

"Heard two shots back there," Tommy Pulaski says.

Boyd says, "Nothing to worry about. Let's haul ass."

From the other side of his waist, Liam pulls out a smaller pistol and charred notebook, drops them near the door. The operators help him and Boyd load up the containers, and they go out in a quick line to the van.

The four operators slip inside the rear of the TNT Express–disguised van and assist Liam and Boyd in returning the dolly and storage cases into the rear.

The doors are slammed.

Boyd goes to the left.

Liam goes to the right.

Both get into the van, and before Liam gets his seat belt fastened, Boyd starts up the van and in less than a minute, they are back onto the E-20 highway.

Liam doesn't say anything and neither does Boyd.

The mission is still underway and won't be finished until they and the gear are out of Russia.

Boyd says, "About that woman soldier..."

"Yeah?" Liam asks.

"What would you have done if she hadn't pulled a piece on us?"

A kilometer passes.

Liam says, "Boyd?"

"Yeah?"

"Never ask me that, ever again."

Two more kilometers pass and Liam's cell phone chimes.

What the hell, he thinks, digging it out of his jacket. This is a CIA-supplied burner phone, only to be used among the crew and with the CIA station back in the American embassy in Helsinki, and only in an emergency.

Nobody should be texting him.

Liam calls up the screen.

The incoming phone number says BLOCKED.

But there's a one-line message:

GOOD JOB. SIERRA.

Boyd is still focused on their driving.

"What is it?" he asks. "Some car warranty company from Moscow checking in on you?"

Liam puts his phone away.

Sierra is the Secret Service code name for President Barrett.

"Our boss just said good job," Liam says.

Boyd looks at him with amazement. "Barrett? How the hell does he know already?"

Liam says, "Former head of the Agency and

Secretary of Defense, he's still got friends and assets in high places."

Boyd says, "Nice to know, but I don't want him looking over our shoulders if we screw up."

Liam says, "Simple solution to that."

"What?"

He folds his arms. "We can't screw up. Ever."

CHAPTER 17

TWENTY-FOUR HOURS later they are relaxing in another CIA safe house, this one near the town of Puntala, Finland, northeast of where they had started yesterday morning. Liam thinks "house" is stretching it, since their quarters is an old log home. A fire is burning in the fireplace to cut through the damp, and Liam finally unwinds, drinking a can of Karhu beer. Back outside of Saint Petersburg, he and the crew had driven about a half hour before getting to another industrial park, where the van was stripped of the interior and the fake exterior and left behind a building with keys in it. They had scattered in returning to Finland, either taking a bus or a rental car, and after rendezvousing here, the captured hard drives and files were brought to the CIA station in the American embassy in Helsinki.

Liam checks the time. Those materials were probably arriving this moment at Langley.

Yet two things are gnawing at him, like little rats coming out at night to chew at the base of his skull.

One was the woman soldier—probably attached to the GRU—whom he had shot back at the bot farm. A righteous kill, since she was armed, she was in a place that was designated as a target by President Barrett, and she was in uniform and about to shoot either him or Boyd.

Yet armed and in uniform, she was still a young woman, and the only woman in the GRU building.

Damn.

But he remembers the last time he saw his brother, Brian, when he was on leave before his final tour to Afghanistan. They had been drinking late into the evening in the basement of their parents' home, and Brian suddenly said, "You know what you learn out there in the 'stan, Liam? I'll tell you. Your job is to get home alive, you and your troops. Nothing else matters. And sometimes you gotta make a hard decision. Like that goat herder coming your way. Is he just a kid? Or is he carrying a grenade in that pouch? And what do you do if he doesn't stop advancing? I'll tell you. You remember job one."

All right, he thinks. He's done jobs in Syria and

Iraq and Suriname, and has been up against bad guys and had done what had to be done...

This time, a young woman.

But a woman with a pistol.

If Liam had been a few seconds slower, a bullet could have drilled him, or could have killed Boyd Morris. And how to pass that news onto Boyd's wife and kids? *Sorry your husband and dad got killed, but I hesitated...*

All right then.

The other concern is the president. He had given Liam and Noa Himel wide latitude and depth in choosing their teams, weapons, and getting the job done.

But Liam doesn't like the eye-of-God oversight.

Was the president just being cautious?

Or paranoid about his orders being carried out?

Overall Liam is pleased with the mission outcome. Last year that bot farm had hijacked some social media platforms in Myanmar and had spread false stories and rumors about atrocities being conducted from a mountain tribe up north, leading to thousands of innocents being massacred. That led to a lockdown by the military government, which then led to international sanctions— except from Russia—which signed some lucrative development contracts for its *Gazprom Neft* oil corporation.

Now Russia paid a price for its killing of

innocents. At the end of the day, Liam will put this op in the win column.

One of his team members sits down next to him on the sagging couch. The fire crackles and sparks.

"Ask you a question?" he says.

Liam says, "Ask away."

"Back at the GRU bot farm, just as we were leaving, you dropped a pistol and a notebook. Looked like some of the pages were charred."

"Good eye."

"Thanks."

"So what was that about?"

Liam says, "Just a bit of fun. That pistol has a serial number that will trace it back to the KDB, the intelligence agency for Belarus. The notebook has handwritten notes about the layout of the building, how to gain entry, how best to destroy the servers inside. Anybody reading it will think it came from a KDB operative, also from Belarus."

"Damn," the other man says. "Belarus and Russia..."

"They currently hate each other," Liam says. "And it's in our interest to make sure that non-lovefest continues."

"Hell of an idea," the operator says, who is Benjamin Lucas, another officer borrowed from the CIA's Special Activities Division.

Liam nods. "Glad you approve."

CHAPTER 18

IN LOS GATOS, California, Noa Himel is parked in a black Chevrolet Suburban on Kennedy Road, a neighborhood of this Silicon Valley city, with her fellow team member Wendy Liu behind the steering wheel.

The homes here are one-story ranch houses, most with very small yards, though the street is lined with lots of trees and shrubbery. There are even white picket fences along some of the yards. Noa has been on her own share of overseas missions, but she's feeling a sense of pride and anticipation on this one, her first domestic op.

A domestic operation like this is usually illegal, but these aren't the usual days.

Wendy Liu says, "Want to hear something interesting?"

"Always," Noa says.

Wendy says, "My grandfather left China after Mao

and his gangsters took over, back in 1949, and went to Taiwan, and then here, to California. Was a laborer, construction worker, and then started his own contracting firm. Built a lot of houses in this valley, and when he built those houses, you know what?"

"What," Noa says, waiting for another vehicle to show up as planned in this pleasantly rich and tidy American neighborhood.

"He built these one-story ranch homes back when a regular family, you know, Dad, Mom, and two point four kids, could own a home like this. Now? You know what these homes cost?"

"Not sure, but I think you're about to tell me."

"Yeah, the initial cost of fifteen or twenty thousand dollars is now, a million, maybe two million, dollars."

Noa spots a white van with red lettering coming down the street, bearing the logo of Comcast Xfinity, the cable company.

The driver of the van is not in fact an employee of Comcast Xfinity.

"God bless America," Noa says.

"You're damn right," Wendy says. "Where else could a nearly illiterate peasant arrive and build homes that now sell for two million bucks?"

The van stops in front of a light-blue ranch house that looks nearly identical to its neighbors.

Noa says, "Well, the nearly illiterate peasants

that didn't join your grandfather sure have made something of themselves."

Wendy laughs. "That's the truth. Thirty or forty years ago, who the hell was worrying about Chinese espionage?"

The van opens and a male worker in a blue uniform and black baseball cap comes out of the front and goes up to the front door. He rings the doorbell and the door opens.

"That was then," Noa says. "This is now."

Two of her team carrying pistols and wearing ghillie suits—making them blend in with the home's shrubbery and brush—get up from the small yard and storm the house through the open door.

Wendy starts up the Suburban's engine.

"Preach it, sister," she says, putting the vehicle in Drive.

CHAPTER 19

NOA AND WENDY put on blue windbreakers with ICE in yellow letters on the back to confuse any nosy neighbors, and go up the gravel walkway to the house, and then into the main living room.

It's a crowded place.

There are six people sitting on the floor, four Chinese males and two Chinese females. All are dressed Silicon Valley casual, Hawaiian or polo shirts, khaki slacks, comfortable footwear, and all have their hands flex-cuffed behind them. There's a single couch and that's it for standard furniture. Four computer workstations, with monitors, keyboards, and stacks of system towers, gently humming, are clustered in a semicircle. Cables and other equipment hang from the plaster ceiling. No television or music system. The floor is bare hardwood.

Three of Noa's crew—Phil Cannon, Aldo Sloan,

and Juan Rodriguez—are working to pile up file folders, hard drives, and other materials in the middle of the floor. Phil still has his cable television repairman uniform on while Aldo and Juan, faces sweaty, are wearing their ghillie suits, looking like extras from some sort of shrubbery horror movie.

Noa looks at the house's occupants and sees one male face that stands out. She grabs a folding chair and puts it in front of him, casually sits down, and nods.

"Zhou Lieu Wei, so nice to meet you."

He's the oldest in the group, with a fleshy face, thick black combed hair, and black-rimmed eyeglasses. He doesn't reply. His polo shirt is black with a white IBM logo stitched in.

"Mr. Zhou, I hope you and your fellow agents are in good shape," she says. "We don't want to hurt you, but we also didn't want you to destroy any computer files or hard drives as we came in to make your acquaintance."

Noa leans over, grabs a thick black cable running in front of the workstations, gives it a tug. "Ingenious little setup you have here, Mr. Zhou. A power cable installed to send an electromagnetic pulse throughout this entire house, to instantly fry every computer in here, erase every file and system, and pretty much wipe clear the evidence of what you and your mates have been doing these past couple of years."

Noa tugs it again.

"Didn't work, right?" she asks. "Last week a Comcast technician came in to fix a modem problem and managed to fix this as well. When my team came rushing in a few minutes ago, one of your young ladies did her very best to set off the EMP pulse. Nothing happened."

More and more gear is being piled up in the center of the room.

Noa says, "Nothing to say, Mr. Zhou?"

He stares at her with utter hatred and contempt, and says in good English, "I demand to call my attorney."

Noa smiles. "Say again?"

"You heard me...woman. I demand to call my attorney. Now. Or after we're taken to whatever location is prepared for us. Immediately."

Noa says, "Why?"

For the first time since entering the house, the older male looks concerned. "Because...it's the law, that's why."

Juan Rodriguez says, "Damn, Noa, you wouldn't believe how much stuff is squirreled away in those back rooms. It'll take us at least another half hour to get it all packed up. They didn't even use the bedrooms...just slept side by side on futons in the hallways. Everything else is keyboards, servers, and filing cabinets."

"Thanks, Juan," she says. "Mr. Zhou, you and

your comrades have been quite busy, haven't you? Stealing various types of software programs and other systems, all for the greater good of the Middle Kingdom. And you folks delight in taking what's been developed here for our uses—like facial recognition software to identify terrorism suspects—and use it for your own purposes, like inputting the faces of dissidents you wish to arrest and scanning for them on the streets of Hong Kong or Shanghai. Or stealing the software we developed for administering our Bureau of Prisons and using it to crush the Uighurs."

He says, "I did not come here to be lectured by you, woman. Take us to where you plan, and I will make my phone call."

Noa smiles once more. She shouldn't be feeling this way, but she's enjoying this. Unlike that spy ring in Cambridge last year that's probably still hard at work conducting espionage thanks to the FBI, this one in Los Gatos is *gone*.

Their superiors in Beijing at the Ministry of State Security at 14 Dong Chang'an Jie Avenue will try for hours, days, and weeks to communicate with their spy cell here in Los Gatos and will get no answer at all.

Disappeared.

Noa likes the sound of that word.

"What phone call?" she asks.

"Do not joke with me, woman. I know the law."

He lifts his head, spits at her, and a splatter of saliva strikes her face. Aldo Sloan and Juan Rodriguez stop in their tracks, and she holds up a hand to keep them from moving forward.

She quickly gets over the shock and says, "But there's a new law, haven't you heard? There's a secret memorandum of understanding between Washington and Beijing. We're going to treat you the same way your folks would if they arrested a group of American spies in China. Same kind of rights and legal representation that Beijing would provide if the roles were reversed."

Now the Chinese leader seems to understand what's going on.

"But . . ."

One of the cuffed women begins to weep.

Noa stands up. "You're not a citizen, you're here illegally, conducting attacks against the United States. Therefore, no phone call, no attorney, no one-way trip back to China. I hear Cuba might be nice this time of year, or maybe the Marshall Islands, or Guam."

The captured Chinese agents stare on in silence.

Noa carefully wipes the spittle off her face, and then leans down and gently rubs her right hand on Zhou's left cheek.

Noa says, "Get used to it. Papa's got a brand-new bag, and his name is President Barrett Keegan."

CHAPTER 20

THE APPLAUSE AND cheers coming from the attendees at the annual Humphrey-Mondale Dinner in Minnesota warms President Barrett Keegan and lifts his mood. The support and the love rolling up from the packed crowd inside the packed auditorium feels almost substantial, as he could lean into it, like one of those weathermen reporting on hurricane-force winds.

Accompanied by party officials, his own White House staff, and members of the Secret Service, Barrett is quickly escorted offstage, the applause and cheers still echoing in his ears and in the corridors of the building.

Briskly the Secret Service takes him outside, where the Beast—his armored limousine—is waiting, along with two other limousines, police cars, and Suburbans making up his motorcade, ready to take him back to Air Force One.

Standing next to him is Stephanie Martin, the head of the Minnesota state party. She says in an awed voice, "Mr. President, look at that!"

"That" happens to be what looks like thousands of residents, crowded behind hastily constructed rope lines set up in the large parking lot. Additional Secret Service personnel and Minnesota State Troops are valiantly working to keep the cheering crowd under control, as Barrett waves back at them, standing on his toes to get a greater view.

Look at that, he thinks, *look at my people.* The trust and love they have for him, Barrett Keegan.

He will never betray that trust and love, and that insistent voice inside of him says, *You belong here, this is your time, your destiny.*

Stephanie has to lean in closer to make herself heard over the cheering crowd. "This was unscheduled, sir," she says. "It was just spontaneous. Sir, the people…they are behind you, one hundred percent."

Barrett waves once more before ducking into the limousine. "I intend to keep that support, Stephanie, as I make them and their families safer than they can even imagine. Thanks for this incredible day."

"You're welcome, Mr. President," she says as the heavy door is swung shut. "You've earned it."

CHAPTER 21

LAS VEGAS

IN A PRIVATE dining room at the luxurious hotel Waldorf Astoria on Las Vegas Boulevard South, Secret Service Special Agent Marianne Harrison is feeling just a bit more comfortable at seeing her protectee, Alamo, settle down to a leisurely meal.

Alamo, also known as Laura Hernandez, former congresswoman, former governor of Texas, and now vice president of the United States, has spent a busy day with a variety of Nevada politicians, going out to the Hoover Dam for a speech on alternative energy sources, and then back to the famed annual Consumer Electronics Show. Alamo toured the various display booths at the CES, tried everything from a VR system that approximates the surface of Mars to a medical bracelet that could "read" vitals from heart rate to cholesterol level, and throughout the tour Special Agent Harrison—the detail leader—and about a dozen or so Secret Service agents kept close watch.

Even though the place was secured and there were undercover agents mingling in with the crowd, Marianne still wishes Alamo wouldn't expose herself so much.

Which is hard to do, since as a former governor, Alamo loves to press the flesh and be out with the public.

But here, inside this closely guarded dining room, Special Agent Harrison is feeling more in control. This room is heavily secured, there's a squad of agents in the kitchen area, and every chef, line cook, waiter, and waitress have been thoroughly vetted.

With Alamo are the governor of Nevada, the majority leaders of both the state senate and state house, and various business leaders and government officials. Alamo's husband is back in Austin, where he's a history professor at the University of Texas, and her two daughters are in schools in and around the Austin area.

The low-ceilinged, wood-paneled room is hung with burgundy draperies and decorated with antique paintings and sculpture. The piped-in jazz music is a soft backdrop for loud conversation and lots of laughs, and then someone starts having a coughing fit.

She looks to where the coughing is coming from.

Alamo's table.

Harrison starts moving and there's a crash of silverware being dropped and glass breaking, and she sees Alamo sliding to the floor, as her seatmates cry out and stand up.

She brings up her wrist microphone from her two-way Motorola radio that's belted to her waist and says, "Alamo is down, Alamo is down, MERT, get in here now!"

Harrison gets to the fallen vice president, calls out, "People, give me room, please, step away!" Back to her wrist microphone she says, "All stations, Alamo is down. Shut down the perimeter. Nobody enters or leaves."

Other members of the detail come through to her, pushing people and chairs and tables aside. The voices are louder now, with calls of "What's wrong? What's going on?" from the other diners.

Harrison's training comes right to her as she instantly responds.

Alamo is on her back, eyes closed. She's wearing a red linen skirt and jacket ensemble, black blouse. She checks her pulse at the side of her neck. Weak but regular. Harrison checks her mouth, makes sure her airway is clear. Alamo is fifty-four years of age, dark complexion and black hair, and is an avid jogger and tennis player.

"Madam Vice President," she says, speaking loudly as the other Secret Service agents push away her dining companions. "Can you hear me? Madam Vice President? Can you hear me?"

A door slams open and four Secret Service

agents run in ahead of members of MERT (Medical Emergency Response Team) carrying canvas bags of medical gear shoving people aside.

Harrison gets up. "Alamo had a coughing fit," she says. "Collapsed. She's breathing and has a steady but weak pulse. But she's unresponsive."

The lead medic says, "Okay, she's ours," as bags get unzipped and monitoring equipment, a green oxygen bottle, and other gear is swiftly removed.

"Amy, this is Marianne," she says, speaking into her wrist microphone.

"Marianne, this is Amy," comes the quick reply. "Status?"

"MERT is on scene. We're going to need transport soonest," she says.

"Ambulance and escort vehicles are already at the rear kitchen entrance," the Secret Service agent says. "We have a gurney and three Las Vegas Fire Department EMTs en route, they should be there in about a minute."

"Roger that," she says, catching her breath. Whenever Alamo or the president, known as Sierra, go to public events like this, her agency always ensures there's a trauma unit within a ten-minute drive.

She catches the eye of Agent Frank Chan. "Frank, everything on this table is evidence. Alamo might have been poisoned. Guard it until the FBI gets in here."

"Roger that, Marianne."

Harrison brings her wrist microphone up, takes a breath. "Rudy, this is Marianne," she says, calling the agent in charge of covering the hotel's kitchen area.

"Marianne, this is Rudy, go."

"Shut down the kitchen. Nobody leaves or enters, none of the food or scraps or dirty pots and pans get touched. Understood?"

"Yes, Marianne."

"I don't care if the chef or the restaurant manager go apeshit, nothing leaves, enters, or gets touched in there."

"Understood," he says.

Marianne stares at the table, at the uneaten food—prime rib or salmon—and the overturned glassware.

Failure, she thinks. Something's happened to Alamo. A strong, athletic woman like that collapsing and going right into unconsciousness, with no warning?

What just happened here?

A medical emergency?

Or an assassination attempt?

BULLETIN

LAS VEGAS (AP)—Vice President Laura Hernandez was rushed to the University Medical Center hospital here after collapsing and becoming unconscious at the Waldorf

Astoria on Las Vegas Boulevard South.
Witnesses told reporters at the scene that
the vice president had a spell of loud coughing
before falling to the floor of a private hotel
dining room. Secret Service agents and EMTs
from the Las Vegas Fire Department provided
immediate assistance before she was transported at 5:46 p.m. Pacific Standard Time.
Her current condition is unknown.
—MORE—

CHAPTER 22

WASHINGTON, DC

PRESIDENT KEEGAN BARRETT is working late again in his quiet and small office on the second floor of the White House. A tray with the remains of his dinner—a simple egg white omelet—is on the coffee table in front of his old desk as he works through a thick file that two hours ago was couriered over to him from Langley.

Like his predecessors, Barrett is working on a list whose name has changed over the years, with its recent, innocent permutation being the Disposition Matrix. But no matter how much lipstick one puts on this bureaucratic pig, it is still known as the "kill list," those enemies of the United States who had been determined to be an imminent threat, and who, upon Barrett's signature, would imminently receive the latest version of a Hellfire missile in their lap.

But Barrett's personal "kill list" has widened,

ever since he set up the two CIA teams under the direction of Liam Grey and Noa Himel, and their initial confidential reports back to him have been encouraging.

Yet he knows, deep down, that his window of opportunity to strike first against his country's enemies may close at any time. What the various pundits and experts, generals and admirals who still want to fight the last war don't understand is how damn flexible and pinpointed one has to be in this new age. Army armored divisions, squadrons of Air Force bombers, and fleets of Navy ships are huge sledgehammers, ready to kill and destroy at a moment's notice.

But today you have to be precise, you have to be quick, and, most of all, you have to be quiet.

And then there's the iron confidence and will—which he's had for decades, urged on by a whisper that he was unique—that he was put on this Earth to do great things.

Which is why he is working so diligently at this late hour.

He reads again the summary of this update, prepared by a team of analysts back at the CIA who are still personally loyal to him, and who didn't feel it was necessary to go through official channels to supply the detailed information he needs.

This update regards one of the biggest banks in South Korea—BK Financial Group—and how for years it's been secretly bypassing and undercutting the many financial embargoes in place against their neighbor to the North. Even though North Korea is a sworn enemy of Seoul, for years this bank has been using distant branches and other financial cutouts to help Pyongyang launder the funds it's stolen from cyber phishing attacks or received from slave laborers sent to China or Siberia, or for coal shipments successfully smuggled to Russia or China.

For years there have been stern messages, complaints, and warnings to Seoul that something must be done to stop BK Financial Group's work in propping up North Korea, but nothing has happened. The various governments of Seoul—who have depended on the BK Financial Group for its campaign contributions and other largesse—have denied the accusations, or promised to "look into it," or have claimed that the rogue bank's actions have ceased.

Enough, Barrett thinks, as he puts the file aside for later action. He mutters, "We keep thirty thousand men and women stationed there…about time you paid the piper."

And as he considers how the piper will be paid— a concealed cyberattack to permanently erase the bank's electronic records, or something old-fashioned like a wayward cruise missile blamed on the South Korea military landing in the main bank's front lobby—the door opens and Carlton Pope, his special assistant, comes in.

"Yes?" he asks, taking another thick file folder from the pile on his desk.

"The vice president has landed at Andrews," he says. "She's being transported to Walter Reed at this moment."

"Good," he says. "What's her condition?"

"Still in a coma," Pope says. "Unresponsive."

"And her husband and children?"

"Air Force transport will be bringing them later tonight to Andrews, and I'll have the Secret Service take them to the hospital."

"Good," Barrett says, opening the file folder.

Pope says, "We have a statement ready for release. Do you want to look at it?"

"Is it good?" Barrett asks. "Do you vouch for it?"

"Yes, sir," Pope says.

"Then give it to the press office, have them release it as soon as they can," Barrett says. "I'm busy."

"Yes, sir," Pope says. "Is there anything else?"

Barrett gestures to the coffee table. "Yes. Get rid of that, all right?"

Pope nods, grabs the dinner tray, leaves his office, and Barrett resumes his work.

One thing he's learned over the years is the importance of picking good people and letting them do their job, whether it's returning a dinner tray to the White House Mess, or crafting a press release, or putting a bullet in the head of an enemy of the United States.

CHAPTER 23

ISLA LA BONITA, VENEZUELA

IT'S A PERFECT sunny day on the Caribbean Sea as Liam Grey gently maneuvers his large paddleboard off the sandy coast of Isla la Bonita. This tourist resort in Venezuela is one of its few places worth visiting as its government keeps on learning the harsh lessons of running an economy into the ground. Liam wishes he could relax in these warm waters, but he can't, since he's deep in work, although any observers out there would have a hard time thinking so.

Which is just perfect, he thinks, as he keeps on slowly paddling, sitting down on the board like he's tired. He's been here on this small island for a week, his dark-brown hair dyed blond, working on his tan and enjoying the nightlife, fitting in with the British, European, and other travelers attracted to these beautiful beaches, waving palm trees, and the ridiculously low prices as the struggling government in Caracas tries to attract more foreign dollars.

Including, he thinks, as he slowly paddles, other visitors who aren't from Britain or Europe, and who don't care much about the beach bars, restaurants, palm trees, and beautiful Venezuelan women.

On the paddleboard is a small black knapsack. Liam removes a bottle of water, takes a satisfying sip, and then grabs a pair of binoculars, gives a quick glance to the rocky promontory at the end of the tourist beach. There's a stone cottage with four black SUVs parked out front, and for the past week, Liam's worked to keep it in view.

The house looks empty, since there are no tourists out there, sunning themselves on the large rocks or splashing around in the tide pools or playing volleyball. Or driving along the dirt road that runs through a collection of boulders and rocks, emerging onto the single-lane paved road running parallel to the beach and the tourist cabins and bars.

No, no tourists.

Just an outpost of the Hezbollah terrorism empire.

He puts the binoculars back into the bag, which is secured to the paddleboard by a set of Velcro straps. He recalls the briefing he received from the president two weeks ago.

"This cell has been active there for at least eighteen months," President Barrett said. "They support drug smuggling, kidnappings for ransom, and killings of tourists, and have attacked numerous diplomatic, military, and business targets throughout Central and South America. Various protests and diplomatic notes haven't caused Caracas to expel them and send them back to Lebanon. I leave it up to you and your team, Liam. Get the job done."

A pleasure, he thinks. Hezbollah's been on both the official and unofficial CIA hit list for more than forty years, ever since the terrorist group kidnapped the Agency's station chief in Beirut and tortured him nearly daily for a year and a half before killing him and dumping his remains on the side of the road.

Ever since then, those assassinations, air strikes, and car bombings against Hezbollah usually blamed on Mossad actually came from their cousins in Langley, though it was never officially or unofficially reported from Washington or Jerusalem.

Some at Langley have very long memories.

Including Liam.

A voice comes to Liam in a flesh-colored earbud via an Agency-owned fishing vessel barely visible on the northern horizon, encrypted with the Agency's latest communications equipment. "Liam, you on station?"

"I am," he says.

Benjamin Lucas, one of his operators back at Saint Petersburg, says, "We're ready, but you need to know there's a Venezuelan Navy patrol boat snooping around about two miles away. If we're a go today, it's gotta be in the next few minutes."

Liam checks his watch. "All right, let's start the countdown. At the mark, now...two minutes."

"Two minutes, roger that," Benjamin says.

Liam takes out a small instrument that looks like a monocular device used by birders, but this device is just a bit more advanced and complicated. He turns it on, checks its vitals as it hums into action, and Benjamin says, "One minute, Liam."

"One minute, roger that," Liam says, stretching out on the paddleboard like he's trying to relax for a moment, the monocular device in his hands.

"Starting countdown," Benjamin says. "Fifty seconds."

"Fifty seconds."

"Forty."

"Forty seconds," Liam replies, bringing up the monocular to his right eye. A light-green reticle with a cross appears, and he adjusts it so that it's aiming at the near window of the cottage. Interior and advanced GPS software ensures it remains centered on the target, even with the motion of the waves against the paddleboard.

"Thirty seconds," Benjamin says.

Liam repeats, "Thirty seconds," and his finger goes to the trigger.

Something's wrong.

A flash of movement catches his attention.

What?

He lowers the monocular device, grabs the binoculars, looks over at the target. A white minivan is coming to a halt near the house.

The doors open.

Four young, laughing women emerge, wearing wide-brimmed straw hats and sunglasses and carrying towels and beach bags.

A slim, bearded man wearing a long-sleeved black T-shirt and long pants emerges from the stone cottage, waves, smiles, and goes back into the house.

One of the young women waves back, and the four women pull coolers out of the van.

"Fifteen seconds," Benjamin says.

Liam says, "Break, break, break. Abort, say again, abort."

"What?" comes Benjamin's stunned voice.

"Abort," Liam repeats. "We have civilians on scene."

Benjamin says, "Liam, we don't have time."

"We're aborting."

"Liam, that damn patrol boat is coming our way."

Liam says, "Handle it. It's an abort."

Benjamin curses and Liam starts paddling, as fast as he can, to the rocky beach where the terrorist cell is located.

CHAPTER 24

THE MOTION OF the waves helps Liam as he gets closer to shore, and when he's a meter or so distant, he leaps out, furiously wades in, quickly dragging the paddleboard up onto the rocks and jumping from rock to rock and over the sand to get to the dirt driveway.

There.

The small knapsack is over his back and he moves up the dirt road toward the four young women, dressed in bikinis and sandals with wraparound skirts. He yells out, "Hey, *chicas*. Wait up!"

One of them turns and replies in English, "Hey yourself."

He comes closer, smiling, and says, "Look, you don't want to go there."

The one who talked to him smiles in return, shakes her head. "What business is it of yours?"

Liam says, "I know those guys. They're ... they're

just lousy. Hairy, don't bathe, treat nice ladies like you like dirt. C'mon, my buds and I, we're having a party in an hour, over at Las Tres Loros. Trust me, you'll have more fun with us."

Two of the young women start talking quickly in Spanish. Liam knows the language, but not this fast. The apparent lead woman says, "I'm sorry, *amigo,* we have made a promise here… and…"

She's ashamed, and Liam knows it. He's embarrassed for her and her three friends, for what they have to do to stay alive in this country teetering on financial and economic chaos, store shelves empty, lines for gasoline miles long, pharmacies barren of drugs.

Damn it, he thinks, there's no time.

There's just no time!

He says, "Look, we're all adults. And I don't want you to get hurt…"

Liam unzips a side pocket, pulls out six one-hundred-dollar American bills. He takes a step forward, pushes it into the near woman's hand. "Take this. See you at Las Tres Loros. All you have to do is have a meal with us, some drinks, and laugh at our bad jokes and bad Spanish. Honest. Please."

The woman looks at the money, talks quickly in Spanish to her companions, and they move back to the minivan.

She says, "The man here...Abdullah. He'll be angry. He might come after us."

Liam says, "Go. If Abdullah comes out, I'll take care of it. Go."

He steps back, watches with satisfaction as they get into the minivan. The engine starts, backs up, makes a U-turn, and heads back down the dirt driveway, kicking up a trail of dust.

Liam starts moving and a man calls out, "You! *Senor!* Stop!"

The man is the same one from before, slim, bearded, long-sleeve black T-shirt and long pants, and thick eyebrows knotted in fury.

Liam holds his hands out. "Hey, I'm just leaving. Have a nice day now!"

He stalks to Liam and takes out a knife from a belt scabbard. The blade is shiny and looks sharp. "What you say, have a nice day? You took away our whores."

Liam says, "They changed their mind. That's all. Why don't you take a walk and cool down?"

Time, he thinks, *time.*

"Walk?" he yells. "I walk into you!"

Liam holds up his hands—not high up—and says, "Hey, hey, hey—"

The Hezbollah man lunges, Liam spins sideways, and as the knife hand goes by, with his right hand, Liam grabs a shirt-sleeve, twists it, and with his left elbow, breaks the man's nose.

He cries out, falls to his knees, and Liam—still holding tight to the sleeve—hammers the man's wrist on Liam's knee.

The knife falls to the dirt.

Liam picks it up.

Shoves it hard up into the terrorist's left armpit, where the axillary artery is located, and Liam draws it up and out.

The Hezbollah man gasps, tries to speak.

Blood spurts out from the severed artery that supplies blood to the arm and fingers and is now supplying blood to the dirt road.

Liam wipes the knife hilt on the man's T-shirt, drops it on his chest.

He leans over and whispers, "In a couple of minutes, you're going to be dead, alone in Venezuela, compliments of the CIA."

He runs back down to the rocky beach, splashing into the water, pushing the paddleboard out. With fast and hard strokes with the paddle—still sitting down—he gets beyond the swell of the waves, turns, and faces the stone cottage.

"Benjamin, this is Liam. Status?"

Just the sounds of the water *slap-slapping* against his paddleboard.

"Benjamin, status?"

He peers out to the north. Hazy and hard to see the boats out there.

"Benjamin?"

His voice comes into his earbud. "Liam...we're a go here."

"Did that patrol boat come by?"

"Affirmative on that."

Liam picks up the monocular aiming device. "Damn...everything okay?"

Benjamin says, "Yeah. A twelve-pack of Corona and a hundred-dollar bill made everything all right. They're off to harass some other poor fisherman. Starting countdown...now. Forty seconds."

He and Benjamin go through the countdown one more time, and he aims the monocular device at the near window, the light-green reticle centered on it, the interior GPS software keeping it right on target.

"Thirty seconds," Benjamin says.

"Roger that," Liam says, as he pulls the trigger.

A laser beam flashes out from his device— invisible to the naked eye—and strikes the center of the window. He keeps it in place, and Benjamin continues the countdown all the way to "Zero, away."

Liam keeps quiet.

Aiming.

A little flash of light from the horizon, like a quiet burst of heat lightning.

Now.

From the deck of the fishing ship on the other side of the horizon, a modified AGM-114R

Hellfire Romeo bunker-buster missile is launched, and instantly locking on to the invisible targeting laser held in Liam's hands, it punches through the stone cottage's window and explodes less than a second later.

Liam sees the windows and door blow out of the cottage, and the stone roof crumple and then collapse in a burst of smoke and gray dust. The shock wave even makes his paddleboard sway in the warm water.

Benjamin says, "Liam?"

Liam puts the aiming device down, starts paddling away from the destroyed cottage.

Liam says, "Nothing finer."

CHAPTER 25

ARLINGTON, VIRGINIA

NOA HIMEL SITS by herself in a wing chair next to a wide wooden desk in a comfortable, first-story home office in a two-story brick home in the Bluemont neighborhood of Arlington, just about fifteen minutes away from Langley. Built-in bookcases are filled with leather-bound volumes and antiques from Turkey, Greece, and southern France rest in decorative cases. Framed photos and certificates hang from the walls. She's pulled her chair opposite an old-fashioned swivel chair and away from the desk so it's facing the open door.

In her career she's met contacts in dingy cafés reeking of cigarette smoke, alleyways ankle-deep in raw sewage, and the top of parking garages where a sharp wind always seemed to cut her through.

Tonight's meeting place is definitely a step up.

She's looking into the entryway of the fine house.

A stairway goes up from the main front door, and on the other side is a living room, dining room, and empty kitchen.

Noa patiently waits. Once she worked with an operator named Callaghan, who could spend hours like this, just waiting. She asked him one long night how he spent the time, and laughing, he said, "My grandmother told me I should take time like this to contemplate my sins."

And she replied, "Ever run out of time?"

"Never," he replied, with a smile.

Poor Callaghan, she thought, killed in a Taliban-led ambush three years ago in some now-forgotten FOB—Forward Operating Base—in the 'stan.

The front door opens. Noa checks the time. It's ten past eleven at night.

She also checks the 9mm Beretta pistol in her lap.

A man comes in, nearly stumbling. He takes off his rain jacket, tries twice then succeeds in hanging it up on a coatrack, and he moves to the kitchen before he seems to sense a presence in his office.

He comes in, carrying a leather briefcase. "What... who... what the hell is going on here?"

Noa reaches over, switches on a green-shaded lamp. The room comes into sharper focus.

"Joshua Mooreland," she says. "So nice to make your acquaintance."

He steps in closer. Late fifties. Dark-gray suit, white shirt, unbuttoned, dark-yellow necktie undone. Eyes blinking. Thick gray-and-white hair, metal-rimmed eyeglasses, fleshy jowls, red face.

"Who the hell are you?" he demands, words slightly slurred.

"Noa Himel," she says. "Directorate of Operations." She moves her chair around so it's facing the desk, waves the pistol. "Have a seat."

"You...you bitch, who the hell do you think you are?" He drops his briefcase on the floor. "I'm making a call right now to DDO Jordan to get your ass fired."

She lets him vent. He goes to his desk, picks up a phone, looks puzzled, drops the receiver into the cradle. Goes to his right coat pocket, takes out a mobile phone. Thick fingers work on the screen.

Nothing happens.

Something approaching comprehension appears on Mooreland's face. He sits down heavily in his swivel chair.

Noa says, "Some work associates of mine are outside, ensuring we have a nice, adult, calm conversation without any disturbances."

He says, "Why the pistol?"

"Due to your sketchy record, Joshua. I can call you Joshua. Correct? Or would you prefer Mr. Mooreland? I understand you asked female subordinates to call you *Mr. Mooreland* when you asked them to parade in your office to give you a little fashion show, whenever you desired it."

He says, "That was consensual. Nothing was ever proven."

"The way you treated local embassy staff in Bogota and Mexico City, was that consensual?"

He turns away for the briefest of moments. "There was evidence that they were in the employ of the Russians. That I was…entrapped."

"Entrapped," Noa repeats. "How convenient for you. Well, that's why I came in here the way I did. I didn't want to be on the receiving end of being entrapped. I'm sure you understand."

He stares at her and she stares back.

First one to talk loses, she thinks.

He says, "What's this all about…whatever your name is."

"Noa Himel," she says. "I've been detached to serve in a special unit to clear out the deadwood at the Agency. After a special review, it's been determined that you're number one on the list. You've had a dull and fairly unimpressive career, bouncing from station to station, division to division, from Athens to Buenos Aires. You barely made the minimum work effort, were always late in submitting reports, and you exaggerated the capabilities of agents you recruited for your division."

Mooreland says, "Whatever's in my record only reflects what my supervisors put down on paper. There are other accomplishments that have not been officially recorded. You know how it is."

"Like the six times you came into work so drunk you had to return home? Or the two times you entered an alcoholic rehabilitation program, promising to halt your drinking, only to have you leave said programs weeks ahead of schedule?"

"Those programs were interfering with my work," he protests. "I had to return to Langley."

Noa says, "I don't know how—perhaps you and your supervisors attended the same schools or belonged to the same fraternity—you failed upward, being transferred and shuffled off to some other poor station chief. Joshua, I'm here to tell you that it ends tonight. Now."

Mooreland says, "Who the hell are you to make such a threat? Damn you, when he was director, Keegan Barrett tried to get rid of me and here I am, still here."

For an older man, Mooreland then moves quickly, hand reaching under the desk, and Noa realizes he's reaching for a weapon.

CHAPTER 26

THE EXPRESSION ON Mooreland's face quickly goes from triumph to despair, as his empty hand slowly comes back from underneath the desk.

Noa says, "Joshua, you were probably hoping to grab that .357 Colt Python revolver you keep in a holster attached to the underside of your center desk drawer. You think I was going to meet with a sexual predator like you, even armed, and leave a weapon within reach?" Noa shakes her head. "Nice try."

He seems to regain some composure. "I'm not going anywhere. And once I get my phone service back, I'm contacting the Office of the Inspector General, to make a formal whistleblower complaint. Once that happens, young lady, I'm golden. And I can't be touched."

Noa says, "Joshua, not only are you a lousy analyst, a pig around women, and an overall drag on whichever division you've been assigned to, there's been at least two instances where you were investigated for unauthorized contacts with foreign agents."

Like a metronome, he automatically replies, "I was investigated in both cases. I passed the polygraph testing. I was cleared."

Noa says, "Just like Aldrich Ames, damn the man, who also passed polygraphs. Joshua, as a smart man, I'm sure you know that Scotland has a different kind of judicial system than their brethren to the south. Instead of having 'guilty' and 'not guilty' decisions, they have a third. 'Not proven.' That's when the jury feels there's not enough evidence to convict, but there's enough evidence to think you probably did it. I've read the reports on your investigations, Joshua. If we were headquartered in Aberdeen instead of Langley, that would have been the Agency's conclusion."

"Go to hell," he says.

"Perhaps someday, but not tonight," Noa says. "You had unauthorized contacts with a Russian agent and an Iranian agent, supposedly random meetings at a bar in Athens and a trade show in Vienna. Following those meetings, networks we were running in both cities faded away, just at the same time your bank accounts were getting fatter, you got your teeth capped, and you purchased a new Jaguar."

"That's all explained in the reports," he says. "My wife and I...we had a lot of gold and jewelry that we decided to sell. It was just gathering dust. We sold it, got cash, and that was that."

"Yes, your third wife," she says. "Supposedly she handled this all on her own, finding the jewelry stores to buy the jewelry, receiving the cash, and losing the receipts and forgetting the names of the stores in the process. Extremely convenient."

Mooreland says, "Now. Get out. Right now."

Noa shakes her head. "Not going to happen."

"Bullshit."

"Nope, not at all," she says. "This is how the next hour or so is going to proceed, Joshua. There's a legal pad on your desk. Find a pen. Start writing down the illegal contacts you made with foreign representatives, what and when you passed on to them, and how much you were paid. Refresh your befuddled mind to the best of your ability and sign and date each page. Begin now."

He tries to regain his voice. "Or what? What can you possibly do to me?"

Noa glances at an old grandfather clock gently ticking in the corner. "Start writing now, Joshua, and when you're finished, you'll resign tomorrow and go find a small town out West somewhere to disappear. You'll receive your full pension and benefits. But it's now...eleven-seventeen p.m. If you refuse to start writing, for every minute that passes, you lose five percent of your pension."

There seems to be a lot going on behind that old man's tired eyes.

Noa says, "Approaching minute one, Joshua."

He waits.

Waits.

Curses and picks up the pen, starts scribbling on the yellow legal pad.

Nearly two hours later, Noa takes the folded legal pages, puts them into her bag, and stands up.

"Your resignation sometime today, Joshua."

He's slumped in his chair, staring out at the office with the plaques, certificates, and collected artwork.

"I need to know something."

"I'll try."

"Suppose I hadn't cooperated, had stood hard, even with my pension zeroing out," he says. "What would you have done?"

Noa smiles, puts her pistol away in the bag as well. "Simple," she says. "I would have blown off your damn head, and claimed self-defense, and I would have been believed."

CHAPTER 27

WASHINGTON, DC

LIAM GREY IS drinking his fourth Sam Adams of the night at Bullfeathers on 410 First Street SE, listening intently as the young woman sitting across from him—Molly Tafer—is telling him about the challenges of selling advertising for the *Washington Post* during this increasingly digital age. He met Molly a half hour ago after dropping in here following a late-night briefing with President Barrett and Noa Himel at the White House, and with the events of the past few weeks, he needs to unwind.

Molly is bright, open, with shoulder-length blond hair and wearing a black, knee-length skirt, and a simple light-pink blouse. She's still working on her first vodka martini.

Over the noise of the bar—packed with lobbyists, staffers, and politicians from both sides of the aisle—Molly says, "My grandfather Jack worked at the *Post,* also in ad sales. He told me that he could make his quota by noon, then have a three-martini lunch and snooze the rest of the day away. Can you believe that? Me, I have to scramble to place pop-up ads that drive both revenue and website clicks."

Liam shakes his head in sympathy, and then she says, "Tell me again what you do at the State Department. Is there a lot of travel?"

"Nah, not as much as you'd think," he says. "In fact—"

A hand is on his shoulder, and a woman behind him says, "Don't believe him, Molly. He travels a lot, and never tells you where he's going, how long he's going to be away, and when he comes back, he keeps his mouth shut."

Molly brightens up in recognition. "Kay! Good to see you. Say...you know Liam?"

Liam feels his face warm and thinks of that old famous *Casablanca* line. *Of all the gin joints....*

Kay Darcy circles around. Her thick black hair is pulled back in a ponytail, she's wearing jeans and a button-front blue blouse, and her smile is engaging yet sharp.

"Liam?" she asks sweetly.

He smiles. "Yes, Molly, we know each other."

Kay says, "Once upon a time we were husband and wife. Before his job conflicted with my job, being a *Post* reporter."

The night quickly takes an odd shift with Molly suddenly remembering she has to meet some friends at another bar, and Liam finds himself with his ex-wife, Kay, whom he hasn't seen in at least eight months.

Kay cheerfully sits down across from him and says, "How far did you get?"

"Apparently not far enough," Liam says. "Is this your new hobby, interfering in my dating life?"

His ex-wife laughs. "She's a good girl, smart about advertising and income stream and internet clicks, but not smart enough to deal with a guy like you, Liam."

"And what kind of guy am I?"

"Oh," she says, "let's not play that song again. We both know the music and lyrics by heart. Let's talk about other things. How're your mom and dad?"

"Doing all right, enjoying the sunshine and their gated community in Florida," he says, once again remembering how those brown eyes and tanned complexion—and, to be honest, those sweet curves—utterly entranced him the first time they had met. It had been at a Saturday seminar at Georgetown University run by the State Department on emerging economies in West Africa, and by evening's end, he had made two acquisitions: her phone number and a healthy dislike for any emerging economies.

"And yours?" he asks.

"Still waiting for me to leave journalism and get a real job," she sighs. "They don't like having their daughter being a quote, enemy of the people, unquote. Mom and Dad want me to move to California, find a job in Silicon Valley, and make a gazillion dollars, so I can support Mom in the way Dad can't."

He smiles at Kay's wit, recalling the six-month frenzy of their early relationship, followed by two years of pretending to be an up-and-coming power couple—her in journalism, him at the Agency—until her working late nights and weekends and his long absences slowly rotted everything, like an underground stream washing away a home's foundation.

"Buy you a drink?" he asks.

She pats his hand. "Oh, aren't you the sweet devil. No, I'm meeting someone here for dinner."

"A date?"

She smiles. "How about none of your damn business?"

Liam says, "Ouch, good point. How are things at the *Post*?"

Kay shrugs, looks around at the crowded bar, and Liam feels a slight pang for the woman he had wooed and loved and promised to spend the rest of his days with, now here, looking for someone new to roll in.

She says, "Oh, you know how it is. Trying to

report stories when nobody wants to talk to you. Trying to determine if a source is leaking you information because they want to see the truth come out, or wants to back-stab somebody on the same floor where they work. Trying to defend the First Amendment when so many people have given up on it, doing my part to ensure democracy doesn't die in darkness, trying not to forget filing my expense reports."

"Makes for a full day."

"Sure does, sport," Kay says. "And you? Subverting freedom anywhere?"

"That was last month," Liam says. "Right now, just following my oath of office, defending the nation against all enemies, foreign and domestic."

Her eyes flash at his last sentence. "Funny you should mention that."

Oh, God, he thinks, *not again.* During their marriage, Kay always teased and needled him about becoming a source for her or somebody else at the *Post*, and the fiftieth or so time she had tried, it had resulted in a night-long vicious fight that turned out to be the first of many.

"Kay..."

"Come on, Liam, hear me out," she goes on. "Covering the military and intelligence agencies, you hear a lot of rumors, a lot of chaff, a lot of crap. Just help me out."

"You know I can't."

"But you can help me by telling me there's nothing there, right? That's not like confirming something I'm working on. For old time's sake."

Liam sits still, not wanting to hear his ex-wife trying to work him.

Kay says, "What you mentioned, about all enemies, foreign and domestic. I'm hearing bits and pieces that your boss might be expanding your Agency's reach, including the domestic part of the world. You can imagine the firestorm if that were to happen."

Liam says, "You really think that a science nerd like Acting Director Milton Fenway would even think of doing something like that?"

Kay laughs. "What makes you think I'm talking about him? No, I'm talking about our second bachelor president, former spook and 'Dark Knight.' The honorable President Keegan Barrett. We're hearing bits of information that he's using his old contacts in Langley and at the Pentagon to set up his own back-channel network to go after those on his enemies list."

There are no real secrets in DC, Liam thinks, *no matter what the dwellers haunting the internet and their moms' basements want to think*, but he's stunned—and a bit sickened—to think President Barrett's efforts have already leaked out.

What to do?

Deny and lie?

Try to dodge around it?

Convince Kay to leave it alone?

He gets up, squeezes her hand.

"Sorry, Kay, I'm late. Good to see you."

He strides out through the crowded bar, not hearing if she is saying anything, but knowing he's just done the right thing.

As much as they unsettle him, questions now echo in his mind:

Who's the leaker?

And why?

CHAPTER 28

WASHINGTON, DC

NOA HIMEL IS slightly buzzed from her fourth glass of white wine, on top of a homemade meal of pasta and garlic bread, and she's stretched out on a small settee in the condo unit of one of her best friends, just relaxing and trying to unwind.

Sitting across from her is Gina Stasio, whom she met when they both started in a training group after their initial hire at the Agency. Gina is short, dark-haired, plump, a wonderful cook, and an incredibly talented member of the Office of Technical Services, the creator and curator of spy gear that's used in the field, all the way from disguises to hidden cameras to encrypted radio systems.

Gina says, "Top you off?"

"In a bit," Noa says. "That means I have to move, and sorry to say, Gina, your comfortable couch here has seized my ass."

Gina laughs. "I can bring the wine to you, girl. And the couch unfolds, so if you want to spend the night, feel free to do so."

The living room is snug and cozy, with low bookcases and two oil paintings of Chesapeake Bay up on the wall, both done by Gina. The television is set to Netflix, some edgy new miniseries about a woman detective in Seattle.

"I might take you up on it," Noa says. "You hear any fresh news about the veep?"

Gina says, "Caught an update when I was cleaning up in the kitchen. Stable and safe condition at Walter Reed, still unresponsive. Poor woman."

To her surprise Noa says, "Maybe she's ashamed of being a part of the Barrett administration."

Her friend laughs. "Noa, where the hell did that come from? You speaking out of school now?"

Watch it, she thinks. Too many careers at the Agency have sunk in the amber waves of booze, even when consumed in the presence of friends.

"I left school a long time ago, Gina," she says.

"Yeah, except for the school of hard knocks," Gina says, getting up and going to the coffee table, picking up a bottle of California Chablis, filling up Noa's wineglass.

Noa doesn't object.

Gina returns to her chair. "Speak."

"Can't."

"That high up?"

Noa takes a healthy sip. "Mount Everest high up."

Gina purses her lips, picks up her own wine-glass. "When I'm in my windowless workshop, doing my best to make a foolproof passport with the appropriate exit and visa stamps showing the exact shade of color and wear, and I sneeze and get droplets on the ink, and I have to dump two days of work and start over again…lots of times, I envy you folks out in Operations."

Another sip of wine from Gina. "But not today. Give your girl a hint or two. It'll make you feel better."

Noa wants to sink into the couch and sip her wine and watch the Netflix episode forever and think of nothing else, and she hears herself saying, "From the Gospel of Matthew, Gina…'Again, the devil took him to an exceedingly high mountain, and showed him all the kingdoms of the world, and their glory.'"

The room is quiet, and Gina says, "You're weirding me out, girl. How does a nice Jewish girl like you know so much about the New Testament? You saying you're Jesus, and the devil is…Acting Director Fenway?"

Noa says not a word, but makes a thumbs-up with her free hand, and gestures to the ceiling.

"Oh, that's pretty high," Gina says.

"You know it."

"And you're tempted."

"Yes, because up there, you can see a lot. And do a lot. But also concerned . . . because . . ."

"The air is pretty thin up there."

Another few seconds pass. Noa looks at the Netflix episode. Unimaginative and simple, but God, sometimes it's good to be unimaginative and simple.

Gina says, "Don't care if the air is thin, or if the view is great, or if all the kingdoms are at your feet . . . if you get pushed off and start tumbling, Noa, where are you going to end up? Besides on that pert ass of yours."

"Probably in a crevasse, so I can keep on falling, just for the amusement factor." Noa rubs at her forehead. "Forget it. Things are fine, I'm doing important work. Just sometimes, you want to be sure you're doing right at the same time."

Gina says, "I had an instructor once, back in the day. She said some of the biggest dangers you'll face in the Agency come from coworkers or supervisors. She said that every time you're told to keep quiet, not take notes, or don't keep records, that's the time to take notes and keep records. You need something to save your butt in case things fall apart."

"Like playing poker."

"How's that?"

Noa sips again and decides she's going to see how this couch feels when it does open into a bed. "My uncle Benny told me once, that if you're playing poker and you can't tell who the sucker is, then it's you."

Gina says, "If you're in an op, Noa, and you can't tell who the fall guy is going to be..."

"Yeah," she says. "Then it's going to be you."

On Netflix, the tough yet tender woman police detective has just tenderly shot someone twice in the chest who was threatening to assault her.

Gina says, "I think I might be able to help."

Noa says, "I was hoping you'd say that."

CHAPTER 29

WASHINGTON, DC

IN HER LARGE and well-decorated office in the Longworth House Office Building, Gwen Washington, speaker of the House of Representatives and a congresswoman from the 43rd Congressional District in California, is staring hard at her three visitors this morning, feeling her mouth go dry with fear and anxiety.

With her are Roget Blaine, her lead attorney; Tiana Grace, her chief of staff; and Shania Greer, her press secretary. All smart, good-looking, well dressed, and, like her, tough Black women in a tough world.

Her office has a dramatic view of the Mall and the Washington Monument, then the rectangular shape of the reflecting pool, and at the end of that—hard to see in the day's haze—the Lincoln Memorial. Nearly two centuries ago the figure in that memorial freed her great-great-grandfather from a Virginia plantation not more than a hundred miles away.

Good job, Abe, she thinks. No matter the setbacks, the challenges, the failures that take place every day, looking at the Lincoln Memorial always sends a jolt up Gwen's spine, makes her buck up and get to the job at hand, to honor her great-great-grandfather and so many others.

She has a healthy self-confidence and ego, deservedly so, having pulled and dragged herself from the poor streets of Berkeley to studying hard and getting grants and scholarships, and getting into Yale, and then coming back, working her way through California politics.

Yet in keeping her eye on the prize, she's never forgotten her roots, never forgot her friends and classmates who didn't have either her luck or drive, and she's made sure that a fair amount of federal scholarship funds and grants get back to her district.

But it's the gentle sound of file folders and papers being placed on her desk that frightens her so, papers and file folders that may do what racist politicians, a biased news media, and even members of her party who dislike someone so powerful and "uppity" have wanted to do to her for years.

Force her out of office.

"How bad is it?" she asks.

"Pretty bad," her lead attorney, Roget Blaine, says.

Gwen shakes her head. "Ten minutes ago, I was on the phone with President Barrett, him support- ing keeping Juneteenth a federal holiday, and promising to give a push to that Department of Justice grant program for better police training, so our folks aren't gunned down in the street. He even said he'd work with us on the economic power zones for the inner cities, so we get more there than liquor stores and bodegas. And now . . . now, all this progress and working with the president, it's all threatened, is that what you're telling me, Roget?"

Her three closest advisers look at her in silence, three Black women carefully made-up and coiffed, wearing power suits and bright jewelry and fine shoes, marking them as part of Gwen Washington's Posse, the gals that got stuff done up on the Hill. There are plenty of photos of her posse up on the wall, along with other photos as well, of W.E.B. Du Bois, Richard Wright, Adam Clayton Powell, Rosa Parks, MLK Jr., Shirley Chisholm, Barbara Jordan, Obama, and so many others who had made her path possible.

And on her desk, in a prominent position, a large portrait of her husband, Hal, dead these past two years, so many hours in the last year of their marriage spent flying red-eye from DC to SF, trying to ease his suffering as pancreatic cancer ate him from the inside.

"Yes, ma'am," her attorney says. "It can all come tumbling down."

"Tell me," she says. "Bad news never ages well."

And she looks one more time out the window, feeling like she's on the edge of falling into a deep hole, failing her people from then, and her people now.

So much to do and so little time to do it.

Less than two hours later, after going through reams of documents, including deeds, government grant paperwork, checking account statements, and property listings, Gwen Washington, speaker of the House, feels a migraine headache coming on. When Roget Blaine finishes the briefing, Gwen sits back and takes a heavy drink of water.

Roget says, "Madam Speaker, as your attorney I'm sorry to advise you that what we have here— in scores of documents contained in the thumb drive dropped off anonymously at your Berkeley office—is enough evidence to show that you and your late husband were involved in a yearslong effort to channel government grants and funds to shell companies owned by the two of you, as well as him getting to the head of the line for his bank—Municipal Financial of Berkeley—to get a federal bailout a week before it was going to be seized by the FDIC."

She taps a thick finger on another folder. "Then there's a host of other petty complaints. You loudly demanding a room upgrade while visiting Las Vegas. Kickbacks to those office supply stores providing stock to your regional offices. Snapping at tourists getting in your way as you tried to board a member's elevator on the Hill. Among other things."

Tiana Grace, her chief of staff, says, "Madam Speaker, we need to get ahead of this story before it gets out."

A vise seems to be slowly constricting around her heart. "But...none of it's true! It's bullshit! I made it clear to him, from day one when I got into politics, that our lives couldn't mingle. He went his way, I went mine, and there's no way on God's green Earth did I do anything illegal." She gestures to the pile of documents. "It's a setup. Forgeries. Clever shit indeed but it's all shit. Russians, Chinese, who knows who's behind it."

Her attorney says, "I'm afraid that doesn't matter at the moment, Madam Speaker. It'll be the first impressions. The news will get out in the near future, and with Majority Leader Deering snapping at your heels...he will want to drag it out as long as possible, to weaken you, perhaps even get you to resign in disgrace. It's going to be hard to prove a negative."

Gwen thinks of the thousands of people she's helped over the years with scholarships, grants, how she served as a role model to those who thought the world was set against them from the day they were born.

Was she going to allow herself to be used to disappoint them and add to the deep political cynicism that's for years afflicted DC?

No.

Not this time.

Gwen says, "Not going to happen. And we're not going to allow this . . . crap, to get out in the news. I don't want a whisper of this leaving this office or getting to Congressman Deering."

Her press secretary, Shania Greer, iPhone in hand, quietly says, "Majority Leader Fritz Deering is going to demand a full investigation."

"Says who?" Gwen asks. "Stop making shit up, Shania."

Her press secretary looks mournful. "I'm not making it up. I'm reading it on CNN."

CHAPTER 30

WASHINGTON, DC

A WEEK AFTER his swim in the Caribbean, Liam Grey is back to meet with President Keegan Barrett and Noa Himel, but instead of being in the White House's family quarters, they are in a penthouse suite at the Hay-Adams Hotel, within walking distance of the Oval Office.

Which is not typical, but which is also not unusual for this president. "With the world's best communications equipment at my fingerprints," he once told a columnist for the *Washington Post,* "why should I stay stuck in a two-century-old house?"

The suite is two large rooms, with an adjoining bedroom and a sitting room that they're occupying, with couches, coffee table, plush chairs, kitchen area, and large-screen television.

Noa says, "You've gotten some sun."

"Yeah, but the trick is to goop up enough so

you don't burn and peel. How about you? Go any place interesting?"

Noa says, "Interesting is where you find it."

Liam stifles a yawn.

"Lots of travel?" Noa asks.

"Some. You?"

Noa says, "You know the setup, it's all domestic. Just stayed in the good old States."

They wait.

Liam is sensing something from Noa, an unease, something making her uncomfortable, out of sorts. "You look like you've just come back from the dentist," he says. "What's up? And I don't mean a rejected expense account or a poor Performance Appraisal Report."

"Liam..."

"Come on, Noa," he says. "We're on the same team, just different squads. Something's bothering you."

She pauses, and says, "The other night I was in a CIA officer's home. A stupid schlump who should have been cut loose years back. And I threatened him until he agreed to confess all and resign. It was a good job...but I felt like taking a long shower afterward."

"The job was done," Liam says. "One given to you by the president. That's all that counts."

"No, that's not all that counts," Noa says. "Who or what's driving the job is what counts. Just before I left, this officer told me that when Barrett was Agency director, that he tried and failed to get rid of him. My mission, then. Something for the national interest, or Barrett getting his long-desired revenge? And you? What's your time been like?"

Liam smiles. "I was on an exotic Caribbean locale, sipping frozen drinks, talking to four amazing Venezuelan young ladies in bathing suits."

"What a burden."

"Yeah, and a while later, I saw a nearby house being rented by Hezbollah tourists suddenly collapse from poor building materials and a modified Hellfire missile, but mostly from a modified Hellfire missile. Awful sight, but you know what? No second thoughts."

"They'll come eventually," Noa says.

"What? Another operation?"

"No," Noa says. "Second thoughts."

"None from me, Noa," he says, crossing his arms. "We got a hunting license, we have all the resources we need, and we have POTUS on our side. What's to worry?"

Liam hears the doorknob turn. Noa says, "You know what they call dedicated CIA officers working on the edge, when they think they have foolproof protection?"

"Tell me."

"Defendants," she says, as the door to the suite opens.

CHAPTER **31**

NOA IS JUST slightly amused at Liam Grey's earlier comment about visiting the dentist, for one rear molar is indeed giving her a dull ache today, but she forgets the discomfort as the president strides in, dressed in a crisp two-piece gray suit, white shirt, and red-and-blue tie, upbeat and positive-looking, carrying two thick, sealed manila envelopes in his hands.

She and Liam stand up when he comes in, and he gently gestures them both to take a seat in their respective chairs.

"Sorry I'm late," the president says, sitting down on the couch across from them. "I was just on the phone with the speaker. She's having a tough day."

"Sir?" Noa asks.

He spreads the two sealed envelopes on the coffee table and says, "Something from her late husband has come up from the grave to bite her in the butt. Loans, payoffs, shell companies in his or her names...looks rough. Times like that make me glad that I never married. Too many chances of something popping up from various family members and hangers-on to take you down."

Liam says, "That sounds serious."

"Yes, poor Speaker Washington," he says. "It may be bullshit but right now it looks like convincing bullshit. You'll see, in the weeks and months ahead, she'll be trying to explain what's going on, while also beating back a leadership fight with her majority leader, who wants her job. Not much will get done on her watch, but truth be told, no matter how clean they are, our congressional representatives are their own worst enemies."

Noa says, "Sounds cynical, sir."

"You know the average yearly salary for a congressman?" Barrett says. "About $174,000 a year. And the average net worth of an American congressman? Nearly eight million dollars. That's some fine financial planning, don't you think? Or lots of luck?"

Liam seems to want to change the subject and says, "Any news about the vice president's condition?"

"Stable and doing fine, except that she's still in a coma." Barrett sighs. "Not to leave this room but the feeling is that some trace poison, perhaps from the Russians, may have gotten onto her silverware or drinking glass. Two physicians from Germany are en route from the Charité University Hospital in Berlin. They have experience in dealing with such toxins."

Liam's face seems to pale. "Russia, sir? I mean..."

"Retaliation?" Barrett says. "Don't worry about it. They're still blaming that action on their Belarus friends, and we expect some border incidents between the two of them in the days ahead. In the meantime..."

Liam and Noa stay quiet as the president goes on. "I want to start off by saying how pleased I am with your initial work. You both have completed four operations with excellent results and no collateral damage, and no extensive interest from our alleged friends in the Fourth Estate."

Barrett smiles. "But as has been said before, 'what have you done for me lately?' Noa, this is yours, and Liam, this is yours." He hands the sealed envelopes to the two of them. "Questions?"

Noa says, "It's been nearly a month, sir. Again, with all due respect, have you made the necessary notifications to the congressional committees? Under the Intelligence Authorization Act?"

"Soon," he says. "I want a few more checkmarks in the win column before I give them a briefing. You know what they say, it's better to ask for forgiveness than seek permission."

He taps his thick fingers on the envelopes. "Liam, you're off to France. Noa, I'm afraid you're off to Virginia again. But at least you'll have no jet leg."

Noa takes her envelope and so does Liam, and the president says, "I need to ask you both something."

Noa takes a view of Liam, who nods, as does she.

He says, "You two ever hear of Stewart Brand?" he asks.

Liam says, "No, sir," and Noa echoes him.

Barrett says, "Stewart Brand was a futurist and environmentalist. He produced books back in the 1960s and the 1970s that he called Whole Earth Catalogues, which were a book form of the internet. Lots of information and technology available between the covers. He once said, 'We are as gods, we might as well get good at it.' Don't you see what he means?"

Noa doesn't know what to say, and it pleases her that Liam is speechless as well.

"Don't you see?" Barrett asks. "What you're doing for me and the nation is vital. We're not engaged in a large-scale war, or fighting to secure trade agreements in our favor, or crushing smaller nations. We are an empire unlike any other that has existed in this world, and I mean to preserve it. We are locating our enemies, foreign or domestic, ones fighting against me and our nation, and removing them, making our nation and our people so much safer."

He stops for a moment. "To misquote Mr. Brand, 'We are an empire, we might as well be good at it.' And I'm counting on the two of you to preserve our empire."

Noa sits still.

As does Liam.

"Any more questions?" he asks.

Quiet.

The president stands up, and so do they.

"Good," he says. "Now get the hell back to work."

CHAPTER 32

ABOUT TEN MINUTES after their meeting, Liam is sitting on a park bench in Farragut Square, one block away from the Hay-Adams Hotel. Next to him, Noa says sharply, "Did you hear him back there? Did you?"

"I was in the room, right? Of course I heard him."

"Help him and the empire? Empire? Do you remember taking an oath to defend an empire, Liam? I sure as hell don't. And then he said something about the 'ones fighting against me and our nation.' You don't think that's odd, him identifying himself as being the nation? Like Louis XIV from France who said, *L'état, c'est moi.* Is that what we're putting our asses on the line for?"

Around them pedestrians, tourists, and district government workers are strolling along, enjoying the sunny day and relatively dry air, and Liam feels the unseemliness of it all, that just a few minutes ago, they were in a nearby hotel suite, talking about destroying the nation's enemies.

Liam says, "The boss was just exaggerating, that's all. Lots of pundits and scholars say we're an empire. Most are too polite to say it out loud."

"The president of the United States shouldn't be saying that, in private or out loud. And shouldn't personally link external enemies to his own safety."

Liam says, "At least he's not using Twitter. Come on, you expect the president to be a constitutional scholar?"

"I expect him to do right, that's what I expect. And not sound like he's losing his grip on things."

"And you're the judge of that?" Liam asks.

"Somebody has to be," she says. "You'll keep on saluting and saying 'yes, sir' all the way to the congressional hearings, with your ass on the line, and me right next to you."

Liam shifts so he gets a better look at her angry face. "All right, Noa, what's your deal? What's driving you? If you're so straight, why in hell did you join the Agency?"

Noa says, "You're ex-military. You wouldn't understand."

"Try me," Liam says.

Noa says, "In this fight . . . I've always felt like we were the civilized ones, fighting against the ones enjoying blowing up kindergartens, taking down civilian airliners, shooting up shopping malls."

"The CIA psychologists would probably think that's a simple and crude assumption," Liam says. "Even though I tend to agree with you."

"Do you think those psychologists know what ZAKA is?"

Liam thinks he's familiar with the term but plays along for Noa's sake. "Probably not. Tell me about ZAKA."

Noa stares out over at the calm and peaceful park, and in a voice that's now slight, tentative, she says, "I've gone back to Israel a few times to visit family. Twice I've seen ZAKA in action. They're a volunteer group that responds with emergency personnel if there's a terrorist bombing somewhere. But they don't work to help the survivors or work on the injured. No, they volunteer to recover the smallest piece of flesh, bone, or brain, so that in the traditional Jewish way, it can be properly buried."

Liam keeps his mouth shut. "So you have our enemies using our technology, from cell phones to bomb-making, and we—the civilized ones—respond by forming squads of volunteers to fulfill a burial obligation. More than two decades ago, the barbarians used the latest in aviation technology to attack this very city. But people forget. They're still out there, waiting to strike again. They've killed your brother, and they killed my cousin Becky in Beirut, years back. And if, by joining the Agency, if I can help knock back the barbarians, I'll work night and day to do so."

"Nice point of view," he says. "I grew up here in DC, long ways away from embassy row and fancy parties, with equally lousy schools. But my parents did the best they could, my dad working as a sergeant in the Capitol Police and my mom as an editor at the Government Printing Office. I saw from them what it was like to work with higher-ups who think they know it all, and I didn't like it. Still don't like it. Especially those bureaucrats who've never been in the field, have never seen what the bad guys can do."

"Glad to hear that," Noa says. "But what was that bit back there, about the vice president and the Russians and you?"

Liam says, "Need to know."

Noa swears and says, "In case you haven't figured it, chief, I'm handcuffed to you on this op. You and I are either going to get promoted, go to prison, or have a memorial star carved in a marble wall at Langley when this is over. I think I have a goddamn right to know."

Liam looks around the crowded Farragut Square, wondering just how many of the people out there knew of Civil War Admiral David Farragut, who led an attacking Union force through Mobile Bay—the Confederacy's last open port—and when he learned that the harbor was mined with objects called torpedoes at the time, issued that famous order.

"Damn the torpedoes, full speed ahead!"

Damn the torpedoes, indeed.

He says, "My crew and I raided a Russian bot farm and took it out."

"Where was it?" she asks. "Africa? Baltic States? One of the 'stans in Central Asia?"

"Just outside of Saint Petersburg," he says.

"Saint Petersburg?" she asks with awe. "The one here or the one over there?"

"Don't be silly," he says. "The one over there."

Noa lets out a low whistle. "That's some damn impressive shootin' there, cowboy. How did it go?"

"Went off fine, without a hitch," he says, and then, correcting himself, adds, "One small hitch. Ops like that one tend to lend themselves to last-minute complications."

"When you say 'raid' and 'took it out,' mind clearing away the sterile language and telling me exactly what happened?"

Liam says, "We got there, pretending to be a domestic package delivery outfit. About a minute before knocking on the door, one of my guys disabled their electronics, surveillance gear, and communications. We then went in and killed everybody in the building, and then set off thermite charges to burn everything, including concrete and steel."

Another low whistle from Noa. "You overseas boys sure don't mess around."

Liam says, "This bot farm was run by the Russian GRU and was responsible for that civil war in Myanmar last year, the one that killed thousands, and also responsible for fouling up that special Senate race in Montana. We also left a calling card. A pistol and charred notebook indicating the raid had come from the KDB in Belarus. Shed no tears for them, Noa."

"I won't," she says. "What was the hitch?"

"The GRU tends to be a chauvinistic unit," he says. "Every GRU officer in there was male and got two taps to the head and one to the chest . . . except for a young woman, hiding out in a bathroom. Maybe nineteen years old. Twenty."

Noa says, "Shit."

"Yeah. We had strict orders. No prisoners, no wounded GRU officers, no witnesses. But the orders didn't say anything about a scared teenager hiding in a WC."

Noa says, "Must have been hard, doing what you did."

Liam is surprised. "How do you know what I did?"

"You outlined your rules of engagement. You don't get to where you are by ignoring them."

Liam says, "You're a cold one."

"If so, we're both hanging out in the same freezer. So answer the question."

Liam says, "She was in a military uniform, in a military facility, and she pulled a pistol on me and a fellow operator."

"Then you did your job," she says.

"I did."

Noa says, "Well, we've got a new job now, friend."

"What's that?"

"Keeping an eye on POTUS, along with me," she says. "He says he chose us for particular reasons, to do what's right. Okay, so far, we've signed off on his targeting plans. They may be a stretch, but they're legitimate. But you know what they say about absolute power and how it corrupts. At some point, we may get a target from Barrett that's not legitimate. What are we going to do then?"

"Respond appropriately."

"That's mush."

"No, that's what we'll do," Liam says. "Like LBJ said last century, better to be on the inside of the tent pissing out, than outside and pissing in. He's trusting us, he's liking what we're doing, and we can be in a position to gently steer him away if he gets too enthusiastic."

"Too enthusiastic? Or too much of something else?"

"Like what?"

"Like it scares me to say it out loud," Noa says. "You have to admit that what he's doing isn't normal."

"Jesus, Noa, what's considered normal when it comes to a president. Do I have to remind you of—"

"No, you don't," she says. "At least this boss stays off Twitter and doesn't claim to be a stable genius. But you and I, we're in a privileged spot."

"No argument there," he says. "And I'll talk to you if I'm concerned about an op or issue, if you promise to do the same."

"Deal," Noa says. "But we've got to prepare for something that's coming our way, Liam. We and our teams are disappearing a number of opposing units. One of these days, our enemies are going to take notice, and they'll respond."

Liam thinks for a moment and says, "Like what we did after we armed the jihadists in Afghanistan when they were fighting the Russians. We walked away from the wreckage we helped cause, and that helped breed the Taliban and al-Qaeda."

"We're causing chaos now, Liam, we need to be eyes open for what happens next."

Liam nods. "Blowback."

Noa says, "Blowback like we can't even imagine."

CHAPTER 33

ON THE OFFICIAL employment list of the Embassy of the People's Republic of China on 3505 International Place NW in Washington, DC, Xi Dejiang is listed as a deputy agricultural attaché, even though it has been years since he's stepped onto a farm or into a slaughterhouse, and that suits him just fine.

He's the senior representative for the Chinese Ministry of State Security for all of North America, and he is pondering a series of problems this morning while holding court in what's known in the embassy as the Cube, or among his enemies in Britain and the United States, a SCIF, a Sensitive Compartmented Information Facility.

It's in a subbasement of a compound that was never officially designed or constructed with the knowledge of local and American federal officials, but Dejiang still takes the necessary precautions.

It's a room made of lead, cloth, Lucite, and radio-frequency-blocking foil and paint. There are no electronic connections that pass through the cube: no power cords, no communications lines, nothing, save for one dedicated and heavily secure phone line. The only furniture is a flimsy wooden table and four equally flimsy and thin wooden chairs, meaning it is nearly impossible to hide any type of listening or recording device in them.

Even then, this room is swept four to five times a day—and never on a regular schedule—and the furniture is also replaced on occasion.

The only bit of decoration in the small and nearly airless room is a framed print of the Grand Admiral Zheng He, who set sail from China in the early 1400s with ships of such size that they would not be matched again until the twentieth century. With his fleet and soldiers, Admiral Zheng had been poised to begin an undefeated march that would have conquered the world, until the idiot Hongxi Emperor and his finance ministers had called him back to shore and sunk his ships.

On days like this, he likes to think of the brave admiral's ships going up the Thames or the Seine, burning London and Paris. He touches the frame and says, "Ah, ancestor, if they had listened to you, we would have taken our rightful place in the world nearly six centuries ahead of schedule."

A tap outside on the cube and he calls out,

"Enter!" The interior of the room is smelly, due to Dejiang's habit of smoking American Marlboro cigarettes. He likes the taste and the nicotine rush and won't toady up to the Ambassador by smoking Zhonghua cigarettes. He has also told the maintenance staff who asked him not to smoke in the Cube to *Gǔn kāi* themselves.

A sliding door opens and his deputy, Sun Zheng, makes a slight bow and sits across from him, the thin wooden chair creaking ominously. Zheng is at least a hundred kilograms overweight and the compound staff tease him that his trouser legs and jacket sleeves clamp him tight, like sausage skins. But behind the flabby jowls is a sharp-rate mind and all-seeing, cold, dark eyes.

His hands are empty, yet Dejiang knows he's ready for the briefing Dejiang requested two days ago. Zheng doesn't need a notepad or paper, and since no electronic devices of any kind are allowed into the Cube, he can still do his job.

"Well?" Dejiang asks.

"The situation has gotten worse," Zheng says. "We've lost another station in Redmond, and two of our Fox teams have gone dark. One in New York and the other in Chicago."

Operation Fox Hunt, Dejiang thinks. Highly classified, highly controversial, with teams of State Security agents being sent undercover to the United States to observe, harass, and—where possible—

seize dissidents, defectors, and suspected state criminals and bring them back to China.

On occasion in years past, Fox Hunt teams had been discovered in the United States, but it has been years since the last one.

And now there's two?

"Any warning?"

"None," Zheng says.

"And no word from the Americans?"

"Officially . . . no."

Dejiang thinks about that for a moment. He says, "In the usual manner, the Americans would make a large production of arresting our people in their country. Somber men in suits behind microphones. Press releases. Warnings from their elected officials about the new emerging 'yellow peril.' Making quiet inquiries through back channels to set up a prisoner exchange. But nothing this time, correct?"

"No, sir."

Dejiang says, "Unofficially, what do you know?"

Zheng says, "I have an asset at the State Department. The asset has made inquiries. It was not local police, or province or state police, or FBI action. It has something to do with President Barrett."

Surprised, Dejiang says, "It was done under his orders?"

"With his knowledge, that's all I can say. But my State Department asset did pass along a message, from someone he's friends with at the White House."

Zheng takes a slip of paper from his side coat pocket. It's white notepaper with the words THE WHITE HOUSE centered at the top. Before reading the typed note, Dejiang says, "Is this legitimate? Not a fake? Or a provocation?"

His assistant looks troubled. "I don't know for sure. But based on what we've seen from this president during the past months..."

Dejiang knows exactly what Zheng is thinking. The president is what his friends and supporters call a lone wolf, operating the government like it was his personal fiefdom yet maintaining a positive popularity rating among the populace and actually getting some legislation passed among the nation's squabbling factions. But he is maddeningly inconsistent, loudly making threats and making confidential messages of goodwill at the same time, rocketing from one position or crisis to another.

For millennia the emperors and rulers of the Middle Kingdom have sought stability above everything else, through wars or trade deals or espionage, and this American president refuses to cooperate, or at least maintain a consistent and predictable position to Beijing's advantage.

He reads the note:

Best regards from John T. Downey and Richard G. Fecteau.

The typed note is unsigned.

He drops it on his desk.

"Who are these two men?" Dejiang asks.

"They are CIA operatives."

"Where are they?"

"One is retired, the other is deceased, of natural causes," Zheng says.

Dejiang asks, "What's the significance of these men?"

"They were prisoners of ours, from many years ago."

"How many years?"

"They were both captured in 1952 when their aircraft was shot down in Manchuria, as part of a CIA mission."

"How long were they kept prisoner?"

"For more than twenty years, and for the first few years of their captivity...our government didn't acknowledge their existence," Zheng answers.

Dejiang pokes at the notepaper. "Highly irregular, don't you think? Not a diplomatic note or demand. An...insult of sorts. Sending a message. But what kind of message?"

"Perhaps the president is gaining revenge for onetime members of the CIA, which he used to head. We know he values loyalty above all."

Dejiang gazes again at the simple paper and simple typeface. Once again, this lone warrior, this solitary tribesman of a president, has done something entirely unexpected, something that will make Dejiang's life more difficult in the days ahead.

"It doesn't make any sense," Dejiang says. "Are we still seeking revenge for our half-million soldiers the Americans killed in Korea? No. We have moved on. But Barrett..."

He thinks again, then looks to his assistant.

"We need to come up with some sort of response, but a measured one. Something to gain the president's attention so we can open some sort of dialogue to determine what he wants."

Zheng says, "I've been working on that, sir. We have an opportunity to get the president's attention with an action in South Africa."

"Good," Dejiang says. "A neutral location. Get to work on it immediately."

Zheng stands up. "At once, sir."

"But..."

"Yes?"

"Your American State Department asset. Quietly and discreetly ask him something from his White House friend, who's been so helpful to us."

"Sir?"

The worrying words seem strange coming from his mouth. "How does he gauge the status of Barrett's mental health?"

CHAPTER 34

THERE'S A LIGHT rain falling this morning as Noa Himel sits in a black Toyota Camry, a cup of Mc-Donald's coffee in her hands, her back molar feeling better. Not a coffee snob—especially after tasting the swill pretending to be coffee from Afghanistan to Turkey—she likes the golden arches coffee for its consistency. A cup in Seattle tastes just like one in Falls Church, Virginia, where she and her crew are currently stationed.

Wendy Liu is again in the driver's seat and they are in the parking lot of a Wawa convenience store on Hillwood Avenue, just across the street from a set of two-story brick condominiums. It's just past six a.m. and already, the road is filled with commuters on their way to and around DC.

"Look at all those good little worker bees, heading off to their jobs," Wendy says. "Inspiring, isn't it?"

Noa says, "Years ago I read one of those apocalyptic novels about a group trying to overthrow the government."

"Who was behind it? The military? The NRA? National Education Association?"

Noa says, "FEMA. Among other discontents. Part of the plan was to hit the District of Columbia with stolen nukes from Russia, and one character, a radio talk-show host, said he would be happy never to hear the phrase 'inside the Beltway,' ever again."

"Some commuting days, I can agree with him. Time?"

Noa checks her watch. "Six-oh-five. Per her schedule, Donna Otterson will be out of the shower and preparing her breakfast. Let's go see what's on the menu."

"Besides betraying one's country?"

"That comes after lunch."

There's an empty parking spot for condo visitors that Wendy pulls into, and Noa joins her outside in the light rain. A Chevrolet Suburban with its engine idling is by a dark-green dumpster, holding the other three members of her crew. Their action this morning is going to be a soft one, since they're going up against a thirty-year-old single woman, Donna Otterson, who is a finance resource officer within the CIA's Directorate of Support, about as far away from fieldwork as one could get and still work for the CIA.

Walking up the brick walkway Wendy says, "Think she's going to put up a fuss?"

"Doubtful," Noa says. "But I've got our three amigos showing up about five minutes after entry, just to be sure."

Wendy says, "What possible kind of secrets can an FRO be passing on to Chinese intelligence?"

Noa says, "Maybe the amount of our mileage reimbursement."

Wendy laughs.

Noa gets to the front door, rings the bell several times, and then pounds on the door.

It opens, revealing a slim blond woman with large, thick eyeglasses, frizzy hair damp from the shower, wearing gray sweats and a Washington Nationals T-shirt. She says, "I'm sorry, what's this?"

"Donna Otterson, my name is Noa Himel," Noa says, displaying her identification. "This is my work partner, Wendy Liu. We're from the Directorate of Operations. We'd like to come in, please."

Noa is expecting an argument, more questions, or some sort of protest, but Donna shrugs and opens the door wider. "I guess so. Just watch out for Bailey, he's an escape artist."

Noa enters in the small entryway. A large black-and-white cat makes for the open door, but Wendy works quickly and the door is shut.

"Cup of coffee?" Donna asks as they go into a small and orderly kitchen. "I can boil up some water, make a cup of tea if you'd like."

"No, thanks," Noa replies, thinking how odd Donna is acting, how she seems resigned to her visit, like she had been expecting someone to come to her front door for some time now.

Another shrug, and Donna says, "Well, I guess we can sit down in here. Bailey, behave!"

Noa nearly stumbles as the cat nips her ankle, and they all go into a living room. It's crowded but neat. Donna sits in a chair with a knit afghan covering it, and Noa and Wendy take the couch. The black-and-white cat jumps up between them, starts licking his paws. On the low table in front of them are neatly stacked copies of the *Economist,* the *Wall Street Journal,* and *Washington Post.* Bookshelves contain equal amounts of paperback and hardcover books, along with a handful of DVDs.

Noa has a feeling that this young single woman sits alone on this couch with her cat, either reading or watching a foreign language film with subtitles, but she instantly tamps down her sympathy for her.

"Donna, you've been a financial resource officer for the Directorate of Support for seven years," Noa says. "Do you have anything to say for yourself before we proceed?"

Another slight shrug. "You two are from the

Directorate of Operations, right?" She smiles slightly. "That's where my dad served. God, he loved the Agency so, and once I got hired and he could tell me some of his old operations...I really wanted to follow his trail—Operations was starting to open to women recruits back then—but this," and she taps her eyeglasses for emphasis, "kept me out. Still, like my dad, I love the Agency."

She waits for a moment. "But why aren't you from the Counterintelligence Mission Center? That's their job for situations like this, not the Directorate of Operations."

"Because they seem to be dragging their feet. Putting your matter at the bottom of their list of priorities. We have other priorities."

Donna says, "That sounds odd. Don't you agree?"

Noa agrees but doesn't want to say it aloud. It is strange, that she and her team would be here, chasing down a leaker who works for the Directorate of Support. But the president had personally given Noa the orders and background to snap Donna out of her job and take her away to be interrogated.

Noa says, "Earlier you said you were proud of the Agency, and the work your dad did. Then why did you do what you did?"

"What's that?" she asks.

"Pass on classified material to unauthorized personnel on at least six occasions," Noa says, feeling like this slight woman is playing a game with her. "I have the photographic evidence to show you if you care to deny it. You chalking a trail sign at Cherry Hill Park, and then placing an envelope underneath a nearby park bench. Ten minutes later, the package is retrieved by an individual we know is stationed at the Chinese embassy."

"You know that for sure, the person is from the Chinese embassy?"

"We do."

Donna looks sad. "Guess I was going to get caught, the longer I did it."

Wendy says, "Why did you do it, Donna?"

"I did it for the greater good," Donna says. "And for the Agency, of course."

Noa doesn't know what to say.

Donna says, "Am I under arrest?"

"No," Noa says. "You're just being detained."

"But you want me to come with you, right?"

"That's correct," Noa says.

"Can I bring Bailey with me?" she asks hopefully.

"I'm afraid not," Noa says.

Tears come to the woman's eyes. "Then what's going to happen to him? I don't want him to be put in a shelter. He'll think he's being punished or did something wrong."

Noa has faced some challenges in her career, but this is a new one, and Wendy comes to her rescue. "I'll take care of Bailey."

Donna's face lights up. "Really? You'd do that?"

Wendy says, "I promise."

The door opens and the three male members of her squad come in, standing still and sheepish, like high school boys on the other side of the gym, working up the nerve to ask a girl for a dance.

Noa stands up. "Donna, we need to get going."

Donna slowly gets up, goes over and scratches her cat's head. "You be a good boy, Bailey. Okay?" To Noa she says, "Can I pack a bag? And brush my teeth?"

"Sure," Noa says, "but Ms. Liu needs to be with you."

A nod. "I understand."

The two go down a hallway and then Phil Cannon steps out in front of Aldo Sloan and Juan Rodriguez. Noa holds up a hand.

"Wait up," she says.

"Don't you want us to start processing the place?" Phil asks.

That is procedure but Noa isn't going to follow procedure. "No, wait until we're gone. I don't want her to see you three lugs going through her belongings."

A loud *thud* cuts through the silence and Wendy shouts, "Noa! Back here! Quick!"

Noa runs down the small hallway, sees an open door to the right, Wendy over the outstretched form of Donna Otterson. One of her slippers has fallen off. Her feet are trembling, and then they stop.

It's crowded in the bathroom and Noa says, "Wendy, what the hell happened?"

Wendy's face is as stern as stone as she feels for a pulse on Donna's neck. Donna's eyes are wide open. There's faint white foam on her lips.

"I'll tell you what happened," she says, voice sharp. "She came here to brush her teeth. I stood here and watched. She opened a new tube of toothpaste, smiled at me and said, 'You'll really like Bailey,' and then started brushing her teeth. About five seconds later she collapsed. She's dead, Noa. Killed herself. Not sure what the poison was but it was certainly contained in that toothpaste tube."

Behind her Phil Cannon says, "Shit. What now, Noa?"

Noa stands up. "Follow procedure. You three do a sweep of the place, and then I'll get a contract clean-up squad to come in."

"Going to be a hell of a thing, securing this one, especially if her dad is retired Agency," Phil says.

Noa says, "Former Director William Colby was murdered more than thirty years ago and whoever did it made it look like a canoeing accident. That's still the official word. I'm not worried about a low-level financial officer. Wendy."

Wendy stands up. "Yes, Noa?"

"You know what to do."

She looks slightly confused. "I do?"

Noa says, "Damn it, you made a promise to that woman, to take care of her cat. Get his food, toys, bedding, whatever, and be ready to leave in five minutes."

Wendy says, "On it, Noa."

Noa takes one last look at the dead CIA financial resource officer on the bathroom floor.

Earlier Noa saw the photographic and video evidence of materials being passed on to Chinese intelligence agents in and around Cherry Hill Park from Donna Otterson.

She would have lost her job, her pension, and probably serve some prison time, but she couldn't have been in possession of anything that dramatic.

Just numbers and budgets and appropriations.

Was that worth a suicide?

Was it?

Phil says, "We're starting the sweep, Noa."

"Good," Noa says. "And be thorough. Really thorough."

One last look at the body.

"This doesn't make any sense," Noa says. "And I need to have it make sense. Sooner rather than later."

CHAPTER 35

PARIS, FRANCE

LIAM GREY IS flat on his belly at about three a.m. in a hot and filthy attic of a tenement building in the Seine-Saint-Denis neighborhood of Paris, also known as "the 93" for it being the *93rd Département* in the country. This cramped district is home to shuttered factories, crumbling tall concrete public housing buildings, and one of the most infamous *banlieues* in France, where certain blocks are "no go" zones for the police. The unemployment rate for the mostly Muslim youth in this area runs at about 21 percent, and, lacking jobs and opportunities, they go out in the streets at night, burning cars and breaking shop windows, and get involved in running battles with the Paris police.

This mission has been planned for months. It's taken just over a week for Liam and his crew to infiltrate this tightly knit neighborhood, where imams and fathers and jihadists fresh home from the various battlefields of the Middle East and Southeast Asia gather on dirty street corners to see who belongs and who doesn't.

Through quick nighttime walks, riding the Metro, melting into the crowds, and hiding in dirty white delivery vans, he and his crew are now in position.

Save for one, Benjamin Lucas, who unexpectedly left France yesterday, saying, "Sorry, Liam, off to Africa for an emerging operation. Can't be avoided."

Which sucks, meaning his team is down one key member, even though it should be a straight in-and-out mission.

He focuses the binoculars, peering through a set of ventilation slats. Across the narrow alleyway is another two-story tenement building, and the windows there are darkened, hiding whatever might be in that small apartment.

But Liam is fairly sure who's in there: three ISIS members who have fled Syria and have found shelter here, near the middle of Paris, and have placed their particular bloody talents up for sale to the highest bidder. It should have been an easy pickup for the Paris Police Prefecture or even France's own intelligence agency, the General Directorate for Internal Security (*Direction générale de la sécurité intérieure*), but as often happens in

France, it's become a sticky situation. A niece of the French president abandoned family and friends to travel to Syria, and she has fallen in love with one of the ISIS terrorist leaders inside that apartment.

Negotiations for him and his two friends to surrender to the French under the protection of the president's niece—always delicate, always lengthy, Liam thinks grumpily—have been going on for months, and now President Barrett's patience has run out.

Those three have raped countless women, have beheaded aid workers, and have burned American pilots alive in metal cages. Their tickets get punched, as soon as you can make it happen.

In other words, this is not a raid to capture these three.

It's a straight kill mission.

In his earpiece, an encrypted message comes in. "Liam, you clear?"

"Yeah," he says. "What's our drone status, Boyd?"

"Our bird is flying free and clear, getting a nice view of the streets and alleys," Boyd Morris says. "No apparent overwatch going on from the target building. What's going on inside?"

"About to find out," Liam says. "Hold on."

He puts the binoculars down, picks up a boxy viewing device that is quietly humming along. Highly classified, the system is called CLARK/K—

SUPERMAN being too obvious for what it can do. He brings up the box to his eyes, blinks to get adjusted as to what he's seeing.

CLARK/K has a variety of imaging and viewing capabilities, including thermal imaging that can go through concrete and brick walls, as well as a form of penetrating radar that can bring living shapes into view.

Liam takes a breath.

There are three men moving around in the second-floor apartment, and two sit down on a couch. Through the imaging and data processing, CLARK/K tells Liam that the shapes have a 95 percent probability of being Haji Omar al-Baghdadi, Abu Bakr, and Abd Samir Muhammad al-Khlifawi, due to height, weight, body temperature, and presence of shrapnel in two of the figures.

"Liam, all stations, targets in place."

Mission parameters say the go order can be issued if the probability rate is above 90 percent, so Liam is feeling pretty good, considering he's resting among rat shit and pigeon droppings, and he and his four team members are here illegally in the eyes of two countries.

Country one, of course, is France. Various political and military pressures on the government and its agencies and the Élysée Palace have proven fruitless, and now, the French being the French, Liam thinks, they're being stubborn just for the hell of it, to show they won't be bossed around by the arrogant Americans.

Country two is the land of the free and home of the brave. Station chiefs of the CIA jealously guard their turf, and the one here in Paris is smart, tough, and has a take-no-prisoners attitude. If she were to find out that Liam and his crew were here without her authorization, they'd be Gitmo'ed so hard and fast she'd make it a point to ship them past the International Date Line so they'd spend an extra day in custody.

Liam says, "Ferris, you have anything?"

"We've got angry yutes in the street, but that's about it," says Ferris Walton, stationed on the top of an adjacent concrete housing building. "Nothing of concern around the target building. Quiet."

"Copy that," Liam says. "Tommy?"

Tommy Pulaski says, "Radio traffic relatively average. A corner store four blocks away was robbed. A guy got knifed in a lobby next street over. Typical night."

Liam says, "Copy that. Mike?"

"Exfil van fueled and ready to roll on your signal, Liam."

He checks the time and looks through the CLARK/K observation monitor. Two of the male subjects are sitting on a couch. The third one...is in the bathroom.

Liam thinks of these three, and the videos he's seen of them in action.

Haji Omar al-Baghdadi, laughing as he beheads four bound female UN aid workers, one after another, taking his time as the hooded workers tremble with fear.

Abu Bakr, tossing a container of gasoline into a metal cage, the cage holding the American pilot of an F-22 aircraft, and then tossing in a lit match.

Abd Samir Muhammad al-Khlifawi, firing pistol shots into the heads of four children, grandchildren of a village leader who wouldn't bow to ISIS.

"Boyd, get the bird into position."

"Roger, that, Liam," he replies.

Liam keeps view through the CLARK/K.

The third terrorist is out of the bathroom. In the kitchen. Now with his two companions in the small living room, each of them with only seconds to live. Within seconds the Thrasher drone will be level to those glass windows with the closed drapes and will fire off four rockets carrying highly classified warheads—Grinder—that minimize any collateral damage in the building. But for anyone in that apartment, the four rounds will explode in shards of fast rotating razor-sharp blades that will turn the place into a slaughterhouse.

Liam knows the specs of Thrasher and Grinder quite well. Two rockets would probably complete the job, but Liam likes to go for the overkill.

"Boyd, are you there yet?" he asks.

The three figures remain in place.

"Boyd, this is Liam. Status?"

A slight trickle of static. "Liam…this is Boyd. We've lost the bird."

CHAPTER 36

LIAM DRAWS IN a deep breath, remembering the "Moscow Rules" that previous officers had devised while going up against the KGB on their hard and sealed home turf, and how one rule always sticks in his mind:

Technology will always let you down.

"This is Liam. Everybody hold," he says. "Boyd, what the hell happened?"

Boyd says, "Not sure, Liam. The bird was heading to the target building when I lost control of it. She spun up and out. Last I saw she was heading to the Seine River, damn it. If we're lucky the damn thing will dive in and sink. No evidence we were here."

The radio net goes silent.

The rest of the team are waiting for his insight, his orders.

On a typical op, with their main weapon out of action, an abort would be the response.

Damn it, though, this mission isn't typical, he thinks. It's taken weeks of surveillance and monitoring to find a time when these three ISIS terrorists would be in one place for a while on this night. An abort would let them live . . . and in a few hours, all three might be gone out into the darkness, preparing to sell their bloody talents to the highest bidder, either some other rogue group or even Russia or China.

Liam says, "All stations, we're not aborting. Ferris."

"This is Ferris, go."

"You're one building over. Can you make it to the roof of the target building?"

No pause.

"You got it, Liam."

"Along the way, pick up some rope, cable wire, anything you can use to hold you up for a few seconds. You're going to come off that roof and through one of those two windows on my signal."

"Roger that, Liam."

"Boyd," he goes on. "With the bird gone, you're with me. In ten minutes, meet me at the corner across from the building, where the bakery is located. We'll go in from there."

"Copy that, Liam."

"Tommy, in fifteen minutes we need a distraction.

Something to draw local and police attention away from this block. Be creative, try not to hurt anyone. But make it happen. And keep an ear on the local radio traffic, alert us if there's anything coming our way."

"Copy that, Liam."

To Mike Cooper, Liam says, "Mike, your exfil is when we come running out of that building. Don't be late, or I'll get your ass fired."

Mike laughs. "I only plan to be late to my funeral, Liam. I got this."

Liam starts to pack up his equipment. "All right, on the move."

Ten minutes later—still smelling of rat and pigeon excrement—Liam is on a dark street, alone in the darkness. Boyd emerges from the shadows around a *boulangerie* and says, "Liam, I—"

"Forget it, it's done," he says. He quickly brings up a night vision monocular and scans the front door. Heavy wood, metal hinges, and—

Damn it.

"Tommy, this is Liam," he says. "You free?"

"Yeah."

"I need you over here, get the front door opened. It's got an electronic lock."

"On my way, Liam," Tommy says. "You're going to get a distraction about one minute after I arrive."

He and Boyd take a look around the narrow

street. Quiet so far. The place smells of burnt food and open sewage, and there's loud Middle Eastern music playing from a nearby flat.

Liam says, "Ferris? Location?"

He replies, "I'm up on the roof. I just took out the local HBO and Showtime, got a coaxial cable secured around me. Ready to go."

Tommy slowly walks down the opposite sidewalk, dragging a leg, like he's injured, and he stops at the front door for five seconds.

From his earpiece Liam hears, "Door is open. Distraction ready to roll in sixty seconds."

Liam says, "Just like the book, gents. Surprise, speed, and violence of action. Disable the non-combatants. When Boyd and I get to the second floor, I'll tell you to fly, Ferris."

"Roger that, Liam."

Liam walks briskly across the street, Boyd next to him, and up to the door. Tommy has disabled the electronic lock and it opens out easily on well-oiled hinges. In the vestibule, two young men with AK-47s in their laps, sitting in chairs, look up in surprise and Liam and Boyd spray them in their faces with small yellow canisters.

The spray is a version of CS tear gas—from which Liam and his team have been immunized—but which will disable the jihadists for at least thirty minutes. They fall from their chairs, yelping and rubbing at their eyes and faces. The wooden stairway is poorly lit, but Liam and Boyd go up as fast as they can, keeping to the side walls so their footfalls won't cause the steps to creak.

From outside there's a muffled *thump thump,* as Tony's distractions—whatever they are—have lit off. As they get up to the second-floor landing, another armed jihadist peers over. In Arabic, Boyd yells, *"It's an emergency! The police are coming!"*

The jihadist hesitates long enough for Liam to spray him in the face, and with a cry he crumples to the floor. At the door now, Liam and Boyd take out their 9mm Ra'ad pistols with sound suppressors.

Just before shooting at the doorknob and two hinges, Liam says, "Ferris, go!"

No answer, but as their gunshots thump out— there is no such thing as a true silencer in the world—he hears glass crashing and shouts.

He and Boyd hammer through the door with their shoulders. A man only wearing dungarees is in front of them, and he and Boyd cut him down with two shots apiece. Another man is on the ground, Ferris standing over him, bits of broken glass sticking to his clothes.

From the other corner of the apartment, behind an overturned couch, gunfire wildly erupts, the bullets whizzing overhead. He and Boyd take quick cover behind kitchen chairs and tables, and with Ferris firing from near the broken window, their pistol fire erupts in hard fashion for less than a minute.

Liam gets up, the smoky apartment lit only by a lightbulb dangling by a cord, and he says, "Finish it, and let's go. Mike, this is Liam, we'll be ready in a minute."

"Roger that, Liam," Mike says through his earpiece.

No prisoners, no captives, nobody left alive, and six shots later—two bullets in each terrorist's head—they go through the apartment door, passing the moaning jihadist on the floor, and take the steps down two at a time. The two guards they had earlier encountered are still writhing on the ground, rubbing at their faces, moaning in pain.

Outside, now.

Speed, surprise, and violence of action.

A battered black van comes to a halt. Doors fly open and Tommy gets out from a doorway, jumps in. Down the street two cars are merrily burning along. Ferris goes in, then Boyd, and Liam brings up the rear as gunfire breaks out behind them. Liam whirls and one of the two jihadists is weaving on his feet, shooting randomly out into the street. Liam takes him down with two shots to the chest.

He pushes Boyd into the van and the door slides shut. Liam says, "Mike, haul ass."

Mike puts the van into Drive, they take a right,

speed by two burning cars with a crowd of young men around it, dancing, laughing, and Tommy says, "No worries, Liam. I wrote down the license plates. We can compensate them later."

Ferris laughs, and so does Mike, their driver, as does Liam. Then he says, "Boyd?"

Boyd doesn't say anything.

Liam gets his mini light, turns it on.

Boyd is smiling, but his eyes look confused.

Liam says, "Boyd?"

Boyd opens his mouth and a spray of blood comes out.

Liam and others frantically go to work.

He's dead by the time they pass the next intersection.

CHAPTER 37

IN A 7-ELEVEN parking lot north of Charlottesville, Virginia, Noa Himel is in a white van bearing the logo of a floral delivery service from nearby Shadwell. Driving this day is one of her team members, Aldo Sloan, a thick, big man who reminds her of the Thing from the Fantastic Four comics, except his complexion is smooth and pale, with a lot of muscle underneath. An ex-FBI agent, Aldo once told her he came to "the other side"—to the Agency—because it had a better dental plan.

Each of them fitted with radio earpieces, pistols hidden in plastic shopping bags on their laps. Two other vehicles belonging to Noa's team are out there in this area of Charlottesville. Nearby is the hum of the Seminole Trail, also known as Route 28.

The 7-Eleven is busy, with lots of vehicles coming and going, most drivers picking up coffee, snacks, and other handheld meals as they head south to Charlottesville.

Noa says, "Aldo, I need a favor."

"Go for it."

"You were assigned last year to the Agency's Counterintelligence Division, to give a seminar on surveillance techniques."

"Yeah."

"You still got friends there?"

"Of a sort."

"What do you mean, of a sort? I need to know, can you go to them, looking for information, and they'll be okay with it? Not complain to any higher-ups?"

Aldo says, "This is about the Otterson case, right? The suicide?"

"Yes, it is," she says. "I want the source documents for the investigation, including photos and videos and any and all surveillance documentation."

"But you already had that before we went in."

"No," she says. "I got a report. That's all. It might have been sanitized, might have been changed. Not good enough. That woman suicided for no good reason. I want the originals. Can you get them?"

Aldo says, "I'll try."

Noa says, "Screw *I'll try*. You either can or can't. If you can't, I'll try somebody else."

He says, "Target vehicle in sight, Noa."

"Answer the damn question."

He says, "I'll get it for you."

"Good," she says. Toggling the microphone of her encrypted Motorola radio, she contacts the other members of her team: Wendy Liu, Phil Cannon, and Juan Rodriguez.

To Wendy and Phil, who are traveling together, she says, "Target vehicle has arrived. Juan, you copy?"

Juan is traveling alone and says, "Got it, Noa," and Wendy also chimes in, "Ready to roll."

Noa watches the target vehicle—a red Chevrolet Impala—pull up to the 7-Eleven, as it has several times during the past three weeks. Three young men step out, laughing and talking to each other on their way inside. Supposedly they are Iraqi refugees, going to the Charlottesville-Albemarle Technical Education Center, about a half hour drive south. One is studying automotive repair, and the other two are studying HVAC systems.

But there are hints the three are not Iraqi refugees, and Noa and her team are about to confirm that today. A quick daytime burglary of their apartment showed nothing of apparent interest, and audio surveillance has them talking about work, girls, and European football.

It's perfect.

Too perfect.

The three come out of the 7-Eleven, paper bags in their hands as well as coffee cups, and get back into the Impala. They all wear hoodies and baseball caps, so facial ID software and imaging hasn't helped in determining their real identities. The Impala backs out and Aldo starts up the van's engine and slides in behind them.

If these three were indeed heading south to their technical school, they would turn right onto the Seminole Trail.

Instead, they turn left, to go north.

Noa whispers, "Once is happenstance. Twice is coincidence. Three times is enemy action. That's what Ian Fleming once wrote."

Aldo laughs. "This is at least the fourth time you've quoted those lines. What would you call that?"

"I don't know, but give me a few minutes."

Back to her radio. "Wendy, Juan, our gang is on the move. Prepare to respond."

And twice in a row comes: "Roger that, Noa."

Aldo speeds up the van. For reasons unknown, the president had suggested this op take place tomorrow. But they have all the intel they need and Noa isn't going to hesitate.

The van is advertising a floral delivery service, but there are no flowers in the back.

Just three mattresses and the gentle *jingle-jangle* of chains and handcuffs dangling from the van's interior roof, ready for the three men, whoever they are.

CHAPTER 38

UP NORTH ALONG the Seminole Trail, the Impala makes a right turn onto a narrow side road called Watts Passage. As Aldo previously noted, these three Iraqis have made this long detour at least five times before, and Noa has a pretty good idea why.

Today she wants to confirm it.

She glances behind her, sees the traffic light quickly go from green to red.

It will remain red for as long as she needs.

The Impala continues along Watts Road. So does a dark-blue Honda CR-V containing Wendy Liu and Phil Cannon, just in front of Noa and Aldo. Juan Rodriguez is approaching them from the other end of Watts Passage, driving a black extended Ford F-150 pickup truck. She checks her watch, and then the SIG Sauer pistol in the bag on her lap.

It's a few minutes from getting very interesting.

"Noa, this is Juan," comes the radio call.

"Go."

"We've got company near the rendezvous site."

"Say again?" Noa asks, looking to Aldo, her driver, who suddenly hunches his shoulders forward, like he's getting ready to be tossed into a football game in the last two minutes of the fourth quarter.

"I've got a Lincoln Town Car, Virginia plates, windows tinted, near the dirt access road. I can't tell if anybody's around."

Noa sees the idle countryside pass by, beautiful and rural Virginia farmland and isolated houses, except for one large government facility, over there to the west and expertly hidden by the trees and brush.

It's the National Ground Intelligence Center, part of the US Army's Intelligence and Security Command. Although there is still no hard evidence, Noa is convinced those three foreign students—in these roundabout trips to their technical school— have been scoping out the place for a future terrorist attack.

Noa says, "All stations, we're still a go. Juan, you're up, get ready. Wendy, you're next."

Aldo says, "I don't like it."

"Neither do I," she says. "But that car could be a breakdown, stolen and abandoned, or out of gas. We're not aborting for that."

The narrow road is curving and looping, but now there's a straightaway. Ahead of her is the Honda CR-V, and in front of that is the Impala. In the distance she sees Juan approaching in the other lane, driving up fast in the Ford pickup truck.

Aldo says, "Sure hope the boy remembered his seat belt."

"Me, too," Noa says, as the black Ford F-150 suddenly swerves into the oncoming lane, blocking the Impala, which slams on brakes and instantly collides into the side of the truck.

CHAPTER 39

FOR THE FIRST time in hours, the main cabin of the scrubbed Air Force Gulfstream G550 passenger jet is quiet. Up forward are the pilot, copilot, and two other crew members, all Air Force, but "sheep-dipped" so they're not officially on duty but are flying as contracted civilians. They have a sense of who they're carrying on this trip, and also have the sense to leave them alone.

In the main cabin, in luxurious leather seats designed for diplomats and officers, Liam Grey sits still with the surviving members of his team. Ferris Walton sits slumped across from him, butterfly bandages on the right side of his face from where he was cut breaking through the second-floor apartment's window, a bottle of Heineken in his hand.

Tommy Pulaski is dozing in his padded seat. Mike Cooper is staring over at Liam, also with a bottle of Heineken in a beefy hand.

It's been a long trip from France, heading out from an abandoned airstrip outside of Montmorency, north of Paris. There had been a debrief, a review of what went wrong and what went right, recriminations and loud curses, and two brawls.

Somewhere in the rear, in a zippered body bag, are the remains of Boyd Morris. Liam knows from cold experience that his family will soon get the bad news, that Boyd is dead, and the bad lie, that he died in a training accident.

Mike Cooper says, "We're pretty thinned out, Liam. What next?"

"We get replacements, and after some training to ensure we click as a group, we head out again once we get our target packages."

Ferris Walton scratches at his bandages. "Liam, besides more guys, we're going to need a change in our ROE. We shouldn't have nailed those guards at the apartment building with CS gas. We should have killed them all."

Liam says, "The target was the three ISIS fighters. Our orders were to go in small, quick, hard, and lethal, and get out. Those were our Rules of Engagement."

Mike says, "Leaving three gunmen pretty much alone."

"They were teenage boys with AK-47s. That's it," Liam says. "Our job was to eliminate the ISIS hardcases before they went somewhere else or hired themselves out. They get zapped, most people cheer. If we kill three local boys being paid a hundred Euros a day for sentry duty, that gets a lot of attention we don't need."

With bitterness, Mike says, "One of those boys killed Boyd."

Ferris speaks up, "Enough. We've already gone through that. But Liam, Mike is right. We need more guys, and we need better orders. When do you think we'll be getting Benjamin Lucas back?"

"Whenever he wraps up whatever he's doing in Africa."

There's a slight jolt of turbulence and Tommy Pulaski is awake. He yawns and says, "What am I missing?"

Mike says, "Talking about when Ben Lucas comes back from his African safari."

Tommy yawns. "He can stay there for another year or two, that'd work for me."

Liam is surprised. "Tommy, I didn't know you had a problem with Ben. He's a damn good operator. What's your problem?"

Another yawn from Tommy. "Yeah, I agree, he's a good operator. Did a good job in Saint Petersburg, did a good job in Venezuela. And we could have used him back in Paris. Maybe Boyd would have made it. But he's too good."

Ferris says, "Man, you're not making any sense."

"He's too good, too lucky," Tommy says. "I've

talked to him a lot, about his career, and you know what I found out? He's never been turned down, for anything. Additional training, transfers to foreign stations, lots of action in the Directorate of Operations, and then to Special Activities and then to us. Every request he's made for advancement has been approved. Liam, why did you pick him?"

"His experience and recommendations from his fellow operators."

"But didn't you see it?" Tommy asks. "Our guy Ben's never been turned down, never been rejected, or faced career disappointment. Nobody's that lucky."

Mike says, "He's got a rabbi."

Tommy nods. "Just like the NYPD. Ben's got a rabbi somewhere in the Agency, someone looking out for him, greasing the skids and making sure he climbs that career ladder. So here's my question, Liam."

Liam says, "Let me guess. Did Ben Lucas's rabbi pull him from the Paris job and send him to Africa to keep him safe, knowing how dangerous Paris was going to be?"

Tommy says, "Yeah, that's what I've been thinking."

Ferris says, "That's a hell of an accusation, Tommy. Pretty out there, pretty conspiracy-minded."

Liam stays quiet. Mike empties his Heineken.

Mike says, "Out there and conspiracies are what we do, gents, every damn day of the week. But I'll tell you this, Liam, we need to have an end game.

I'm sorry for Boyd and I love what I do, but we need more team members, and a guarantee from POTUS that he has a plan to declare victory at some point. I don't want my wife and kids thinking I died in a training accident."

Ferris says, "Nor I."

"Same here," Tommy says.

Liam says, "Guys, I'll make it happen."

And as they arrive to the East Coast of the United States, Liam is still thinking how to make it happen indeed.

CHAPTER 40

WITH THE FORD pickup truck T-boned by the Impala, the CR-V with Wendy Liu and Phil Cannon pulls right up to the rear of the Impala, blocking it in. Aldo stops the van to the left side of the Impala and he and she jump out, taking protection behind the open doors. Up ahead is the dirt access road that leads to the base's fence line. There's the black Lincoln Town Car, but Noa pays it no attention as she and the other members surround the Impala. Wendy and Phil come out of the CR-V, carrying pistols, and up forward, Juan steps out quickly, carrying a cut-down CAR-15 automatic rifle.

Noa yells, "Federal agent, leave the vehicle now, hands up!"

The driver's-side door snaps open and Aldo yells, "Gun!" and the driver starts shooting, as Noa returns fire, joined by Wendy and Phil.

The shooting lasts only seconds, the side of the Impala pockmarked and the windows shattered, the left rear tire collapsing.

Noa starts advancing, holding her weapon in the approved two-handed stance, Aldo next to her, Wendy and Phil going to the other side of the shot-up Impala.

Juan yells, "Noa! Over here!"

An engine is starting up and the Lincoln Town Car is reversing on the dirt road, the rear wheels spinning up dust and dirt.

Noa yells, "Juan! Stop that damn car!"

With the cut-down automatic rifle up to his cheek, Juan quickly fires off two-round bursts, flattening two of the tires and riddling the front end, killing the engine.

Back to the Impala now, the driver is dead, as is his front-seat passenger. Pistols are on the bloody upholstery.

"Drag them out," Noa orders.

Juan yells again, "Noa! Here!"

A man in a black two-piece suit is running into the woods. Noa yells back, "Leave him!"

Good Lord, she thinks, *this is getting way too complicated for a domestic operation,* and she's hoping that permanently stuck red light at the intersection will keep things quiet for the next few minutes. As to the Town Car driver running into the woods, he'd probably be dialing 911 at this moment, but cell service within a hundred meters of this op is disabled.

The two dead men are stretched out on the pavement, hats and hoodies pulled away. Wendy Liu squats down, aiming a digital notepad at each of their faces, and says, "Surprise, Noa, they're not Iraqi refugees. They're not even Iraqis. Facial recognition software positively IDs them as members of the Iranian Quds force."

Noa nods, knowing well the Quds force, specializing in overseas terrorism and special operations activities, and officially listed by the American government as an FTO, Foreign Terrorist Organization.

"Get the third body out of the Impala, get his facial ID as well. I'm going to check out that other car."

Juan is still at the Lincoln Town Car, CAR-15 at his side, when Noa strides up. She says, "Good shooting."

He smiles. "Always aim to be the best. Check this out, Noa."

Juan pries open the rear trunk. Noa leans over and gently whistles.

Four RPG-7 rocket launchers are nestled in a pile, along with canvas carrying pouches with spare warheads. There are also several AK-47s, boxes of ammunition, and what look to be small bricks of plastic explosive, possibly Semtex.

"Looks like we broke up a loud date," Juan says.

"Fair enough," Noa says. "We don't have much time, Juan. Give the car a quick look for documents or anything else interesting, and then help us get the bodies into the van."

Noa turns and heads back to the shot-up Impala, when she hears a loud yelp.

The third terrorist is still alive.

CHAPTER 41

DAMN, DAMN, DAMN, she thinks, as she gets closer to her group of people. The third man is writhing in pain, blood streaming from the side of his head and sopping through his gray sweatshirt. The other two bodies are gone, brought into the rear of the van.

"Wendy?" she asks.

"Quds again, and this one is their superior," she says. "And he's got the worst record of all of them. School buses, cruise ships, even a goddamn day care center in Budapest."

He moans and she stares at his pain-wracked face. And her thoughts turn to her cousin Becky, dead these many years from a visit to Beirut and a meetup with a car bomb.

Aldo says, "Noa...unless he gets immediate medical attention, he's not going to make it."

Noa says, "Phil? Any safe medical facility nearby?"

Safe meaning one under contract to the Agency, with no pesky reports to file to local police agencies about GSWs—gunshot wounds—or patients with questionable immigration status.

After looking at his iPhone Phil says, "One about an hour northbound."

Aldo says, "He won't last that long. Only way he's going to make it is by transporting him to a local hospital. Civilian."

Civilian.

Not like they can drive up and dump him off at a local ER entrance.

Or bring him in officially to a hospital, explaining that his wounds occurred courtesy of the Central Intelligence Agency.

Lots of questions being asked, the word going out quickly about a Quds member being shot and severely wounded on a country road near to one of the most secure and confidential military bases in the region. Add witnesses and surveillance tapes being reviewed, by this time next week, hearings would start up in Congress.

Aldo says, "Noa?"

She says, "Aldo, help Juan unpack that Town Car and dump the load into the pickup truck, if it's still drivable. If not, use the CR-V. Move."

Aldo and Juan quickly move back to the disabled Town Car, leaving Wendy and Phil with Noa and the wounded terrorist.

Becky and Beirut.

Amazing how strong those memories are.

Noa takes out her SIG Sauer and shoots the Quds man in the middle of his forehead.

"Wendy, Phil," she says. "Help me put him into the van."

Wendy and Phil say not a word, but instantly step forward to help her.

Juan and Aldo ignore them all, focusing on their own job, as good operators do.

CHAPTER 42

IT'S A LATE night in Arlington, near the Pentagon and Pentagon City, and Liam Grey is sipping his second Guinness of the evening—appropriate since they are at an Irish pub—sitting across a small table with an old Army buddy of his, Captain Spencer Webster. Back in the day, when Liam was chasing the Taliban up and down lots of rocky mountain trails, Spencer was the platoon's medic, nicknamed—of course—Doc.

He was way overqualified for his medic role, being a top graduate from the Pritzker School of Medicine at the University of Chicago, and then—surprising friends and family—entering the military. Why? During leave one night in Bagram, Spencer said, "Following in my dad's esteemed medical footsteps, I was destined to do lots of surgeries for wealthy patients in safe hospitals. I wanted to do something different. So here I am."

Now Spencer is part of the White House Medical Unit, and it's good to sit tight with him and exchange old stories and memories. The night is going well. Spencer is two years older than Liam, with a thick neck and short blond hair, and both are wearing civvies.

One of the best parts of military and intelligence work is knowing that you can walk into any bar near a military installation and find a familiar face or two, like Doc.

Following that Paris mission and the long hard flight back to the States, Liam is enjoying every minute of unwinding with a Guinness and an old friend in a safe and familiar place, the Sine Irish Pub and Restaurant.

Liam asks, "How's Miriam? And Liz? And Linc?"

"Miriam's enjoying working from home so much I doubt the EPA will ever get her back in the office," Spencer says. "Both Liz and Lincoln are graduating from the 'terrible twos' to the 'thrashing threes,' bumping into the furniture, breaking anything within reach, terrorizing the cat, sometimes going after him as a duo."

"Sounds like fun," Liam says.

"It is," Spencer replies, smiling. "You should give it a go. I mean, sorry it didn't work out with Kay, but like they say, there're plenty of fish in the sea."

"I'm sure there are, but I'm currently in the

wrong sea," Liam says. "Job not conducive to healthy family relationships."

"Yeah, so I've heard," Spencer says, taking a good swallow of his Guinness. "How's the cloak-and-dagger work?"

"It's...work. Too much cloak, sometimes not enough dagger. Travel a bit, poke around some, meet interesting people."

"And kill them?"

Liam keeps smiling but thinks of that wild evening in France, killing the three terrorists, and that long night speeding away in the darkness, frantically trying to save Boyd's life.

He and his crew sure could have used Spencer that night.

A quick sad thought: Spencer probably could have saved his brother Brian back when he was ambushed in Afghanistan.

"When necessary," he says, suddenly feeling morose. "And you? What the hell is going on with the veep? What do you hear?"

"That, my friend," Spencer says, words quiet, staring into his glass of Guinness, "is the daily million-dollar question. Lots of experts are being flown in, tests after tests being run...she's in some sort of coma, but damn right now if anybody can figure it out."

"Good to know POTUS is in good shape, though," Liam goes on. "Saw on CNN yesterday that he's in perfect health. Were you part of the team doing the poking and probing?"

Spencer says, "Sure was. And yep, he's in good shape . . . physically."

That last word sticks with Liam.

"Whoa, back up there for a moment, friend," he says. "What do you mean, 'physically'?"

Spencer quickly shakes his head. "Nope, I've drunk too much, said too much. Forget it."

"Spencer . . . there's no way I'm going to forget it. Give."

His friend's face is bleak.

"Liam, please, don't push me."

"Spencer . . . you really need to tell me. Honest. I'm not asking for my health, or for morbid curiosity, or just to have something to gossip about."

Spencer stays quiet.

Liam says, "Look, the past couple of months I've been seeing POTUS almost on a daily basis. Giving him the PDB, I've been up close to him . . . and I've seen things. If you can confirm it . . ."

Spencer finishes off his Guinness, slaps the glass down, and walks out through the crowded tavern.

"Shit," Liam says, pulling out his wallet, tossing a few twenties on the table, hurrying to catch up with Spencer.

Outside in this popular part of Arlington, there's a lot of foot traffic, but Spencer being well above six feet, Liam quickly spots him. He pushes fast through the crowd and grabs an elbow, and Spencer spins around.

"Hey, come on, leave me alone," Spencer says.

Liam says, "I can't. Spencer, if there's more going on here...you've got to tell me."

Spencer lowers his voice, leans in, and says, "I could lose my license, get court-martialed, and probably arrested if I were to break doctor–patient confidentiality. You know that, right?"

Liam thinks for a moment and thinks again of Admiral Farragut.

Damn the torpedoes and full speed ahead.

He sees a closed stationery store nearby, with an alcove. He gently pushes Spencer into it, and looks back.

"Okay, fair is fair," he says. "I'll go first."

A quick glance to make sure no one is within earshot.

Liam says, "I've been working directly for the president. Highly classified missions overseas. Dangerous ops, not cleared by congressional oversight. At first I wasn't worried...but now you've got me worried, Spencer. Worried about what the hell I'm doing. It feels like we're turning into his own personal Army, settling personal grudges, not missions that benefit the country. Like he's hell-bent on eliminating enemies before they can reach him."

Liam feels he's in one surreal world where the mental health of the President of the United States is being discussed out in the open in a popular tourist district.

Spencer looks to his feet, then looks up at Liam, eyes troubled and burdened.

"Just this once, and don't ever dare bring it up, ever again."

"I promise."

Spencer speaks quickly, like he wants to limit the possibility of getting caught. "We only look into his physical condition. Only. Weight, height, blood pressure, cholesterol level, that sort of thing. We wouldn't dare ask him how he's feeling, or thinking, or his moods. I mean... what the hell would we do if he said he was suicidal?"

"But he didn't say that, did he?"

"No," Spencer says. "He started talking about his health, and how as the most important man in the world, he always has to be on guard for his health. He said that's why he works out every day, watches his diet, and how the Secret Service protects him at the White House with a special ventilation system that can detect viruses, microbes, or even radioactive materials."

Spencer stops, takes a breath.

Liam says, "Was this before or after the vice president got sick in Vegas?"

"Well before," Spencer says. "The president said the Secret Service worked with the White House Mess to check the quality of the food coming in,

and he didn't think they went far enough. He...
started talking quickly, very quickly, like this had
been bothering him for a while. He said that there
should be another level of defense for him and
his health."

Liam feels frozen in place. "Like what?"

Spencer shakes his head, like he can hardly
believe what he was about to say.

"He said the old regimes used to have food
tasters in court, to make sure the kings or queens
wouldn't be poisoned," Spencer says. "The president thought it was time to do that again. Hire
food tasters at the White House, to make sure he
was never poisoned, or attacked. An important
man like him, he said, needed every level of
protection. He had lots planned for the months
ahead, and he wanted to eliminate any chance
of an illness striking him down before he could
achieve what he wanted. Food tasters made sense
to him."

Liam says, "Food tasters? Did he say where he
would find such people?"

A thin smile. "Death row prisoners in federal
prisons, where else. Serve as presidential food
tasters for six months, and then get their sentences
commuted."

Liam knows there is traffic behind him and people talking, but all he can hear now are Spencer's
words.

"God, Spencer, he must have been joking."

Spencer shakes his head. "No," he says. "The way he talked, his loud voice, the look in his eyes.... Liam, I've done some residencies at mental institutions as part of my training. It's my judgment that the president has what's known as a 'Cluster A' personality disorder."

"What the hell does that mean?" he demanded.

The next six words from his friend seemed to punch right through his mind.

Spencer says, "Our president is a full-blown paranoid."

CHAPTER 43

BEFORE HE BROKE his sister's jaw two years ago, Michael Balantic put up with her calling him a mercenary at holidays and get-togethers. Again and again, he tried to gently explain to her that he was a security consultant, until one day at a family reunion in Milwaukee, he had just had enough of her teasing and socked her one.

It put a bit of a damper on the reunion, but nobody—even her wimpy husband Ross—did anything about it, and that had been the end of being teased.

This night Michael is working a shift in Arlington, keeping track of a man that he was told to follow and record. That's been his entire focus, all night long. It's been a pretty easy job, because instead of using his own equipment, he's been piggybacking on the host of surveillance gear that's spread out through this heavily federal part of Arlington, from local police to state police to the FBI and a number of other agencies.

Some of the surveillance equipment and wire-taps out there are even legal.

He's in a dark-red Mercedes Benz SL with Virginia license plates that would trace back to an actuarial firm, and never in the history of the world have the police ever rousted a driver in a Mercedes-Benz in a rich neighborhood like this.

Michael's confident he's just fine.

But the evening is turning into something not fine indeed.

He's wearing Apple earbuds that are connected to a classified drug interdiction program being run by the DEA and a Virginia State Police task force, and listening in to a conversation between two men standing in the doorway of a closed store, just yards away from a Mick restaurant.

"Well, damn," he says.

He goes to the side of the front seat, picks up a cell phone, dials a programmed number.

It's answered on the first ring.

"Yes?"

Michael says, "We have a problem."

"Tell me more," says Carlton Pope, special assistant to the president.

CHAPTER 44

SPENCER TRIES TO walk away but Liam blocks him.

"Wait, wait," Liam says. "What are you going to do?"

"Didn't you hear me earlier? What the hell can I do?"

"You're a doctor, you should be able to tell the president's personal physician what you found out."

Spencer says, "Commander Prentiss? Sure. I'll make an appointment tomorrow and we'll have a nice little chat. Maybe I can convince him that the president has a Cluster A personality disorder, presenting as paranoia. What then?"

Liam says, "Well, there must be some sort of plan, or protocol, or—"

"Or nothing," Spencer says. "What, you think this is some sort of Third World country where a cadre of doctors can get together and declare the president is insane? Do you?"

Liam says, "There has to be something…"

Spencer says, "Ever read a book called *Night of Camp David*?"

"No," Liam says.

"It was published back in 1965, written by Fletcher Knebel, half of the writing team that did *Seven Days in May*. I read it a couple of weeks ago. Not a bad thriller for its time, but damn, the situation is similar. A senator is close friends with the president and is convinced that the president is paranoid, imagining enemies everywhere."

Liam says, "What happens in the book?"

"You looking for a way out, a resolution?" Spencer shakes his head. "It doesn't end that way. The senator tries to convince the secretary of defense, a Supreme Court judge, other officials, that the president is increasingly unstable. But who makes the decision? The Cabinet? A congressional sub-committee? And imagine the firestorm if *anything* got leaked to the press that members of President Barrett's administration are concerned about his mental health? It'll make the Trump administration seem like an Amish barn-raising by comparison."

Liam says, "Answer the question. What happens in the book?"

Spencer says, "A bit of a letdown, honestly. The president…he seems to realize that he's not well, and he resigns. End of book. Unfortunately for you, me, and the nation, I don't think President Barrett is going to follow that plotline."

Liam sighs, runs both hands through his hair. "Something has to be done."

"Like what? Look at our history. Kennedy had enough drugs in him to open a pharmacy. Johnson was so paranoid that he thought his Secret Service detail—all JFK appointees—were out to get him. Nixon had a drinking problem, on top of his paranoia. And we don't have to go too far back in history to find another president who had questions about his stability."

"But something has to be done."

"Certainly," Spencer says. "But not by me, friend. Nope."

"Aren't you worried?"

"Of course I am, but at least there are guardrails out there. Nixon's folks kept it together until he resigned. And there are safeguards in place when it comes to declaring war. As much as he may want to do it down the line, POTUS can't launch a nuclear attack on his own. Even if he is a paranoid."

Somewhere a car honks.

Spencer says, "So that leaves it to you, doesn't it, to do something about it."

"Me?" Liam asks. "Why does it have to be me?"

Spencer walks away, gently tapping him on the shoulder. "Because it has to be somebody."

CHAPTER 45

IN AN ISOLATED alleyway in Georgetown off M Street Northwest is an unmarked wooden door that leads to the Button Gwinnett Club, with access only allowed through a numbered keypad lock.

The code to the lock is given upon a payment of $100,000 to the club, and in exchange, the club offers something rare in the District of Columbia.

Pure privacy.

No cell phones or electronic devices are allowed into the club, and there is a warren of corridors that lead to private dining rooms so the shakers and movers of the nation's capital don't bump into each other while making off-the-record deals with their supposed opponents.

In one room this morning is Hannah Abrams, President Barrett's nominee for director of the Central Intelligence Agency, who is working through a breakfast of tough pancakes and greasy sausages with Senate Majority Leader Cleveland Hogan, trying to get her appointment back on track. She's sixty, unmarried, with big-boned features that make her look striking, but not pretty in the typical sense. Her most remarkable feature is her pale-blue eyes, which look like they've seen a lot over the years and are ready to stare straight through you.

The Senate majority leader is poking at a cold omelet with a fork, looking like a first-year medical student dissecting his first human brain. He says, "Hannah, look, for the moment, my hands are tied."

"Why's that, Cleve?" she asks, trying to keep her voice light and innocent. "I know the votes are there for you on the floor . . . bipartisan, which is hard to believe. But what's the holdup in the Intelligence Committee?"

Cleveland picks up a piece of omelet, chews, and grimaces. The Button Gwinnett Club is not known for its décor, food, or service.

Just privacy.

"Well, Hannah, it's like this . . . the holdup really isn't in the committee. It's from me."

Years of working in different government departments, intelligence agencies, and overseas undercover have given Hannah many talents, including keeping her face bland and calm when the time calls for it.

Like now.

"Cleve, for real?" she asks, trying to keep a

balance of sadness and surprise in her voice. "What could possibly be the problem? When I served as deputy director, I always worked well with the Intelligence Committee and the Gang of Eight, and I've never been reluctant to testify or pass along information about current operations. And us... Cleve, I always thought we had more than just a professional relationship."

Senator Cleveland Hogan looks embarrassed, which is a good start. He's sixty-four years old, wearing a dark-gray suit that cost a thousand dollars and cut to look like it came off the rack at Walmart. A lifetime politician, he has thick, black hair and cold, intelligent eyes behind round spectacles. He's been majority leader for twelve years, is a senator from Tennessee, and like most senators from the South, his unofficial motto is, "The United States Senate: the most exclusive club in the world, with more than 250 years of history unimpeded by progress."

Cleve chews another piece of his breakfast and says, "Oh, Hannah, it's nothing personal, honest."

"Then what is it, Cleve?"

"The president asked me for the delay, that's all."

Hannah is now struggling to keep her composure. "But the president nominated me. He's been public in support of my approval. Why would you let him put the blame on you?"

Cleve says, "He said it was something important,

something about Terrence Grant and his role. It seems...well, Terrence thought the job should have gone to him and President Barrett wants to find the right position for him in government, to sort of ease the pain of his not being named director."

Her right hand is gripping the fork so hard it's a miracle it doesn't bend. "Terrence's been director of National Intelligence for two years and if he's accomplished anything, it's been one of the most well-kept secrets in Washington. You and I both know that. And he's tried several times to take control of the CIA, when that's been a dead issue since Leon Panetta was director and cut off the DNI at the knees with such force he walked with a limp for the rest of his life."

The majority leader looks miserable and Hannah pushes her advantage. "Senator, you know your reputation both here and abroad, as one who takes the Senate's responsibilities seriously. How many times have you gone on the Sunday talk shows and in front of microphones on Capitol Hill to say that Congress, the legislative branch of government, is equal to the executive and the judiciary? True?"

"Hannah..."

"Senator, are you telling me that you're allowing the president to set your agenda? To take control of the Senate's prerogatives and responsibilities? To push you around?"

The Senate majority leader's eyes grow cold and hard. "That's not what's going on, Hannah."

She says, "Perhaps. But what do your colleagues think? Or the minority leader? Or the op-ed writers once they figure out what's driving the delay in my confirmation? Do you think they'll see the entirety of the situation, or see a majority leader who's letting the president interfere?"

The cold look remains. "I don't care what any of them think."

"That's very honorable of you," she says. "I know how much President Barrett values unquestioning loyalty."

He stares at her, carefully wipes his fat fingers on a white napkin, and says, "If you'll excuse me, Hannah, I've suddenly remembered that I need to get back up to the Hill."

Hannah says, "I see."

He backs his chair away from the table. "And if I were you, I'd keep the rest of your day's calendar clear."

Her inner voice is whispering *victory,* and she says, "Why, thank you, Cleve, that's quite thoughtful of you."

Cleve smiles. "You're welcome, Director Abrams."

CHAPTER 46

AFTER RECEIVING HIS morning briefing from Carlton Pope, his special assistant, President Keegan Barrett pours himself another cup of coffee in his second-floor office in the family quarters of the White House and says, "Well, ain't that a kick in the head."

"Agreed, sir," Carlton says.

"I want increased surveillance on them both, especially that doctor, Captain Webster."

"Yes, sir," he says.

Barrett sips at the coffee, the finest he's ever tasted. "The White House Mess is one of the best, don't you agree?"

Carlton says, "Agreed, sir."

"But there was a time when it wasn't so," Barrett says with reflection. "Back in FDR's day, his wife Eleanor wanted the kitchen to serve simple food, to show that they were all sharing the pain of the Great Depression. And the food was horrible! There are memoirs from that time of prime ministers, kings, and generals being served crap like cold jellied bouillon, salmon salad, and bread-and-butter sandwiches for lunch. At the White House!"

He puts his coffee cup down. "I'll miss their great food when I leave after my second term is complete. That's a state secret, Carlton, just so you know, because even though I've been in the job less than six months, I intend to run for a second term. And win. I know the American people love me, support me. All of the poll numbers reflect that. I won't disappoint them."

"Yes, sir."

"Because there's so much to do ... and I've been chosen at this time and place to finally take care of America's enemies," Barrett says wistfully. "Do you see what I mean, Carlton? Call it kismet, fate, or God, but when I was running second in the primaries and Governor McCall died of that brain tumor, clearing my way to get the nomination and eventual victory, I knew that something larger than me—than all of us—wanted me to become president."

Carlton says, "You've done a tremendous amount of work in such a short time, sir. You should take satisfaction in that."

"Perhaps," he says. "But I don't want to start feeling any true sense of accomplishment, not yet." He takes a look around his spartan office. "Some successes, but not nearly enough. Which is why I do most of my work here, or at the Hay-Adams Hotel, or Blair House, and not the Oval Office. When I leave office, there will be some who think what I did was so monstrous that if it had been done in the Oval Office, it would be forever tainted. And those who oppose me..."

He pauses, like he's trying to come up with the correct words, not wanting to tell even the trusted Carlton, the voice inside of him from years ago that's promised him greatness. He says, "They will probably nail the door shut here to this office, to ensure it's never used again," Barrett says. "I expect that. But the next president, whoever they might be, they can go into the Oval Office clean, knowing it's unsullied, that certain orders were never issued from there. The Oval Office can return to being a shrine, and my successor—though they will never admit it—will secretly thank me for handing over an America devoid of its most ruthless enemies."

Carlton starts to speak and the phone rings. Barrett picks it up and says, "Yes?"

"Mr. President? It's Quinn Lawrence."

Barrett smiles at Carlton, who smiles right back. He says, "Quinn, always a pleasure to hear from you. What's troubling my chief of staff this morning that you need to call me?"

"Er, well, it's not me, per se, Mr. President," he stammers. "It's Senate Majority Leader Cleveland Hogan. He wants to talk to you."

"At this time, the feeling's not mutual," Barrett says. "Set up a time for tomorrow. Or the next day."

"I'm sorry, sir, I don't think that will work," Quinn says. "He's quite insistent. He says it's an urgent matter, and he won't take no for an answer."

Barrett looks to his special assistant, shrugs, and says, "Oh, all right. Put him on."

"Thank you, Mr. President."

A faint *click* and then, "Mr. President? It's Senator Hogan."

Barrett leans back in his chair, puts his feet up on his desk. "Cleve, so good to hear from you. What's going on?"

There's an odd tone to the Senate majority leader's voice. "What's going on, Mr. President, is some good news. The Intelligence Committee has voted on Hannah Abrams's nomination, and it's passed eleven to four. I'm fast-tracking it to a floor vote today and—"

Barrett slips his legs off his desk, sits up straight. "Cleve! What the hell is this? You told me you'd hold off on the vote!"

"I did, because you indicated it was a matter

involving the DNI. With all due respect, Mr. President, I got tired of waiting. The Senate has a job to do and we did it."

"You...Senator, you know how important this was for me!"

"Was it?" the senator shot back. "You made the original request of me to delay the vote. The vote was delayed. And what I did for you was professional courtesy. Not a blank check that lasts forever. With all due respect, Mr. President, you can't order the Senate around."

With his teeth nearly clenched, Barrett says, "I wasn't ordering."

"That's what it felt like," the senator says. "Now, to put a nice shine on everything, I expect the full Senate vote sometime early this afternoon, and then I plan to escort Director Abrams to the White House, where you can have a nice meet-and-greet with her in the Oval Office."

Barrett says, "Cleve, you shit, that sounds like you're ordering me around."

"No, sir," he quickly replies. "The Oval Office visit and your congratulations are tradition. For the good of your administration, you should remember that. You certainly don't want to be embarrassed when we show up and you won't let us in."

After slamming the phone receiver down, Barrett stares for a few seconds at the paperwork and folders on his desk, his plans for future targeting operations, all these plans tossed in the air because of that damn Tennessee ward heeler.

"Damn it," he says, "damn it all to hell."

Carlton remains quiet.

With restrained fury in his voice, Barrett says, "I was counting on for another month or two without that smart bitch in charge. I know her. She's going to start turning over rocks and asking hard questions. The more I could get done in her absence, the more networks off the CIA's grid and oversight I could set up before she took office, I was counting on her absence to make it happen. Now some old fool who bellows 'tradition' whenever it suits him has screwed it up. The only reason I nominated her was because I needed Senator Carson's support to win California last fall, and she insisted that a woman head up the CIA. So I picked Abrams and dragged it out as long as I could. I needed California to get here, so I compromised. Damn it."

Carlton says, "Do you need a job done, sir?"

"No, not yet," Barrett says, a headache coming on. "But we need to keep a closer eye on our people in the weeks ahead. Their loyalty to me might be challenged, might be called into question. The Fates have put me here at this vital time, Carlton, and I will not be denied." He pauses. "I'm going to want all options available to me, and soon."

"You can count on it, sir."

Barrett returns to his coffee cup, thinking of all the black and bloody jobs this man has done for him in the past.

"I know I can," the president says.

CHAPTER 47

THE *BLINK-BLINK* of the camera flashes that Hannah Abrams is enduring—check that, CIA Director Hannah Abrams—are irritating as hell, but she keeps a pleased and professional smile on as the news media pool in the Oval Office toss questions to her and President Barrett.

They're both sitting in yellow upholstered armchairs just a couple of yards apart, and boom microphones are hovering over them, like spears suspended in midair.

"Mr. President, were you surprised at the Senate's quick confirmation today?"

"Director Abrams, were you insulted at how long it took for the Senate to finally confirm you?"

"Mr. President, do you still have confidence in Director Abrams's abilities despite the lengthy confirmation delay?"

Keep smiling, Hannah thinks, as the president

holds out his big hands and does his best to charm the unruly group of reporters, photographers, and videographers.

"Oh come along, now," he says, his voice strong and confident. "Of course I have full confidence in Director Abrams. She's highly experienced, is a veteran of the CIA and other agencies, has great relationships up on the Hill, and I know she'll hit the ground running in assuming her job."

A smiling Barrett turns to her and she feels the full force of his political charm, when he says, "I bet the director spends the next twenty-four hours at Langley, sleeping on a cot, just so she can get caught up. Am I right, Hannah?"

"I'm sorry, sir, that's classified information that I can't share with the public."

A few laughs from some of the reporters, and one asks, "Director Abrams, what do you see as your first challenges when you arrive at Langley?"

"The building has undergone some renovations since I was last there," she says. "My first challenge will be getting around without getting lost. Personally, I'd be embarrassed, but professionally, I'm sure all of you would love to report that story."

A few more laughs.

"Mr. President," the next question begins. "Was it a surprise to you that the Senate took action earlier today? The matter certainly wasn't on the Senate's agenda."

Just like that, the smile is gone, and the full force of the president's personality—now anger—is focused on the young Black woman reporter who had raised the question. The carefree and light mood of the Oval Office has instantly changed.

"Pamela? It's Pamela Hall, right . . . from the Inner City News Consortium? Correct?"

"That's correct, Mr. President."

"Before I answer that silly question, and please, we all realize here the silliness of that question, please tell me which president has done more for the inner cities in such a short time. By setting up empowerment zones to revitalize distressed areas, additional federal police training to ease the conflict among the citizens and local police, and a host of other new programs."

The Oval Office is quiet, and Hannah keeps her slight smile.

"I'm sorry, sir, I'm not in a position to answer that question," Pamela replies, not backing down.

To Hannah it looks like the president is about to let loose another bit of rage against the Black woman reporter, and then it fades away, like a heavy dark fog being swept away by a rising sun.

What the hell was that all about?

"I'm just needling you, Pamela, and forgive me if I took it too far," he says, his voice instantly more calm. "As to your initial question, no, I wasn't surprised. Senator Majority Leader Hogan and I have been in close contact these past weeks, trying to untangle whatever mess Director Abrams's confirmation was entangled in. Today I pressured him to get the job done, and as you can see"—holding a hand in Hannah's direction—"the job is done."

The president stands up, as does Hannah. He says, "Speaking of jobs, I've got a busy afternoon ahead of me, and so does Director Abrams—"

"Any updates on the vice president's condition?" a reporter calls out.

"I'm afraid not."

"Mr. President, any comment on the allegations against Speaker Washington?" another reporter chimes in.

The president says, "I've known the speaker for a number of years. She's a trustworthy and honorable woman. And allegations are just that: allegations. Now, I must leave."

One of the president's press aides, a young man with an aura of importance about him, said importance not quite matching his scuffed black shoes, starts calling out, "Thank you, folks, thank you...come along, it's time to leave."

The door to the Oval Office swings open and the reporters are gently herded out, still tossing out questions like children sending out last-minute pleas to a store Santa Claus. Then it's just her and the president and his special assistant, Carlton Pope.

"Thank you, Mr. President, it's going to be an honor working for you."

"Well, remember that, when certain hotspots start boiling over—"

"Mr. President," she interrupts. "May I have a few minutes with you. Alone?"

The briefest of glances between the president and Carlton Pope, and the squat, rugged man nods and leaves, gently closing the door behind him.

President Barrett remains standing.

Doesn't offer her a seat.

So that's how it's going to be, she thinks.

"Sir, I'd like to start out our relationship on a good footing, and I believe the key to that is regular meetings and communication."

The president remains silent.

She says, "You get the PDB on a daily basis, and between you and me, I'm glad that you've gone to the old-style way of being presented the information in printed form. I guess I'm a dinosaur as well, because that's how I like to work."

"Hannah," he says. "Get to the point."

She says, "I think it would be greatly productive if we had weekly meetings. I can give you additional information above and beyond the PDB. It's also a productive way for you to give me your concerns directly, without it being filtered."

Barrett says, "I think such meetings are overrated, to tell you the truth."

"I would politely disagree, sir," she says. "It's a great tool for the two of us to work together for the benefit of the intelligence community and the nation."

His eyes seem to get colder. "You're a big fan of meetings, aren't you, Hannah?"

"Sir?"

His eyes are now frigid. "Meetings and phone calls with the majority leader. So damn eager to get into your job. Going around me—the president!— who had nominated you for this post. Is this what loyalty means to you?"

"Mr. President, I assure you that—"

"From now on," he says, "you'll only communicate to me via the PDB unless we're under attack. Do you understand?"

"Yes, sir," she says.

"Good," he says. "You stay on your side of the Potomac, and I'll stay on my side, and we'll get along just fine. In the meantime, the dog and pony show for the press is over. Get the hell out of my house."

My house, she thinks. Not the People's House, or the White House.

My house.

"Yes, Mr. President," the director of the CIA says, turning on her heel and striding to the door leading out.

CHAPTER 48

SOMEWHERE IN SOUTH AFRICA

BENJAMIN LUCAS ISN'T quite sure, but he thinks he's been held captive in this single-room cell for at least three days. His SERE training back at the Farm years ago pounded him into knowing that the captors have control not only of food and water, but the environment itself.

Meaning they control the lighting, the temperature, and the quantity and quality of the meals—and his ability to gauge the passage of time.

Still, he's sensing rhythms of a regular schedule. At what feels like the morning hours, the sole metal door is opened and a meal tray is placed on the floor by a smiling yet uncommunicative young Chinese male, and then quickly closed.

It's breakfast—made from American MREs, how ironic—with orange juice and coffee. Sometime later the door is opened again, and the tray is removed. Lunch and dinner arrive in the same way, except the evening meal is accompanied by three South African newspapers: the *Daily Sun,* the *Cape Times,* and the *Star.* At some point the recessed lights overhead in the concrete ceiling dim enough to allow him a troubled sleep.

Three meals a day, and a solid metal toilet and sink in the corner, standard issue for any prison. Black slippers, orange shirt and pants. He knows that despite the aches and bruises from his being captured at the meeting location, he's being treated reasonably well. No loud noises. No flashing lights. No sub-harmonic frequencies to make him feel anxious. No screeching music from Yoko Ono or out-of-tune bagpipes.

He's sitting on his carefully made bed, sheets and blanket in place, thinking.

He knows he's under constant surveillance, so he's been as boring as possible, though inside, he's still pained over Chin Lin, their sweet embraces and first steps to getting her back to the States, and then—

The room being broken into.

Him being seized.

Her tossed against a wall.

Shot three times in front of him.

He blinks at the tears forming in his eyes.

Chin Lin.

Had she betrayed him, taking the role of "honey trap" used in so many espionage stings over the years?

If so, why?

Honey traps are used to hook in an opposing intelligence operator, make them turn so their embarrassment of having sexual relations with a foreign spy isn't made public.

But he and Lin?

He wasn't an ambassador, a high-level diplomat, or anybody of influence.

Just a field operator.

And in honey traps...the traps aren't shot and killed in front of the target.

Chin Lin...

What happened?

The door is starting to get unlocked. There's no handle on his side, the hinges are hidden, and overall, this cement and metal cube is pretty secure.

But he doesn't feel hungry.

Are they finally screwing with him now?

The door opens and there's no meal tray, just a well-dressed Chinese man, black suit, black shoes, white shirt, and red-and-blue striped necktie. He's wearing brown-rimmed glasses and his short black hair is trimmed well.

The door is closed behind him.

Benjamin doesn't like sitting in front of him, so he stands up.

The man slightly bows. "Benjamin Lucas, I'm pleased to make your acquaintance."

"You have me at a disadvantage," Benjamin says. "I don't know who you are."

A smile. "Han Yuanchao. I'm the station chief in Pretoria for the Ministry of State Security."

Benjamin says, "There must be some sort of mistake. I'm a freelance writer—"

Yuanchao holds up a hand. "Please. Let's start off as relative equals in our respective professions, and let's not insult each other's intelligence. You are Benjamin Lucas, a GS-12 assigned to the Directorate of Operations, although we've gotten indications that you've been working these past two months in a special unit of the CIA. Do I need to recite more of your biography?"

Benjamin keeps quiet.

"Anything you'd like to say?" Yuanchao asks.

"Yes," he says. "I demand to be allowed contact with the American consulate in Johannesburg."

Yuanchao smiles. "I'm afraid that's not possible. You're here illegally in South Africa as a spy and my government and Pretoria have a confidential understanding concerning these matters. At this moment, you are in our custody."

"This is intolerable."

"Oh, yes, it certainly is," Han says.

"Your men . . . they murdered Chin Lin. Why?"

A slight shrug of his shoulders, like he is being asked about an expense account error. "It was an act of mercy."

Benjamin nearly shouts. "Mercy? You call that mercy?"

"But of course," he goes on. "She was guilty of being in contact with an American intelligence operative, she was in possession of a large amount of classified material, and she was about to defect. These actions mean the death penalty in my country. Better that she received her sentence here, promptly, without enduring months of . . . *interrogation* back in Beijing. Don't you see?"

"I suppose I should prepare myself for such interrogation, right?"

"Good heavens, no, not really," Yuanchao says. "What could we learn from such techniques that we don't already know about you, your training, and your tradecraft?"

The Chinese intelligence operative checks his watch. "Dear me, I must be going. But is it safe to say that at a later time, you will say that you feel you've been treated well, all things considered?"

Yuanchao steps back to the door, knocks on it twice. It's immediately opened and Benjamin says, "In fairness, yes, I've been treated well. Does this mean you'll be contacting Langley for the terms of my release?"

Yuanchao steps through the door, turns, and looks puzzled. "Langley? Why should we deal with Langley?"

The door slams shut and is locked.

CHAPTER 49

NOA HIMEL IS about ten feet away from the West Wing entrance to the White House, off the closed Pennsylvania Avenue, when her cell phone chimes.

She answers with "Himel" and it's her team member, Aldo Sloan, the former FBI agent who's now with the Agency.

"Noa?" he asks. "You got a minute?"

"Barely," she says. "What's up?"

"I got a briefing on that matter you asked about." The Otterson suicide.

"Go on," she says.

"Not here, not now," he says. "I need to show it to you personally."

"That important?"

"Like you wouldn't believe," he says. "Can we set a time for a meet?"

"Depends on how this session goes with POTUS," she says. "I'll call you when I'm free."

In his small office on the second-floor family quarters, President Barrett says, "I've had some connections of mine in the Virginia State Police and FBI tracing the license plate to that Ford Town Car that was at your seizure location. Good job, not letting that car distract you, even if you were a day early—"

Noa is sitting in a chair next to the president's desk and interrupts him. "Sir, sorry to interrupt, but have you done the required notification to the Gang of Eight as to CIA activities on American soil?"

She's expecting him to explode, or snap back at her, but instead he shakes his head in what looks to be amusement and says, "Our Miss Himel, looking to dot the *i*'s and cross the *t*'s."

Noa says, "This Miss Himel wants to ensure that her actions are legal. Sir, have the notifications been made?"

Simple answer, and to the point: "No."

All right, she thinks, *here we go.*

"Sir, it's been two months since I began operations in the United States, which is against the CIA's charter and the law," she says. "I cannot proceed in the future under your direction."

"What do you propose to do, then?" he asks, voice still cool and calm. "Go squeal to the *New York Times* on how poor Noa Himel is being mistreated by that bad man in the White House?"

Noa's voice rises in response. "Frankly, sir, what you've just said is beneath you. I won't break my vows of confidentiality and I won't leak to the press what missions I've accomplished."

"Even if they were good missions, designed to protect me and the nation?"

Noa says, "If the missions were done on American soil without congressional approval, it doesn't matter what kind of missions they were."

He shakes his head. "Sorry, Noa, I can't let you go. You will continue doing your job."

Noa stands up, knowing she's losing it and not caring. "Mr. President, go to hell. We're becoming your personal hit squad—assassins—like some Central American dictatorship. It ends with me today, and you can't stop me."

"Give me ten seconds," he says.

She remains standing. Takes a breath.

"All right, sir, ten seconds."

The president opens a desk drawer, takes out a computer tablet, wakes it, works a few keys, and rotates it so that Noa can see the image on the screen.

An apparent drone photo, taken at about a dozen feet or so in altitude, but showing in great clarity the Virginia landscape and her team and the stopped vehicles, but, most important of all, her with a pistol aimed at the forehead of the Iranian Quds member lying on the pavement.

"It's also on video," he says. "Do you want to see it?"

"No."

"Then sit down."

Noa returns to her chair, legs weak. The president sighs, closes the tablet, and returns it to the desk. "If I were to show this to a member of the attorney general's office, how long before you were indicted on a first-degree-murder charge? And what evidence could you provide on your behalf? Was the man threatening you? Was he armed? Or were you performing an extra-legal execution?"

Noa speaks but it's like someone else's voice is coming out of her mouth. "I had to make a tough field decision, in an operation sanctioned by you, Mr. President."

"Really?" he asks. "Do you have in your possession a memorandum from me, authorizing you to shoot wounded and unarmed prisoners in your custody?"

Noa is trapped. She knows it and the president knows it. If she were to go to the press now and reveal all, it would be the president's word against hers, and he has the video evidence—*slippery bastard that he is*—to prove his point.

Noa Himel executed a wounded prisoner in cold blood.

The president says, "Noa? Anything to say?"

"No, sir."

He puts his hands together and leans toward her. "We're taking a break for a little while. You, me, and Liam Grey and his team. And when we start up again, you're going to continue to be a valued member of my domestic team. Do you understand?"

Noa hates how faint her voice has become. "Yes, sir."

"To make it even more clear, so even a woman like you can understand, I own your ass. You will continue to operate in the United States, and screw the laws, and screw Congress."

A weird, odd laugh comes from the president. "That's funny. You know why? Because you do have a cute ass, and I could take you now, toss you over my desk, and screw you six ways to Sunday, and you couldn't do a damn thing about it. Because I've got evidence that you're a stone-cold killer, Noa Himel, safely kept in my hands."

Noa can't say a word, can't move, can't even bear to look at the man.

"But that's beneath me, as you said. So think of this. You leave the White House and if I feel like doing it, within the hour, I'll come for you. You will no longer exist, your records will be wiped, you will become an un-person."

"Are . . . you threatening to kill me?"

"Worse," he says. "I'm threatening to make you

disappear. Like you never existed. You think I can't do that?"

Noa's mind is a blank.

"Now I will allow you to leave," he says. "So do so."

Defeated, face warm with humiliation, Noa gets up and tries to walk leisurely to the door leading out and away from this man, but she feels like running.

God, she feels like running out of this place.

CHAPTER 50

LIAM ISN'T SURE what time it is, consumed as he is by an internal struggle to prioritize two sworn duties: to uphold and defend the Constitution of the United States and to keep confidential—*forever*—his work within the Central Intelligence Agency.

He's sitting on a park bench, nearly in the dark, waiting. He's in Maywood Park on 22nd Street North, in Arlington, waiting, his senses at high alert, looking and listening and just feeling.

It took him more than an hour to get here, going dark, doubling back and checking and rechecking, and he's convinced he's "gone black," avoiding all surveillance. Liam has left his cell phone at home and he's wearing new clothes and sneakers he bought at a local Walmart. So unless he's got a transponder implanted in his skin, he's sure he's clean.

He hears traffic whiz by and then spots a shape

coming in through the open gate of the small park. The woman's stride is instantly recognizable, and in a few seconds, his ex-wife, Kay Darcy, sits down on the bench next to him.

Liam says, "You left your phone, iPad, anything electronic back at your condo?"

"Hey, nice to see you, too, Liam," she says. "The answer is yes, and my question is, what the hell is going on here?"

"Besides me violating my oath along with a number of federal statutes, just a little meet and greet to see how single life is treating you."

Even in the dying light, he senses a change in Kay's attitude and body language. "Got it, Liam. Sorry. Go on."

He keeps moving his gaze around, checking and rechecking the landscape. They are under a grove of trees, meaning no drone surveillance. Scanning the traffic, he doesn't see any repeats, like a white van going by again and again.

Liam says, "Thanks for meeting me. Means a lot."

His ex-wife says, "It was interesting to be in your world for a while. The anonymous text message. Me going to a Barnes & Noble, picking up the latest Lincoln biography, turning to the page number associated with our wedding date and finding a note with the time and place of this meeting. Liam, what's this all about?"

"I need to ask you some questions."

She laughs. "Nice change of pace."

Liam says, "But I need to set the ground rules. Whatever is said here, stays here. On deep background. Not even mentioning anyone connected with the CIA. Only a government official. Agreed?"

"Agreed," Kay says.

"Last time we chatted at Bullfeathers, you said you were working on a story about the president. How he's using his connections in Langley and the Pentagon to set up a back-channel network to go after whoever's on his enemies list. True?"

"Quite true."

"How's the story going?"

"Slow," she says. "Practically nonexistent."

"How did the story start? A source at the Agency?"

Kay says, "Sorry, we're going to need a bit of quid pro quo here, Liam. You don't get to haul me out here and grill me. I'm going to need some information in exchange."

Liam remembers back to his Army training when he stepped out of a perfectly good aircraft, in his first parachute jump. That initial step out into air and nothingness, hoping you knew what you were doing and that your equipment was going to work.

He says, "Your story is correct. One hundred percent. President Barrett has set up a back-channel and probably illegal network to attack terrorists abroad and in-country, without Congressional oversight or knowledge. It's been going on for just over two months."

"How do you know this, Liam?"

The words seem to come out weighted with lead. "Because I'm leading one of the teams. How's that for a quid pro quo?"

"Pretty damn good," she says. "You're right, I've got a source in the Agency."

"Who is he? Or she?"

"Sorry, Liam, I'm not burning my source. But... you're confirming my story. What now? Can you tell me more?"

"Not at the moment," he says. "But you've got the story. Work it, work it hard, and tell your editors that it's the real deal. Where and when I can, I'll pass on information to help you. But only on my schedule and terms, Kay."

"Agreed," she says. "But why are you telling me this? What's going on?"

"Bad things are going on," Liam says. "That's what's going on... and I can't stand it anymore."

"Good for you," she says.

Liam says, "There's something else developing."

"Like what?"

"Like something so out there I can't even wrap my mind around it," he says. "Sorry. But if I can convince this guy to talk to you... it'll be a game changer."

She sighs. "Sounds like our marriage, Liam. Over-promising and under-delivering."

"Keep on thinking that, Kay," Liam says, irritation growing, "but when it hits, it's going to be like nothing you've ever reported on."

They sit in quiet for a few long seconds, and Kay says, "What now?"

"You keep on pushing, you go back to your source, and work hard. I'll help when I can, but we have to do it the right way. Which means no phone calls, no email messages, no texts. Same kind of tradecraft as before. All right?"

Kay says, "That sounds a bit much, Liam."

He says, "You know your *Post* history?"

"As good as anyone who works there," she says.

"So you remember Watergate," he says.

Kay sighs, "Oh, for God's sake, some of our editors and staff are still going out to lunch on that old story. You got something to add?"

"Yes," Liam says. "When Woodward and Bernstein were working on their initial stories, talking to Mark Felt—their Deep Throat—they were once warned that their lives might be in danger. Later they realized that the warning was overwrought and over the top. Didn't think much more of it as the story went on."

A pause. Kay says, "And?"

"Back then it was probably a bullshit warning, that their lives were in danger," he says. "Kay, what's going on now and what you're digging into...it's not a bullshit warning. Be careful. Walk in well-lit public places. Don't agree to meet a new source alone. Be aware, Kay."

She doesn't reply. Liam says, "Time for you to leave. Go straight home and lock the doors, put a chair under the doorknob, and don't let anybody you don't know in. All right? I'll leave here in ten minutes."

She says, "Liam...you're scaring me."

"Good," he says.

He waits to see if she'll say anything else, but she doesn't, walking briskly out of the park, not looking back once.

CHAPTER 51

NOA HIMEL IS at home in her condo when the intercom rings and she answers, "Hello?"

"It's Aldo," says the voice coming from the speaker. "You never called me."

She rests her head against the wall. "Aldo ... it's been a bear of a day. Sorry."

"Can I come up?"

"Aldo ..."

"Trust me, Noa, you're going to want to see this."

"Okay."

She buzzes the lobby door open and goes into the kitchen, makes a gin and tonic, and when there's a knock on the door, she gives a quick glance through the peephole—yep, there's Aldo—opens the door, keeping the chain in place.

"You alone?" she asks.

"Suspicious?" he replied.

"After the day I've had ... yeah. Hold on."

She closes the door, unlocks the chain, and opens it wider, letting in Aldo. He's wearing blue jeans, a white shirt with a button-down collar, and blue blazer, looking like a hockey player in his first year of retirement.

He holds up a thick manila envelope. "Here it is."

"What's that?"

"The reality behind Donna Otterson and how she got into trouble. Long story short, Noa, the official story is so much bullshit."

She feels both relief and fear. Her suspicions about something wrong taking place in that single woman's apartment are coming true...

But at what price?

"Come on in," she says, leading him to the small kitchen. It's clean, well ordered, with pots and pans hanging from a wooden beam above an antique-looking gas stove.

Aldo says, "Impressive. My place has takeout menus and carryout boxes."

Noa says, "Don't be too impressed. I keep it clean for whenever my parents take the train down to visit their wayward daughter. Get you a drink?"

He sits down in a wooden kitchen chair, starts undoing the clasp to the manila envelope. "Nope, want to keep a clear mind."

Aldo spots the Beefeater gin bottle on the kitchen table and says, "How clear are you, Noa?"

She sits down. "I'm at that weird place where I think I could polish off that entire goddamn bottle and not slur a word. But don't test me. Show me what you got."

Aldo slides out a thick file folder, with the appropriate red slashes and TOP SECRET and NOFORN and Noa feels unease at seeing such confidential material out of a secure area. An immediate firing offense if caught. Aldo seems to notice her attitude and says, "I wouldn't have gone out on such thin ice if this wasn't important, Noa."

"Show me," she says.

He opens the folder. Noa recognizes the documents and color photos on Donna Otterson that she got from POTUS.

"This is what we worked from, right? And he... where did he get this information?"

"Don't know," she says. "It must be his own contacts and friends back in the Agency. He's pretty close-mouth as to sourcing."

She looks down at the surveillance reports, the photos of Donna Otterson going to Cherry Hill Park on three separate occasions. The photos show Donna walking to the park's sign, looking over it, and with a quick move, marking the lowest part of the wooden sign with blue chalk.

The photos shift.

She's sitting on a park bench.

Bends over like she's adjusting a shoe.

Sticky-tapes an envelope to the bottom of the bench.

The next photo shows Donna getting up, walking away.

The next series of photos show a young Chinese woman approaching the bench.

She's pushing a baby carriage.

She sits down on the bench and then retrieves the envelope.

Two other sets of photos show young Chinese males making similar pickups.

Aldo says, "About as clear as it can be, right?"

Noa nods.

He goes back to the envelope, pulls out a similar manila file folder, with the same letters and markings. Aldo says, "This is where it gets interesting, Noa."

"I hate interesting," she says. "I prefer clear-cut and to the point."

"Well, prepare to be disappointed, Noa," Aldo says. "I have a friend who works in the Counterintelligence Mission Center. During my training module, I gave this friend some…extra guidance to pass the course."

Noa says, "Female friend, perhaps?"

Aldo says, "Please, stay focused. I asked him about Donna Otterson. He didn't recognize the name. I said Donna Otterson, financial resource officer, who had been dealing with the Chinese. That confused the crap out of him and did some digging, and sure, Donna Otterson was under investigation. For this."

The same photos from before are spread out, showing Donna marking the sign with chalk.

Aldo waits, and then spreads out a new sheaf of photos.

In each photo, the same envelope was being retrieved from under the park bench.

But not by a Chinese resident spy.

"Aldo..."

He puts a thick finger on the photo. "Yeah. White woman, early thirties, working quickly to retrieve the envelope, her hair up in a baseball cap so we can't capture a photo of her face. So no facial recognition. But Noa..."

She picks up the photos and stares at them.

"Donna Otterson wasn't leaking information to the Chinese," Noa says. "We were set up."

"Big-time," Aldo says. "And I hate to point out something that seems pretty obvious, Noa, but it was the president who set us up."

"Shit," she says.

"Yeah," he says.

CHAPTER 52

SOMEWHERE IN SOUTH AFRICA

IT'S THE CHANGE in the lighting that first awakens Benjamin Lucas. As he rolls over on his bed in his cell, the door is unlocked and a Chinese man walks in, carrying a tall paper sack with twin handles, from which a smooth wooden handle sticks out.

Behind him another, younger Chinese man brings in a comfortable chair, and after a brief exchange of murmured sentences, the second man leaves and the first man sits down. He's about Benjamin's age, wearing blue jeans, black sneakers, and a white, button-front shirt, top button undone.

"Benjamin Lucas," he says, in good English.

"That's right."

He doesn't offer a hand but the man says, "Chang Wanquan. I'm the deputy agricultural attaché to South Africa. Officially, that is. You wouldn't believe the amount of time I waste going out and pretending to be interested in wheat and corn, along with citrus fruits. Then I have to go back to our embassy and do my real job, looking into South Africa's most important exports. We all know what the most important exports of South Africa are, don't we? Diamonds and rare minerals. That's what I work on, when I can scrape enough time together. It can be a real...drag. Yeah, that's it. A drag. You ever feel that, Benjamin Lucas?"

He stays quiet.

"Still trying to be the stoic CIA officer, right?"

The man's smile grows wider. "First time I've ever gone face-to-face with a CIA agent. Knowingly, that is. I'm sure I've run into some of your chaps at embassy parties and other random events. All working under some sort of diplomatic or industrial cover."

Benjamin says, "I like your accent. British, it sounds."

Wanquan nods. "Not bad," he says. "You have a good ear for language. I suppose growing up in San Francisco helped, with all the different Chinese from Taiwan to the mainland and Singapore, Malaysia, Indonesia...but for me, it was Hong Kong. I spent my formative years there, thanks to my father, a wealthy banker in Shanghai."

Wanquan puts his hands on his knees. "And Hong Kong is where I grew to hate you, Benjamin Lucas."

"Why me?" he asks, confused. "I'm not even British."

A laugh. "Sorry, old habit. No, that's where I learned to hate the West, for how they had humiliated us and had stolen Hong Kong and the New Territories."

"Britain returned it to your control nearly thirty years ago," Benjamin says, wondering just what in hell is going on with this slim man from the Ministry of State Security. "Still carrying a grudge?"

He says, "Many of us in positions of authority and power have been holding grudges for what the West did to us, even when it was centuries ago. Now, after all these years of oppression, we're taking our rightful position in the world. We started with Hong Kong, and soon, we will have Taiwan back, and the rest of the Pacific will belong to us, either overtly or covertly."

Wanquan pauses. "Hong Kong...my father thought they would teach me manners, grace, and how to fit into a culture that prizes business and profits above all else. And you know what I learned? I learned they hated us from the Mainland. Thought we were barbarians. Not waiting in queues like ladies and gentlemen. Spitting on the sidewalk. Pissing in alleyways."

He rustles around in the paper bag.

Benjamin says, "I didn't realize captivity includes a history seminar."

"Oh, it doesn't," he says. "But you remind me of Hong Kong. Arrogant, above it all, part of the West. They thought they could remain alone and aloof, with their own laws and way of life, while under our governance and protection. They were wrong."

Benjamin sees now what's attached to the polished wooden handle sticking out of Chang's paper bag.

It's a cricket bat, flat and heavy-looking.

"One of the sports I was forced to learn in Hong Kong was cricket. Can you imagine that? Me, a child of a wealthy member of the Party, learning to play the game of our enemy? And nobody plays cricket in the Middle Kingdom. Nobody."

He expertly spins it in the air. "Father thought I would be more like Hong Kong when I came back. Open to business, democracy, what you in the West call essential freedoms. He was wrong. I wanted nothing more than revenge against that renegade island. My good friend Han Yuanchao, who believes he is in charge of this operation, thinks that when the time comes, you will be freed with little or no discomfort."

Benjamin takes a breath, focuses, knows what's coming, stands up just as Wanquan moves toward him.

"Like Father, Yuanchao is wrong. You need to be punished. If you are ever returned to America, I want to ensure that you bear the wounds of those who go against us."

The cricket bat snaps at his head. Benjamin blocks it with his wrist, but the jolt stuns him, and despite his training and experience, in a few minutes, he's on the floor, the thick wooden bat hitting him, harder and harder, until he blacks out.

CHAPTER 53

ALDO SLOAN SAYS, "What now, Noa?"

"Now?" she says. "For the moment, the president has halted our operations, and those of our overseas group. That gives us some time."

"To do what?"

Noa says, "For you and the others, time to hire your own lawyers. Unless there's divine intervention from whatever god or goddess is out there, BOHICA time is coming. Be prepared, lawyer up, and you and the others have my permission to toss me under whichever Metro bus is closest. I hate to use this phrase because of its origin, but you were following my orders."

"But you were following President Barrett's orders."

Noa freshens her drink. BOHICA: Bend Over, Here It Comes Again. A Vietnam War–era phrase that has lasted for decades, meaning those folks in the field—military or intelligence—are going to be the sacrificial lambs once again to protect the ones issuing orders.

"That's right, and at some point, some congressional oversight committee is going to determine that his orders were illegal, and whoever followed his orders should have known better."

"Why don't you get the story out first?"

"Leak?" she says. "Not going to happen. Plus, the president has something he's holding over me. A nice clear video of me executing a wounded prisoner in CIA custody."

Aldo says, "What? Surveillance camera?"

"A drone, it looked like."

He says, "Noa, you made a tough decision. There was nothing else you could have done. That Quds terrorist was dying. Bringing him to a civilian hospital was not an option. Besides, there was a good chance that he'd probably die even if we did get him there. If it was an execution, it was a battlefield operation against a known terrorist who shot first."

Noa smiles. "I love your attitude and support, Aldo, but getting a jury of twelve in Virginia to agree with your thoughts are nil."

"What are you going to do?"

"First," she says, getting her phone in her hands, "some photos, just in case the evidence you found disappears at some point."

Noa takes photos of the mystery woman picking up Otterson's envelopes.

"If it does, I'm being disappeared as well."

"You're too big to disappear, friend," she says, as she puts the phone down. "Meanwhile, I'm going to lawyer up myself, I suppose," she says. "It's coming, one way or another. Once Director Abrams gets her footing and starts digging and asking questions, she is going ballistic, and shit is going to fly, and you know how shit all flows downhill in circumstances like this."

"Well," Aldo says, gathering up the photos and reports. "I'm not lawyering up, not quite yet." He taps a thick finger on the original photo of Donna Otterson and the unidentified woman who three times retrieved drop-offs.

He says, "I'm going to find out who this woman is, and what in hell Otterson was passing over that made her want to kill herself. I mean, she was a finance resource officer, for God's sake. What kind of classified information could she have that was so important to pass on, and to end in her suicide?"

"You don't have to do it, Aldo."

He puts the rest of the photographs away. "Not an option, Noa, and I can tell you, the rest of the team feels the same way. We're together on this, and there's no bus out there that we're going to toss you under. So don't worry about that."

Noa takes one more swallow of her drink. Sharp and cold, she finds it refreshing, and she says, "Good. That leaves me with a host of other things to worry about."

"Such as?"

"Such as President Barrett has been giving us mission packages because of the people in the Agency who are still personally loyal to him," she says.

"That's obvious."

"Sure is," she says, "and what else is obvious is that he still has people at the Pentagon and elsewhere who are loyal to him as well. He's told me that he believes the Fates or divine providence— not the American people—made him president. Besides our two CIA teams, what else could POTUS be up to, using Navy or Air Force assets?"

Aldo's voice is bleak. "I don't want to even think about it."

Noa says, "Wish I had that luxury."

CHAPTER 54

ABOARD THE USS *DAN HEALY*

EAST CHINA SEA

COMMANDER JAKE UNGER, commanding officer of the USS *Dan Healy* (DDG-129), is in his cabin this early morning at five, mug of coffee at his elbow, when there's a knock on the door.

"Enter," he calls out. The heavy door swings open and his executive officer, Lieutenant Commander Natalie Chung, comes in, folder under her arm, wearing an officer's khaki uniform, just like his.

She says, "Captain, I've got the preliminary on the test mission," as she puts the folder down on his clean and orderly desk.

"And?" he asks, opening the folder, glancing at the formal report and attachments.

"The first test Tomahawk we fired was perfect, flew past all the designated waypoints and true to the target latitude and longitude, just off that Philippine island."

He looks up. "Meaning the second Tomahawk wasn't perfect."

"No, sir," she says. Natalie is second-generation Korean American, is a good XO, tough but fair, and he's been impressed with her since she arrived aboard ship two months ago.

"What happened?"

"The Raytheon Technologies team is still reviewing the telemetry and other information, sir," she says. "It appears it flew along the programmed route, started a sudden descent, and that's when we lost all contact, about ten minutes after launch. Early indications seem to suggest an engine failure, and she splashed down about thirty nautical miles out. Even the two E-2 Hawkeyes following the test lost it at the same time."

"Our Chinese Navy escort still in the area?"

"Yes, sir," she says. "The watch told me that the Type 815G electronic surveillance ship is still about five nautical miles to the west, maintaining their distance."

"Maybe they know what happened," he says, "but they won't tell us, will they?"

His XO smiles. "Not likely, sir."

He thinks it through. The *Dan Healy* is here on two missions: officially, to test the latest Block VI Tomahawk cruise missile variant capable of stealthy, low-altitude flight to avoid detection; unofficially, to "show the flag" in this part of the East China

Sea. The goddamn Chinese PLA Navy was starting to think these waters were their personal lakes, and his ship and others were determined to show them otherwise.

"All right, Natalie," he says. "From here and now, it's Raytheon's problem, not ours. Looks like this new version needs some tweaks. Lucky for all, that Tomahawk is probably still sinking to the bottom of the ocean."

"Yes, sir," she says.

"Okay, thanks, XO," he says, going back to the folder.

"Yes, sir," and she leaves his cabin.

CHAPTER 55

JIEYANG, GUANGDONG PROVINCE

ZHANG DELUN OF the State Grid Corporation of China is up early this morning, desperately trying to take control of the situation here in Jieyang. Approximately thirty minutes ago, a good part of his city of more than one million people went dark. He's at one of the city's main electrical switchyards, trying to figure out what the hell has just happened. There had been no electrical storms, no loss of power stations, and no collapse of transmission lines.

Just a quick *flick* and the lights went out.

Lights powered by portable generators are starting to illuminate the scene. Workers carrying flashlights and wearing yellow slickers and hard hats and orange safety vests are streaming into the switchyard, and Yang Jing, also from the State Grid Corporation, comes up to him, phone up to his ear.

"Look at this."

Delun aims his flashlight at Jing's hand. It looks like Jing is holding...what?

Some very fine strands of...thread? Silk?

He gently touches the material, and instantly knows what it is.

Graphite.

"Oh, fuck," he whispers.

A black utility van comes in, slides to a stop. It's followed by two others.

From the lead van a uniformed military officer comes forward, with another man wearing a dark, two-piece suit. Each are carrying phones in their hands. The man with the suit looks determined yet friendly, but the military officer—*Shit, is that man a general?*—Delun thinks with terror, spotting epaulettes with two large yellow stars and a wreath on his broad shoulders. The man comes up to him and says, "Are you the engineer in charge?"

"Yes, sir, Zhang Delun, of the State Grid Corporation."

"What happened here?" he asks.

"Sir, approximately thirty-five minutes ago, the electrical grid suffered massive failures at three switchyards and one substation."

The general growls. "At the same time?"

"Yes, sir."

The civilian says, "Any idea of the cause?"

Delun gestures Jing to come forward, and he

holds out his hand. The general says. "What am I looking at?"

"Graphite fibers, sir," Delun explains. "Enough graphite fibers like this, distributed over sensitive sites like a switching station or substation, can cause it to fail, creating a power blackout."

The civilian peers down. "And how are these graphite fibers distributed?"

Dejiang swallows. His mouth is dry. "Considering how many sites were struck, and at the same time, I would think...er, I would say, that a series of bombs, sir. From a ground attack, perhaps. Hidden mortars. Or tossed grenades."

The general says, "Or from the air. Like the Americans did to the Iraqis, and NATO did to the Serbs. An act of war, this is."

The civilian says, "How long before power can be restored here?"

Delun feels sweat trickling down his back. "Normally, a day or two, but..."

The general snaps, "But what?"

The sweat down his back seems to flow faster. "Sir, some of these switchyards needed vital equipment insulated just to prepare for such an event. Two years have passed since the request was made for such an upgrade. If the insulation had been installed, power could be returned in a day. Now...depending on the damages, perhaps up to a week, sir."

In the harsh illumination from the spotlights, the general looks like he's about to explode, but Delun is pleasantly surprised when the civilian smiles and says, "A week?"

"A week, sir."

The civilian takes out a thin black leather wallet, extracts a business card, hands it over. Zhang Delun examines it in the light.

It has a name—Huang Zemin—and a phone number.

He says, "Call me at any time, night or day, to get the personnel and equipment you need, or to override any fool who is causing you trouble. If you can restore power in two days or less, you will be handsomely rewarded. Have I made myself clear?"

Delun is afraid to move, afraid his hand holding the business card might tremble.

"Extremely clear, sir," he says, and Huang, the civilian, gives him a gentle slap to the shoulder and says, "Now, we mustn't keep you from your vital work."

The civilian Huang Zemin—whom Delun is convinced belongs to one of the security forces—walks away with the general, talking between themselves, and the general raises his voice once more, saying, "An act of war, and I will report it as such!"

His worker Jing, still grasping the graphite filaments, says, "What just happened?"

Delun says, "I've just made the best friend in the world, or the worst enemy."

"How will you know?" comes the puzzled question.

Delun says, "If the lights come back on Wednesday, and not Thursday."

CHAPTER 56

LANGLEY, VIRGINIA

CIA DIRECTOR HANNAH Abrams touches her desk once again, like a holy talisman passing on power and knowledge, here, on the nearly sacred seventh floor of CIA headquarters. She is here, she has made it, despite the long hours, the trips away from home, her two divorces and the knife scar along her left ribs from one busy night in Belgrade years back, and the many sleepless nights and nearly inedible meals.

She has made it.

Although a cautionary voice inside her whispers, *Have we gotten here in time?*

The door to her office opens and Jean Swantish, her deputy director, steps in, shaking her head.

"Still getting nothing from Beijing or their embassy about their capture of Benjamin Lucas. They're polite but they have no interest in talking to you."

Hannah taps her fingers on her desk. "What do you think their game plan is? Why the delay?"

Jean sits down across from her, notebook in hand. They first met years back during training here and at Camp Perry and other secret training sites on the East Coast, and their respective careers have steamed along in parallel, like two old cruise ships pacing each other out in the seas.

In those years they've watched out for each other, have passed along tips and information on job openings and shitty supervisors, and Jean has done the same "night soil circuit" Hannah has done, taken every crap Third World assignment offered.

According to her personnel file, Jean is fifty-one, single, with thick brown hair, but Hannah also knows that hidden behind her dark-gray slacks, white blouse, and dark-blue jacket is a long, furrowed scar across her belly, courtesy of a Boko Haram gunman in Nigeria.

Deputy directors usually don't serve as the director's immediate right-hand person, but Hannah has ideas on how she's going to run things, and Jean is a vital part of it.

Jean smiles brightly, says, "I could make a joke about the inscrutable Chinese, but besides being racist, it's a lousy joke. They're up to something. We just don't know...for now."

Hannah says, "But it was a straight exfil mission.

Benjamin Lucas was captured by the Chinese, his old college friend was shot at the scene, and... nothing. There wasn't anything particularly cutting-edge about the operation, was there?"

"No," Jean says.

"But they won't even admit they have him. And they're not letting me talk to my counterpart in Beijing or their resident in DC. Which means they're either extremely pissed at us, or something larger is going on."

"Agreed, Director."

Hannah smiles and says, "Don't get into the habit of saying 'agreed' that much, Jean. When I screw up or you think I need advice, don't keep your mouth shut."

"I won't."

"Good," Hannah says. "What did you think of my speech to the troops in the Bubble?"

"Straight and to the point," Jean says, going back to her notebook. "You said, 'I'm honored to be here, you're the most talented group of patriots and workers in the world, and if you follow the law and rules, I'll have your back, forever.'" Jean looks up. "Not up to Henry V's speech before the Battle of Agincourt, but I think most of them were pleased."

"You took good notes."

"You didn't talk for long."

Hannah says, "That's because there's too much to

do. All right, next up, I want the personnel files on Noa Himel and Liam Grey."

"Who are they?"

"That's what I want to find out," Hannah says. "The head of Operations told me last night that he was concerned that President Barrett had pulled them away—along with nearly a dozen other operators—for some operation. It was approved by Acting Director Fenway, but what they're doing for POTUS is still not clear. I don't like it. I've been here for only a day and I've heard rumors and tales. I want the facts."

Jean is scribbling in her notebook and Hannah says, "Strike that, I want more than their personnel files. I want a fresh look, like a Red Cell committee, digging deeper and further. And while they're at it, I want to know all about Carlton Pope, the president's special assistant."

Jean looks up from her notebook. "Director... that might not be wise. President Barrett has a fair number of friends and allies in the Agency. Word will probably get back to him that we're doing that."

"Good," Hannah says. "I don't have a problem with that. And Acting Director Fenway... no idea where he is?"

Jean says, "No. He left his condo at McLean and told his neighbors that he was taking a long-overdue vacation. He told one neighbor he was going to hike the Appalachian Trail, told another one he was going to learn to scuba dive in Mexico, and a third that he was going to find a secluded beach in Hawaii and learn tai chi."

"Not the typical change of command ceremony one expects," Hannah says.

"Think of it as a funny chapter in your auto-biography someday."

"Sure, someday," she says.

Jean says, "Anything else, Director?"

The director of the CIA's office is traditionally large and well furnished, but Hannah hasn't had time to bring in any personal belongings or souve-nirs, but there is one new object, taking up most of the free space in the room.

A fold-up government-issued bed.

Jean says, "How did you sleep last night?"

"Passable, but I've slept in worse," Hannah says, and after a pause, says, "And so have you. And, I'm sorry to say, prepare to sleep again tonight in your office. There's too much going on, too much at stake."

"Yes, Director," Jean says, getting up and closing her notebook.

As Jean heads out of Hannah's office, that earlier phrase returns to Hannah.

Have we gotten here in time?

CHAPTER 57

LIAM GREY IS getting onto the George Washington Memorial Highway for his drive home, his mood foul, honking the horn at a commuter who was a few seconds slow getting into traffic.

He had a brief meeting with President Barrett yesterday that didn't go well, concerning Boyd Morris, his team member who was killed in Paris.

Liam had asked that a Memorial Star at Langley be carved for Boyd, and Barrett instantly refused.

Boyd didn't die for the Agency or the nation. He died for me, so there can be no record.

He speeds up on the highway, trying to maximize the distance between him and CIA headquarters and its Memorial Wall, three of its stars for fellow operators he's known to have died in the field.

And for what?

Like the others marked on the wall in the lobby, they had died for their country.

Not a politician.

A noise distracts him and Liam realizes his cell phone is ringing from where he leaves it during work, the center console of his Jeep Wrangler.

It continues ringing as he pulls over to the side of the road. Virginia has a hands-free phone law and getting ticketed by a Virginia State Trooper will certainly not improve his mood.

He puts the Jeep in Park, picks up his phone.

The caller ID says WEBSTER.

He answers, "This is Liam."

Spencer Webster says, "You in a good place to talk?"

Liam says, "Fair enough, Doc, although I might get rear-ended any second. I've pulled off on the George Washington. What's going on?"

He says, "You got time for a chat?"

"Absolutely," he says. "Name the time and place."

"How about that place we were the other night? In an hour? I've got to stop at CVS and pick up a prescription first."

"Fair enough," Liam says. "Spencer…have you changed your mind?"

"Yeah."

Nothing else is said and Liam wonders if they've been disconnected. He says, "Spencer?"

Another slight pause, and the doctor says, "Miriam and I were putting Liz and Linc to bed last night. After we switched off the light and left the bedroom, I was wondering what their lives were going to be like...and that got me to wondering about our conversation."

Liam keeps his mouth shut, thinking Spencer is going to go on.

Which he does.

"What I got to thinking was what kind of world I was going to leave the twins, if...nothing changes in the next three and a half years, or longer, God forbid."

"I see."

"Gotta go, see you in an hour."

Liam disconnects the call, puts his Jeep into Drive, and eases his way out back onto the crowded George Washington Memorial Highway.

He whispers, "Maybe your ghost, George, does protect the republic."

Ninety minutes later he checks his watch again.

No Spencer Webster.

He's gone in and out of the Sine Irish Pub and Restaurant at least a half dozen times, including checking the men's room, and has walked around the block three times, looking for the familiar tall shape.

Nothing. And damn it, he was planning to convince Spencer to talk to his ex-wife, the *Washington Post* reporter, about what he knows about the president's mental state.

He's outside again, gets his cell phone, dials Spencer's number.

Like the five times before, it goes straight to voicemail, and he leaves another brief message. He disconnects the call and thinks, *One more time. One more time.*

He dials Spencer's home number and there's the briefest of pauses, and then it rings.

It rings!

"Come on, come on, pick up, pick up, pick up," he whispers.

It rings six times and goes to voicemail, with Spencer's calm voice saying, "You know the drill, after the beep, please."

He leaves another message and starts running to his Jeep.

Spencer Webster lives with his family in a fairly nice part of DC, the neighborhood of Cleveland Park. It takes about forty minutes with Liam racing through two yellow lights and one red light to get there.

Upon turning down Woodland Drive Northwest, he speeds up, and then instantly slows down when he sees what's parked in front of Spencer's house.

A white District of Columbia police cruiser, with its POLICE in blue against red stripes. Parked in front of it, a black Chevrolet Impala with a whip antenna on the trunk.

"Oh, no," Liam says, as he pulls in tight behind the cruiser, nearly hitting its rear bumper.

He jumps out of the Jeep, runs up the short driveway and to the front door of the two-story brick house, doesn't bother knocking, just opens the door, pushes past a female uniformed DC cop, right to the living room. Miriam is sitting on a couch, face pale and drawn, eyes red rimmed, her arms nearly crushing three-year-old Elizabeth on one side and Lincoln on the other, their eyes wide and fearful, not sure what's going on with Mommy, only that something very, very bad has happened.

A male in civilian clothes with a police shield on a chain dangling around his thick neck looks at Liam when he comes in. Liam says, "Miriam?"

"Oh, Liam, he's dead...my Spenny...he's dead."

Her chin quivers and tears start rolling again. He says, "What happened?"

Miriam forces the words out. "Liam, he was shot. Murdered."

CHAPTER 58

PRESIDENT BARRETT IS alone in his office in the family quarters area of the White House when the door opens and Carlton Pope comes in and takes a chair without asking, his usual approach.

"Well?" Barrett asks.

Carlton says, "Taken care of. Made to look like a random robbery. Like that's a rare event in DC. Doubt it'll even make the late-night news, even with his record."

Barrett shakes his head. "A pity. He was a good doctor, a good officer. But still..."

A variety of emotions are roiling along in him, anger at knowing that this doctor had betrayed him, both personally and professionally, and guilt for ordering what had to be done. So much had been accomplished here in such short time, and to have it be betrayed now is intolerable.

He couldn't—*wouldn't*—allow it.

The destiny that's been promised to him for years awaits him.

Nothing can stop that.

Barrett says, "Robert E. Lee—that famed traitor—once said, 'To be a good soldier, you must love the army. To be a good commander, you must be willing to order the death of the thing you love.'"

He goes on. "I love the army, and all of our armed forces, and our intelligence services. But in my years of service, I know I've sent young men and women to their deaths…and I've been comforted in knowing that it was for a greater good, a greater cause. You can't rise in the ranks and take on this heavy burden of command without knowing it. Or letting it haunt you."

Carlton said, "You did the right thing, sir. Our progress has been impressive, but if the doctor started talking to the press, getting rumors started, we would be finished before we even started, before your goals were met. Before we could say, 'Mission Accomplished.'"

Barrett smiles. "Well, at least I'm not going to make Dubya's mistake and put up a big goddamn banner to announce it."

"Glad to know it, sir."

He says, "When we're at the mission accomplished stage, Carlton, nobody except for you, me, and a few others will know that we've won.

That the nation has been saved, and that I've been protected, to keep her great."

"It'll be a historic day, like none other."

"But there will be casualties. Like Captain Webster. If he had just kept his mouth shut, had followed his professional and military obligations, hadn't reached out to Liam Grey, and hadn't called him to say he was going to cooperate . . ."

Carlton says, "In some ways, it's his fault."

Barrett is pleased with his special assistant. "True. That's a very good point."

A knock on his door, and he calls out, "Come."

The door swings open and one of his aides comes in, a young Black woman, staff lanyard around her neck. She holds out a manila envelope to him. "Sir, here's the package you've been expecting."

"Thanks . . . Grace. That's right? Grace Tilly. How are you doing?"

"Fine, Mr. President."

"And your grandmother? How did her hip replacement go?"

She smiles. "Just fine, sir. Thanks for asking."

He says, "She's at George Washington, correct?"

"Yes, sir."

"Think she'd like a 'get well' bouquet from the White House?"

Her smile is bright and happy. "Oh, Mr. President, that'd be wonderful."

He nods. "Then I'll make it happen. In the

meantime, could I bother you to fetch Carlton and me some coffee?"

"It'd be a pleasure, sir," she says. After the door is closed, Carlton smirks.

"You're too nice," he says.

"Never can be too nice to your inferiors," Barrett says as he tears open the manila envelope. "She's clumsy, dumb, and she'll screw up the coffee order, but you know what? She'll say nice things about me to her friends and coworkers, and they'll pass it on to others, and if you do that to everyone you meet in the White House, the nasty leaks won't happen, the anonymous sources won't drop a dime, and there're no tell-all books telling the world the secrets of the Barrett White House."

He tugs out a business-sized white envelope, thick and creamy.

"That's one of my many goals, Carlton," he says, "is to dry up the tidal wave each year of the White House tell-all books. Ahhh, look at this, will you?"

He rotates the envelope so that the return address is visible:

Embassy of the Russian Federation
2650 Wisconsin Ave, NW
Washington, DC 20007

No other marks appear on the outside of the envelope.

Barrett opens the envelope, takes out a folded sheet of paper, unfolds it. The same address is centered at the top, and there're two lines of handwriting:

Agreed

Josef

He grins, pushes the sheet of paper over to Carlton, who takes it in his large hand. Barrett says, "How do you like them apples?"

Carlton gives it a quick scan. "Well done, sir."

Barrett takes the letter back with satisfaction. "Halfway there, Carlton. Halfway there . . . now that we've got the Russians where we want them. Stop the cyberattacks, leave us alone, and we'll leave them alone. Quid pro quo. Set up spheres of cyber influence. If they want to mess around with the Poles, Germans, or Chinese, have at it. Just leave us be."

"Think it'll stick?"

"I made them an excellent offer, going back more than forty years from ye olde CIA playbook," Barrett says. "They've just finished their fourth Nord Stream natural gas pipeline project from Russia to Germany. I told Josef that if they quickly agreed to my proposals, I, in turn, would tell them which parts and computer software bugs were placed within that pipeline and its sisters while I was running the CIA. A time bomb, if you will, that could cause billions of dollars in damage, help crater the Russian economy, and break relations with Germany."

Barrett grins. "Reagan and the CIA did the same thing, nearly fifty years ago. The Russians were just starting to steal our technological secrets, and we allowed them to do that for a natural gas pipeline in Siberia. When it exploded, the force was so huge and bright that astronauts in space thought it was a nuclear bomb going off. Oh, they'll stay bought. I have no doubts."

He folds up the sheet of paper, puts it back in the envelope. "For decades we've been scared to death of the Russian bear, thinking it's ten feet tall with razor-sharp claws and big sharp teeth. Truth is, their GDP is less than Italy's. If it weren't for their nukes, the rest of the world would laugh at them. They're a bear, all right, one of those old sad sacks with a muzzle over its mouth you see at a second-rate circus."

He puts the victory note aside. "What they crave most is respect. This agreement is secret, just between me and the Russian government, via Josef, the SVR *rezident* at their Embassy. One spy to a former spy, who know how to keep secrets. We get what we want, we stop giving them painful lessons, and we never, ever publicize it. Or even hint at it."

"And the Chinese?" Carlton asks.

"A tougher nut," Barrett says. "But we'll crack them, sooner or later. No matter how bloody and long term."

"Your two terms, I imagine," Carlton says.

"I hope not," Barrett says. "We got the Russians in less than a half year. I can't see our efforts lasting eight years. That's too much time, but we'll still do it, no matter what."

"Only if your efforts are kept…confidential."

Barrett says, "Talking about Liam, I suppose."

"Yes, sir."

A knock at the door.

Their coffee has arrived, he thinks.

"You know what has to be done," Barrett says.

"Sir."

"So do it."

CHAPTER 59

LIAM GREY SAYS, "Murdered? Oh, my God, Miriam."

He walks forward, bends over to hug her, and with her face buried in his chest, she starts weeping, her arms around him. Little Lincoln and Elizabeth, seeing Mommy crying, start weeping as well.

He continues the hug, turns to the DC police detective and says, "What the hell happened?"

The male detective looks like he's been wearing his tan suit for a week. In a tired voice, he says, "Apparent robbery followed by a shooting. Like it or not, the damn crime rate in DC is climbing again. No matter what the mayor says, the stupid fool."

"But . . ."

"I'm Detective Joe Mazzaglia, and who are you?"

"Liam Grey," he says, still holding tight to Miriam. "I served with Spencer in the Army. We were in the same platoon in Afghanistan. Been good friends ever since."

"I see," the detective says, looking to a worn notebook. "This is what it looks like. Captain Webster was exiting a CVS pharmacy on Georgia Avenue Northwest. He had picked up a prescription, and it looks like he was robbed and shot just as he was getting to his Volvo."

Liam slowly pulls back. Miriam's face is pale, and her arms are now back around the twins.

Liam says, "Witnesses?"

"None so far."

"Surveillance videos?"

"The store has them, but only for the interior and the door leading in. Nothing for the parking lot."

Liam thinks of what he's just heard.

Captain Spencer Webster.

Doctor Webster, ambushed in a CVS parking lot, after surviving three tours in the 'stan.

He remembers.

Up in the Korengal Valley in eastern Afghanistan, one very cold night at FOB Eversmann. He was with Gus Lumberg and Doc was treating Gus's feet by a red-lens flashlight that Liam held, so their night vision wouldn't be spoiled. Doc was trimming away dead skin from the pale feet, and then powdering it up.

"There," the doc said. "Got a pair of clean socks?"

"Nope," Gus said.

"Clown," Spencer said, going into his bag, pulling out a pair. "I know it's a chore, but try to keep your feet dry, best you can."

Gus started tugging on the socks, wincing. He said, "I'll do what I can, Doc, but Jesus, humping up and down these trails all day, crossing streams..."

"Yeah, well, do your best," he said, packing up his gear. The three of them are in a fire hole, covered with sandbags and heavy logs, overseeing one of the trails leading up to the FOB. A fully automatic SAW—also known as the M249 light machine gun—was fastened to the rock wall, pointing out and down to the trail, with full magazines of 200 rounds of 5.56mm ammunition nearby.

"Thanks, Doc," Liam said.

"House calls are what we do," Spencer said. "Which reminds me. The Taliban are coming by for a raid later tonight."

Gus said, "What, the ell-tee told you?"

"Nope," Spencer said.

"First sergeant?" Liam asked.

"Nope."

Gus said, "C'mon, who told you?"

Finished with his packing, Spencer sat up against one of the walls. "I'll tell you, but don't think I'm crazy."

Liam said, "We won't."

Spencer sighed. "Well, it happened during medical school, and when I did residency. I always had this . . . feeling, or sense, that something was about to happen. A patient coding on my floor. The ER being swamped with victims from a multi-car crash. Some person sitting calm in the waiting area suddenly going berserk and taking down two security guards."

Liam said, "That's what you're feeling now?"

"Oh, yeah," Spencer said, his smile barely visible in the red light. "The T-man is coming here tonight. I can just feel it. So eyes open and don't rack out. Call it extreme situational awareness or a seventh sense, I just know they're coming."

As Doc started to leave, Liam said, "Crap, Doc, why the hell are you out here anyway? You could be back in Chicago, working nine-to-five, sleeping in a nice safe bed every night."

One last smile from Spencer, who said with an exaggerated drawl, "Cuz I love Amurrica, boys. Don't you?"

As predicted, the Taliban struck an hour later.

Liam thinks, *Situational awareness.*

Possible seventh sense.

There's no way on earth that an experienced soldier like Doc would allow himself to be ambushed.

Detective Mazzaglia says, "I've already asked Mrs. Webster, but do you know if Captain Webster has any enemies? We're still regarding this as a robbery gone bad, but we have to consider all possibilities."

Liam thinks, *Sure, President Keegan Barrett, wanting to keep his mental state secret.*

He says, "No, I can't think of anyone."

Liam goes to Miriam, holds both her hands, and says, "Is there anyone coming here to keep you and the kids company?"

A shaky nod. "My sisters are coming over, and Spencer's parents...they're trying to catch a flight out of Chicago tonight."

He kisses the top of her head. "Miriam, I'm sorry, but I have to go...urgent business. But I promise I'll come back as soon as possible."

Her teary-eyed face looks hopeful. "Something to do with Spenny?"

With Detective Mazzaglia and the uniformed officer looking on, Liam needs to lie, as much as it hurts him.

"No, I'm sorry," he says, "but I'll be in touch. Honest."

He turns away and gets out of the house, running to his Jeep Wrangler, hurrying to get away from here and the District of Columbia.

He gets in, starts it up, and backs onto the street without even looking. At the first stop sign, Liam reaches up to the windshield, tears down the transponder for toll roads in the state of Virginia, and at the first service station he comes to, pulls over, parks, and tosses it into the rear of a Chevy pickup truck bearing Maryland plates.

Then he continues going north, driving with one hand while working hard to take out the SIM card from his powered-off phone.

There are hunters out there in the darkness, and he knows they're now coming after him.

CHAPTER 60

IN THE SENSITIVE compartmented information facility in the subbasement of the Chinese Embassy on International Place Northwest, Xi Dejiang of the Chinese Ministry of State Security looks to his assistant, Sun Zheng, and says, "That's one hell of an escalation from the Americans."

Zheng says, "The investigation isn't completed yet, but what is known is that the city of Jieyang, in Guangdong Province, suffered a major utility blackout about twelve hours ago, and it looks like sabotage."

Dejiang says, "Really?"

His assistant passes over a red folder. "Without a doubt. There's a substance, graphite fibers—looks like fine silk or thread—that if deposited over a sensitive area of a switchyard or electrical substation, causes a system-wide short circuit, blacking out a portion of the city. This portion, sir, included our Building 14."

"From Unit 212, conducting cyberspace operations."

"Correct."

"Was the building or its equipment damaged?"

"No, but it'll be out of service for a few days, at least."

"How did the graphite fibers get there? Hand grenades or something similar?"

His assistant shakes his head as Dejiang opens the folder, reads the first few sentences and says, "A cruise missile?"

Zheng says, "No doubt, sir. Witnesses saw it fly over the area, and saw it eject objects, which were the bomb canisters carrying the graphite fibers. Then the missile self-destructed over the Rangjiang River in the middle of the city. The local harbor police and a boat from the PLA Navy are dragging the area now."

He continues to read the dispatch, then closes the folder.

"A cruise missile," he says. "This isn't one of their 'freedom of the seas' ship passage. It's an escalation."

What to do?

Despite publicly following the aggressive Party line and doing his intelligence job to the best of his abilities, Dejiang has come to admire the way these people live, learn, and work.

His son is at Harvard Business School, and he enjoys the brief moments he's been allowed to visit him up in Boston, seeing how his boy has thrived without being under the heavy thumb of the Party.

Secretly, Dejiang also sees his role in DC as being an unofficial intermediary, preventing these two Colossi from stumbling into a confrontation.

Or worse, a war.

He glances at the framed photo of old Admiral Zheng He. His had been a powerful military fleet back then, charting new lands, but it was also a fleet filled with trade goods. The fist and the open hand.

What would you do here, Admiral? he thinks.

"It's a provocation," Dejiang says. "But what is the point? They've rolled up some of our networks here in the United States, understandable. But to strike at our homeland like this? Unheard of."

His assistant says, "The generals in the Joint Staff Department of the Central Military Commission are probably howling for retaliation at this moment."

He takes a moment to think, lighting up a Marlboro. He knows he should be seen smoking the semi-official cigarette of the Party—Chunghwa—but despite their many faults, the Americans do know their tobacco.

Dejiang says, "Let's get ahead of the military. We'll send an emissary to President Barrett. See if we can learn what is driving him. A cruise missile attack like this would only come from his direction. No underling in their military would dare do such a thing."

"The ambassador?"

"That simpleton? Of course not ... it will have to be someone the president knows and respects. An American. A friend of ours."

Another satisfying drag as he thinks through the options. "Dale Loomis. From Boston. The former congressman who set up those software companies and trading firms. He does a lot of business with us, and elsewhere in the Pacific. He was also an early supporter of President Barrett, did a lot of fundraising for him. Just the man to talk to the president and quietly ask him what the hell is going on. Before our generals get permission to sink an American warship near the Spratly Islands in retaliation."

"Do you think he'll do it?"

Dejiang says, "The Industrial & Commercial Bank of China and the China Construction Bank both have him by the balls. He's overextended in China and elsewhere. He'll do it or we'll bankrupt him by this time tomorrow. Make it happen."

Zheng stands up. "Absolutely, sir. But the matter in South Africa ..."

Dejiang waves a hand. "That's a powerful instrument, only to be used at the right time. Now's not that time."

CHAPTER 61

LIAM GREY IS walking to his condo in the Southwest Waterfront section of DC, near where he grew up, having taken nearly an hour to get here after driving a circuitous route to get to a near lot and taking several stops on the Metro, finally getting off at the aptly named Waterfront Station. The night is pleasant and lots of residents are out and about, going to the bars, bistros, and restaurants in this up-and-coming neighborhood.

Yet Liam feels more exposed, more at risk, than at any time in his military or CIA career. During those dangerous times, at least he had support, backup, from fellow soldiers or operators in the field, or the full might and fury of any nearby Air Force or Army assets.

Not tonight.

He is utterly alone.

He sits on a park bench that's up against the

concrete wall of a building next to his, spending a few minutes surveilling the sidewalk traffic.

A line from a great movie about CIA operatives comes to mind:

"Whenever there is any doubt, there is no doubt."

In other words, trust your gut.

Maybe the DC detective was right.

Maybe Doc was caught up in a robbery gone bad, ending with a bullet to the head.

This is the unfortunate way of life in the District of Columbia.

But Liam's gut tells him otherwise.

Doc being shot down in the street right after his phone call to Liam, saying he was ready to come forward about what he knows about the president's mental state?

No.

Either the president or someone in his employ ordered the hit.

And are he and Noa the only ones POTUS selected for illegal activities?

Stupid assumption.

Barrett has lots of allies still working in the DoD and the CIA.

Who else is out there, working in the shadows?

He gets up and quickly walks to the entrance of his condo unit. He flashes his keycard to the electronic lock and after the satisfying *buzz*, opens the door and walks into the small lobby.

It has a tile floor, two chairs, a short hallway to the left and two elevator banks, and, most important, a semicircular desk where there's a doorperson, 24/7.

On duty at this hour is Belinda Roper, a Black woman who's a retired Navy chief petty officer with a ready smile, a sharp tongue, and a sawed-off baseball bat under the counter. She's wearing black trousers and a light-tan uniform shirt.

Liam goes up to her and says, "How's it going tonight?"

"Just fine, Liam," she says. "How about you? Traveling again anytime soon?"

Near Belinda is a bank of CCTV monitors, covering the front door, alleyways on each side, and the rear door for maintenance workers and deliveries. There's no one visible on the screens.

"No travel for a while, I hope," he says. "Hey, has anybody come by looking for me? Or calling for me at the front desk?"

Belinda shakes her head. "I've been here two hours, Liam, and no one's looking for you." Her smile broadens. "You got some woman pissed off, stalking you for not returning her texts?"

"I wish," he says. "Have a good night."

He goes to the elevator banks, punches the Up button, and waits.

A *buzz* at the door and he turns.

Mrs. Lucianne from upstairs, and her two young boys. The two boys start fussing about something and when the elevator door opens, he quickly steps in and hits the Close button, and waits.

Rude to his neighbors, but he has to keep moving.

In his unit on the third floor, he makes a quick sweep of the place. He doesn't have a house cleaner, and he always leaves little telltales around the unit to see if any unauthorized visitors have come in, from the arrangement of magazines on the coffee table to a piece of thread tied across the bedroom doorway.

Nothing.

Finding a lockbox in the main closet, he dials the combination, opens it, and takes out a 10mm Glock semiautomatic pistol with three spare magazines. Also coming out is a waist holster and a thousand dollars in one-hundred-dollar bills, and a passport that marks him as a citizen of Canada with the name Lee Grayson.

Last out are two burner phones, placed in each jacket pocket, and then he leaves the unit, not knowing when he's coming back.

Liam goes back to the elevator bank and keeps on walking, taking the fire stairs down to the lobby, peering over at every landing as he descends to make sure the stairwell is empty.

It is.

At the lobby floor Liam quietly opens the door, walks the few short yards to the lobby, and stops, taking a quick glance at Belinda.

She's not alone.

He slides back into the hallway.

Recalls what he's just seen.

Two large men with matching dark suits and sensible shoes, talking quietly and forcefully to Belinda, trying to intimidate her by leaning over the counter.

Liam knows that's not going to work, but he's not sticking around to find out.

He walks quietly down the hallway, to the outside door marked EXIT, pushes the bar and gently closes the door behind him, then starts moving quick, just in case one of the men back there saw him leave via the CCTV system at Belinda's station.

Liam returns to his pace of walking, backtracking, and taking the Metro and getting off to make sure he's not being followed.

But what now?

With Doc's death, does that mean he's next?

Or is he still a useful enough tool for POTUS and his people to be kept alive?

He steps out of the Union Station stop—the busiest in the Metro system—and backs up against a concrete wall, takes one of his burner phones out.

He could call his former supervisor at the Directorate of Operations, but then what?

His old boss would tell him to come into Langley for Liam's own safety, and a debrief.

But that assumes Liam would get there alive.

There've been a few rumors and stories—just a few, but enough—of operators being recalled back to Langley after some dark development, and having a car accident, a drowning, or having their head struck by a steel pipe fall on a construction site before getting to safety.

That's not happening to Liam.

But he will make a call.

It rings once and is picked up.

He nearly sags from relief. Maybe he is ahead of the game for once.

"Hello, who is this?" the woman's voice says.

"It's your partner in crime," he says. "Need to make it quick. We have to meet...in two hours. At the place we had drinks after delivering the PDB. Understand?"

"Yes."

"Get there as a ghost, and for God's sake, be on time."

"Two hours?"

"That's right."

"All right," Noa Himel says, and she disconnects the call.

CHAPTER 62

SOMEWHERE IN SOUTH AFRICA

BENJAMIN LUCAS DISCOVERS that if he doesn't move—no matter the temptation—the aches and pains along his ribs, arms, legs, and head don't hurt as much, but no position eases the pain and shame inside of him.

With his training he should have made quick work of that Chinese intelligence officer with the heavy wooden cricket bat, but that son of a bitch—Chang Wanquan—was equally strong and well trained. Liam had gotten in a few good shots, splitting the shit's lip, for one, but the Chinese intelligence officer had gotten the best of him.

Bastard.

He has to ease his breathing because of the pain in his ribs. He thinks through the past couple of days, especially that cryptic comment the other intelligence officer had made before leaving.

Why should we deal with Langley?

What the hell did that mean?

Even when an officer is "off the books," like he was back in Johannesburg, there is an understanding that while the State Department wouldn't lift a finger to help in the event of a capture, it was in recovery that Langley would do what it could.

Either the quiet diplomatic way of making back-channel deals for a prisoner swap, or a more aggressive approach involving helicopters, black-clad men, and lots of firepower.

What's it going to be, then, if the Chinese refuse to deal with Langley?

Does the Agency even know where he is?

As grim as it sounds, it seems like Benjamin is on his own.

In the years he's served in the Agency, there've been tales told around drinks about contract agents and other operators "left behind," in places ranging from Tibet to Vietnam to countries in Africa, when the higher-ups decided it would take too much political capital and trouble to get them free.

Is he now on that list?

He moves slightly, winces at the pain radiating among his left ribs.

Some resistance back there, sport, he thinks. He should have been more aggressive. When that clown started talking about cricket and playing with his bat, Benjamin should have taken the initiative and blasted at him, taking him out at the knees.

Oh, the outcome would have been about the same, but at least the son of a bitch would have left with more bruises.

He rolls onto his right side, where his ribs don't hurt as much.

Tries to focus on his surroundings, what possible weaknesses there might be in this concrete cell, and what he can do to escape.

He smiles at that. The brave, captured CIA officer, limping off to freedom.

The sound of the door unlocking.

Doesn't feel like mealtime.

Maybe it's Chang Wanquan, coming in for a second round.

If so, Benjamin is going to do his best to get within biting range, either a finger or ankle or cheek. This time he's going to draw blood.

He hears the door opening.

Still on his side, Benjamin says, "Is this the brave Wanquan, coming in to beat up an injured man?"

A woman's voice says, "No, it's not."

He blinks hard, slowly rolls over onto the other side, ignoring the shooting pains and burning in his ribs, bones, muscles, and tendons.

Standing in front of him . . .

It can't be.

"Hello, Ben," says Chin Lin.

CHAPTER 63

DALE LOOMIS OF Loomis Worldwide is sitting nervously in a comfortable chair just outside of the Oval Office.

What an afternoon he's had.

A scheduled meeting with engineers who had the latest schematics for a wind farm off Catalina Island was about to begin over at a conference room in Crystal City, when he had gotten a phone call from an old friend of his who is the deputy minister of the Ministry of Commerce in Beijing. It must have been very late at night or very early in the morning when the urgent call came through. His friend was direct and to the point:

"You need to see your president as soon as you can, and tell him that talks need to take place."

"Talks?" Dale asked. "What kind of talks?"

"He'll know. Just do it. As soon as you can."

Dale protested, "Wait, this is way out of line.

How do you expect me to see President Barrett on such short notice? His day is scheduled down to the minute!"

"Find a way," came the sharp voice from the man. "Or you and your various companies will never do business, ever again, in China or elsewhere in the Pacific, and certain documents will be released to the news media that will ruin you. Your choice."

And after the call was disconnected, Dale realized that his old friend was anything but.

Yet a miracle of some sort had occurred, because he had called the deputy chief of staff—everyone in DC knew Quinn Lawrence, the supposed chief of staff, was a weakling—and here he is, just outside the Oval Office.

"Five minutes," the deputy warned him. "That's it."

Dale rubs his moist hands across his pants.

Five minutes will be plenty.

But what the hell is going on now between the United States and China? Oh, the relationship is strained over human rights issues, trade, foreign policy, and China's aggressive moves in the Pacific, but all of those issues are decades old.

From what he's observed in the news over the past weeks, nothing untoward is going on with China that's not expected, and that frightens him.

A man in his position and with his responsibilities needs to be ahead of the news, and he doesn't like knowing that something huge is going on that he knows nothing about.

Something triggering a phone call from Beijing and an urgent visit to the president.

A check of his watch.

He's been waiting for nearly an hour.

And he has to find a bathroom, and quick. His bladder is screaming for relief. He's due in two weeks for a prostate procedure that will ease the eight to ten times a day he needs to visit the toilet, and now he wishes he had scheduled the surgery last month.

Another rub of his hands against his pants leg.

A young and confident-looking Hispanic male White House aide comes around the corner and says, "Mr. Loomis? The president apologizes for the delay, and he'll see you now."

He feels the warmth of embarrassment.

He really needs to urinate but he can't afford to wait, and doesn't want to anger the president.

"Thanks so much," he says.

He gets up slowly—afraid that if he moves too quickly his bladder will let loose—and the two of them walk to a door guarded by a female Secret Service agent, who whispers something into her sleeve. The aide opens the door, and he walks in.

CHAPTER 64

THIS IS THE third time Dale has been in the Oval Office, but the previous two times he was part of a delegation. Here he's all alone with President Barrett, who's sitting behind his desk.

He says, "Hey, Dale. Take a seat. Sorry for the delay but I was caught up in the nation's business."

"Thank you for seeing me, sir, on such short notice," he says, slowly taking a chair, not wanting to put any quick pressure on his bladder, looking over at the president—dressed in a dark suit, white shirt, and striped red-and-yellow necktie— and Dale takes a glance at his desk.

There are the phone banks and a paper desk calendar, and the president is moving his hands and Dale leans over and sees—

Solitaire.

The president is playing solitaire.

What the hell?

Dale slowly sits back. Okay, he thinks, give the man a break, he's juggling a lot of responsibilities, and if playing solitaire helps him unwind and relax at the end of the day, well, so what?

Eisenhower and others would putter around on a small golf green on the White House grounds, Nixon had a bowling alley, but so what if the man wants to play cards?

But Dale feels just a bit of annoyance that he was made to wait, over a card game.

Especially since he so desperately has to visit a bathroom.

Barrett says, "Ever play solitaire?"

"Sometimes, sir."

"No, I mean, really play it. With actual physical cards you can hold in your hand."

What the hell is going on here?

"Ah, no, sir. Usually, it's on my laptop or phone."

The president shakes his head in apparent disgust. "Not the same. You need to actually hold the cards in your hand. Have the physical touch. Like other games on the internet, from chess to go to so many others. When things exist on the internet, they fail to exist in the real world."

He puts down a card and looks up from the game. "Years ago, my parents were schoolteachers, even though my dad was a disabled Marine. Sunk all their savings into the teachers' union pension fund. Everything, because they trusted the fund managers and they trusted the people who worked for them. One day, there was a burp, a blip, something electronic went south on the Chinese international markets, and they lost nearly everything. Instead of living out their years comfortably in a condo in Hawaii, they lived in a rental apartment in a tough neighborhood in Oakland. Because their money turned from something real into something electronic, something that could disappear in seconds."

Dale crosses his leg, tries to ignore his full bladder. "Mr. President, if I can—"

"Same thing happened when I was in the Army," he says, looking back down at the cards. "We have the best soldiers in the world, Dale, everyone knows that. But what happens if all of their communications systems, firing software, and logistics programs disappear? You think they can fight and win like they've gone back in time to being an army from 1945?"

Dale doesn't know what to say.

The president says quietly, like he's talking to himself, "Like the poet once said, 'the center cannot hold.' You see what I mean, about my parents and the Army? The center isn't holding, and sometimes I think I'm the only one who can see that."

A heavy pause, and the president says, "Ah, got you," and then scoops up the cards, carefully puts them back in a little cardboard box, and focuses on Dale.

That look...he feels like squirming under this man's attention.

"Here you are," Barrett says. "For two reasons. One, you did a hell of a job raising funds and asking your fellow technocrats to join you, giving me a good push to win the White House. That was always my future, to be sitting in this office, making the tough decisions that need to be made. Decisions never even considered by any prior president. I'm in your debt for that, which is why I allowed you to come by today."

"Thank you, sir."

"And the second thing...I understand you come bearing a message from the government of China?"

"Yes, sir, I was asked, as a favor—"

Barrett shakes his head, opens the top drawer of his desk, drops in the deck of cards and pushes the drawer back.

"Dale, shut your trap," he says, voice still sounding calm and reasonable. "I know why you're here, and the message you're bringing. You've been doing business for decades with the Chinese, and now a crisis is emerging because of the foolishness they've done for years in cyberspace and beyond. They've dispatched you here as a messenger. Correct?"

"Well, yes sir," Dale says, desperately trying to salvage the situation. "I've worked alongside the

Chinese for many years, and above all, they desire stability and—"

"And that's your message, isn't it, Dale? Please beg President Barrett to be a good boy, stand down, and let's work things out."

Dale squeezes his legs tighter. *God, please don't let me piss myself in the Oval Office.*

The president smiles. "Screw that, and screw you, Dale. You can leave. If there's anything to be discussed, I want to talk to the puppet master, not the puppet. So tell whoever's waiting for your call that President Keegan Barrett will only talk to the *rezident* here at the Chinese Embassy."

"The who? Aren't they all residents?"

"The *rezident,* spelled with a *z,* not an *s,*" Barrett says. "They'll know what that means, you can be sure of it. Now leave, before I ask the IRS and the SEC to investigate your ass. And ruin you. That would make me smile, and trust me, smiles are currently rare around here."

Dale nearly stumbles out of his chair, goes nearly blindly to the door, opens it, and there's the same aide.

"Help you, Mr. Loomis?"

A bathroom is what he needs, but instead he says, "Please, show me the quickest way out of here, please?"

"This way," the aide says. When he's out on the driveway near the West Wing, he starts walking faster, fearing both the pressure in his lower gut and what kind of response he's going to get when he calls the Chinese Ministry of Commerce.

Nothing good, he's sure, and whatever the secret crisis is out there, it's going to get worse.

He urgently texts his Uber driver to pick him up at the near White House gate. As he passes through the Secret Service checkpoint, something warm and wet suddenly spreads through his pants.

Dale looks down in horror, realizing that with all these people around, some staring at him, he's just wet himself in public.

CHAPTER 65

SOMEWHERE IN SOUTH AFRICA

BENJAMIN LUCAS WHISPERS, "You…why…I saw you get shot, Lin. In the apartment."

That smile that's haunted him for years breaks out as she comes over and gently kisses him on the lips.

His mind is racing, but one thought above all comes to him.

What is going on here?

"My poor boy," she says. "My chest and ribs still hurt from the three wound squibs I was wearing when I last saw you…but you're hurting even more, I'm sure."

She kneels on the concrete floor, takes his hand, kisses it. "I only have two minutes. A girlfriend of mine who went to Columbia is controlling the surveillance system. She promised me she'd screw up the system long enough for me to get in and out to see you."

"But Lin...why? The fake shooting..."

She squeezes his hand. "They wanted to frighten you, scare you so much that your resistance would weaken, make you more malleable."

"No, I mean—"

"Why did I betray you?" she asks, voice flat. "Because I was following orders. They found out I had reached out to you, and they made threats. They had a whole script for me to follow, and I had to do it. Or...Mother."

Lin's eyes water. "She has an aggressive form of leukemia. If I cooperated, then she gets the travel documents to fly to the States and go to Sloan Kettering. If I didn't cooperate...she'd have to make do with a provincial hospital."

He squeezes her hand back.

Is she telling him the truth? Or something else?

Despite the pains and aches, he still holds on to his training.

"That I can understand...but why me? I'm just a field operative. No special talents or knowledge. The equipment I had was standard trade items. Why did they use you to get me to South Africa?"

She gets up from the floor, releases his hand, gently kisses him. The kiss brings back so many wonderful memories and hopes and desires...

But what is really going on behind those sad brown eyes?

Is she still following orders, coming here to talk to him?

To lighten his mood, give him hope, give him...

What?

"I don't know," she says. "But they wanted you, wanted you in their custody."

"The other man who talked to me..."

"Yes, the station chief. Han Yuanchao."

"He told me that they weren't contacting Langley for an exchange. Or anything."

She shakes her head. "Don't know that, but know this. I'm getting you out of here."

"Lin..."

"Trust me on this. I love you, Ben."

The slightest of hesitations.

Who is talking to him at this moment?

Chin Lin, Stanford student?

Or Chin Lin, operative for China's Ministry of State Security?

He says, "I love you, too, Lin."

She reaches into her slacks pocket, takes out something, presses it in his hand.

"Best I can do," she says. "Two Extra Strength Tylenol. It'll help take the edge off."

He looks at the familiar pills, squeezes them.

"Thanks, Lin."

She smiles, goes to the door.

"Hang in there, sweetie. I'll get you out."

Then she works the door and she's gone.

He rests there, thinking of what just happened.

Lin is alive.

Alive!

He slowly rolls over, so he's facing the concrete wall.

But what does that mean?

Is she still following orders? Was this still the process of softening him up, make him more hopeful that at some point he'll be freed through her actions?

Was she the proverbial honey pot?

Fairly sure he's out of view of the surveillance cameras inside his cell, he brings his clenched fist to his face, opens it.

The two caplets are white with red numbers.

They certainly do look like Extra Strength Tylenol.

But could they be something else?

Could she be trying to poison him, kill him so he doesn't suffer anymore?

Benjamin closes his eyes.

I love you, Ben.

He opens his mouth and swallows the two pills dry.

She's alive.

Chin Lin is alive.

CHAPTER 66

NOA HIMEL IS walking across the dirt and gravel parking lot of the Tuckerman Roadhouse outside of Langley when a black Jeep Wrangler with over-sized tires roars up and suddenly brakes, tossing up bits of dirt.

The passenger door swings open, and Liam is leaning across.

"Hurry up, get in."

She clambers up and Liam starts driving out of the parking lot. She tries to close the door and fasten her seat belt at the same time.

He barely brakes at the road, and takes a left, speeding up.

Noa says, "Nice to see you again, Liam."

"Yeah, same here," he says. "You ghosted your way here?"

"Yes, and did you?"

Liam says, "I did. I also took a gamble, picking

you up here so close to headquarters, but they probably wouldn't think I'd be that crazy."

A traffic light is ahead and the light turns yellow. Liam speeds through it. She grabs a door handle, takes a calming breath, not wanting him to see that he's shaking her up.

"Who's 'they,' Liam?"

He makes another turn, gets on an exit to I-495. Joining the heavy flow of traffic seems to ease Liam, and he lets the Jeep's speed match that of the surrounding traffic.

Liam says, "Think I'm getting a bit nutso? Losing it?"

"No," she says.

"Wish your voice was more convincing."

Noa says, "I'll work on it. What's going on?"

Liam says, "A few hours ago I was talking with an old Army friend, a doctor, now assigned to the White House Medical Unit. Yesterday he told me that he believes the president is mentally ill, a paranoid. About an hour after we got off the phone today, saying he would let the right people know about the president's state, he was murdered. That's what's going on. Give me a few minutes. I'll park my Jeep and we can talk things through."

"Great," she says. "Because I have something to tell you, as well."

"Fantastic," he says. "Gonna be a hell of a night."

She says nothing, just looking at the white

and red lights from the surrounding traffic move quickly along.

About thirty minutes later, Liam pulls his Jeep into a crowded Walmart parking lot in the town of Vienna, and he finds an empty spot at the far end of the lot. He switches off the engine and settles back in his seat, rubbing at his face.

Liam says, "Mind going first?"

"No," she says.

"Thanks."

"The president is losing it," Noa says.

"No disagreement here. I'm feeling that, and so was my friend Doc. Go on."

She says, "I had a meeting with him this morning. I asked him if he had informed the Gang of Eight as to what we've been doing. Check that, what my team and I are doing. Liam, you've got cover, you're operating overseas. But unless Congress signs off on what we've been doing in the States, my team and I are all facing decades in jail."

Liam swivels in his seat. "I bet he took that well."

"I was surprised, he didn't shout or bellow or toss papers around the office. He just said, no, he hadn't informed the Gang of Eight. I told him I was done. He told me otherwise, but I was still working for him, no matter what."

"Then what?"

Noa feels that little flame of shame for what Barrett showed her and did to her in his private office.

She says, "Our last action got complicated. We were trying to capture three Iranian Quds members who were planning an attack on the National Ground Intelligence Center in Charlottesville. They decided to fight it out. One of them was severely wounded, and we couldn't take him to a civilian hospital, and an Agency-affiliated ER was too far away."

"What did you do?"

"What I had to do," she says. "And Barrett showed me a drone video of me doing just that. He said that my ass belonged to him, and that if I tried to leave, that drone footage would be given to the AG's office. Oh, and to round it off, he said he could rape me in that office, and I couldn't do anything about it. Or he'd make me disappear. Permanently."

Liam murmurs, "Oh, damn," and turns away for a moment, like he's embarrassed for her. Noa wants to say, *What, this is news to you? That powerful men have always taken what they wanted from us women?*

"And you?" she asks. "Tell me about your Army captain."

Noa listens carefully as Liam talks about his friendship with Captain Spencer Webster—Doc—their time together in Afghanistan, and how Spencer later got to the White House Medical Unit.

She nearly shivered when Liam repeated the phrase the doctor said.

Our president is a full-fledged paranoid.

Liam says, "Last night, I tried to convince him to pass that information along to somebody, anybody, who could do something with it. He refused. But a few hours ago, he called me, saying he changed his mind. Thought of his kids. Wondered what kind of future was ahead for them. He agreed to meet with me again, talking to me on his cell. An hour later, he was dead. Shot in the head in a parking lot. Apparent robbery, the DC cops say."

Noa says, "It could just be an awful coincidence."

"No. Not ever. Not with Doc. He had too much situational awareness to be caught like that. No, either the president or someone working for him knew about our meeting and were monitoring his cell. Maybe even mine."

Noa says, "If that's true, Liam, you might be next."

"Right."

"What are you going to do?"

"Me?" Liam says. His next words seem so out of place and bizarre in a typical quiet suburban parking lot of a Walmart. "Noa, I'm going straight to the director, confess all."

"That's a career-ender, going around the chain of command."

"Don't care," Liam says.

"Me neither," Noa says. "I'm going with you."

CHAPTER 67

CIA DIRECTOR HANNAH Abrams says, "Good job, Jean. Didn't expect it so soon."

Her deputy director yawns, and without fail, Hannah yawns as well.

It's been a very long and grueling forty-eight hours since she was sworn in as director in the Oval Office by President Barrett. So far, that little ceremony has been the highlight of her career.

Jean says, "There's a cadre of pros in the Agency who are glad you are back and are going to go the extra distance for you, Director. In the meantime, we still don't have the full picture yet on Benjamin Lucas. There are some inconsistencies that need to be nailed down."

Hannah runs her hands across the thick manila folders, opens two of them, starts glancing through them both. "Liam Grey and Noa Himel. Good, solid backgrounds, equally solid careers in Operations.

No disciplinary actions or letters of reprimand. Exactly the operators we claim to Congress we have throughout the Agency. And then, a couple of months ago, they drop out."

Jean says, "On orders President Barrett gave to Acting Director Milton Fenway, Liam and Noa were given authority to recruit from within the Agency and the military to form two separate teams, and that's all we've got. Paperwork is minimal so far, with their salaries being logged in the President's Special Access Account."

Hannah nods. "POTUS's own slush fund, when you want to try to kill Castro or fund the Contras or subsidize an Israeli bunker-buster bomb to use in Iran. It would be nice to get a briefing from Milton, but we still don't know where he is, right?"

"Not yet. But we're working it. Along with that other thing you asked for."

Hannah picks up a third folder with distaste, like she's picking up something nasty that the cat had deposited on the kitchen floor at two a.m.

"Carlton Pope," she says. "Good God, how did this . . . creature get to be at the president's side?"

Jean says, "Carlton Pope, previously a sergeant assigned to the 615th Military Police Company, of the 709th Military Police Battalion, stationed in Grafenwöhr, Germany. Did two tours in Kosovo during the renewal of hostilities years back. During his second tour his unit provided protection to the

809th Military Intelligence Battalion, commanded by Colonel Keegan Barrett."

"Remind me of the nasty bits," Hannah says.

"There was a temporary facility set up for processing prisoners from Serb militia units operating in the area. There were at least three complaints filed against Sergeant Pope for excessive force, one case leading to the death of a prisoner. Not sure how it happened, but all three charges against him were broomed. Next time we hear from him, he's been an honorably discharged graduate of George Washington University and think-tank employee. When Barrett announced his campaign, Pope volunteered and POTUS rewarded him with a top job in the White House. Does that make any sense at all?"

Jean says not a word, and Hannah yawns again, picks up a cup of coffee, takes a strong sip, realizes it's cold.

She doesn't care.

Hannah finishes it off.

Thinks.

Hannah says, "The president has as his right-hand man, one with tremendous influence and power from the Oval Office, a former military police sergeant with a very sketchy record."

She gets up from her desk, stretches her back, and walks around her office, crowded with the bed in the center.

Hannah stares out the window at the lights of her CIA campus.

"What in hell is he doing over there?" she asks.

"Carlton Pope?"

Hannah says, "No. The president. The vice president is in a coma. His chief of staff has no real power. He's working on his second national security adviser since his inauguration. His secretary of state is a former Silicon Valley tycoon, currently on his third listening tour out in Europe. The secretary of defense is a former military contractor who loves visiting bases where his company's jets are being used."

The lights burn brightly over there, on the other side of the Potomac.

She goes on. "Barrett's isolated, alone, with a thug at his side. As others have said, power corrupts, but absolute power corrupts absolutely. Jean, that sure as hell is what's keeping me up at night. How absolute Barrett's power is, and what he's doing with it."

CHAPTER 68

THE MOST POWERFUL woman in United States politics is sitting in front of President Barrett's Oval Office desk this early evening, looking like she is struggling not to lose control.

Barrett likes the look. It's good to be the alpha dog in situations like this.

Speaker of the House Gwen Washington says, "Mr. President, thank you for seeing me."

"Good to see you, Madam Speaker," he says. "How are you holding up?"

"In public, I'm keeping it together, but in private... it's been tough."

Barrett's hands are folded in front of him on the *Resolute* desk. He's known the speaker for years but that doesn't mean she gets to go to his upstairs private office.

"What's the latest?"

She wipes at her left eye. She's well made-up, hair coiffed, wearing whatever latest women's clothing is in fashion today, but the clothes seem not to fit her, like she's lost her stand and stature.

"I've tried to head it off by calling in favors and twisting some arms, but hearings on the Hill are guaranteed, thanks to my asshole majority leader. You know that line from *The Art of War*, 'Keep your friends close and your enemies closer'? Well, only if your enemies aren't holding a knife, ready to plunge it in your back."

"You're probably regretting asking Deering to be majority leader."

"Every damn night," she says. "But I needed his support and that of his caucus to get to the speaker's chair, and now he wants my job. He's spreading rumors, leaking like mad to the press, and he's gotten enough members to go along to start public hearings."

Barrett says, "I like the way the wormy little bastard set it up. *I'm doing this just to help Speaker Washington clear the air, to give a full and frank accounting of the charges being posed against her.* Have to give him credit. Hard to believe we both belong to the same party."

"But the charges are false," Gwen says, voice brittle. "I know they are."

Barrett shrugs. "Unfortunately, the paperwork accusing you looks legit. You know what they say:

a lie can travel halfway around the world while the truth is putting its pants on."

With weariness in her voice, the speaker says, "Yes, and preparing a defense and hiring forensic accountants to prove my innocence is going to take time. While that's all going on, Mr. President, it means my job as speaker is crippled, and your agenda for the next few months is going to be stalled."

Barrett decides it's time not to say a word. She has no idea of what his real agenda is, which is just how he wants it.

He lets the speaker look at him, dismay in her eyes, and waits for her to break.

Which she does.

"Mr. President, I need your help."

"Of course, Madam Speaker. What do you have in mind?"

Gwen lowers her eyes, lifts them, and says, "They haven't said it publicly, but I'm sure the attorney general and the FBI are going to start an investigation."

Barrett says, "You're probably right."

"And sir," she says, voice tinged with desperation, "I know you can't interfere in their activities. I wouldn't even consider asking you that. But if you could see your way clear to making a public statement, perhaps with me at your side in the Rose Garden, as the party leader, that you have faith in me and are confident that I'll be cleared of all charges, that would make a world of difference."

He lets her dangle there for a few seconds.

"Sorry, I can't do that, Madam Speaker."

"But Keegan," she pleads, "I've been with you right from the start! I hosted fundraisers and rallies for you when you were fourth in the polls, when you started running in the caucuses and primaries, and I got the California delegation sewn up for you ahead of the convention. Sir, I . . ."

Barrett softens his voice. "As much as I do believe in your innocence, Gwen, I can't do that. A public statement on your behalf would seem like I was interfering in an upcoming investigation. And second, as much as it pains me to say this, standing next to you and announcing that I totally believe in your innocence, it would make me incredibly vulnerable if the worst were to happen and you were found guilty."

"But I'm innocent!"

Barrett says, "I'm sure, Gwen, but I can't take that risk. Sorry. I need to let the process take place, as painful as it's going to be for you."

The speaker's face is a mixture of anger and sadness. Barrett says, "Look, this is what I can do. Later today I'll have one of my staff members leak something to one of our friends over at the *Washington Post*. Say that 'while the president is concerned about these allegations, the speaker is still a close personal friend and is confident she will be cleared of all charges.' Best I can do, Gwen."

She nods, gets up from the chair. "I wish you could do more, but I understand, Mr. President."

Barrett steps up from his desk, goes around and gives her a hug. "I'm with you, Gwen, as much as I can be. God bless you."

"God bless you, too, sir."

About ten minutes after the speaker of the House leaves, his special assistant, Carlton Pope, steps in and says, "Well?"

Barrett is gathering some reports and folders, wanting to quickly get back to his private office and refuge upstairs.

"It went," he says. "But I want you to contact one of our friends at the *Post*. I need an article in tomorrow's paper."

Pope says, "What do you need?"

"A White House source says the president is watching with keen interest the alleged charges against Speaker Washington and supports a thorough and transparent investigation into her activities."

Pope nods. He's got a great memory, and Barrett is sure that quote will appear tomorrow just as he dictated it.

"That doesn't sound particularly supportive," his special assistant says. "It's like you're letting her dangle out there, probably guilty."

Barrett checks his desk, makes sure he's leaving nothing behind.

"The speaker made a huge mistake," he says.

"What's that?"

"She trusted me," Barrett says.

CHAPTER 69

IN HIS JEEP Wrangler with Noa Himel, Liam Grey says, "Right from the beginning, when POTUS called us into his office, you were spot-on. Saying it wasn't going to end well."

Noa says, "Bet those words burn coming out of your mouth."

"No, they don't," he says. "I'm looking at reality. We thought we could exert a restraining influence on Barrett by being on the inside with him. We were wrong."

He shifts in his seat, looks behind him.

Just a typical parking lot at a typical Walmart.

But he's as jumpy as if going on his first overseas op.

Liam turns around, taps his fingers on the steering wheel. "I had a meeting with POTUS yesterday as well, and it wasn't as bad as yours, but it was bad enough."

"Tell me," Noa says.

Liam says, "We lost a man in Paris. Boyd Morris. Good guy, good operator. And earlier I learned that another member of our team, Benjamin Lucas, was captured by Chinese authorities in South Africa while on a failed exfil operation. He had been TDY'd from my team back to the Directorate of Operations."

"You've been thinned out, haven't you?"

"Yeah. I told him that my team members and I wanted a review of our rules of engagement before any more temporary duty assignments get made. He basically told me to shut up, salute, and go up the hill."

"And?"

"It just got worse. I told him that Boyd Morris needed to have a star carved for him on the Memorial Wall. He flat-out refused. I said I could understand if there was a delay, in order not to upset his current planning, but he said no, not ever. A former director of the CIA refusing to let a star be installed? Unheard of. Especially when he said Boyd died for him. Get that? Boyd didn't die for the country or the Agency. Nope, in Barrett's mind, Boyd died for him, and him only."

"Jesus," Noa says. "Now I'm thinking that somebody might visit me later tonight. With a box of flowers and a bullet to my forehead."

Liam watches the happy shoppers out there,

wondering if they could even imagine what was being discussed in this old Jeep.

Nothing major.

Just a nice peaceful talk about President Keegan Barrett's current mental health, and what can be done about it.

Liam says, "Like I said, we need to see Director Abrams. Dump everything in her lap and let her take the lead."

"Do you trust her?"

"More than I trusted Acting Director Fenway."

"And how do you plan to talk to her? You know her extension? Think her admin assistants will let us talk to her?"

Liam says, "My plan is for us to go into work tomorrow, just like we belong there, and take the elevator to the seventh floor, and demand to see her."

"Bold, but what if we get pulled aside before we get through the lobby? Start a fight? Pull a pistol?"

"How about you and I just stage a sit-down strike, hook our arms together, and start singing, 'We Shall Overcome'? That will get us what we need: public attention."

"All right, we get to Director Abrams. It'll be our word against the president's."

Liam says, "She's one tough and smart cookie. She'll at least look into it."

Noa says, "Hold on," and starts going through her

purse. "Hold on, I've got something to show her. Something that will tilt the case in our favor."

Liam watches her take her phone out and before he can say anything, she leans over and starts flipping through the screens.

"Look. A week ago, my team went to pick up a Donna Otterson from the Agency. She was suspected of passing along information to Chinese agents. These are photos of the surveillance operation...see?"

"Noa..." he starts.

"Three scenes of her dropping off information at this park, and the envelopes were retrieved by individuals that we assumed belonged to Chinese Intelligence. But something happened that made me question what was going on. I mean, why us, Barrett's domestic crew? Why not someone from the FBI or Counterintelligence?"

Liam says, "What was her job?"

"Get this," Noa says. "Finance resource officer in the Directorate of Support."

"What the hell, what could she be supplying to the Chinese? Payroll data? What did she tell you after you picked her up?"

There's a change of tone in Noa's voice. "She didn't. She was quiet, seemed unsurprised that we were there. Otterson asked to brush her teeth and get dressed. While in the bathroom, she suicided. Cyanide in a closed toothpaste tube."

"Shit," Liam says. "That's when you wanted to dig deeper."

"Yeah, and this is what I found out. I had one of my team members call in some favors ... look at these photos."

Noa flips through the phone and there's the same photo as the first one, except that the Chinese woman with the baby carriage has been replaced—

Oh, shit.

"Noa! I told you to ghost your way here ... is that a burner?"

"No, I—Oh, shit. I was in a goddamn hurry."

She switches off her phone, starts tugging at the rear plastic plate to remove the SIM card, just as Liam starts up the Jeep's engine.

The engine just *clicks.*

Disabled.

Too late.

All four windows and the windshield to the Jeep Wrangler implode, showering Liam and Noa with shattered glass, smoke, and a shock wave that pushes both of them back into their seats.

CHAPTER 70

IN THE SCIF in the subbasement of the Chinese Embassy to the United States, Xi Dejiang of the Ministry of State Security crisply says, *"Xiānshēng zàijiàn,"* and then hangs up the phone, connecting him to a secure line to Ministry headquarters in Beijing.

He sits still for a moment, as his assistant, Sun Zheng, looks at him questioningly.

It's so quiet in the SCIF that Dejiang imagines he can hear his heartbeat, as well as Zheng's.

"Sir?" Zheng asks.

"Wait," Dejiang says in disgust. "I am to wait for further instructions from Beijing. Bah."

His hand reaches for the familiar Marlboro cigarette box and then he pulls it back. Too much lately, smoking the American tobacco, wondering and thinking of what's going on in the American White House, barely a fifteen-minute drive away.

He says, "You know what will happen. It's very late in Beijing. That means phone calls must be made, superiors must be woken up, and they will have to be briefed. In turn, they will call their respective bosses, there will be committee meetings until someone decides that the president himself must be informed . . . all while hours pass and who knows what President Barrett might do next."

Sun stays silent. Dejiang knows that Zheng one day wants this job, but he's fairly certain Zheng doesn't feel that way at this moment.

Dejiang says, "The president has asked for my presence, specifically. With every minute that passes, each hour that goes by without a response, what do you believe he is thinking?"

"One would hope he would realize scheduling such a meeting takes time."

With irritation in his voice, Dejiang says, "In normal times, yes. But these are not normal times. President Barrett is what the locals here like to call a lone wolf. Check the past briefings on the White House inner workings. He has no close circle of advisers, of men to advise him and control his impulses. A bad way of doing business."

He shakes his head, succumbs to temptation, takes the Marlboro package and removes a cigarette.

"No, I think the president is there, mostly alone, wondering why his request for our nation's *rezident* to visit him is being ignored. He's not seeing it as a delay for typical reasons, no, he is a man of action, a former general, used to having his orders and requests instantly obeyed. Trust me on this, Barrett is sitting over in that White House, feeling humiliated and ignored. A dangerous combination."

Zheng says, "What do you propose, sir? A phone call to the White House, perhaps?"

Dejiang shakes his head. "No. A phone call will not do."

He reaches for his lighter, given to him last year from his son. It is maroon in color and has the symbol of Harvard on its side, and was made by his son and the fellow members of his social club—whatever that means—as some sort of joke.

From his small, framed portrait, Admiral Zheng He stares out with cool composure and courage.

Dejiang says, "I will go to see him myself at the White House, as soon as it can be arranged."

His assistant is stunned. "That's too dangerous, sir. Going against Beijing's instructions...extremely dangerous."

"As dangerous as sitting on our fat asses, waiting for Beijing to respond?" He brings the cigarette to his lips, anticipating that first sweet inhalation of smoke and nicotine. "I can't allow that. I'm here, I'm close by, and the American president has requested my presence. I will go and see what he wants. If we were to wait longer, he will get angrier and angrier, and if he has demands, they will increase proportionately."

Zheng's face goes from shock to placidness. "A brave move, sir."

Dejiang says, "But just a few minutes ago, you said it was dangerous."

"You've convinced me otherwise."

"*Fèihuà*, comrade," Dejiang says. "I've done no such thing. But a thought has crept into that busy mind of yours, Zheng, hasn't it? Perhaps when I leave to see the president, you will cable Beijing, and tell them what I'm doing. Sabotage my efforts to learn the president's mind and perhaps keep the peace. Leading to my dismissal and a trip back to Beijing."

Zheng's expression doesn't change.

Dejiang takes the Harvard lighter, flicks it open, and with a steady flame, lights up the cigarette. He takes that satisfying drag and slowly lets it out.

Dejiang says, "Don't forget, my deputy, that this SCIF is entirely secure. What is said in here stays here. And if I find out otherwise, that what I've said here somehow finds its way out, and if I'm going to prison, why, you'll be joining me. Right up to the point when we're both marched out to a courtyard, forced to our knees, and dispatched with a bullet to the back of the head."

Another drag of the cigarette.

"Do I make myself clear, Sun Zheng?"

It seems a bit of perspiration is developing on his assistant's forehead.

"Absolutely, sir."

"Good," Dejiang says. "Now make yourself useful and call the White House and tell them I'm ready to visit."

CHAPTER 71

LIAM GREY IS sitting in a dark room, bound to a chair, his eyes still burning from whatever chemical or narcotic agent was sprayed into his eyes. He blinks a few times trying to get some tear action working to flush out what was used, which was professional and good indeed.

After the engine to his Jeep was disabled and the windows were blown in, men dressed in black tactical gear swarmed them, spraying their faces. He instantly lost consciousness—the same for Noa, he's sure—and when he woke up, here he is.

And where is here?

He tests the bonds holding him to the chair.

Velcro straps, of course. Tight around his wrists, chest, and ankles. Not too tight but tight enough.

The air smells clean.

He can't hear any outside noises.

His eyes are still burning but they're beginning to adjust to the darkness.

Liam slowly rotates his head, using what astronomers call averted vision, because the human eye has more light-sensitive rods in the corners.

Something is out there in the room.

If he stares directly, there's nothing.

But a sideways glance...

A shape.

What kind of shape?

Angular and curved.

Time for a gamble.

"Noa," he says. "That you?"

Her voice comes right back. "Sure is. I was wondering when you'd notice me."

Liam says, "How long have you known I was over here?"

"Long enough," she says. "How are you feeling?"

"Tired," he says. "Sore. Eyes burning, getting better. You?"

"The same," she says. "Liam, it was my fault. I should have taken the time to transfer those surveillance photos to another device. I was in a hurry. I made a mistake."

Liam shifts and wiggles, but the damn Velcro straps won't budge.

"Well, at some point I'll send a memo to your supervisor, advising you go for some fieldcraft retraining."

"My current supervisor is POTUS. I don't think he's in any mood to listen to either one of us."

True, he thinks, trying to think ahead to what words he might speak or action he might take once their captors enter this room, no doubt working under the direction of President Barrett.

"Liam?"

"Still here," he says, trying to move the chair.

No joy.

Fastened to the floor.

"I've been thinking of something," she says.

"If it's an escape plan, I'm all ears," he says. "But make it quick. No doubt we're under surveillance in here."

She says, "The president used us, right from the beginning. He anticipated what we would do, how we would do it, until at some point, we were wounded, killed, or decided to rebel against his actions. But he knew we would both say *yes* when he asked us to set up the two teams, even if it was off the books."

He jerks the chair back and forth. Very safely secured.

"Well, that was pretty apparent, right?"

Noa says, "No, I don't think either one of us picked up on it. Remember what he said, when we were first interviewed? He said, *You have the perfect backgrounds and history of heartbreak to do what must be done.* Remember?"

"I do now," Liam says.

"No, I don't think you do," she snaps back. "Because it stuck with me. 'History of heartbreak.' Your heartbreak was your older brother, right? Killed in Afghanistan?"

"Yeah," Liam says. "My older brother Brian. A captain in the 10th Mountain Division. The Taliban did it. And you, it was a cousin, right?"

"Yes," comes the voice through the dark room. "My cousin Rebecca. She was an executive with Magen David Adom, part of the International Red Cross. Becky was meeting secretly with her counterparts in the Red Crescent Society in Beirut, but her presence there was uncovered by the usual tribe of bad actors. Becky died from a car bomb."

"Sorry," Liam says.

"Do you see it now?" she asks. "He praised us for our skills, our backgrounds, which operations we successfully achieved. But he wanted more from us. He knew we had revenge in our souls, enough so we wouldn't ask the tough questions, or turn down the tough assignments. He baited us and reeled us right in, even though deep down, we both knew we were operating illegally."

Another tug of the straps.

No joy.

"Good call, Noa," he says.

"Thanks."

"And if you can come up with a way to get us out of here, let me know."

Noa says, "I'm working on it."

CHAPTER 72

SOMEWHERE IN SOUTH AFRICA

THE DOOR TO his cell is unlocked, and Benjamin Lucas is resting on his right side, the aches and throbbing pain exhausting him. Whatever comfort the two Extra Strength Tylenol Chin gave to him earlier has worn off. His eyes flutter open and he sees two men walk in, and then he closes his eyes.

To hell with them both.

He's not going to greet them, and if they want to talk to him, they can go first.

They start talking in Mandarin and Benjamin recognizes the voices: Han Yuanchao, the Chinese intelligence officer who had first talked to him here, and Chang Wanquan, the little shit who had tuned him up yesterday with that thick cricket bat.

Yuanchao says, *Who gave you the authority to come in here and torture this prisoner? I couldn't believe what I heard. Which is why I had to see for myself what you did.*

Wanquan replies, *There was no torture. He attacked me and I responded. I know he is a trained CIA operative, quite dangerous. What else should I have done?*

Amazing coincidence that the surveillance system in this cell failed at that moment you entered.

Wanquan says, *It has its problems, you know that.*

And what was your intent in questioning the prisoner without my permission?

You were unavailable. I wanted to see for myself a captured CIA operative.

And did you get your questions answered? Yuanchao asks.

No, the younger officer says smugly, *but I got what I wanted.*

To hurt him? Perhaps to kill him?

Wanquan says, *If and when he is returned to the Americans, I want them to see what happens—personally—if you work against us.*

Fool, Yuanchao says. *Suppose you had put him in a coma? Or killed him? What value would he have then to us?*

Benjamin keeps his eyes closed, his breathing regular.

Wanquan says, *Why are you babying this man? Why do you protect him so?*

Benjamin hears footsteps as Yuanchao heads to the door.

Because he is vital to us, and to the Americans.

Vital how? He's just a spy, nothing notable about him.

You are wrong, Yuanchao says, knocking at the door. *He's the key to it all.*

The key to what?

Preventing World War Three, Yuanchao says. The door is opened and closed and locked, and Benjamin opens his eyes.

Preventing World War Three.

Him?

How is that even possible?

CHAPTER 73

SOME TIME HAS passed in the near darkness, and Liam says, "You awake over there?"

"I am," Noa says.

"You still working on our escape?"

Noa says, "Somewhat. But due to ears and eyes on us at this moment, I'm keeping it secret."

"Well, do pass it on when the time comes."

Liam is feeling better but he's thirsty, and he says, "Hope they haven't dumped us here and forgotten about us. Could use a drink."

"I could use something practical. Like a bucket."

"Oh."

"Thanks for saying 'oh.' Makes me feel a lot better."

"What's going on? Need a bathroom?"

Noa says, "I need something to eat. Sometimes I get a bout of hypoglycemia when I don't eat and my blood sugar craters. Next up is a heavy bout of nausea, followed by vomiting."

Liam thinks for a moment and says, "Remember SERE training? In Virginia?"

"Oh, yeah, one of my favorite memories when I was training for Operations."

Liam says, "Yep. Survival, evasion, resistance, and escape. Dumped into the wilderness of Virginia, brought into a mock prisoner-of-war camp, starved, and slapped around by our coworkers in the Agency. One day blending into another. Cold, little water, crappy, cold food, lots of shouting interrogations. Sometimes you could hear your fellow classmates screaming in pain or fear."

Noa says, "If you're trying to buck me up, you're failing."

"No, there's a point," Liam says. "One day pretend commandos raided the joint, shot our captors with paintball rounds, and we were freed. We were brought out to the compound, the flag of the terrorists was hauled down, Old Glory was run up the pole, and we all sang 'The Star Spangled Banner.' Us and our pretend captors. Then there were hugs and handshakes and, hey, no hard feelings all around. You do that to the folks from the Agency who tortured you?"

"I don't remember."

Liam says, "I remember. I didn't shake anybody's hands. I had no feelings of love and forgiveness. I went up to one of the camp's deputies—we called him Hardcase—and he was smiling at me and I punched him out and broke his nose."

"And yet you made it."

"Exigent circumstances," Liam says. "I was under pressure, that kind of crap. But what I'm getting to is this: a price must be paid. These guys were doing an important job, prepping us in case we got captured, but some of them had too much fun, were too enthusiastic. Hardcase was one of them. I wanted him to hurt."

Noa says, "Please tell me there's a point."

"Not to be vulgar, but if you can't stand it any-more, let it go. Lean over and puke your guts out. It'll be uncomfortable but you'll be hitting back at those who captured us. You'll make a smell, you'll stain your surroundings, you'll give them extra work to do. Not much but it'll be some-thing, Noa."

"And you?" she asks, skepticism in her voice.

He's about to say that he'll come up with something, when lights overhead suddenly come on. Liam blinks his eyes hard and the room comes into focus. The room is carpeted beige and seems to be in a basement, with small casement windows before him and to the left. Other items are covered with white sheets, like this area is also a storeroom. At the right is a wooden door. The room is wood-paneled and Noa is about ten feet away, sitting in a leather chair fastened to the floor, strapped in with Velcro like Liam.

She blinks, too, and Liam says, "Hold on, it's going to get interesting."

Noa says, "Liam?"

"Yes?"

"Great working with you," she says. "However this ends."

"Right back at you," he replies, and the door opens.

A woman comes in, accompanied by two large men with ill-fitting suits that say security to Liam, but his focus goes back to the angry woman coming in.

CIA Director Hannah Abrams.

She stops and looks at Noa, and then straight at Liam.

"You two," she says. "Can you think of any good reason why I shouldn't put you both on a rendition flight right now and Gitmo your respective asses?"

CHAPTER 74

PRESIDENT KEEGAN BARRETT is in a living area on the second floor of the White House, sitting alone on a couch, a bowl of oatmeal in his hands as he watches the morning cable news, keeping the sound off.

Coffee and low-sugar orange juice are on the table before him. He frowns as he eats his morning meal. Despite the addition of low-fat milk, organic strawberries, and imported Ceylonese cinnamon sugar, he still feels like he's shoveling a tasteless lumpy sludge into his mouth.

He'd much rather have an omelet or French toast or two eggs over easy, with plenty of bacon and hash browns as a side, but if he wants to keep healthy for the rest of the years left to him in the White House, he needs to eat well.

Doctor's orders.

Which brings a pang of memory, of how that nice

Captain Spencer Webster had been shot and killed yesterday, to keep Barrett's unfolding operations secret. Painful, but it had to be done.

At some point Barrett will make it right to Spencer's widow and kids, but not now.

The sound is off on the television as he flicks through the channels. He has a high tolerance for necessary pain and suffering, but that tolerance doesn't extend to listening to the chattering "journalists" from the various studio sets, all trying to portray themselves as expert and hard-nosed with empathy and sympathy for the masses.

He has a dim childhood memory of watching a special about the famed CBS news anchor Walter Cronkite. Now that was a journalist who commanded respect, a guy who came up through the ranks, risked his life a couple of times—in World War II he rode along in a bombing raid when the Army Air Force was suffering horrible losses, and even flew in with troops in a glider during Operation Market Garden, when many of those gliders destructed against trees or stone walls—while these talking heads would probably collapse sobbing if they stubbed a toe.

But Barrett keeps an eye on the graphics, on the videos, as familiar stories roll by.

Vice President Laura Hernandez still in a coma, cause unknown.

Speaker of the House Gwen Washington facing

investigation from at least three Congressional committees.

Barrett's Secretary of State in Germany, laughing while posing with the German chancellor, both of them wearing lederhosen.

His own approval ratings holding steady at 59 percent, and he nods with satisfaction at that number.

No news of Russia.

No news of China.

"How's breakfast?" Carlton Pope asks, walking into view, sitting down in a near chair.

"Sucks, as always," he says. "What's going on?"

"Bad news, good news, for the moment," Carlton says. "We still haven't located Liam Grey, but we're working on it."

Barrett says, "It might take longer than you think. He's experienced."

"Well, so are my guys," Carlton says. "With the advantage that they don't play by any rules, except getting the job done."

He looks at the remaining gray mush at the bottom of his bowl and thinks it's a hell of a thing when the leader of the free world can't eat what he wants, just a few days away from everything coming together. He puts the bowl down, the seal of the White House bright on the side of the porcelain.

"Pass on the good news, then," he says.

"The Chinese have bit," Carlton says, grinning.

"Their *rezident* contacted us. He wants to come for a visit."

"Xi Dejiang, correct?"

"Yes, sir."

"When does he want to come by?"

"He requested this afternoon."

The president picks up his coffee cup. "He'll get tomorrow afternoon, and he'll like it. He's in my country, not his. Screw him."

CHAPTER 75

CIA DIRECTOR HANNAH Abrams walks into the furnished basement and says to her two security officers, "Bruce, Ralph, let them out, will you?"

Liam Grey and Noa Himel stay still as the two men remove the Velcro restraints. Hannah sees that Noa takes a moment to rub her wrists and stretch out her legs, while Liam defiantly sits still, like he doesn't want to show any appreciation of being freed.

Despite all that's going on, Hannah likes seeing the toughness of her officer.

She steps closer.

Noa and Liam both look at her, no fear or favor in their faces.

"Well?" she asks. "That wasn't a rhetorical question, Liam. Or Noa."

Noa says, "You shouldn't send us to Gitmo because we need to tell you what we've been doing under the president's orders."

Liam says, "I'm with Noa."

Hannah reaches over to a sheet, tugs it off, revealing a chair.

She drags it over, sits down.

Bruce and Ralph stand still behind her.

"Okay," she says, reaching into her bag, taking out a white legal pad and pen. "Start talking."

About thirty-five minutes later, Noa and Liam have visited a toilet in the basement, and the three of them have coffee that Bruce brought in from Starbucks, along with some pastries to take the edge off Noa's hunger. A larger breakfast is promised.

Hannah looks down at her notes.

"Just to recap, Liam and Noa, operating without the proper authority from the Agency and—"

Liam interrupts her. "The president told us that he had buy-in from Acting Director Fenway. What, we should have gone to him up on the seventh floor and double-checked?"

Hannah stares at him. "That would have been fine, out-of-the-box thinking, wouldn't it? But as the good former Army officer you once were, you thought you had the proper orders. You didn't."

Noa says, "But what about Fenway? Won't he confirm what the president ordered?"

Hannah says, "Mr. Fenway has gone to ground at a point between the Florida Keys and the Aleutian Islands. He wasn't around for a debriefing after I was sworn in, and his secretaries told me the day before I came on board, most of his paperwork and files were dumped into burn bags. If you're hoping for him to bail you out, forget it."

She lets that bit of news sink in and she tells the two officers more. "When the congressional investigations start up, you two will quickly find out that there was no Agency paperwork, no official presidential finding, and to put a cherry on top of this bloody mess that's going to make Iran–Contra look like an overdue library book scandal, there was no notification to Congress."

Liam still looks defiant, but it looks like Noa has aged about ten years since Hannah started speaking.

Hannah says, "In a normal world, and if I was in a good mood, I'd advise the two of you to lawyer up, and then I'd contact the attorney general and confess all, and then I'd next arrange an urgent meeting of the Gang of Eight in Congress to give them a full debriefing, and wait for the flamethrowers to kick in, and the leaks to the news media to start a few hours later."

She pauses. "Even though I haven't been on the job three days, you two and your rogue teams are still my responsibility."

Hannah quiets for a moment, gauging what might happen next with Noa and Liam after this bracing blow of reality.

Liam looks to Noa, she looks right back at him, and Liam says, "I guess what you're saying, ma'am, is that we're not in a normal world."

Hannah is pleased the two of them have caught on to what she's just said.

"Correct, Liam. We are not in a normal world. We're in a world where you and others have unwittingly helped a very sick man attack our adversaries in secret, to take this nation to the brink of a world war, a war that will eventually turn off our lights, kill our farms, and destroy our cities. That takes precedent over your respective violations of the law and the Constitution."

Hannah glances down at her notes on her legal pad, looks up, and says, "The question now, of course, is what are we going to do about it?"

CHAPTER 76

FOR A PLEASANT few seconds, Liam Grey thinks he and Noa are going to slide unscathed through this thundering avalanche coming down on them both, but that feeling quickly disappears when the CIA director says "we" when mentioning stopping the president.

"Ma'am," he says. "What do you mean, 'we'? We don't have the authority or power to do anything to President Barrett."

"True," she says. "Do you think that's just a coincidence? Of course not. The president has used his CIA and military background, connections, and experiences to put himself where he is—untouchable."

Liam says, "Impeachment, then. Failing that, the Twenty-fifth Amendment. If the three of us testify on Capitol Hill as to what happened, what illegal orders he's issued, then Congress will have to act."

Noa speaks up. "Do they? Liam, the usual system is broken, don't you see that? The vice president is in a coma. The speaker of the House is fighting for her political life. Do you think she's going to do anything to upset those representatives who are Barrett true believers, who think he can do no wrong? Like it or not, Barrett has positioned himself to where he has absolute and unchecked power. The secretary of state and the secretary of defense belong to him. His chief of staff can't even order pizza without POTUS agreeing. There's no national security director in office."

Liam sees what Noa is saying, but doesn't want to acknowledge it. This was the United States, damn it, not some South American republic that could change its president or constitution at the drop of a hat.

He takes a breath, trying to calm himself. "This... it can't be done. You're talking treason. We have to let the system work, no matter how clumsy and slow it'll be."

Noa says, "Liam, you mentioned the Twenty-fifth Amendment. Congress has no power to bring that into effect. It's up to the vice president. Who's in a coma."

The room falls quiet for a moment.

Hannah says, "Noa, you told me that Barrett nearly threatened to rape you in the White House, or even kill you. Liam, you told me that you think the president had something to do with Captain Webster's murder."

Liam just sits still, not wanting to hear what comes next.

"Ever since this Republic came to life, nearly every president has been accused of being a mentally ill madman, and always by their partisan opponents," Abrams says, voice suddenly weary. "But now it's happened, for real. And I'm afraid we're running out of time."

CHAPTER 77

JOINT INTELLIGENCE CENTER PACIFIC

PEARL HARBOR, HAWAII

LIEUTENANT COMMANDER CORNELIUS Johnson is the night duty officer at the facility supplying intelligence to the Indo-Pacific Command of the US Navy. One of his deepest secrets is that he loves every minute of being here. During meal and coffee breaks he'll join in with the general bitching and moaning of working for the Navy, resisting the urge to tell his fellow sailors and officers just how damn lucky they are.

Cornelius grew up poor in a housing project in the Cherry Hill part of Baltimore, where the sounds of gunshots and sirens kept you awake at night, where too many of your neighbors were on street corners, hustling or nodding off in abandoned doorways. But he found his escape via a Navy recruiting station in a broken-down strip mall. The Navy fed him, clothed him, paid him well, and, considering he was a child of Cherry Hill, also gave him one hell of a responsibility.

In this large, darkened room with workstations with large computer screens and enormous illuminated wall displays, he and a dozen other Marine and Navy personnel kept watch on almost everything on the move in the Pacific and associated waters. Civilian airliners, commercial freighters, factory fishing craft, and, of course, every military aircraft and ship and submarine from every navy operating in the Pacific.

When he first arrived here, he had been overwhelmed by the complexity of the screens, the symbols and numbers marking targets of interest, but now, a quick glance tells him all he needs to know.

Right now, things are relatively calm.

His station is a cluttered desk that overlooks the rest of the room—called the Pit—and his evening is suddenly interrupted by one of his secure phones ringing. Since 9/11, when one glaring error was revealed on how each intelligence agency and law enforcement organization jealously kept their work to themselves—called siloing—a move went afoot to break down the barriers and allow cross-communications and intelligence sharing.

He has six secure phones on his desk: one each connecting him to the Indo-Pacific Command duty office, the Pentagon, the Defense Intelligence

Agency, the FBI, the CIA, and the National Security Agency. In his nine months here as duty officer, the phones from the FBI and CIA have never rung once.

But the teal one from the NSA is ringing. He smiles, hoping Tina—his night duty counterpart—is on the line.

She is.

"Hey, Corny," she says, "how goes it tonight?"

"Looking forward to my hula lessons in the morning, how about you?"

Soft and pleasing laughter from this intelligence analyst at Fort Meade. He doesn't know her real name or what she looks like, but she's smart and he loves talking to her.

He says, "Always a delight to hear from you, Tina."

Her voice suddenly gets serious. "You might not keep thinking that when I sign off."

"Oh?" he asks, grabbing a pen and pad of paper. "What's the situation?"

Tina says, "We're seeing increased communications and orders being issued for the PLA Navy bases in Haikou, Guangzhou, Shantou, and the Yulin Naval Base in Hainan. It looks like they're prepping for something. I'd advise you to immediately start focusing your assets on those locations."

Cornelius says, "Are they prepping for a training exercise?"

"Doubtful," Tina says. "It takes months to prepare for a naval exercise. This seems much more serious. And to make things even more interesting, we're getting a similar chatter increase from their cyber-warfare facilities. There's a bunch of lights burning late tonight here and at the Pentagon, and I wanted you in on the fun."

Cornelius says, "Thanks for the heads-up, Tina."

Her laughter returns. "That's what I get paid for."

"Tell me," he says, "what does your gut tell you?"

"Not my job."

"I know that, but between you and me, what's going on?"

She laughs. "Some *between you and me,* considering these calls are recorded."

"Humor me," Cornelius says, feeling out of sorts.

A bit of silence, then Tina says, "Hold on tight. The Chinese are pissed at us for something, they're preparing a strike, and they're coming at us heavy."

CHAPTER 78

CIA DIRECTOR HANNAH Abrams has brought her two operators upstairs and after a number of minutes, they are dining on eggs Benedict, hash browns, toast, and more coffee and juice, prepared by one of her security officers, Bruce, who is a graduate of the other CIA—the Culinary Institute of America—before joining the Agency.

The dining room is well furnished, with a smooth polished table, wooden chairs, and bookshelves and cabinets holding antique plates and bowls.

Liam looks around and says, "This is one hell of a safe house we've got here, Director Abrams."

She smiles. "It's not a safe house."

Noa asks, "Then where are we?"

Hannah says, "It's my house. I wasn't too sure how many of Barrett's allies are still in the Agency and reporting to him, so I did the safe thing and brought you here, after the snatch team picked you up at the Walmart parking lot. Sorry about your Jeep, Liam."

He says, "Not a problem, Director. But you've got an . . . interesting setup in your basement."

"Just temporary, that's all," she says. "Amazing what you can get done quickly if you ask the right people."

Hannah forces herself to eat. She's not hungry but she knows the hours and days ahead are going to be brutal, requiring her to be sharp and have energy. She thinks of what she just told these two, that Barrett still has allies in the Agency—which they already had figured out—and wonders just how deep the rot goes.

"Liam, your targets have been a Russian bot farm, a Hezbollah outpost in Venezuela, and three ISIS fighters in Paris. But nothing involving the Chinese."

"No, ma'am," he says.

"Noa, your targets have been a mix, but you have rolled up Chinese assets operating here."

"Correct, ma'am."

She says, "For the past two months, you and your teams have been going after a number of targets, and so far, so good. The Russians have stayed quiet. The Iranians and Hezbollah are secretly wondering why it took us so long. But the Chinese . . . This is the first time that we've gone after their people without offering a trade or any other accommodation. The

Chinese won't like that. And it seems like Barrett has upped the stakes."

Noa asks, "In what way?"

Hannah says, "Two days ago, a city of nearly a million people in China lost power, and in that city was a cyberattack facility operated by China's Ministry of State Security. A cruise missile did the job, dropping graphite fibers over parts of the electrical grid, shorting it out."

Liam says, "Director, it couldn't be one of ours."

"Why not?" she says, now having entirely lost her appetite. "Hours before, an American destroyer in the East China Sea was conducting a test of a new generation of cruise missiles. One flew straight to the target coordinates. The other supposedly disappeared after launch. I think the second flew according to plan, right to China."

Aghast, Liam says, "That's an act of war."

"Surely is," Hannah says. "The president used you and your teams to muddy up the waters while he goes after his real target. China."

"Why not go see the president, Director?" Noa asks. "Tell him you know of his illegal actions involving the Agency and military and tell him it has to stop."

Hannah says, "You left out the 'or else,' Noa. Or else what? Go to the press? Go to Congress? We've already discussed how that won't work. I serve at President Barrett's pleasure. If I do meet him, he'll just pull out a blank piece of White House stationery and demand my resignation, then and there. I'll be gone and he'll still be there, un-accountable, stirring up trouble."

Noa and Liam look on. She feels like the school-teacher whose students can't solve a complex math problem, and they're looking for her to come up with something, anything.

Hannah says, "Richard Helms was director dur-ing the latter part of President Johnson's term. Each time Helms briefed LBJ, he told him the same news. That CIA analysts and operatives on the ground in South Vietnam were unanimous that our intervention there was a losing cause. LBJ would just nod, say thanks, send him away, and not change a damn thing. Here, though, I'd be going to President Barrett and saying his personal actions and orders are illegal. He won't stand for that. I'll be forced to resign, and that's all she wrote. Folks, we need more if we're going to stop the president."

Liam speaks up. "Madam Director, is Noa's cell phone in your possession?"

"My security detail has it."

"Get it," he says. "Noa has something we both need to see."

Hannah listens carefully as Noa once again goes over the mission concerning Donna Otterson, a relatively obscure finance resource officer in the

Directorate of Support. Noa has her phone in hand as she goes on.

"We were scammed by the president," Noa says. "We thought she was engaged in espionage with the Chinese, and we had these surveillance photos to prove it. It looks like she was passing along information to Chinese intelligence. I had my team dig deeper. It wasn't the Chinese at all. It was this woman."

Hannah peers closer at the photos of the woman with the dark clothes and baseball cap pulled down tight over her face. "Do we know who this woman is?"

Noa says, "No."

Liam sighs. "Yes."

She and Noa both stare at Liam. "Who is she?" Hannah asks.

"That's a *Washington Post* reporter," Liam says.

Noa says, "Are you sure?"

"Positive," Liam says. "Her name is Kay Darcy, and she's my ex-wife."

CHAPTER 79

SPEAKER OF THE House Gwen Washington is sitting in her luxurious office, thinking, staring at the confident man sitting across from her, Congressman Fritz Deering of Ohio, the House majority leader and the traitorous son of a bitch who wants to be sitting on her side of the desk.

He's wearing a cheap black suit, white shirt, and yellow tie. His thick toupee is gray and white, and with his black eyebrows, it makes him look like some sort of angry badger or possum.

Besides being the majority leader, he's also the unofficial head of the Old Party Caucus, seeking to return the party to the roots of the working person, old-style manufacturing jobs, and dreams of the 1950s where the average man could support his wife and two kids on one salary, and have a comfortable life.

An average white man, of course, but Gwen

doesn't feel like explaining that sensitive point once more to Fritz.

Gwen says, "You asked for a meeting, so here it is. You have five minutes, Fritz. Go."

He folds his arms across his plump belly. "I've been trying to keep our House members in line, and it's not working. There's a move afoot to combine the three different House committees looking into your financial dealings into one investigative committee, with full subpoena powers. It won't be pretty."

Gwen feels like her hands and feet are freezing from this news. "There's no evidence that those documents are real. I assure you that they are not."

Fritz shrugs. "At this point, what difference does it make? The investigations here on the Hill and no doubt from the FBI are underway, and that work will take weeks to conduct, weeks where the people's business won't take place, and things here and in the Senate will be in lockdown."

She says, "Fritz, I really admire the way you say 'the people's business' without that rug on your head bursting into flames. It sounds so noble, so pure, only being concerned with the people's business. That's utter horseshit and you know it."

Gwen glances over at the old wind-up clock in the corner of her office, once belonging to her great-grandfather, the son of slaves, alive, still working.

"You have two minutes now," the speaker of the House says. "Don't waste them."

His face flushes. Gwen knows how much he hates his toupee, but it's part of his "street cred" or whatever with his fellow caucus members and constituents that he wears something so cheap on his scalp.

"It's like this," he says. "You have two choices ahead of you. Let the investigations kick in and have the Hill and the nation suffer. Or resign."

"The way you're saying that, Fritz, it sounds pretty simple," she says.

"It's the best thing for the party and the country, and you know it, Gwen," he says. "Step down with your name and dignity intact and retire back home to California. I'm sure you can get a comfortable teaching job at some university or college."

"You think that's what I really want? A comfortable teaching job?"

"Why not?" he asks. "Leave the charges behind, slip on out—"

Cold fury seizes her. "Congressman, my whole life I've never 'slipped on out' on any damn thing, and I'm not going to start it today."

"I was just suggesting—"

"Take your suggestions and shove them where the proverbial sun don't shine, Congressman," Gwen says. "The charges are false. And I'm going to fight them every second, minute, and hour of every day, even with you egging on your Stone Age caucus."

"Fine," he says, abruptly standing up. "The president is wavering on you, every day I get another phone call from a member who wants to see you gone. There's too much that has to be done with a weakened speaker in charge. I came here in good faith, to help you out. I should have known I was wasting my time with the likes of you."

Gwen clenches a fist and gives him a steely smile. "What do you mean, the likes of you? An uppity Black woman who doesn't know her place?"

"Whatever," he says, walking quickly to the door. "But I guarantee you, Gwen, in a week, my place will be here."

CHAPTER 80

LIAM LOOKS TO Noa and Director Abrams, and says, "Kay's working on a story about Barrett. She knows he's funding and supporting private paramilitary teams, here and overseas. She doesn't have all the pieces, but she's got enough to keep working on it."

He takes in the surveillance photo. "That's her. The way she's dressed, the body frame, the way she holds her arms and the way her head is cocked. That's Kay."

Noa says, "But why is she meeting with Donna Otterson? A finance resource officer?"

"Kay's thorough," he says. "There has to be something there. She won't go through official channels to get to her story. And as another incentive, she also hates the Agency for breaking up our marriage."

The director says, "Is she right?"

Liam says, "Of course she's right."

"Can you still see her?" Hannah asks. "Will she talk to you?"

"If she thinks she can get a story out of it, yes," Liam says. "I talked to her a couple of days ago."

Hannah says, "What about?"

Liam stares at the director of the CIA. "My violation of my oath. I was confirming her information about President Barrett's illegal activities, about setting up paramilitary teams here and abroad."

His boss's eyes darken and narrow. "One hell of a violation, Mr. Grey."

"Yes, ma'am. But it was the right thing to do."

"Says who? Your supervisor, or your conscience?"

"Me, only me," Liam says, realizing that even in the midst of this crisis, he is out on a long, thin, creaking branch.

The director smiles. "With what's going on, that was minor, indeed, Liam. In fact, it's going to help us. We have a reporter in the most respected and prestigious newspaper in this part of the world, and she's already working on the story."

Noa says, "At the right time, Director Abrams, she could release a number of stories that would help you."

Abrams nods. "That's what I'm thinking. Liam, can you meet with her? Safely?"

"It'll take some time, but yes, I can do that."

"Good. Meet up with her and we'll set up a

confidential pipeline to her. Feed her information, have her tell us what her editors think, have her tell us what she's finding out from her own sources. A quid pro quo. It won't do the job entirely, but it'll be a help."

Noa clears her throat. "With all due respect, Director Abrams, what is our job?"

Abrams says, "To have President Barrett resign before he kills us all."

Nearly an hour later, after more discussion, brainstorming, and setting up plans to contact his former wife—*boy*, he thinks, *she is going to get one hell of a surprise in a few hours*—Liam says, "With what the snatch team did to my Jeep, I'm going to need transportation, Director."

Hannah is about to reply when one of her two security officers, Ralph, steps into the room and says, "Sorry to interrupt, Madam Director, but there's a phone call."

She gets up from a couch and says, "Probably my deputy director, wondering why in hell I'm so late getting to work."

Ralph's tone is apologetic. "I'm sorry, Madam Director. The phone call is not for you."

Liam is frozen at the next words Ralph says.

"The call is for Liam Grey."

CHAPTER 81

J. EDGAR HOOVER BUILDING

WASHINGTON, DC

FBI DEPUTY DIRECTOR Edie Hicks is in Director Warren Jablonski's office on the seventh floor of the FBI building at 935 Pennsylvania Avenue NW, trying to keep her patience in place.

The director looks at a two-page memo that Edie had earlier deposited on his wide, shiny, and spotless wooden desk. He stares at it like a dinner at a fine French restaurant, ready to send the *blanquette de veau* back to the kitchen because it's two degrees too cool.

The office is huge, with a conference room table, fine furniture, bookshelves, and, behind the director, American flags and the flag of the FBI. Edie has been in this office numerous times, with both Jablonski and his predecessor. Edie came up the ranks of the FBI the old-fashioned way, assigned to the Criminal Division in the New York Field Office, working the streets, even joining the SWAT team. More assignments followed, from Counterterrorism to even serving two tours in Afghanistan, and running the FBI office in Chicago before being promoted here.

The FBI director talks in a slow voice, like every word is being carefully weighed and chosen.

"That's quick work, Edie," he says. "Very impressive. A nice reflection on the agents you chose to do such a sensitive job."

"Thank you, Director."

Then he shuts up.

Edie feels like sighing. The gaunt man in front of her with the sad basset hound eyes and thick black hair has come up a different way through the Department of Justice, by never making waves and never doing anything controversial. Not an approach that was respected by most of the FBI field agents, but when a crisis ever hit the DoJ or the attorney general's office, he was always the compromise candidate who'd get the job to "clean things up."

She doubts he's ever made an arrest in the field in his entire career.

But now he's here, as director, and Edie loathes one of his habits, which is keeping his mouth shut and letting the other party speak.

She waits.

A grandfather clock in the corner goes *tick-tick-tick.*

Screw this, she thinks.

"Do you have any questions, Director?"

He still stares at the offending memo. "No, you did a thorough job, thank you."

Another pause.

Tick-tick-tick.

"In case you have any questions, Director," she says, "I'll just point out that we were able to get a jump on the investigation because of the accusation that the speaker's deceased husband used some sort of influence to secure funds years back after Congress passed its latest version of the Emergency Economic Stabilization Act. His bank seemed to be first in line to get the financing, weeks before it was set to be seized by the FDIC."

The director just nods.

Not a word.

Words are weapons and can be used against you once uttered.

Edie says, "For lack of a better phrase, that accusation was the low-hanging fruit from all those charges made against the speaker. Following the attorney general's request, we had a forensic accounting team examine the records in question at the Treasury Department."

"I see," he finally says.

Edie is now losing her patience. "Director, our accounting team reached the conclusion that the documents were fake. A clever fake indeed, but the type of paper used in those records recovered from the Treasury Department were the wrong bond used during that year. There was also a mistake in recording the address of Mr. Washington's bank, and the name of the primary bank inspector listed belonged to a Treasury official who had retired three weeks earlier. Other supporting documents that should have been there were missing. To my team, it looked like the documents were made up and planted there."

He stays quiet.

Tick-tick-tick.

"Director, do you see what we've discovered? Speaker Washington is correct. The charges against her are fake. Well-done and apparently incriminating, but fake nonetheless."

"So?" he asks.

CHAPTER 82

DEPUTY DIRECTOR EDIE Hicks clenches her jaw at the director's response.

"Sir, I hope you're understanding the gravity of this situation."

The barest of nods, and he stirs himself just a bit, like an old man waking up after twelve hours of sleep. "But that's just one charge. There are many others. And your teams haven't completed their initial investigations."

"Yes," she says, frustrated. "But the fact that the most devastating accusation is fake...well..."

The director seems to be finally paying attention. "Well, what, Edie? What are you trying to say?"

Edie is never sure of her status with the director, and what she's about to say next will probably mean a big hit to her career, but so what?

What is right is right.

And the women in this horrible town need to watch out for each other.

"Sir, my gut is telling me that somehow, somewhere, an enemy or enemies of the speaker are working to either weaken her politically, or to force her out."

Another slow nod. "Sounds like a reasonable position."

"Sir, someone is attacking a constitutional officer of the United States. We need to do something about it."

He says, "We *are* doing something about it. We're conducting a quiet and professional investigation."

"Yes, sir, but once we're finished, it'll be too late," she says. "There are hearings being planned up on the Hill. Even if they don't force her out, they will weaken her tremendously, impacting how well she can perform her governmental responsibilities. Saying months later that oops, it was all false ... the damage will already have been done."

Tick-tick-tick.

More waiting.

"Well," he finally says, "I don't see any way around it. As unfortunate as it might be for the speaker."

"But you can do something, Director. This afternoon. Today."

His eyes look troubled. "What is that?"

She says, "With your permission, Director, I can reach out to a friendly reporter at the *New York Times* Washington bureau. On deep background, no direct connection to the Bureau, we can have a story appear tomorrow that according to a reliable source, the initial investigation into Speaker Washington's affairs show that fake documents are being used to smear her."

There.

It's out.

Dangling like a balloon between them.

He clears his throat. The balloon turns into a dirigible, then to the *Hindenberg,* and everything bursts into flames.

"Not on your life," he says.

"But Director—"

"No," he says, voice more firm and resonant. "You know how many previous directors got into trouble for appearing to interfere in political investigations? Too many. And I'm not going to join that list. Not ever. My term of office is not going to include charges that my Bureau was politicized. We're going to do this by the book, and that's it. And to make it clear, you are forbidden to discuss this investigation with anyone not in the Bureau. Do I make myself clear?"

"Utterly," she says, disgusted.

"Good," he says. "Now, if you'll excuse me, I have another appointment."

"Thank you, Director," she says, getting up and walking away.

Back in her office and restless, Edie thinks about making a call to a friend of hers, at the "other agency," but holds off. What would that call accomplish, except for a chance for Edie to bitch at the unfairness of it all? Besides, her friend is no doubt busy with her own problems.

Edie picks up a copy of that day's *Washington Post,* with yet another update on the continuing mystery of the vice president's coma and condition over at Walter Reed.

There were days when she and others in this building thought Director Jablonski was in a walking coma, by the way he acted, and one thing that continues to puzzle her is why he's still here. There were rumors some months ago, after President Keegan Barrett's inauguration, that he would ask for the director's resignation and put in one of his own to run the Bureau.

But no, President Barrett kept this bland and nearly lifeless cipher on board.

Why the hell would he do that?

CHAPTER 83

CIA DIRECTOR ABRAMS leads Liam and Noa into her office at the other side of her home. Liam feels like he's in the audience of some play and has just been dragged out of the seats to come up onstage and start performing, with no idea of the story or script.

Her office is neat with built-in bookshelves and only a few framed photos on the walls, and two large windows overlooking a wide rear lawn. Liam has been in offices for military or intelligence leaders where the walls fairly groaned from holding up all the plaques, awards, and light boxes with challenge medals.

But not her office.

Liam likes the contrast to the other "look at me" offices he's been in. Three chairs are near her desk with three phone systems on it. Her security officer Bruce is holding a handset out to Liam. The director picks up another handset to listen in.

Bruce steps back and Noa stands beside him.

It's reassuring to have Noa next to him, he realizes.

He takes the handset. "This is Grey."

"Hello," says a woman's voice. "How are you doing this morning, Liam? If I may call you Liam."

"Who is this, and how did you find me?"

A quick laugh. "Are there really any secrets left in this world, Liam? A request is made and various technical avenues are searched, until there you are, at the home of Hannah Abrams, director of the Central Intelligence Agency."

"Yes, here I am. And where are you? And again, who are you?"

"South Africa, in Johannesburg," she says. "My name is Chin Lin, and I bring you best wishes from Benjamin Lucas."

The director's eyes widen and she grabs a legal pad, pen, and waits.

Liam says, "I'm not sure I know what you're talking about, Lin."

She sighs. "Let's not play these games, Liam. You and Benjamin work for the CIA. You have been on a team conducting paramilitary operations overseas. Benjamin left your team to come to Johannesburg to exfil a defector from China's Ministry of State Security. That defector is me."

The director slides over the legal pad.

Get her to the point.

"Then what happened to the exfil?"

"I was forced by my superiors to betray Benjamin. He's currently in our custody in Joburg. We only have a short window before he gets transferred to one of our black sites."

A laugh. "We learned that from you, after your Iraq war. Funny world, isn't it?"

"What do you mean, 'we only have a short window'?"

"Oh, haven't you figured it out? Ben and I had a romantic relationship when we went to Stanford. We still love each other. And I want to free him, and you're going to help me do it."

Another scribble from the director.

The word is straight and to the point.

No.

CHAPTER 84

LIAM LOOKS AT the single word.

No.

As if.

"Why should I do that?" Liam asks, as the CIA director glares at him.

"Because he's gettable at the moment. In a couple of days, he'll be unreachable."

"Tell me more," Liam says.

The director's face reddens. The pad goes back to her and then back to Liam.

NO!

Chin says, "He's your teammate. I hope that gives you incentive enough to come here and help me rescue him."

"Hope is not a strategy," Liam says. "I can't go on a one-man crusade to rescue him, as much as I admire him for his service and expertise. You have him, and your government will eventually work out a deal with my government to free him. Don't bring me into this."

Lin says, "Are you not listening to me? That's not an option. He needs to be rescued. And by you only. I can't have one of your Special Activities Division teams roaring in with their black gear and weapons. It has to be done quietly. With only you."

Noa is looking at him, Bruce's face is blank, and the director looks at him with the expectation that he will follow her orders to a T.

"I admire what you're doing," he says. "But it can't be done. I can't pop overseas like this. Especially if this is a trap and you're trying to capture me."

A slight laugh. "You're a field operative, Liam. Not a director. Don't puff yourself up like that."

A pause.

Liam still feels like he's onstage, making it up as he goes along.

"All right," Lin says. "I'll sweeten the offer."

"I'm listening."

Lin says, "You come to South Africa, help me free Benjamin, and I'll tell you how your vice president fell into a coma, and how to safely and quickly revive her."

Another scribble on the legal pad from the director, but Liam doesn't have to look at her note.

"Lin, you've got yourself a deal," he says.

CHAPTER 85

DIRECTOR HANNAH ABRAMS feels like she's on a treadmill that keeps speeding up, and she can't get off. All she can do is keep upright and make it work, no matter how much the speed dangerously increases.

Listening in, she hears the Chinese intelligence operative say, "Very well. Contact me at this number"—and she recites a series of numerals—"once you're in-country. We'll meet and go over how we're going to get Benjamin Lucas out. Once the three of us are in a safe place, that's when I'll tell you about the vice president."

Abrams captures Liam's eye, writes a quick question on the pad, and pushes it over.

"Did you and your agency do it?"

Lin says, "No. But we know how it was done, where it was done, and how to make her well. I've been on this call too long. Call me when you're in South Africa."

Click.

The call is disconnected.

Hannah replaces the phone receiver, as does Liam.

Noa says, "I just caught part of the conversation, but is Liam going to South Africa?"

Hannah says, "It appears so. Not to sound cold and callous but rescuing one operative is too dangerous. But if we can help the vice president, well, it'll be worth it. Especially if she's well and in place in the days and weeks ahead."

"Ma'am," Noa says. "You've said time is of the essence. Even if Liam was to leave right now, it's at least a twenty- or twenty-one-hour flight to Johannesburg. That's nearly a day, ma'am."

"If he flies commercial, you're right," she says, reaching for a different phone that has a secure line for sensitive communications. "But he won't be flying commercial."

Hannah picks up the receiver from her secure phone bank, strikes a button that rings a prerecorded phone number.

It's picked up after just one ring.

"Two-eight-three-one."

"I need to speak to General Pease."

"He's unavailable," the male voice says. "He's on the flight line."

"This is CIA Director Hannah Abrams," she says. "Make him available. Now."

"Hold one, ma'am."

The phone line goes quiet.

It's also quiet in her office.

Liam and Noa look at her. Bruce is doing his job, which is looking around the room, at the open doorway, and the two windows looking out to the rear yard.

A faint *click* and a male voice says, "Pease here."

"Harlan, this is Hannah Abrams."

"Good morning, Director. To what do I owe this pleasure?"

"How goes the A-22 project?"

No answer.

"Harlan, this is a secure line. Don't worry."

The general says, "We're a bit behind, but nothing we can't make up later on."

"When's the next test flight scheduled?"

"In two days," he says. "Director, what's this all about?"

"Don't hate me because I'm asking, because I'm asking," Hannah says. "I need you to bump up that test flight to today, preferably in a few hours."

"Director..."

"And to make it worse, I need to have an observer on board, and your destination is whatever facility we might be able to use in South Africa, as close as possible to Johannesburg."

She senses the general isn't talking right now because he's building up to an explosion of anger and arguments. She quickly says, "Harlan, you and your team have done incredible work with minimal funding and technical support, and this isn't a request. I hope I don't have to go into the details of how the Agency owns two-thirds of your black budget for this project, and if I decide to cancel our share before Congress finds out and gets pissed at being kept in the dark, well, what can you do with one-third of an aircraft?"

His voice sounds like he's being strangled by someone. "It won't be much of a flight test."

"If you can get my man in South Africa soonest, then I'll consider it a successful test, Harlan," she says. "His name is Liam Grey and he works directly for me."

The air is dead on the other side. She feels sorry for the general, who has done a lot with minimal budgeting and not enough staff. He says, "All right. Tell him where to go."

"I won't forget this, Harlan," she says. "In the meantime, I'm going through the Agency's budget next week, and I'm going to try to squeeze out another ten million dollars in additional funding for the A-22. How does that sound?"

"Director," he says, "that sounds great," but Hannah still feels like she's defeated an honorable man, and it wasn't a fair fight, since the Agency does own two-thirds of this highly classified, black aircraft.

She's about to say thank you once more, when she hears him hanging up on his end.

Fine.

Hannah replaces the handset and says, "It's done. I'll give you directions to the base, Liam, and we'll arrange transport."

Liam says, "Do I have time to pack? Arrange some gear?"

The director shakes her head. "Only what we can scrounge from my closets. You see, Liam, if you haul ass from here in the next few minutes, you'll be in South Africa in just over two hours."

CHAPTER 86

THIS MORNING MICHAEL Balantic is tracking Liam Grey, the rogue CIA operative, and the search isn't going well. His vehicle of choice today is a burgundy Mercedes-Benz SL with Maryland license plates, and he's temporarily parked in a lot next to the Coppa Enoteca restaurant on Prospect Street NW in the District of Columbia.

It's busy, with lots of foot traffic, and he only has five minutes or so before he has to move his surveillance to another tracking location, back to Liam's condo. After that, to a Starbucks barista he dated six months ago.

Not that Liam is in this restaurant or any other restaurant within walking distance, but from the comfort of this Mercedes, Michael is keeping watch on the Georgetown home of CIA Director Hannah Abrams. On the dashboard of his luxury vehicle is a video display that looks like it's showing a

GPS-sourced map of the District of Columbia to anyone passing by and peeking in.

But the eyeglasses he's wearing have special lenses, so Michael sees something entirely different: a drone-eyed view of the CIA director's home on O Street NW in Georgetown, a two-story brick house with black shutters, gated driveway, and a two-car garage with a breezeway connecting it to the house.

The feed from the drone is holding steady. It's one of the latest black budget drones from General Atomics designed to look like a sparrow. At the moment it's resting on the branch of a maple tree across the street from the director's home. There's not too many bells and whistles packed into the tiny package, but the thermal imaging tells him there are five people inside.

What are they saying?

He can't tell.

The drone is passive, meaning it's designed to observe and record. Anything more intrusive could be detected by whatever surveillance systems are hidden in the CIA director's house. He also knows that some high-tech detection devices could sense the sparrow drone if it got any closer to the residence.

He waits.

Shadows move across the bay window at the front yard.

Using a control system in his lap, he lifts the drone and brings it closer.

Through the window, he sees Director Abrams.

She passes by.

A male comes into view, putting on a brown farmer's coat and a Baltimore Orioles cap.

It's Liam Grey.

Michael starts up the Mercedes and gets back into traffic.

He drives as fast as he can without breaking any traffic laws, keeping one eye on the display screen set into the dashboard. Liam moves away from the window. The drone pulls back some.

A shadow passes through the breezeway leading to the garage.

Move, move, he thinks, cursing a Range Rover dawdling in front of him.

The door to the garage swings up.

A black Audi Q7 SUV pulls out, one person in the driver's seat.

Wearing an Orioles cap.

He types in a command to the drone, which will lock on to the Audi.

The Range Rover finally turns and gets out of the way.

He picks up a burner phone, punches in a programmed number.

"Pope," comes the voice.

"I've got Grey," he says. "He's moving. Looks like

he's taking the Francis Scott Key Bridge, heading into Virginia."

Pope says, "Good. First chance you get, end it."

"On it," Michael says, disconnecting the call.

Within twenty minutes he catches up with the Audi, heading north on the George Washington Memorial Parkway. He keeps at least two other vehicles between him and the Audi. A few times he drops back, letting the sparrow drone keep the tail going, just in case Liam is being paranoid, which would be the smart move on his part.

He has no idea where Liam Grey is heading and doesn't really care.

All he needs are the few seconds to finish the job.

The Audi starts slowing down, moving to the right-hand lane.

Michael smiles.

Those seconds he needs seem to be coming right into his lap.

The Audi turns into a combination convenience store and service station, the Langley Mart, and pulls up to a set of pumps.

Talk about luck, he thinks, pulling out his 9mm Beretta pistol. Just like the job against that Army officer, this one was going to be quick and to the point.

The Audi stops.

The driver's-side door opens.

Liam steps out.

No time for fancy maneuvers, just get the job done.

Michael turns and stops the Mercedes at an adjacent series of pumps, gets out, leaves the door open, and quickly takes three steps before opening fire, the man crumpling and falling, the gas hose and pump handle dropping to the ground.

Two more steps, put a kill shot in the skull, and the job is done.

CHAPTER 87

SWEATING AND HOT underneath a black wool blanket in the rear seat of the Audi, Liam hears gunfire break out and tosses the blanket aside. Grabbing his pistol, Liam throws open the rear passenger door opposite the gunman, giving himself cover.

He hits the pavement, rolls and comes up, sees a man in a leather jacket and jeans approaching the Audi, pistol in both hands. Liam doesn't hesitate, puts two rounds into his chest.

The man drops and hunches down. Liam goes around the rear of the Audi, spots the gunman writhing on the ground, pistol still in hand, and shoots once more.

Bruce, the director's security officer, is sitting up against the near gas pump, hand over his left arm, breathing hard, blood soaking through his fingers. The Baltimore Orioles cap is on the cement next to him.

"Shit," he says.

"How bad?" Liam asks.

"Took two rounds in the back," he says. "Vest saved me, but I've got cracked ribs for sure. Third round went through my arm. Burning and hurting like a son of a bitch. The shooter?"

"He's dead."

"You sure?"

Liam says, "He was wearing a vest, too. But my last shot went into his left eye."

Bruce grimaces and says, "There's a first-aid kit in the rear of the Audi. Get it."

Liam moves quickly, retrieves the hard plastic white case with the red cross symbol on it, and, going back to Bruce, opens it. The security officer shakes his head. "I'll bandage myself. We need to trade weapons. What are you carrying?"

"Glock, ten millimeter."

"Good," Bruce says. "Same here. I can't reach it. It's under my right arm. Take it, leave yours, and get the hell out of here. Any later forensics will show the pistol in my possession was the one that did the shooting."

"Bruce, let me work on you first."

"Shit, there's no time. Get out of here before the EMTs and cops show up."

Liam slowly stands up. "What are you going to tell them?"

"Self-defense, what else? Move, Liam, move."

He gets into the Audi, starts the engine, roars out of the store parking lot, gets back on the highway, and speeds away.

Time.

Bruce is right, as much as Liam hates to admit it. Leaving a wounded comrade in the field is a huge violation of what passes for a warrior's code, but Liam has no choice. If all goes well, the EMTs will get there in time and get him stable, and then to a hospital.

As to what Bruce is going to say to the cops, at the moment it isn't Liam's problem.

Getting to his meeting place is.

He speeds up the Audi.

Nearly an hour later, bumping down a potholed and cracked single-lane country road, Liam comes to a waypoint: a rusting metal gate, spanning a dirt and gravel road.

He parks the car, gets out, and goes to the gate. It's fastened to a rusty, wide metal pipe stuck into the ground, and a Yale combination lock holds a thick chain around the post.

He dials the combination—15, 1, 15—and the lock snaps free. He opens the gate, keeping a sharp eye on the surroundings, drives the Audi in several yards, stops, and closes and locks the gate behind him.

The dirt road is rough and bumpy, and he's thinking about what might be waiting for him up ahead. Something highly classified, black budget, and deeply guarded.

The trees and brush thin out. He sees buildings coming into view. He gets his ID ready from his wallet, curious as to how deep the security is going to be in this rural part of Virginia.

The dirt road comes to an end against an open access road.

He's expecting triple-fencing with razor-wire curling on top, armed guards and warning signs saying photography and trespassing are forbidden, and that use of deadly force is authorized.

But the way ahead of him is empty.

There's a long runway.

Three hangars clustered at one end of the runway, and a larger one, set off at a distance from the others.

Not even a control tower.

Five civilian planes—Cessnas, Beechcrafts, Pipers—are parked on grass aprons, their wings tied down to the ground. Two gas pumps sit on a concrete island about twenty feet away.

Liam turns right, drives down the narrow road running parallel to the runway, and a small building comes into view, looking like a small one-story Cape Cod cottage with black shingled roof and a door at the center.

A Harley-Davidson motorcycle is parked on the grass.

He parks the Audi next to the motorcycle, gets out, and walks into the small building. There's a metal desk, two mismatched chairs, another motorcycle in pieces on a tarp on the cement floor, and a tall woman in jeans and a black tank top working a wrench. She has purple hair and both arms are heavily inked with tattoos.

She looks at Liam. "If you're looking for storage for your private aircraft, sorry, we're full."

She stands, wipes her hands on a white greasy rag.

Liam says, "I'm supposed to meet someone here, at nine." He looks at the round clock with black hands next to a tool calendar from Dewalt. It's 8:55 a.m.

She smiles. "Well, best as I know, I'm the only one here. A couple of folks park their Lear jets in the other hangars, and I'm here just to make sure nobody steals the joint. Sorry."

Liam says, "Not a problem."

He steps outside in the bright morning sunlight.

Now what?

He checks his watch.

One minute to nine.

What to do when time runs out?

He hears a whisper of a sound and looks off to the south.

A jet is approaching.

A big jet.

One of the biggest in the world, a four-engine

C-17 Globemaster III transport, made by Boeing, and—

The damn thing is landing here!

The landing gear lowers and Liam takes another good, hard look at the place.

The runway is less than a mile long from what he can tell, which is plenty of room for the C-17. It lands gracefully, the engines throttling back, and it slows down and then maneuvers its way to the large hangar sitting apart from the others.

Liam goes to the Audi, takes out a black duffel bag, starts running to the Globemaster. All Air Force aircraft have serial numbers and squadron lettering on them, but not this one. The only identification mark is a small, dark Air Force roundel on the fuselage.

The aircraft lurches to a halt. A wide door slides up at the hangar and a set of stairways is pushed out by two men wearing plain, dark-green jumpsuits. It gets to the forward door of the aircraft, which swings open. Within seconds a line of men and women come off the aircraft, while others emerge from the warehouse and go in.

He gets to the stairway.

A woman with her blond hair tied up in a bun and a sun-worn face looks him up and down. She's wearing a standard green zippered Air Force jumpsuit, with no insignia, rank, or name tag.

"You Grey?"

"I am," he says.

"Then get in," she says.

"But..."

"But what?"

He thinks, *I'm supposed to be in South Africa in less than two hours. This can't be right.*

"Thanks," Liam says, and climbs up the several steps and into the dark interior of the aircraft.

CHAPTER 88

NOA HIMEL IS waiting in the living room of Director Abrams's home when the director comes out of her office, face drawn, accompanied by her security officer Ralph and says, "Liam's made it. Bruce, I'm not so sure."

"What happened?" Noa asks.

Hannah says, "There was a shooting at a service station off the George Washington. Liam escaped, but Bruce got shot in the arm. Lost a lot of blood before the EMTs arrived on scene. He's en route now to a hospital in Tysons Corner."

Ralph looks like he's carved from some mobile type of granite, but Noa sees his dark-blue eyes and looks away. Death is in those eyes, and she quickly feels a bit of sympathy for whoever shot his fellow officer Bruce. *Ralph is coming for you,* she thinks, *whoever you are, and whoever ordered you to do this.*

Noa says, "I'm ready, Director, if you think it's a good time to head out."

Hannah sits down on the near couch. "Nothing right now is a good time, but we'll have to make do. Ralph, when you get a moment, make a call. I want increased protection for me, Deputy Director Jean Swantish, and this house."

"Yes, ma'am."

"Also get a firearm for Miss Himel here."

"Thank you," Noa says.

A tired smile from the director. "Better to have it and not need it, than the reverse, correct?"

Noa says, "I'm going to need transportation to get to Kay Darcy."

A shake of the director's head. "With my personal Audi gone, I'll have Ralph drive you out in my Agency Suburban. But you be careful out there, Noa. You milk Kay as much as you can and you promise her the world and the universe. We need to know what she knows about President Barrett. But make it quick. There's already been one death and today, an attempted murder. Forces are in play."

"Where are you going, Director?"

"To Langley, where else? I've got to be there, showing the flag, working like I don't have a care in the world. Otherwise, Barrett's allies in the Agency will tell him something is amiss. I can't have that."

"Ma'am, you being in the office is going to be dangerous."

Hannah gets off the couch. "We're all in danger today, aren't we? You be careful at your meet with Kay and get back here as soon as you can. I'll leave instructions for the additional security officers that will be showing up here to let you in."

Noa stands up as well. "Director, I need to tell you something. About the president's threat to rape me or kill me."

Hannah says, "Is it important?"

"Very important," Noa says, feeling embarrassed again at the incident, but also strengthened as to what she's about to say to the director.

Hannah sits back down on the couch. "Then tell me."

CHAPTER 89

ONCE LIAM IS inside the interior of the large transport aircraft, the door shuts behind him, and the engines start whining into power. Next to him are the short set of stairs leading up to the cockpit, and to the aft—

He's puzzled.

Where did all the personnel go?

There's a forward metal bulkhead with a center door here that doesn't belong, that Liam hasn't seen on previous trips he's taken on other C-17s. There's a narrow row of seats in front of the bulkhead, and the woman who escorted him in is sitting down, buckling in.

"Have a seat, Mr. Grey," she says, voice loud over the engines.

He puts his bag at his feet, sits down, buckles up, and looks around. Typical C-17 interior with cables, access panels and lights, except for the bulkhead behind him.

"You can call me Liam," he says, matching her voice's volume. "What's your name?"

A slight smile and the briefest hesitation, telling Liam that she's about to lie to him.

"You can call me Betty," she says. "Welcome aboard."

"Thanks," he says, surging back in the seat as the C-17 starts rumbling down the runway.

About fifteen minutes later a small red lamp forward turns green, and Betty unbuckles and gets up. "We're at altitude. Grab your gear and follow me, and for God's sake, don't touch anything."

"I won't," he says, and she opens the door to the bulkhead and he follows in, stopping in awe at what he's now seeing.

The huge storage area of the C-17—eighty-five feet in length and eighteen feet in width—is jammed with personnel at monitoring stations, large cylindrical tanks with hoses running out of their bases, and other workstations and—

In the center, taking up most of the free space, is a small aircraft, the oddest he's ever seen.

It's flat and shiny black, with two stubby fins at the rear tail assembly, and a narrow fuselage that ends in a needle point, with thin wings nearly touching each side of the C-17's fuselage. At the stern of the aircraft is a series of eight rocket nozzles, all in a row. Hoses from the shiny metal tanks are being hooked up to the underbelly of the aircraft by workers in hazmat suits. What looks to be part of a cockpit is resting on the deck.

Betty says, "I'll find a place for your bag. Go forward and get prepped, and again, don't touch a damn thing. The leading edges of the wings can cut your fingers off."

He recalls what he heard back in Director Abrams's office. "Is this the A-22?"

Betty says, "Aren't you the informed one. Just a test bed for now."

Liam walks with her to the front of the aircraft. "Hypersonic, correct?"

"From Point A to Point B anywhere on the globe in two hours or less, or your next delivery is free," she says. "You need to use the latrine?"

"No."

"Good."

Up forward is man dressed in an orange pressure suit, not unlike an astronaut's space suit. Two women in plain Air Force flight suits are checking readouts from the suit—one holding a clear helmet in her hands—and the suited man with close-cropped black hair sees Liam and frowns.

Liam doesn't blame him.

"Okay," Betty says, as two other technicians come forward, carrying a similar suit. "Strip."

Some minutes later he's helped into the rear of

the tiny cockpit. Hoses and communication cables are hooked up, and then a helmet is lowered over his head and fastened on a rigid collar. Liam feels the suit pressurize around him and his mouth is dry, and he's feeling so out of place that part of him wishes he was still back in the Army, facing the Taliban at night. At least you knew what you're doing, who and what you were up against. Straps are lowered over his shoulders and tightened.

The pilot is sitting in front of him, with a large instrumentation panel separating the two of them. The cockpit cover is lowered by four Air Force technicians and Liam hears the pilot up forward press a set of switches, shackling it in place.

His earphones crackle in his ear. "Mr. Grey?"

"Yes," he says.

"I'm Jeff, your pilot," he says. "You secure back there?"

"I am," he says.

"Good," he says. "Just one thing."

"Don't touch anything," Liam says.

A soft chuckle. "You're learning. Drop-off and launch is in five minutes."

The dark interior lightens with red light. Just above and forward is a windshield, but it's less than a foot in height and maybe a yard in width.

Liam says, "One hell of a setup you folks have here."

Jeff says, "Thanks. Wish I could say I thought of it

but no, others figured out that CONUS was getting too crowded for classified flight tests, even in the most remote desert areas. Too many people with cameras and phones. So we hide in plain sight, and when it comes to doing tests, we just fly off to an empty part of the Atlantic and let loose."

"Makes sense," Liam says, realizing the tightness in his chest isn't coming from the tight straps, but from his racing heart.

"Yeah," Jeff says. "Now, if you'll excuse me, I'm about to get real busy. Don't talk to me unless it's an emergency, and trust me, you won't recognize an emergency until it's too late."

"Roger that," Liam says.

He blinks his eyes, trying to move his head, but there's not much room in the helmet. He looks to the instrumentation panel and sees the various dials and screens have been covered. Whatever classified clearance level Liam has is worthless here.

The quality of the light changes, and Liam thinks the rear cargo hatch of the C-17 is opening. He's going to ask Jeff that and he remembers his orders.

Okay, he thinks.

We wait.

Shuddering gets his attention, and various squeals and whines, and—

A heavy lurch, a sense of falling free.

He can't see much but he's sure the A-22 is now free of the C-17.

In the helmet's earphones Jeff says, "Get ready for a kick in the pants."

Liam keeps his mouth shut and there's a heavy, deafening roar, and then he's on his back, as the classified hypersonic jet leaps into the air. G-forces crush his chest, legs, and arms, and he looks up through the helmet visor and tiny aircraft windshield.

Liam thinks he sees stars up there before he passes out.

CHAPTER 90

CIA DIRECTOR HANNAH Abrams is sitting in one of the conference rooms on the seventh floor of CIA headquarters. Across from her is a man that she thinks was approaching his teens before he could reliably tie his shoes by himself.

But she keeps that opinion to herself—not even sharing it with her deputy, Jean Swantish—because this man is Terrence Grant, the director of national intelligence, retired admiral from the US Navy, and nominally her boss.

After 9/11 and the intense failure that was the search for Iraqi weapons of mass destruction, legislature was passed years back for one intelligence position that would oversee all of the alphabet intelligent agencies, from the National Security Agency to the Defense Intelligence Agency.

Terrence is a tall, slim man with brown-rimmed glasses, black hair, and a look and presence that he doesn't feel quite comfortable either in his skin or his pricey gray pinstripe suit.

He says, "Hannah, with all due respect, I need more than just a fifteen-minute session here with you. We need to have a meeting of deputies and principals, clear up lines of communication and responsibility, and get the intelligence community moving forward as one."

Terrence waits and looks around the empty conference room table. In a traditional meeting, there would be a coffee and tea service, with some sort of late-morning snacks, but Hannah isn't feeling traditional.

"Sorry, Terrence, but I'm doing a lot of catch-up," she says, smiling sweetly, remembering her meeting with the Senate majority leader at the Button Gwinnett Room, where he said the president was delaying Hannah's confirmation due to Terrence's objections.

She adds, "I'm sure you know exactly what I'm facing."

Terrence says, "Not entirely. Which is why I think this meeting is imperative."

No, it's not, Hannah thinks. Keeping the president in his lane and ensuring he doesn't stumble this country into war is her imperative. And she's wasted fifteen minutes that should have been spent dealing with that problem, instead of this worthless meet and greet.

But appearances must be kept.

"Sometime soon, Terrence, I promise," she says. "We'll get the biggest conference room here at the campus, and you can bring in as many principals and deputies you'd like, and we'll get the job done."

"Why not later in the week?"

"Like I said, I'm quite busy, my confirmation having been delayed so long."

Plus, Hannah thinks, after spending this time with the DNI, the Four Ds—the directors of Operations, Intelligence, Administration, and Science and Technology—will be pushing her hard for a meeting.

Just not enough time!

"I hear you've set up a bed in your office," he says. "As well as your deputy."

Hannah says, "You hear right. I guess some of my folks here are sending you back-channel information. You must be thrilled. Our relatives' plates are overflowing, and we're trying to play catch-up by staying here, twenty-four/seven."

He purses his thin lips, shakes his head. "I can cause a lot of trouble for you and the Agency, Hannah, if you don't cooperate."

"I'm sure," she says, checking her watch. He has one more minute left and enough is enough. "But now we've run out of time."

His face flushes and he says, "What makes you think you're so special?"

"Excuse me?" she replies, nearly laughing at his question. "I'm here, aren't I?"

A soft knock on the door, and one of her security officers, Gary, walks in and says, "Sorry, ma'am, but Deputy Director Swantish says she needs to see you right away."

"Thanks, Gary," she says, and stands up. "Thanks for coming over, Terrence. And I will make it up for you at a later date. If you're still talking to me then."

She takes a few steps and then turns. "You're ex-Navy, Terrence. I'm sure you remember Admiral King, the CNO during World War II."

"Absolutely."

"Well, remember this," she says. "After one of his unexpected promotions, he supposedly said, 'When they get in trouble they send for the sons of bitches.'"

Hand on the conference room's doorknob, Hannah says, "Well, we're in trouble, and they've sent for the bitch."

CHAPTER 91

LIAM GREY FEELS out of time, out of place, standing on a flat stretch of scrubland in South Africa, back in his civilian clothes, sweaty and tired and still stunned at what the past two hours have been like, flying so high and so dark. There's an empty runway and a distressed-looking hangar that is holding the A-22 hypersonic jet that brought him here, and not much else.

The wind is blowing hard and all around this empty land is lots of sand and low brush, and a dirt road leading away to the south. Mountains are on the distant horizon. At this end of the dirt road is a dusty, black, two-door Volkswagen Polo sedan with Northern Cape province license plates.

A side door to the hangar opens and the pilot, Jeff, comes out, holding a plastic shopping bag, which he passes over to Liam. He's wearing blue jeans, black polo shirt, and an LA Dodgers jacket. His close-cropped hair is still matted down with sweat.

"Some water and energy bars," he says. "Best I can do."

"Thanks," Liam says. "I appreciate it. And thanks for the fantastic flight. What do you do now?"

"Me? Sit my ass down, maybe take a nap, read a book. The C-17 we launched from won't be here until sometime late tonight. Then we load up and fly back home."

Liam says, "Where are we?"

"Closest thing to the 'middle of nowhere' you'll ever experience, Mr. Grey," Jeff says. "Namibia is over there, and Botswana is over there, and there's not much in between. Anything else?"

With a bit of humor, Liam says, "You never showed me the ejection handle."

Jeff says, "That's because there isn't one. That's why it's called a test flight. And like I said before we launched, by the time you figure out there's an emergency, it's too late."

"Oh," Liam says.

Jeff turns to go back into the warehouse. "But what difference does it make? This place doesn't exist, this aircraft doesn't exist, and neither do I." He pauses. "Pity, because you've joined a very exclusive club."

"Unauthorized civilians hitching a ride on a nonexistent aircraft?"

"Nope," Jeff says, opening the side door. "We flew fifty miles above the earth's surface. Congratulations, Mr. Grey, you're officially an astronaut. But no one will ever know."

CHAPTER 92

LIAM FINDS THE key to the Polo on top of the left front tire, and it takes three tries for the engine to start.

"Some astronaut," he murmurs, sitting in the right seat, thankful the little car is an automatic, so he won't have to worry about shifting on the "wrong" side of the car. On the passenger's seat is a worn map of this part of South Africa, with a tiny red dot he hopes marks his location. A faded dotted line for what looks to be a dirt lane goes on for—crap, fifty miles?—before it connects with a paved road.

He shifts in his seat and slowly starts driving away from the hangar, the dirt road barely visible, and it doesn't take long for the hangar to disappear in the rearview mirror.

Once he finds a paved road and eases out, he forgets for a moment that here, driving is on the left side of the road. A roaring dual-cargo tractor-trailer truck nearly collides with him, honking its horn, and he flips the steering wheel so he's in the left lane.

Hell of a way to end this mission, he thinks.

Eventually he sees a sign telling him that he's on the N14, and the drive quickly becomes monotonous and monochrome, the only color being buses and cars that scream by, passing him, or others heading in the opposite direction.

Following the map, he's heading east and eventually to Johannesburg. He pulls the car over and takes a quick pee break, and then on his Company-issued phone, taken from Director Abrams's home—a cautious woman, to have such supplies in her house—dials the number provided to him less than three hours ago. There's low brush and trees not much taller than him, and an incredibly deep blue sky.

It rings twice and is picked up by a woman speaking Chinese.

Liam says, "I'm sorry, is this Chin Lin?"

The woman switches to English. "Yes, this is Chin Lin. Who is this, please?"

Another double-trailer truck flies by, spitting gravel and sand into his face. "Liam Grey."

Her voice sharp, she says, "I told you not to call me until you were in South Africa."

"That's where I am," he says. "A desolate spot, but that's where I am. On the N14. About forty kilometers from a place called Kakamas."

"Impossible. I only spoke to you about three hours ago."

"Yet here I am."

"How did you get there so fast, Liam Grey?"

"I clicked my heels three times and said *There's no place like deserted South Africa*," he says. "I'm here, I've called you. What now?"

"Hold on," she says.

Liam looks around some more. His first time in South Africa, and there's a desolate beauty here, if one has the time to appreciate it.

Which he doesn't.

Lin says, "Stay on the N14. About four hours from now you'll enter a town called Olifantshoek. Look for a large truck stop called Engen Fuel A Lot. I'll see you there."

"Alone, I hope."

She laughs. "Of course. Don't you trust me?"

"No," Liam says, disconnecting the call.

Four hours later, as promised, Liam spots the signs for the Engen Fuel A Lot Convenience Center and pulls in and parks. He's tired, worn, and, above all, he needs to refuel the Polo before he goes any farther.

But he steps out instead and goes into the one-story building divided into a little store and a Steers fast-food restaurant. He goes into the cool interior and smells fried food and grease, and sees a Chinese woman sitting alone in a rear booth.

Other booths are filled with truckers and one Black family—Mom, Dad, two girls—apparently on some sort of family trip.

Liam goes up to her. "Sorry to be so blatantly racist, but are you Chin Lin?"

"I am," she says. "Please join me."

Liam sits down and she pushes over a cardboard drink carton with a straw poking out. "A cold Coke," she says. "Hope you like it. I've already had two servings of fries so I could keep my place."

He takes the Coke, then pushes it back. Did she really think he was going to accept a drink from her?

"First things first, you know where Benjamin Lucas is located?" he asks.

"I do," she says, her long black hair tied in back with a simple ponytail. She's wearing a red turtleneck and short leather jacket.

A very attractive woman indeed, Liam thinks. *No wonder Benjamin fell for her back in college.* He swivels in his seat so he can keep an eye on people entering and leaving the restaurant. His 10mm Glock—originally belonging to the director's bodyguard Bruce—is at his waist. He wonders how Bruce is doing. Liam's also glad he's armed, because there won't be a second CIA officer captured by the Chinese this week in South Africa, not if he can help it.

"And you also know how to treat the vice president's coma?"

A nod.

"And you've got a plan to free Benjamin?"

"I do," she says. "An old friend named Bo-Bo is going to help."

Liam turns so he's looking at her. "Who the hell is Bo-Bo?"

A delicate but chilly smile. "Did you know the Romans knew of the Chinese empire, even back then, nearly two thousand years ago? Yet even though we are centuries old, the West never wanted to understand us, or more importantly, respect us."

Liam stays quiet. It's like the Chinese intelligence agent across from him is retelling an old story.

She says, "In the nineteenth century an English writer named Charles Lamb explained the origins of barbecued pig. It seemed hundreds of years earlier, a dull farm boy in China named Bo-Bo burned down his father's house, along with their herd of pigs. While clearing it out, Bo-Bo discovered how delicious roasted pig tasted. His father agreed, and that's how barbecued pig came to be. But the ignorant Chinese thought the only way they could correctly cook a pig was to burn their houses down. It supposedly took years before they realized house burning was a waste. Hah-hah-hah."

Liam says, "Point taken. Admiration and respect. You got it from me. Now, how are we getting Liam out?"

Chin smiles. "We're going to have a barbecue tonight, featuring you."

CHAPTER 93

HANNAH ABRAMS WALKS into her office and Jean Swantish joins her from the door leading in from her own office, Jean's clothes wrinkled and slightly stained from late-night and early-morning meals, and her hair is a mess.

But Jean's eyes are bright and smart, and she sits down in front of her just as Hannah sits down as well. There's a turkey club sandwich on Hannah's desk and Hannah takes a healthy bite.

Jean says, "Before I start, Director, do we know the status of Noa Himel and Liam Grey?"

The sandwich suddenly tastes like it's made of compressed sawdust. Hannah swallows one more piece, then drops it on the plate.

"Noa is on her way to see the *Post* reporter, Kay Darcy," Hannah says. "I'm hoping she has helpful information that she'll be willing to trade. Liam is probably on the ground now in South Africa, looking to meet up with the Chinese intelligence agent. And it also looks like Bruce is going to recover."

"It's going to be a hell of a thing, keeping that shooting quiet."

"It's what we do," Hannah says. "What do you have?"

"Got him," she says, her smile wider.

"Who?"

"Benjamin Lucas."

"You mean, we got him out of Chinese custody?"

"No, no, I'm sorry," she says. "I got his record, but the further afield we went from the official paperwork, there were some questions we got answered."

Good for us, Hannah thinks, as she takes a sip from her now cold coffee. *But couldn't it have waited?*

"Lucas grew up in San Francisco, graduated from Stanford, and then got his master's degree in Asian Studies at Boston University, where an asset of ours recruited him. Went through training without difficulty, went to various specialty schools and did some fieldwork with Army and Navy units. He was in the Directorate of Operations before he was recruited into President Barrett's arms. But one thing bothered me."

"Go," Hannah says.

"His accomplishments and advancements all came off without a hitch, a setback. He got everything he asked for, every school, every transfer."

"Somebody here was clearing a path for him."

Jean nods, eyes still bright. "That was the most recent question. Who was that wizard clearing things for him? Then I had a couple of my people really dig into his upbringing, and I mean, dig."

Hannah recalls what she knows about Benjamin's upbringing.

"An orphan, wasn't he?"

Quick nod. "That's right. Two months old, given up for adoption to Catholic Charities of California, and later adopted by the Lucas family of Los Gatos. The records were sealed, of course, but...through various means, we've gotten access."

"Jean, please tell me nothing illegal happened."

"Director, at this moment in time, nothing illegal happened."

"Jesus...go on."

"His birth mother was Roberta Tyler. She was a civilian contract worker for the Department of Defense. Father listed as unknown, but my folks went further, even did some out-of-the-box thinking involving DNA analysis...Director, you will not believe who Benjamin Lucas's father is."

"Tell me," Hannah says.

CHAPTER 94

THE MEETING NOA Himel is having with Kay Darcy, *Washington Post* reporter and ex-wife of Liam Grey, is not going well. It took one long and cryptic phone call before Kay grudgingly gave up her address, and now Noa is sitting in her tiny kitchen, cluttered with unwashed dishes in the sink, piles of newspapers on the floor, and an overflowing trash can. Noa pushed to have this meeting somewhere else, someplace public, but Kay would have nothing to do with that.

"You think it'll do me any good to be seen in public with a CIA officer?" she said. "Bad enough I was married to one. Forget it."

So here Noa is, in Kay's apartment. No water, no juice, no coffee or tea offered.

Kay says, "This is a first, having a CIA officer reach out to me that I've not been married to. I better mark this day on my calendar. Why me, then?"

"I've been working with Liam," Noa says. "He's told me what he revealed to you, about President Barrett's illegal actions. I'm here to confirm that and pass along additional information about the program."

Kay crosses her arms. It's her day off and she's wearing black sweatpants and a gray Washington Nationals sweatshirt, sleeves pulled up on her arms.

"Out of the goodness of your CIA heart?"

"No," Noa says. "For a quid pro quo. We supply you with information, on background with no names attached, and you let us know what you've learned. And you also agree not to publish until we say it's safe to do so."

Kay shakes her head. "Why isn't Liam here, making this offer?"

"He's otherwise engaged," Noa says, feeling like she's starting a delicate dance with this woman, trying to gently get her to see what must be seen.

"Really?" Kay says. "You dating him?"

"No," she says. "Not my type."

Kay leans back in her kitchen chair. "This sounds too weird to be true. Maybe a setup."

"What kind of setup? To get you in legal trouble? Or embarrass you and the *Post*?"

"It's a thought," Kay says.

"It's neither," Noa says. "I've been sent here as a representative of CIA Director Hannah Abrams. I have the authority to reveal highly classified information to you."

"In exchange for what, again?"

"That you tell us what you know, and that you will cooperate in the timing of the story's release."

Kay says. "Not convinced. Tell me what you've got, and I'll consider it."

Noa says, "I need better than that. Sorry. This story is going to be worth it. I can promise you that. What Liam told you was true. I can tell you much more, with the blessing of the director."

The kitchen is quiet, smells of old coffee and microwaved popcorn. The apartment block is in the Westchester section of the district.

Kay says, "Okay. It's a deal. Truth is, I've been running in circles on this damn story. It would be nice to have some facts to play with."

Noa nods. "All right," she says. "The facts are, Liam and I have been in charge of CIA teams, appointed by the president, to operate illegally here in the States and abroad, without congressional notification, to capture and kill those deemed enemies of the United States."

Kay slowly reaches over to a pile of papers on the kitchen table, pulls out a notebook and pen.

"Can I have more details than that?"

"You can," Noa says. "But now I need something from you."

"I'll try," Kay says.

"Do better than that," she says. "We know you've been receiving information from Donna Otterson, a finance resource officer with the Agency. We want to know what she was passing on to you."

Kay smirks. "Why not ask her yourself?"

"I can't."

"Why? She lawyer up?"

"No," Noa says. "Because she's dead."

CHAPTER 95

NOA SENSES A chink in Kay's hard journalist armor, and says, "It's up to you now, Kay. With Donna's death, whatever she was passing on to you only rests with you."

Her voice is quiet. "And you want me to tell you."

"Yes," Noa says, "and we'll pass on more information to you, so that generations from now, when people think of the *Washington Post,* they won't recall Woodward and Bernstein. They'll think of Kay Darcy."

Kay picks up her pen, then lowers it. "How did Donna die?"

"Suicide."

"How?"

"Cyanide, hidden in a toothpaste tube. My team and I were there, taking her into custody, when she killed herself."

Noa is surprised to see tears come to Kay's eyes. "Donna loved the Agency, loved her father, too," the reporter eventually says. "That's why she joined. She wanted to be in the Directorate of Operations, but it didn't work out. She was determined to do a good job, not embarrass the Agency, but something came across her desk that concerned her. That's why she came to me."

"Why you?"

Kay says, "Sorority sisters, back at Northwestern. Funny, eh?"

"What did she bring you?"

The briefest of hesitations, and Noa says, "Your turn, Kay. We're going to see this through, the two of us."

A small shake of the head. "Donna was part of a division that oversaw the president's Special Access Account."

"The president's own slush fund for pet projects. What didn't she like?"

"A number of officers who were in the Directorate of Operations and the Special Activities Division were now being paid from the Special Access Account. Paying salaries from that fund, that's never done. There were also unauthorized transfers of huge sums of money to FEMA, earmarked for Mount Weather and Raven Rock. That's also never done. Donna told me that it was like President Barrett was beefing up those government retreat bunkers without any oversight, like he had advance knowledge that a war was going to break out."

Dear God, Noa thinks.

"Go on."

"Donna said there were odd purchases here and there. Special surveillance equipment. Hacking programs from people that populate the dark web. Firearms, C4 explosives...hell, even the purchase of a Town Car through a series of cutouts so it couldn't be traced."

Noa freezes at the last phrase.

"A Town Car? Really?"

"Really," Kay says. "Why in the world would the President need C4, weapons, and a damn Town Car?"

She recalls the ambush in Virginia, near the National Ground Intelligence Center, and the Town Car that was recovered, stuffed with weapons and C4.

Why in the world, indeed?

Noa is about to say something when the lights flicker in Kay's apartment.

They blink again.

"What the..."

Noa gets up from the table. "You ever have utility problems or brownouts here?"

"Never."

She reaches into her purse, pulls out her 10mm Glock.

"Call 911, right now. Someone's breaking into your apartment."

"But . . . nothing's happening!"

Noa says, "Trust me, they're coming."

She goes to the front door in the living room, makes sure it's locked. There's a chain and lock that she additionally secures, which will only slow the invaders by a few seconds, but she'll take it.

Kay steps in, voice trembling. "I can't make a call."

"Service here is blocked," Noa says.

Noa goes back into the kitchen, grabs a chair, brings it to the door and shoves the back under the doorknob. She looks into the living room and says, "Help me with the couch."

The two of them drag the couch so it's nearly blocking the door.

The lights flicker and stay out.

Noa says, "Where's the bathroom?"

"Over here."

Noa goes to the bathroom, takes a quick glance, and says, "Do you have a weapon? Any kind of firearm?"

"What, no, I mean—"

Noa says, "Get into the tub. Now. Keep on dialing 911 in case service is restored. I'll be back in a moment."

Move, move, she thinks.

Kay calls out, "What's going on?"

"Into the tub!"

Messy bedroom. More books and papers on the floor, along with piles of clothes. Noa strips off the top sheets and blankets, hauls the mattress out, knocking over a lamp, and pushes and shoves the mattress into the bathroom.

"Stay here, no matter what," Noa says. "Keep on dialing."

"But—"

Noa drops the mattress over Kay, steps out, locks and closes the bathroom door.

Move, move, move.

The couch is tipped over.

She thinks she hears low voices.

Route of escape?

On the other side of the living room is a set of sliding glass doors, leading to a small outdoor deck.

Three floors up, but still.

Noa kneels behind the couch, takes a throw pillow, unzips it, and tugs out the foam insert. She tears off chunks of the foam, wets them with her mouth, rolls them into tight little balls and puts them into her ears.

Weapon now in her hands.

Waiting for what's coming.

Sharp, twin blasts from a shotgun in the hallway takes out the door hinges, and a battering ram breaks down the door. Noa opens her mouth, waiting for the flashbang grenades to go off, but, surprise surprise, the two-man crew wearing helmets and black tactical gear start shooting, no flashbang grenades in play.

No yells of *Police!* or *Search warrant!*

You started it, she thinks, and starts shooting back.

CHAPTER 96

IN THE LONG minutes that it takes to pass through the West Wing of the White House, Xi Dejiang of the Chinese Ministry of State Security keeps a slight smile on his face, enjoying every moment of being in the so-called belly of the beast, the center of America's imperialist government.

Yet he is under no illusions, as each White House staffer, all wearing those silly lanyards with colored cards that make them look like farm animals being sorted for later slaughter, gives him looks of anger or distaste as he strolls along. They don't know who he is, only that he's a high-ranking Chinese diplomat, coming in for a face-to-face meeting with their increasingly irrational boss.

That's fine.

He's not concerned at all about their looks, or their hate.

It is expected to receive such discourteous looks

from a class of people who sense within their very bones that their famed American empire is in decline, to be replaced by another. With their internal squabbles, their willingness to bend over to give the Middle Kingdom technology and knowledge, and the opening of their finest universities to train the next generation of Beijing technocrats, what do they expect?

"Just this way, sir," the unctuous young male aide says, walking Dejiang down an elegant hallway, and thus to the first surprise of his visit: being brought to an open elevator door.

Dejiang says, "I'm sorry, what is this? I've always thought the president's work area was the Oval Office, on the first floor."

A knowing smile from the aide. "Not *this* president."

Just a few seconds later the elevator opens to an old-fashioned living area, decorated with antique American paintings, furniture, and sculptures that should be in a dusty museum instead of this supposed powerful house.

They go down a short corridor with a female Secret Service agent in a black suit standing guard. The aide raps on a door, opens it, and says, "Here you go, sir. The president."

Dejiang gives a slight bow of thanks, walks in, and a host of familiar smells come to him. The room is small, with a wooden desk, no windows, two couches facing each other, two chairs, and a small table.

On the table are platters of breakfast foods—Chinese—and President Barrett stands up from the far couch and waves him in.

"Mr. Xi, do come in, please," he says, in that pleasant baritone voice of his. "I know it's late and practically lunchtime, but I asked the White House Mess to prepare a traditional breakfast for you, and I hope they've done you a service. Have a seat."

Dejiang slowly sits down on the opposite couch, still staring at the food. The president gives a quick tutorial of what is available, saying, "Here's your steamed *baozi*, half with pork and the other half with vegetables. This one I think is called *jianbing*. To me it looks like a French crepe that ended up in the wrong neighborhood."

Barrett laughs but Dejiang doesn't join.

What is this man doing? Is he becoming even more mad, after that note mentioning the two old CIA agents, and the cruise missile attack?

"And lastly, *youtiao*, fried flour sticks and warm and sweetened soy milk. You know," he says, sitting down, "those *youtiao* look mighty fine. I think I'm going to try one."

He picks up a napkin and Dejiang sits there, feeling out of order, slightly humiliated, like he's some junior official from the Ministry of Trade, here to finalize a contract about soybean deliveries.

The president starts munching on one of the fried sticks and he says, "Damn, that tastes pretty good. I might have the White House Mess put this on the regular breakfast menu."

Focus, he thinks, and says, "Mr. President, thank you for seeing me on such short notice. There are evolving issues involving our two nations and I hope that we can talk out our differences this morning, reach some sort of understanding, some way to reduce tensions."

The American leader finishes off his *youtiao* and gently wipes his fingers with the white cloth napkin. "You ready to stop suppressing the Uighurs?"

"Ah, well—"

"Abandon your illegal military bases on your man-made islands in East China?"

"Mr. President, I—"

"Return autonomy to Tibet and Hong Kong?"

Dejiang keeps quiet. The man is ranting.

"Or stop stealing our technological information? Hacking every computer system from local water works to the federal government? Are you telling me, Mr. Xi, that Beijing is prepared to do all of this? For real?"

Dejiang feels color come to his face. "Those are unreasonable demands, sir. And you know it. We are a great and proud nation. We will not be humbled."

The president says, "Unreasonable or not, that's all you're going to get today. And if I hadn't made myself clear, I love and admire the Chinese people, but you and your Communist government can go fuck off."

A heavy, cold pause, and Dejiang is now regretting this unofficial visit.

The president says, "Get you something else to eat?"

CHAPTER 97

NOA HIMEL IS limping down a side street, maybe three blocks away from Kay Darcy's apartment, hoping the *Post* reporter is still alive. When the shooting started Noa was under no illusions, she wasn't going to bravely hold off a tactical team intent on killing them both. No, she just wanted a delay.

A delay for the neighbors to call the real police, and for her to escape.

After the shooting started, she returned fire. When there was a pause, she escaped out through the rear deck glass door and over the railing. Something stung her hard when she started to drop, and when she hit the ground, she sliced her wrist on a nail sticking out from one of the deck beams.

Walk calmly, she thinks, as she strolls down the sidewalk, hearing sirens out there near Kay Darcy's apartment. *Don't walk with hesitation or a limp, even though your left arm and your side hurt like hell, because you will stand out, you will be noticed.*

No time to be noticed.

She comes across an alleyway between two apartment buildings, the narrow row crowded with trash bins and piles of collapsed cardboard boxes tied with twine. Noa sidles in, takes a series of deep breaths, takes stock of the crappy situation.

Her left wrist was shredded when she struck the exposed nail. Noa takes off her torn jacket, sees the ripped sleeve and blood. From her purse she takes out a Leatherman tool—essential gear for nearly everyone—and slices off the torn sleeve and its opposite. She wraps the good shirt-sleeve around the bloody wrist, ties it as best she can.

Sirens still sound off in the distance.

Now to her left side, just below the ribs. One bloody mess. Either she was shot bailing out of the third-floor apartment or was grazed.

Shit.

From the near trash bin, a burst-open green trash bag reveals old sheets and towels. A bit more work and later, she's made a compress against the wound and has tied it in place with twine.

Noa is hurt, she's light-headed, and needs to get on the move.

The hospital?

Nope, not with a gunshot wound. That would

immediately get police attention, or uniformed men and women claiming they were police.

Call the CIA? Even with their usual and customary objections against working in CONUS—hah-hah, she sourly thinks, remembering what she's been doing these past months—there is a phone number she could call and get help within minutes.

But who would respond? The domestic CIA quick reaction force, or officers whose lasting loyalty is to President Barrett?

Gina Stasio? Her friend from the Office of Technical Services? She nearly sobs at the memory of her last meeting with Gina, relaxing in her cozy apartment, drinking wine, sharing secrets.

A call to Gina would get her here for sure.

But it would take too long, and who knows what kind of danger Noa would put Gina in, by reaching out to her.

No, she thinks, walking farther down the alleyway.

She needs to get to Director Abrams's house, as fast as possible, before it is too late, before she bleeds out here.

The end of the alleyway ends in an old wooden fence, falling apart, and she slips through, wincing, finding a parking lot for another apartment building.

It's crowded with cars, SUVs, and a few pickup trucks. Noa takes her time, walking and examining every vehicle she passes by, until she stops with relief at a dark silver Toyota Celica with some rust and dings, made back in the 1990s.

She moves in and tries the driver's door.

Locked.

Well, finding an old car here was going to be luck enough. She walks out and returns a few minutes later with a good-sized rock in her right hand.

"Sorry," she whispers and, with one sharp blow, shatters the passenger's-side window. Reaches in, unlocks the door. The inside of the car is filthy with sweaty gym clothes, empty water bottles, crumpled-up food wrappers from Popeyes.

Noa gets into the front seat, leans down—moans from the pain radiating up from her side—and with the Leatherman tool, gets to work, undoing the low plastic panel next to the steering wheel, tugging it free.

Three clusters of wires dangle in front of her.

She ignores the one to the left and the one to the right, focusing on the middle set of wires, consisting of three: red, yellow, and white.

Noa blinks her eyes. Things are looking shaky.

Focus!

Leatherman tool in hand, she cuts all the wires away, strips off some of the insulation.

"Eddie, old boy," she whispers, thinking of one of her instructors back at the CIA's Farm years ago, "I sure hope I remember this right."

Using part of a T-shirt she found in the car's rear seat as insulation, she wraps the bare ends of the red and yellow wires together.

The Celica's dashboard lights up.

There you go.

She takes the last white wire, and gently touches it to the twisted red and yellow wires.

The engine roars into life.

She feels like fainting.

No, not yet.

She slowly maneuvers her way back so she's sitting in the driver's seat.

Grabs the steering wheel.

It's locked.

Noa finds the rock she used earlier and hits the metal keyhole on the side of the steering column as hard as she can. On the fourth blow, it breaks, and she tugs it free, digs out a spring, and tries the wheel again.

It moves smoothly under her touch.

She puts the Celica in reverse just as she hears, "Hey, hey, hey, what are you doing to my car!"

"Stealing it, silly," she murmurs, heading to the lot's exit. "For the good of the country."

After some turning and driving—avoiding potholes and manhole covers, so the twisted wires don't loosen up—she's heading south on Wisconsin Avenue NW, heading for O Street NW, where the director lives.

Her wrist is burning and every breath she takes causes a jagging pain in her left side. She keeps glancing at the side view and rearview mirrors, looking for district police cruisers to come racing up to her, lights flashing, siren wailing. The breeze coming in through the smashed window makes it one chilly ride indeed.

Noa gets off on O Street NW, into a pleasant avenue lined with Georgian-style homes. She figures she's about six blocks away from Director Abrams's home.

Just six blocks.

We can make it, she thinks, *we can get there.*

We've got to tell the director what's been learned.

The unauthorized spending from upgrading the government retreat at Mount Weather, to paying for the weapons and car those Iranians had—a setup, had to be a setup—the extent of Barrett's actions are getting more terrifying with each passing hour.

Three blocks to go.

Noa reaches a four-way stop at 31st Street NW, looks both ways, and gently eases into the intersection.

A flash of blue on the right catches her eye and in seconds her stolen car is T-boned by another car. The Celica spins, hits something, and Noa loses consciousness when the airbag deploys, hammering her face.

CHAPTER 98

THE PRESIDENT PICKS up another *youtiao*, examines it for a moment, and then puts it down on the crowded coffee table. "Okay, Mr. Xi, I've made my points. The ball is in your court. It's your turn at bat. You've got the conn."

"Sir?"

Barrett waves a hand. "Get on with it. What does Beijing want?"

Now we're finally getting somewhere with this strange man, Dejiang thinks.

He says, "From your communities in the United States to our city of Jieyang, you have made your displeasure about our past activities quite apparent. We hear your messages, and we are eager to engage in high-level talks to ease the tension, reach an understanding before events escalate and spiral out of control."

"Another negotiation?" Barrett says. "Wow. Color

me shocked and impressed, that the *rezident* of the Ministry of State Security for the United States would come to the White House and offer additional negotiations. Gosh."

Even though he knows he's being mocked, Dejiang says, "Sir, this makes sense. You know it does."

Barrett says, "You a student of history?"

"In a manner, yes," Dejiang says, feeling like he's on a slippery set of stone steps, like a tour he took once on the Great Wall, where one false move would end in injury or death.

"Back in 2001, after long negotiations, China was allowed to join the World Trade Organization," Barrett says. "Negotiators from the West, including my predecessor here, thought it was a wise decision. By opening markets to you and a greater exchange of information and goods, it was thought that you were on the road to democracy, and that a great liberalization would take place in Beijing."

Barrett returns to the fried pastry, breaks off a piece, chews, and swallows. "Guess we messed that one up, eh? You got the enormous economic trading advantages of being part of the WTO, but your government in Beijing thought it also gave you license to raise hell around the world. But it ends now, with me."

Dejiang's face is still flushed, but now his hands are cooling.

"Ends how, sir?"

Another wipe of his fingers on the napkin. "You've come here to ask me to stop my activities, in finally paying Beijing back for the years of economic theft and cyberattacks. And I'm telling you, no, it's not going to happen. Sorry. Oh, hold on a moment, I forgot I have something for you."

Dejiang looks on in astonishment as the president of the United States pulls a bulging white plastic bag from underneath the table, and hands it over. Dejiang takes the bag and looks in.

Four cartons of Marlboro cigarettes.

With pride Barrett says, "Had one of my aides bounce over to the 7-Eleven on 19th Street Northwest. Your favorite brand, correct?"

Dejiang drops the bag on the couch and sharpens his voice, saying, "Mr. President, I came here in good faith, to offer talks to reduce tensions and stop the situation from escalating, and you're not taking me, or my nation, seriously. I won't stand for it."

Barrett says, "Yeah, if I was in your seat, I probably wouldn't, either."

Now it happens, Dejiang thinks, *now I will use the weapon I've been saving.*

"Sir, you must know that we have a CIA operative in our custody, in South Africa."

He shrugs. "You forget, I was CIA director for a number of years. Having an operative captured is part of the business of espionage."

Dejiang says, "This CIA operative is Benjamin Lucas. I have been instructed by my government that if you do not agree to these talks, and stop your attacks on my nation, that this CIA operative will be executed by my government as a spy, as is allowed by international law."

Dejiang stares at the president's face, looking for some flicker, some bit of emotion or something to cross his face, but his expression remains bland.

Barrett says, "Price of doing business. I know it well. Go right ahead. There are greater things in play than one man's life, who has sworn fealty to me and this nation."

Dejiang feels like he's at the Great Wall again, but this time, he is falling, falling hard to the ground.

"But Mr. President, surely you will agree to our requests."

"Why?"

Dejiang licks his dry lips. "Because Benjamin Lucas is your son."

CHAPTER 99

CIA DIRECTOR HANNAH Abrams says, "Excuse me, say that again? Benjamin Lucas is the son of President Barrett?"

"Yes, ma'am," says Jean Swantish.

She leans back in her chair, just staring in disbelief at her deputy director.

"Jean," she says, "tell me what you got, and it better be good, to have been hidden all these years."

Jean has a thick manila folder in her lap but doesn't refer to it as she begins.

"You asked us to go deep, and deep is where we went," she starts. "Roberta Tyler was Benjamin's mother. At the time of his birth, she was employed as a civilian contractor for the Department of Defense, working at Fort Ord in California before it was closed. The birth certificate said father was unknown."

"Did we talk to her?"

A sad shake of the head. "She's been dead for a number of years. Car accident. But we did talk to her neighbors from that time, and one said she was sure Roberta's father was stationed at Fort Ord. We did a check of personnel records, to see who was stationed at Fort Ord at the time, and to see if there was any connection that led to Roberta. Nothing…but one of our analysts found that Barrett Keegan, then a lieutenant, was stationed there. That just raised questions, especially considering Benjamin's golden career here at the Agency, with someone clearing the way for him."

Hannah shakes her head. "Not nearly good enough."

"That's what I said, and knowing how fast you wanted confirmation, we skipped a few steps. Actually, a lot of steps."

"Where did you end up?"

"DNA analysis," Jean says. "We have Benjamin Lucas's DNA on file, of course, and we ran a match against the president's DNA and—"

"Hold on, where did you get the president's DNA?" Hannah asks. "Did you access the Secret Service's cold storage? They keep some of the president's blood for emergency use, but that supply is well guarded. That would be an incredibly dangerous move, Jean."

"Er, no, we didn't get his blood from the Secret

Service. Or Homeland Security. We got it from our own medical office."

Hannah feels her eyes widen. "We have blood samples from President Barrett?"

Jean nods. "Not just him. We have blood samples going all the way back to Kennedy."

"Kennedy . . . ?"

"Yes, ma'am. Er, a little-known program called the Manchurian Project. Named after that—"

"Book and movie," Hannah recalls.

"Correct," Jean says. "It seems at the time there were concerns about, well, a body double assuming the presidency during a moment of crisis, and having samples of the real president's blood on hand would be key in—"

"Enough," Hannah says, resting her head in her hands for a moment. "Holy shit on a cracker, if we spent more money on real programs and technology, instead of this James Bond nonsense like exploding cigars for Castro, the Cold War would have ended a decade earlier."

"Is it possible the Chinese know?" Jean asks. "And that's why they've captured him? And won't talk to us about his release?"

"Possible," Hannah says. "They're good at sucking up petabytes of information from Social Security numbers to payroll records for every damn company in the country. Why not?"

Hannah pauses for a moment, then sits up. "All

right. A good piece of intelligence we didn't know before, about Benjamin's parentage. Good job to you and your operatives. Barrett has based his entire political career on being the lone wolf, utterly dedicated to the nation, with no family and no distractions. Doesn't drink, doesn't smoke, doesn't chase women. But now, you and yours have given me something I didn't have before."

"What's that?" her deputy asks.

Hannah says, "A weapon to use against Barrett, at the right time and place."

CHAPTER 100

THE FIRST THING Noa Himel notices when her eyes flutter open is the sharp acrid smell of firecrackers being shot off, and then there's white dust everywhere. She coughs, comes to full awareness.

Her stolen Celica is up on a sidewalk, the front end smashed by a utility pole, and the passenger's side is caved in by a blue Chevrolet Tahoe. Steam is rising from under the Tahoe's hood.

They're here, she thinks, grabbing at her bag, unbuckling the seat belt, needing to get out of the X, the kill zone. *Setting up a fake car accident to stop me from getting to Director Abrams's home and safety. The ones who shot Kay Darcy and me, they're here.*

It takes one good shove before the door opens— her wincing hard from the burst of pain—and she steps out, 10mm Glock in her hand, and there's a yell. She turns, saying, "Hold on, right there!," pointing her weapon at the people closest to her.

She takes in the scene, best as she can, with her chest aching after the hard blow of the airbag deployment, her eyes burning from the dust coming out from the now deflated safety device.

A few people are on the sidewalk, gaping in awe at the accident. Other cars that don't want to be held up slowly drive around the wrecked vehicles.

In front of her are two teen girls, weeping, one holding up her freshly manicured hands to her face, saying, "My parents are gonna kill me! My parents are gonna kill me!"

Her friend has an arm around her. "It was an accident, that's all. Just an accident."

The weeping girl says, "The cops are gonna call up my phone records, they'll see I was texting when I hit this woman's car." She drops her hands and says, "You okay, lady, it was an accident, right? Are you okay?"

Noa is definitely not okay, but she's feeling like karma has just bitten her, hard.

To survive that shootout back at Kay Darcy's apartment then to be stopped by a high school girl looking at her phone? Stuck without transportation just two blocks away from safety?

"Lady," the second girl says, voice quavering. "Put the gun away, will you? You're scaring us."

Noa ignores them both, goes back into the Celica, retrieves her bag, starts walking. No time to stay here, no time to make sense of this traffic accident.

"Lady, you gotta stay here," the other driver says. "You just can't walk away! The cops are coming and we'll have to fill out paperwork."

Noa keeps her mouth shut, limping down O Street. Other voices call out. "Hey, she's leaving the scene of an accident. She can't do that. Somebody stop her!"

She keeps on moving, bag over her arm, wrist, side, and most everything else hurting. The sidewalk is rough and cold against her right foot. She looks down, sees she's lost a shoe along the way.

"Lady, you gotta stop. You just gotta!"

The driver's passenger races up, grabs her arm, and Noa turns, displays her Glock.

"No, I don't," she says firmly. "Go away and leave me the hell alone."

Noa takes a couple of deep breaths, keeps on moving.

Crosses a street.

Just one block to go.

Sirens are coming clearer.

Noa looks back.

A DC fire truck and ambulance have stopped at the accident scene.

Then a blue-and-white DC police cruiser. Three people are pointing in Noa's direction.

Move it, she thinks, *move*.

Up ahead, her energy draining, she sees that

brick wall and wrought-iron gate of the driveway belonging to Director Abrams.

Just a few yards away.

Just those several feet.

The roar of a car comes up behind her.

No need to turn around.

Noa gets to the metal call box set into the brick.

She presses the buzzer.

Again.

Again.

A car breaks to a halt.

Quick glance.

DC police cruiser, of course.

"Yes?" a tinny male voice comes out of the speaker.

Noa takes a breath. "This is CIA Officer Noa Himel. I need to get in here."

"Director Abrams isn't home."

Noa says, "I don't care if she's orbiting Jupiter… she gave permission for me to come here."

From behind her, a strong male voice. "Ma'am, freeze, right there. Don't move. Don't you dare move!"

Over the static coming from the little speaker mounted on the gate, two males seem to be talking over one another, and then a second male voice says, "Okay, the gate's opening now."

Noa looks back at the male cop, who's joined by a female companion, both with service weapons in hand.

To the call box Noa says, "I need somebody here. The cavalry has arrived and they're not happy."

A buzzing sound and a *clank,* and the gate starts rattling to the left.

"Ma'am, don't you dare move!"

Two tall and hard-looking security men step out and Noa brushes past them, going up the cobblestoned driveway.

More shouting from behind her—

"...hey, we're all on the same team..."

"...she's walking away from an accident scene..."

"...we can sort it out later..."

"...the hell we will..."

The small front lawn of Director Abrams's home looks so green and luxurious. Noa sits down and stretches out. She feels like some Cold War refugee, gaining sanctuary at some church or embassy.

The voices lower.

It's quiet.

The gate starts rattling shut.

Even her various pains and aches seem to fade out.

Safe.

Noa fights to stay awake.

Safe. But for how long?

CHAPTER 101

PRESIDENT KEEGAN BARRETT is enjoying the stunned expression on the Chinese intelligence officer's face after he shrugs and says, "So what?"

It seems like nearly a minute passes before De-jiang regains his composure. His otherwise quite good English stammers some as he speaks.

"But—again—sir. We have your son. Your only child—Benjamin Lucas—in our custody. In South Africa."

Barrett shrugs. "Keep him."

It grows increasingly silent and uncomfortable in his upstairs office, and Barrett is enjoying every second, seeing this opponent before him squirm. How could this poor man know what he's up against? Not only a president, but a president who's about to fulfill his lifelong fate. What man or nation could defeat that?

"But... sir, this is highly irregular."

"Certainly is," Barrett says.

Dejiang says, "I am forced to tell you something, Mr. President, that circumstances have led us to this position."

He pauses, swallows. "If you do not cease your operations against the People's Republic of China and agree to a summit to reach an understanding of our respective areas of concern, especially concerning cyberattacks and cybersecurity, it will not end well for your son."

Barrett just stares at the man. "You've already threatened him with execution, What, you're going to kill him twice?"

Dejiang says, "However you phrase it, the choice of whether he lives or dies remains with you."

Barrett keeps his stare on the man, the same stare he's used on fellow politicians when he was back in Congress, at recalcitrant generals and admirals when he was secretary of defense, and at bureaucrats deep in the bowels of the CIA's swamp.

He bursts out in laughter.

"Go ahead," he says. "You think that will do anything to sway me? The death of my son, dying in the line of duty?"

Dejiang looks on, still stunned. "Sir..."

"You ever hear of John Marshal?"

The intelligence officer stammers for a moment. "One of your early American jurists, correct?"

"No," Barrett says, suddenly impatient. He has a

long day still ahead of him and he wants this man out of his office.

Barrett says, "You folks always whine about outside forces and tyranny of history. Well, get ready for a history lesson you won't ever forget."

CHAPTER 102

CIA DIRECTOR HANNAH Abrams hangs up one of her secure phones, looks again with dismay at the foldout bed taking up a good chunk of her office. How long will that damn thing remain here? How soon before she can have it hauled out when circumstances get back to normal?

And what the hell is normal anyway?

A knock on her door and Jean Swantish steps in from her office, her face concerned.

"Madam Director, I—"

"Just a moment," she says. "I just got off the phone with one of my new security officers at my house. Noa Himel is there, injured."

Jean slowly sits down.

"What happened?"

Hannah says. "Kay Darcy insisted on meeting Noa at her apartment. Noa had no other choice.

They met and within fifteen minutes, the place was raided."

"The DC cops?"

Hannah says, "Not on your life. It was an outside force. They broke in, shot up the place, and then left. Noa bailed out of a third-floor deck, messed up her left arm and got a gunshot wound to her side. Thankfully, it's a through-and-through. There's an Agency medical team heading to my house now. She also asked that I send over a friend of hers, Gina Stasio, who works here. Make that happen, will you? Give her a security escort, complete with lights and sirens."

"At once, Madam Director," Jean says. "What about Kay Darcy?"

"Shot, in serious condition, now over at GW Hospital. I want her guarded, twenty-four/seven, through one of our contract companies."

"Yes, ma'am."

Hannah lets out a sigh.

"You came over here for a reason, Jean," she asks. "What is it?"

Jean says, "I got a secure phone call from a friend of mine, works at the FBI in their Counterintelligence Service. Xi Dejiang, the *rezident* here for China's Ministry of State Security, is currently at the White House, meeting with President Barrett."

Hannah lets that last sentence roll heavily around in her mind. The president secretly meeting with the Chinese ambassador, that could happen. Or with an official from their Trade Ministry, or some other flunky at their embassy.

But the head of their intelligence service?

One-on-one, in secret?

"I need to go back home," she says. "I want to get a fuller debrief from Noa Himel."

"On it, ma'am."

"What the hell is Barrett doing with the Chinese *rezident*?" Hannah asks, getting up from behind her desk. "Making promises, or making threats?"

"I don't know, ma'am."

"Neither do I," she says, getting her bag ready. "And that is scaring the crap out of me."

CHAPTER 103

PRESIDENT KEEGAN BARRETT says, "You know about John Marshall, one of our most famous chief justices of the United States. Well done, sir. As much as I despise your government, your education system is first-rate. Most American college and high school students, if asked, would probably think Mao was the sound a cat makes."

Xi Dejiang doesn't say anything. The man before him, the most powerful man in the West, is starting to rave.

Barrett says, "Damn it, Mr. Xi, I just paid you a compliment. Don't you have the courtesy to at least say *thank you*?"

Dejiang remembers whispered tales of old men he had met on his rise up the ladder of power, who when they were younger, worked for the Great Helmsman, Chairman Mao himself, and how the old man would slur, stutter, and talk madness at the end of his days.

He now knows how those old men must have felt.

Dejiang nods, his voice just above a whisper. "Thank you, Mr. President."

Barrett smiles. "You're quite welcome. Now, the John Marshal I was speaking about was an Englishman several hundred years older than our famed chief justice, and spelled his last name with a single *l*. In 1152, there was a civil war in England between a King Stephen and a Queen Matilda. King Stephen wanted to hold on to his throne and John Marshal, an ally of Queen Matilda, was holding on to a strategic castle. You following so far?"

The slightest of embarrassed nods. His homeland and this nation are about to trade deadly blows and Barrett wants to talk ancient Anglo-Saxon history?

"Well done," Barrett says. "There was a long siege, and John Marshal offered a truce. To seal the deal, Marshal gave up his five-year-old son William to King Stephen as a hostage, so Marshal wouldn't violate the terms of the truce. But that's exactly what Marshal did. He brought in fresh troops and supplies. King Stephen was outraged and threatened to kill his son, the hostage. You know what Marshal said?"

The slightest shake of Dejiang's head. A mistake, it had been a mistake, trying to come here and reason with this man, who is clearly mad.

Barrett said, "Marshal basically said, so what. Kill the boy. He still had the hammer and forge to produce another son, even finer. Got it?"

Dejiang says, "I'm not entirely sure, Mr. President."

Barrett leans over and says, "You can kill my son and dump his body on the South Lawn, and it will not make a lick of difference in my actions. I'm doing what is best for my nation and its people. There will be casualties. And if by some odd chance in the future, I wish to have another son..."

Barrett quickly stands up, slaps his crotch.

"I have the hammer and forge to produce another son, even finer."

"This...makes no sense."

"Sense? I'll show you what makes sense from where I sit." Barrett goes around to his wooden desk. From the lower right-hand drawer, he pulls out a Colt Model 1911 .45 caliber semiautomatic pistol. He comes back to the couch, puts the pistol on the table.

"See that?" he asks. "Designed more than a century ago. One of the finest sidearms ever developed for our military. This one was carried by my grandfather, when he was in the Marines, in Korea, and nearly got killed at Chosin Reservoir. I'm sure you know about that battle...hundreds of thousands of your ancestors came at my grandfather and other Marines. He survived, but he lost both feet, frozen from the cold."

Barrett touches the pistol. "My father carried this in Vietnam, until a round from a Chinese-made SKS-56 blew off his right knee. For the rest of his life, even as a schoolteacher, my father was a bitter drunk, thanks to you folks. But now... your aggression, your violence, ends with me."

Enough is enough, Dejiang thinks. He has to get out of here and report back to Beijing the condition of this nation's president. Quickly.

He abruptly gets up. "You have made your position quite clear, Mr. President. We have offered you a way out from our dilemma. You have refused any consideration, any compromise. You have until noon tomorrow to reverse course."

The president of the United States stands up as well, face red, eyes wide.

"Fine," he says. "And you have sixty seconds to get the hell out of my White House."

CHAPTER 104

LIAM GREY IS driving the beat-up Polo into Johannesburg, yawning, desperately trying to stay awake.

It's taken nearly nine hours to get here from the truck stop where he had met Chin Lin. She left before him, allowing him time for a burger, fries, and refueling the Polo before driving east. Along the way he pulled over for a nap, refueled the Polo twice more, and kept on going with water, energy bars, and coffee. Now he's on Stiemens Street, following the directions Lin gave him.

There.

A bulky, concrete parking garage, part of the Joburg Theatre complex, consisting of four separate theatres in the Braamfontein area of the city.

Liam slowly drives in, notes that it costs twenty rands to park—money supplied to him before he left the States—and then he goes into the complex, up a level, and finds a certain spot. He parks the Polo, takes his duffel bag and steps out, stretches, and a voice says, "You're cutting it close."

Lin emerges from between two parked cars, walking to him, feet echoing on the concrete.

"Had to pass through a herd of water buffalo, sorry," he says. "I'm ready if you are."

She nods, gestures him over. She has on gray slacks and a white, button-front blouse with the same leather jacket as yesterday. Lin is alert and looking smart.

"Come along," she says, leading Liam to a dark-gray Mercedes-Benz S-Class sedan. She toggles a key fob and the rear trunk pops open, makes a gesture, and Liam says, "No."

"What?"

"I'm not getting in that trunk, not now."

"You agreed."

Liam says, "No, I've agreed to this op because it's the only way I see to get Benjamin freed and find out how to help the vice president. But this op goes against every bit of tradecraft I've learned over the years. And climbing into a car trunk in a parking garage, trusting you'll take me to the right place? That's not going to happen."

With anger in her dark eyes, Lin says, "Then what *is* going to happen?"

Liam goes around to the passenger's-side door, opens it. "Lady, I'm trying to minimize this big-ass risk. Which means I need to see the target building before we begin. I'm not going in cold. All right?"

"What difference will it make?"

"It'll make me happy," he says. "Aren't you in favor of improving Sino-American relations?"

"Only for one particular American," she quietly says.

"Making me happier will help," he says. "Now, you have a choice to make."

"What's that?"

"Which one of us drives?"

It's about a twenty-minute drive north along a busy Jan Smuts Avenue. As Lin drives, Liam presses her again about the upcoming op, what she has planned, the fallback and alternatives if the plan goes wrong.

As they talk, Liam takes in the bustling side streets and sidewalks of Johannesburg, and knows that even if this op is successful, getting Benjamin Lucas out and learning the cure for the vice president's condition—a long shot indeed—he will probably never be able to operate in Africa, ever again. The Chinese will make sure of that, passing along his information to every other intelligence agency on the continent.

Big deal, he thinks.

If it works, that will be all that matters.

He feels wide awake now, tingling in anticipation

of what is ahead, realizing he's on the knife edge of disaster. No matter the promises and reassurances the attractive young woman next to him has professed, she's still an intelligence officer from a nation that hasn't made secret its desire to turn the United States into a Second World nation.

Add in the fact that the local CIA station chief doesn't know he's here, and there's no time to do a surveillance detection route, just to see who might be out there with eyes watching. This op might end up making the disastrous Bay of Pigs Invasion look like the successful D-Day of 1944.

Lin drives smoothly and expertly through the narrow streets off Jan Smuts Avenue, into residential areas, all of which have tall concrete walls and gated entrances. Lin slows down as they pass through a roundabout, and she says, "Killarney Street. That's where Benjamin is being held."

Liam says, "One street over from your consulate on Cleveland Road. How convenient."

"You are distressingly well informed," Lin says, slowing down in front of 24 Killarney Street, marked in bronze colored metal letters and numbers on the concrete wall. Underneath that is Burnham Associates, in the same letter style. Liam gets a quick view of a gate and beyond that, a one-story concrete building with small windows, painted a dull yellow.

Lin speeds up. "Anything else?"

"Yes, I wish I had a day to surveil the joint," Liam says, turning in his seat for one last glance. One way in or out. Easy to block to prevent any escape. Hell, it looked like it could be blocked by a damn golf cart.

"There must be a utility or access tunnel connecting the consulate to your satellite building," Liam says. "What happens when the action starts? Every armed person at your consulate will come at us."

Lin pulls into a driveway where a building seems to be under renovation. But while there are piles of stone and pallets of lumber, no workers are visible. Lin drives to the rear where there's an open green bin filled with broken plaster and chunks of lumber and parks the car.

"That's taken care of," Lin says. "When we start, the tunnel closes off automatically at each end. There should be minimal occupation and resistance in the building where Benjamin is being held. Anything else?"

Liam can think of another half dozen questions or so but he knows they don't have the time.

"No," he says. "Let's do this."

They both get out and Lin opens the car's trunk— *or is it called a boot over here?* Liam randomly wonders—and he starts to get dressed from the gear Lin earlier placed in there.

As he puts on the gear, Lin sees him placing his borrowed 10mm Glock into a pocket.

Lin says, "I can't let you bring that in there."

Liam zippers the pocket shut. "Too late now. Lady, if I'm going into a trap, I'm not going in unarmed."

"You still don't trust me."

"Yes, but at least I'm polite enough not to point it out all the time," Liam says. "Let's get this thing done."

This time, he gets in the trunk for the short drive to the op.

CHAPTER 105

AT HER GEORGETOWN home, CIA Director Hannah Abrams sits in her kitchen, cup of coffee in hand. Her security officer Ralph says, "The DC police have come here twice, looking to talk to Noa. The next time they come, they'll be coming with a search warrant."

Hannah rubs at the side of her head. "I'll make some calls, see if I can get them to hold off for a while. How's everything else?"

"We have six additional security officers on the grounds, and I've got two other officers watching from vehicles parked on the streets," he says. "Noa's friend from the Agency, Gina Stasio, arrived about an hour ago. Do you expect any other visitors?"

"Probably Deputy Director Swantish, either late tonight or early tomorrow morning," she says. "Any news about Bruce?"

Ralph works his massive jaw. "In surgery at the

moment. Months of rehab ahead of him. But he'll bounce back, if it takes months or years."

Hannah stands up, briefly touches Ralph's shoulder. It's like touching a cloth-covered chunk of granite. "Thanks for the update."

Even though it's late in the evening, Hannah needs to check in on her overnight guest. Up on the second floor she gives the guest bedroom door a quick knock, and opens it and slips in. Noa is asleep on one of the two guest beds. Her friend, Gina Stasio of the Office of Technical Services, is sitting on the other bed. She stands up and Hannah gently raises a hand.

"No, don't bother," Hannah says. "How's she doing?"

Sitting back down on the bed, Gina says, "She's woken up a couple of times, but has slipped back into sleep. What did the doctor say?"

After Noa arrived, bleeding and injured, Hannah arranged for one of the Agency's medical teams to come in and treat her. Hannah says, "The wound on her wrist has been stitched and bandaged, as well as the bullet wound to her left side. It was a through and through, and the doctor cleaned and stitched that as well. Gave her an IV to replenish her lost fluids."

Gina says, "She should be in a hospital."

"She will be," Hannah says. "Once I talk to her."

"Director, that's—"

"Hold on, hold on," Hannah says, walking closer to Noa, whose head is moving back and forth on the pillow. The room is small but Noa notices that Gina had arrived with two large pieces of rolling luggage. *Talk about overpacking,* she thinks.

Hannah sits on Noa's bed, gently strokes her forehead. "Noa, are you awake?"

Her eyelids flutter open, her eyes move, and then focus.

"Director," Noa whispers. "You've got to...hear what I have to say..."

Hannah leans in. "Go. Tell me what you found out."

"Kay...Darcy. Is she alive?"

"Yes," she says. "Wounded but alive. She's at GW, and we're guarding her. But currently unconscious. What else?"

Noa licks her lips. "Donna Otterson...the financial officer...she was telling Kay Darcy about... illegal payment requests from the president's Special Access Account."

"Like what?"

"I'm so thirsty, can I get something to drink?"

Gina says, "On it."

She leaves the bedroom and Noa says, "The fund...it's been used to pay the salaries of Barrett's teams, so it was hidden from standard oversight."

Gina comes in with a glass of water. She holds up Noa's head and Noa takes a healthy drink.

"God, that tastes good," she says. "Director…the president has been buying other things as well. Automatic weapons. C-4. Even a damn Lincoln Town Car."

"A Town Car? Wait—"

Noa nods. "Yes…the Iranian Quds unit we ambushed. They had C-4, AK-47s, and they were in a Town Car. All provided by President Barrett. A setup. But that's not the worst of it."

Hannah feels the temperature of the room seemingly plummet. "Go on."

Noa says, "He's illegally transferred millions of dollars to FEMA, for upgrades to the continuity of government bunkers at Mount Weather in Virginia and the Raven Rock Mountain Complex in Pennsylvania."

She coughs and catches her breath for a cold moment.

"Ma'am," Noa says. "He's preparing to go to war."

CHAPTER 106

LIAM GREY IS finding it hard to breathe in the trunk of the Mercedes-Benz, wearing some of the gear Chin Lin has provided, but he's thankful the drive will be a short one.

His hand touches the shape of his Glock.

It'd better be a short one.

He feels the car stop, barely hears a rattling noise—the gate moving aside—and the car surges forward.

Moves a few seconds, then halts.

He hears footsteps outside.

His pistol in his hand.

The trunk lid opens and there's Lin.

Alone.

Good.

He stiffly clambers out of the trunk, wearing heavy boots, thick pants, and a black firefighter's jacket with Chinese characters on the front and back. Firefighters' bunker gear, identical to those used by the fire brigade at the consulate. Earlier Lin had said, "We don't trust the Joburg firefighters, so we use our own. But you'll have to be quick."

Reaching back in the trunk, he pulls out an air pack, shrugs it on his shoulders, pulls the straps tight, and applies the face mask, tightening that as well around his face. A helmet with rear flaps goes on, the helmet also bearing Chinese characters. Liam twists the valve and starts breathing the air, puts on heavy gloves, and picks up a heavy folded length of firehose, which he puts on his shoulder.

Lin leans into him. "Hurry up, now, the barbecue's just started. And remember what to say. Now go get my Benjamin!"

He walks quickly around the Mercedes, parked and hidden near a small garage, hears an alarm ringing from the building, and sees two nervous-looking young Chinese women moving quickly out of the front door. His hearing and vision are obscured, but that should work in his favor.

Just bull through, he thinks, *just go.*

Inside the glassed-in lobby. The door is open. He goes through, smelling now the heavy smoke that's coming up through the elevator banks. Two more young women and a man emerge from a stairwell, and Grey calls out, his voice muffled, *"Shūsàn jiànzhú wù, shūsàn jiànzhú wù!"*

Which Lin says, means, "Evacuate the building!"

He hopes she's right.

He goes into the stairwell, starts descending, his boots heavy on the steel and concrete steps. Another door opens and four or five men in suits look up at him, and, just for a moment, he feels trapped—these guys are intelligence officers, just like him, smart and probably tougher—and he keeps on keeping on.

He waves his hand up the stairs and repeats, *"Shūsàn jiànzhú wù!"*

They go by him, racing up the stairs.

Basement floor, two levels down now, where Benjamin's cell is located.

Close.

Getting real close.

And then the lights go out, plunging everything into absolute darkness.

CHAPTER 107

HANNAH ABRAMS WALKS down the cobble-stoned driveway of her home this morning, her lead, Ralph, matching her stride for stride. There are at least four other security officers in the yard, all with radio earpieces, wrist microphones, and weapons under their jackets. Hannah has a brief, funny thought of the local historical commission filing a complaint that her security force isn't fitting in with the nature and style of the neighborhood, and that they should have to dress in period clothing, circa 1850 or something like that.

Earlier she got off the phone with Jean Swantish, who is now en route to her home. When that call was complete, she was notified that someone was at the gate, demanding to see her.

Two more security officers are at the closed gate and a big-boned man—even larger than Ralph—

nods at her and says, "Sorry to disturb you, Madam Director, but I didn't know where else to go."

"What is it, then?" she asks, looking past the iron bars of the driveway gate, spotting an unmarked DC police cruiser parked in front of a hydrant.

The man says, "My name is Aldo Sloan. I've been working for Noa Himel these past couple of months, working on some delicate domestic operations, and now she's disappeared. I mean, people who should know about her whereabouts now claim they don't know anything about her and her job. Which is bullshit, ma'am. Excuse my language."

"I've heard worse. Go on."

"The last op we were on, we intercepted an Iranian terrorist cell that looked like it was about to strike at an intelligence center in Virginia."

Hannah says, "Yes, I know. The National Ground Intelligence Center."

Aldo allows himself a slight smile. "Good. You know about it. Well, that day we smoked three of the Quds guys, but there was something else there, too. A black Lincoln Town Car, filled with C-4, RPG-7s, and AK-47s. It looked like we got to the Iranians just before a transfer was to take place. Noa, she was going to wait a day, but decided to hit them early."

Noa last night, telling her that the president had authorized the purchase of a Lincoln Town Car, along with weaponry and explosives.

"Wasn't there a man with the Town Car who made an escape?"

Aldo reaches into his coat pocket, pulls out a folded-up piece of paper.

"Noa tasked me to find out who the driver was, what connection he might have with those Iranian terrorists," Aldo says. "It took a while—I mean, the ownership of that Town Car was behind so many cutouts you'd think it was made of cardboard—but then I thought about going back to the source. Or the scene."

He slips the paper through the ironwork.

Hannah slowly unfolds it.

Sees a man running in a dark suit, necktie flopping, holding a pistol, running past a large pine tree.

"From the outer perimeter surveillance cameras at the National Ground Intelligence Center," Aldo says. "He's on government property but not close enough to the perimeter fence to cause a response. But . . . there he is."

Hannah stares at the man, caught in mid-run. Thinks of a phone call she will be making shortly to an acquaintance of hers, FBI Deputy Director Edie Hicks, with whom she spent several miserable weeks at the Farm years ago.

Aldo says, "Noa said it was very important. But with her absent . . . I thought I should give it to you. Is that all right, ma'am?"

"It is," Hannah says.

"So it's important?"

Hannah folds up the paper, puts it carefully in her jacket pocket, like it was a loaded weapon. "Like you wouldn't believe."

CHAPTER 108

IN THE UTTER darkness in the basement of the Chinese intelligence facility, Liam's first response is, *Oh, damn it all to hell.* He starts fumbling through the pockets of the firefighters' coat, looking for a flashlight, but there's a *bang* and *hum* as a distant generator kicks in, and the lights return.

Shit, he thinks, *that was too close.* Lin had slipped him a couple of key pieces of equipment but he doesn't want to waste precious seconds looking for a light.

He shoulders the door open, breathing hard through the air mask, holding the heavy hose over his right shoulder, as he emerges into a concrete corridor.

Alarms are ringing and red lights hanging from the concrete ceiling are flashing.

Breathing is hard through the mask—the air tank and hose must weigh close to a hundred pounds.

Add in the turnout gear and heavy boots and helmet, and it's hard to keep balance, hard to keep moving fast and true, but he has no choice.

He's got to get Benjamin out.

He moves past a locked metal door and finds the standpipe Lin told him would be here. He thankfully drops the rolled-up hose, spins the cap off the standpipe, and hooks up the hose, for the benefit of anyone passing by or any surveillance cameras that may be operating.

Move, he thinks, unrolling the hose.

Smoke is starting to drift into the hallway, drifting up to the concrete roof.

Past another door—someone in there is screaming in terror, but he shuts that off in his mind— he comes to the fourth door.

Liam drops the hose, digs deep into the side pocket of his coat—right by his 10mm Glock— and pulls out a rubbery object the size of a schoolboard eraser, from back in the day. He pulls off one of the heavy fire-resistant gloves, tears off the strip on the rear covering the adhesive, and slaps the device against the lock.

He turns and there's a flare of bright light— highlighting his shadows in this gloomy corridor— followed by a sudden *thump*.

Liam pushes the door open.

Simple cell with metal toilet and sink, a bed, and a barefoot man in dull-orange pants and shirt.

The man looks up, mouth agape, eyes wide. Liam's first thought is that *Lin, damn you, you've got the wrong cell, or the wrong prisoner, or*—

The man croaks, "What the hell is going on?"

Liam shudders. Even with the bruises, the black eyes, the bloodied swollen lips and bent and twisted fingers on one hand, Liam knows it's Benjamin Lucas.

"Well?" Benjamin demands.

Liam loosens two straps to the air mask, pulls it out for a moment, and says, "Benjamin, can you stand? Can you walk?"

"Liam, how—"

"Shut up," Liam says. "Move. We don't have time before the entire goddamn PLA comes down that hallway."

Benjamin starts to get out of the bed, wincing, standing up in bare feet, weaving, and he says, "Ah, shit, Liam, I'm really messed up."

He tightens the mask back onto his face. "I can see."

Liam grabs Benjamin's good arm, pulls, lowers himself, and lifts him up in what's known as a fire-fighter's carry. Benjamin's torso goes across Liam's shoulders, and he shifts so that Benjamin's right hip is next to his head, allowing Liam's hands to be free if necessary.

His voice muffled via the air mask, Liam says, "Hold tight, we're moving!"

Benjamin's legs extend in front of him and his head and shoulders extend behind him, meaning he will fit through any door, but Christ, even with the hose gone, the weight of his fellow officer is damn heavy. It would be quicker if he dumped the air mask and tank, but the mask obscures his features and the tank is part of the outfit of the rescuing fire brigade member.

Outside the smoke is heavier. Benjamin starts coughing. He goes by the same door where a prisoner inside is screaming, banging on the door.

Liam stares ahead, at the stairwell door.

All right, get there, and don't think how you're getting up those flights of stairs, carrying this gear and injured CIA officer.

Just move.

He's about two meters away from the door when it swings open, and an angry Chinese male, mid-thirties, in black slacks and white shirt, comes out yelling.

Liam waves an arm, repeats the evacuation order.

"Shūsàn jiànzhú wù, shūsàn jiànzhú wù!"

The man doesn't move, yells at Liam in a long sentence of angry Chinese, which Liam doesn't understand, and Liam tries again, forcefully waving his arm, yelling even louder.

"Shūsàn jiànzhú wù, shūsàn jiànzhú wù!"

The man comes closer, yells more, then halts, frozen, as he apparently recognizes who's on Liam's back.

The Chinese intelligence officer yells one more time, reaches for something at his back. Liam is trapped in this basement, alarms ringing, smoke getting thicker, weighed down by Benjamin Lucas on his back.

He needs to get Benjamin out.

Getting Benjamin out means Lin will tell them how to save the vice president.

But this intelligence officer is pulling out a pistol and coming right at them both. With the combined weight on his back, Liam can barely move.

CHAPTER 109

PRESIDENT KEEGAN BARRETT is in his office in the family quarters of the White House, getting an update from Carlton Pope, his special assistant. No coffee, no pastries, no distractions. Barrett recalls those times back in the military, the Pentagon, and at Langley, when plans that had been prepared and reviewed for months—years, even—were about to be put into place.

There was always a buzz of excitement, of anticipation, of watching the clock wind down until it got to zero hour. Like Shakespeare said, they would cry havoc and let slip the dogs of war.

But you had to be careful. As that old buzzard Prussian Marshal Helmuth von Moltke said centuries ago, "No plan survives first contact with the enemy."

Which is why you have multiple plans and backups.

"Well?" he asks Pope. "Where's Liam Grey?"

Pope looks uncomfortable. "We don't know. Our last sighting was when Balantic tried to eliminate him yesterday at that convenience store off the George Washington."

"Tried," Barrett says. "You mean he failed, and Liam got away. And wasn't there a drone following him?"

"Sir, that drone had a limited operating life. The last it was reporting before its batteries died was that Liam's vehicle was heading northwest."

"And his bitch partner, Noa Himel? Another screw-up on your part? The *Post* reporter is still alive, and Noa's still alive. Who the hell are you hiring? The gang that couldn't body bag straight?"

Pope tenses up. "They are good contract personnel—most from overseas—as good as we could get without facing Immigration questions. Liam will be found. Noa is injured and is at Director Abrams's house. Give me the word and we'll go in and get her."

Barrett says, "Keep your eye on the prize. We can't afford having a firefight in the middle of Georgetown when we've got so much going on. But do what you can to keep her quiet. Has General Peterson confirmed his visit today?"

"Yes, sir, at ten a.m."

"Good. I'll want transport prepared for evac to Mount Weather at noon. That should give me plenty of time to be in a secure and safe place once the Chinese realize what's going on and begin their retaliation. Let's look to do an address to the nation at one p.m., explain what's going on."

"The networks might drag their feet, unless they know exactly what's going on."

Barrett says, "When they see the Staten Island Ferry lose control due to some teenager in Shanghai and ram into the USS *Intrepid,* they'll let me talk whenever I want to."

Pope nods. "You're correct, sir."

Barrett bristles. "Of course I'm correct. How else did I get here? Anything else I should know about?"

"Not at the moment, sir."

"Good." He decides to lighten the tone. "How does it feel to be on the cusp of history?"

"Truthfully? I'll be glad when this day and this week is over, Mr. President. There's a lot of balls in the air. I admire your juggling skills keeping them all in motion."

Barrett says, "Nice job of kissing ass, Carlton. I appreciate the metaphor. But I'm not juggling balls. I'm juggling hand grenades with the pins pulled, with only a short amount of time before I can start tossing them without getting a face full of shrapnel."

Pope slowly nods. Barrett says, "Remind me again of Balantic, your man killed at the convenience store. Was he TDY from the Agency?"

"No, sir," Pope says. "A domestic contractor I met in Kosovo. Untraceable. And easily replaceable."

"Good," Barrett says. "What I don't need now is somebody else bitching at me about getting a memorial star carved in Langley's lobby."

CHAPTER 110

IN THE BASEMENT of China's Ministry of State Security's annex, the smoke is getting thicker and the Chinese official a couple of meters in front of Liam is pulling a pistol out from a rear waistband holster.

No time, Liam thinks, and rotates a few feet. Benjamin Lucas is now blocking, only for a second, and the Chinese official pauses.

Liam grabs his 10mm Glock from a coat pocket and shoots the man twice in the chest.

The alarm continues to screech.

The man falls flat in the concrete corridor, his pistol skittering out beyond his hand, and Liam moves Benjamin so he's facing the original position.

He heads to the stairwell, opens the door, starts thumping his way up the stairs, breathing hard through the air mask, the mask fogging up, obscuring his view but also hiding him from others who might take a close look at this particular fire brigade member.

One more flight.

Just a handful of stairs.

His chest feels like it's going to burst.

Every step seems like Benjamin is gaining another pound.

He slams the door open. The first floor and reception are empty, but it's hazy with the smoke, and Liam thinks that's one hell of a barbecue Lin must have set.

Outside in the sunshine, he resists the strong temptation to tear off his air mask. He's got to keep up the appearances and, above all, keep moving. There are small groups of consulate officials gathered, talking, pointing, some even smoking. Two large dark-red vans with flashing red lights on top are parked, and fire brigade members from the consulate—the real ones—are gearing up, pulling out air tanks and rolled-up hoses. He keeps on moving.

A childish thought but a real one: *If I don't look at them, they won't look back at me. I'm invisible.*

Now.

Around the small garage, Lin is standing there, her hands come up to her face, and, even covered, Liam sees the thankful smile.

She opens the rear door to the Mercedes and

helps Liam roll off Benjamin and put him in the rear seat. Liam tugs off the helmet, rips off his face mask, loosens the straps, and shrugs off the air pack. He tosses it all onto the rear floorboard and gets the gloves off.

"Lin, give me the fob," he says. "I'm driving. You sit back with Benjamin and see how badly hurt he is."

He expects her to hesitate or object, so he's surprised when the fob is tossed his way. Liam catches it and within seconds, she's in the rear seat and he's in the driver's seat. The Mercedes starts up.

Liam lowers his head, drives out through the small area, past the groups of Chinese intelligence staff looking at him, and the two consulate fire brigade vans.

The open gate is ahead.

He clenches his hands on the steering wheel.

Just a few seconds more.

Close.

Two Chinese consulate workers come in from the outside sidewalk, dressed in gray business suits, both wearing eyeglasses, looking like standard-issue Chinese government bureaucrats, but these two are carrying QBZ-95 bullpup assault rifles slung over their shoulders.

Both hold up their hands and yell and bring up their respective rifles.

Liam stops. "Benjamin, hide your face, best as you can."

Shit.

He could run them down but there was a good chance one of them would be able to fire off a burst from a thirty-round magazine and ventilate this Mercedes-Benz and its passengers.

The two men come closer, yelling louder. From behind him, Lin says, "Lower your window, Liam."

He's not sure why she's made the request but he does so. Lin lowers her window as well, and starts yelling back at the two armed Chinese men.

Liam doesn't know what they're saying to each other, but it doesn't look good.

Lin seems to focus on the armed man to the right. She's pointing at him, raising her voice, and he matches her tone, syllable to syllable.

Then the second man moves around the front of the Mercedes, stepping closer, and Liam realizes both shooters are now on the same side of the car, and in a split second, knows what's going to happen next.

Lin propels herself across the seat back, buries her hand in his coat pocket, comes out with his 10mm Glock, shoots the near man in the face, and fires off two more rounds that hit the second armed man in the chest.

Liam's ears are ringing and the interior of the car

smells of burnt gunpowder. Lin is shouting at him. He can't quite hear her, but he doesn't need to.

He slams the accelerator down and the Mercedes speeds out of the compound and takes a left on Killarney Street.

CHAPTER 111

IN THE SCIF in the subbasement of the Chinese Embassy on 3505 International Place NW in the District of Columbia, Xi Dejiang of the Ministry of State Intelligence feels like an utter and complete failure.

Sitting across from him, like an old wife who won't leave you alone, is his assistant Sun Zheng. Dejiang knows that Zheng so desperately wants his job that he's tempted to scribble out a letter of resignation and let the fat bastard take control.

The inside of the SCIF is thick with smoke, and Dejiang's throat is raw from all the Marlboro cigarettes he has burned through. He's out of smokes yet he doesn't regret taking that bag full of cigarette cartons offered to him by President Barrett and throwing it at the stunned aide who escorted him out of the West Wing.

Zheng clears his throat. "Well, sir?"

He shrugs. "Failure. Complete and utter failure. Beijing has been trying other avenues of communication with that madman, and none are working. He is intent on giving us a punishment he thinks we deserve, and nothing is holding him back. Now Beijing is through with trying to talk to him."

Dejiang checks his watch. "In approximately four hours, the attacks will begin. How and where they will start is still a guess...but I have failed. Terribly. I thought I could reach him personally, intelligence professional to intelligence professional, but I was a fool. He's too far gone."

He reaches for a cigarette pack, to see if he's perhaps overlooked a cigarette, but it's still empty. He crumples it and throws it to the floor.

Zheng says, "I wish it went otherwise."

Dejiang nearly smiles. "I'm sure you do. No worries, Zheng. If and when they come for me here—because by this time tomorrow I doubt any airlines will be flying—I will say you were innocent, that it was my decision alone."

A brief nod, nothing else, but Dejiang senses the relief from his deputy.

"In the meantime," Dejiang says, "tell the Ambassador to commence the *Zhurong* operation immediately, before our embassy is ultimately breached. And get as many staffers as possible to go shopping.

Batteries, freeze-dried or canned food, and plenty of bottled water. Tell them to try to be as discreet as possible, but to get as many supplies back to the embassy before noon."

"Yes, sir," his assistant says.

He lifts his right hand, fingers nicotine-stained.

"Go, now," Dejiang says.

His assistant gets up, nods once more, and in a matter of seconds, is gone from the SCIF.

Dejiang rubs at his forehead. Not the place nor the time he imagined his career and his life would end, as he's under no illusions. He has failed in stopping the madman in the White House, and he will pay the ultimate price.

He looks at the crumpled cigarette packs and ash over the table, next to the cigarette lighter that was a gift from his only son.

Dejiang picks up the phone. It is expressly forbidden to use the embassy's secure phone system for a personal phone call, but so what. He will warn his son to leave Cambridge immediately and travel north, perhaps even across the Canadian border.

It is a day of reality. He knows that his wife and daughter in China will die in the upcoming attack, or be arrested and shot, and that there is no way to safely communicate with them from here in the United States.

But if his only son and his line is to survive,

then that will be the sole blessing to come out of this day.

The confident face of Admiral Zheng He stares at him from the small, framed print, mocking him. He turns it away as the phone rings and rings.

CHAPTER 112

LIAM GREY IS speeding through the crowded streets of Johannesburg, sweaty and achy after hauling that air pack and Benjamin Lucas up three flights of stairs back at the consulate building, ears ringing from having his own pistol shot off right behind his head.

Right behind his head!

The interior of the Mercedes smells of burnt gunpowder and whatever happened back there, one thing was proven: this Chinese intelligence operative just demonstrated her love for Benjamin by blowing away two of her own.

In the rear of the car Lin and Benjamin are talking low to each other, which is perfectly fine with Liam.

Benjamin's weak voice comes from the rear seat. "Liam ... how did you ..."

"Just part of the job," he says, stopping fully at

each traffic light, trying to see if anyone out there is tailing them.

So far, so good, but it doesn't mean that there's not a drone out there as well, flittering through this city's streets.

"Liam."

"Still here, still driving. Let's talk more later, okay?"

"Once you got me out of my cell, you had a confrontation with someone…I'm pretty sure it was Chang Wanquan. I recognized the bastard's voice. And you rotated me. Why?"

"To block him from shooting me."

Lin says, "What?"

"You were captured for a reason, Benjamin. Meaning you were worth something. Me using you as a barrier made that guy hesitate for a couple of seconds. All I needed."

Another traffic light, another stop.

"Good call," Benjamin says.

"Thanks."

"Wait," Lin says. "You shot Chang Wanquan?"

"Well, I was thinking of giving him a kiss to surprise him into stepping back, but I couldn't get my face mask off with just one hand. Why are you complaining after what you did back there at the gate?"

The light changes.

He resumes their quick drive.

About seven minutes later Lin says, "Hold on, you're going the wrong way! You're supposed to be heading north on the M1, not south."

Liam drives with his eyes flickering from the side mirror, to the rearview mirror, and then the other side mirror. So far so good, but for how long?

"Just a bit of tradecraft, that's all."

Lin says, "You do what we planned."

"Sorry, I don't remember the 'we' part, Lin. You were just giving orders. This isn't your op. It's mine. Hold on."

He takes an exit off the M1, slows down, and in another minute, Liam is slowly driving through the crowded parking lot of the Kelvin Village Shopping Centre. He goes up one row and then another, until he spots a black Jeep Cherokee with a neon-orange flyer stuck in a windshield wiper.

Liam pulls into a near space, switches off the engine.

Lin says, "What is this?"

"Change of vehicles," he says, opening the door. "I'm sure you gave this Mercedes a clean sweep earlier, but I didn't do it, so I don't trust the results. Hurry along."

He walks over to the Cherokee, finds the key fob in a small magnetic box under the driver's-side rear tire, pulls it free. Back at Director Abrams's residence, before he left, she promised she could help in a few areas, like this transportation. He unlocks the Cherokee, brings his gear to the rear of the vehicle, and helps Lin and Benjamin get into the rear seat.

Lin says, "What the hell is this?"

Liam is happy to see two shoeboxes and clothing in plastic bags. "New shoes and clothing for both of you. Don't take your time changing. I'll close the door for privacy. I'm not taking the chance that tracers are in your clothes."

He shuts the door.

Looks up into the cool June sky.

Nothing airborne up there yet.

Maybe he's being too cautious, but that's like saying there's too much bacon.

No one in the Agency ever says those words.

Lin opens the door, passes over a bulging plastic bag, which he tosses into the trunk of the Mercedes, and in a few minutes, he's driving the Cherokee and his two passengers back south on the M1.

Lin says, "You're still driving the wrong way."

"If you mean I'm driving away from your safe house, yeah, that's exactly what I'm doing."

Benjamin speaks up. "Liam...you can trust her..."

"No, I can't," he says. "Even with her shooting those two armed men back there. A good sign but I'm inherently suspicious, sorry. We're about an hour away from *my* safe house, which I can vouch for. In the meantime, Lin, get working on your end of the deal."

"What?"

"Your man is rescued," he says. "Time to make the call, to give up what's ailing the vice president."

"No," she says.

Liam feels something hard and cold punch his chest. If this was all a lie and a setup, just to get Benjamin freed without the quid pro quo of saving the vice president, he's about ten seconds from coming to a halt, opening the rear door, and shoving her out onto the busy highway.

"Better explain yourself, and now," he says.

Lin says, "Once we're safely in place at your facility, knowing we've not been followed, then I will make the call. Not sooner."

Liam chews his lower lip.

Lin says, "Don't like being on the other end, now, do you?"

He keeps quiet, just looking at the time, converting it to what must be early morning back in the District of Columbia.

Just what in hell might be going on back at home?

CHAPTER 113

IN HER HOME office in Georgetown, CIA Director Hannah Abrams is focused on the clock on her desk, a gift from years back from the head of MI6. It's a piece of tourist kitsch, the Big Ben clock and tower, done up in red, white, and blue, with a grinning bulldog sitting at its base.

Jean Swantish says, "Staring at it won't make it go any faster."

"It should," she says. "Liam's been on the ground for nearly a day, and not a word."

"That's what you wanted," Jean says. "For him to stay mission silent until he had Benjamin and the medical information for the vice president."

The clock says it's approaching eight a.m.

"Will it chime when it hits the top of the hour?"

Hannah says, "Thank God, no."

Then she smiles, taps the tower. "Test time. What is this?"

Jean says, "More like trick time. It's Big Ben, right?"

Hannah says, "Ha, I have you! Nope, Big Ben is the name of the clock. The name of the tower is the Elizabeth Tower. Even when everything is widely known, it can also still be wrong. Good thing to remember."

She keeps on looking at the clock, but there's a knock at the door, making her jump. *Keep your cool, girl, you're almost as jumpy as when you spent your first night at the Farm, wondering and dreading what was coming for you in the months ahead.*

"Come in," she says.

Ralph comes in, face tense. "Ma'am?"

"Yes?"

"We're under attack."

CHAPTER 114

THERE'VE BEEN SOME sharp words between Liam Grey and Lin, who is gently caressing Benjamin's forehead, but Benjamin doesn't care. He's lying down in the rear of the Cherokee, and even with the aches, throbs, and jolts of pain, he feels like he's in bliss. His legs are twisted some but his head is in Lin's lap. She looks down at him and smiles, her eyes filled with tears.

She whispers, "See, I told you I'd get you out."

"You did," he whispers back. "What now?"

"We leave South Africa. Liam says he will take care of it."

"I'm sure," he says. "You can trust him on that."

The Cherokee hits a pothole and Benjamin gasps with pain. She strokes his forehead again. He says, "When you say 'we,' you mean me, Liam, and you, right?"

Lin smiles, touches her lips with two fingers, gently presses them against his lips.

"Yes, Benjamin, that's exactly what I mean."

Liam drives, staying on a straight route, but every several minutes, taking an unplanned exit or turn, glancing at the rearview and side mirrors, checking for ground surveillance.

No.

So far, so good.

The city has given way to the countryside, with lots of farms and low trees and brush. Following the narrow two-lane R563 state road, they enter the small farming village of Hekpoort, about sixty klicks northwest of Johannesburg. At a dirt road next to a service station, Liam makes a left. The land is reddish dirt with some trees and barbed-wire fencing, with a mountain range to the north.

He says, "Sorry, Benjamin, it's going to be bumpy for a bit."

Lin says, "I'm holding him. He'll be all right."

Liam keeps his view moving left and right as they go down the remote road, until a small, one-story wood-and-dark-stone farmhouse comes into view, with an attached one-bay garage. He pulls the Cherokee into the garage, gets out, and swivels the door down.

The next few minutes are occupied with getting his gear into the interior of the cool house, as well as Benjamin and Lin. Liam helps Benjamin cross the stone floor and stretch out on a dusty couch near a fireplace. Throw rugs, heavy wooden chairs, and empty bookcases occupy the main room. A small kitchen is visible, along with two doors, one leading to a bathroom, and the other to a bedroom.

Snug and to the point, which is all they need, Liam thinks.

To Lin he says, "We weren't followed, and we've safely arrived at this place. Time for you to seal the deal, complete your side of the bargain. Make the call."

Lin says, "But I don't have the number."

Liam digs out his Agency-issued phone, thumbs the touch ID to bring it awake. He quickly scrolls through and finds the number for Director Abrams's home, and pushes it.

"Here," he says, passing the phone to Lin. "I'm calling Hannah Abrams, the CIA director. Be polite but get the damn message out."

Lin takes the phone, holds it up to her ear, waits, and returns the phone to Liam.

"You must have misdialed," she says. "It's not ringing."

"The hell I did."

"Then you call," she says.

Liam looks again at the number, then swipes the call feature.

He brings it up to his ear.

The phone rings once.

Then clicks off.

"Shit," he says.

He does it again.

Same thing.

One ring and the call doesn't go through.

He says, "Lin, you've got a phone?"

"Of course. A fresh burner so we couldn't be traced."

She pulls her device out of her purse and Liam displays the number for Director Abrams's house.

Same thing.

Lin says, "Just rings once and signs off."

"Damn it!" Liam says. He goes into the small kitchen, sees an old-fashioned phone up on the wall, complete with curling cord. He lifts the receiver and is relieved to hear a dial tone. Agency safe houses are equipped to receive—on zero notice—visitors in need of water, power, food, and now, most important, a landline.

Holding his Agency phone in one hand and cupping the receiver between his shoulder and right ear, he punches in the right sequence of numbers to get an international line to the United States.

There.

It rings once.

Twice.

He turns and smiles at Lin.

"I think we're going to make it."

The phone is answered. Liam hears a woman's voice and says, "I need to speak to Director Abrams, right away."

But the voice pays no attention.

"...no longer in service. No other information is available for this number. Good-bye."

Click.

Liam slowly replaces the receiver back to the wall phone's cradle.

"The director's been blocked," Liam says.

"Meaning?" Lin asks, while Benjamin looks up from the couch.

"She's dead, disabled, or captured," Liam says. "We're on our own."

CHAPTER 115

JOINT INTELLIGENCE CENTER PACIFIC

PEARL HARBOR, HAWAII

US NAVY LIEUTENANT Commander Cornelius Johnson is getting a cup of coffee in the small galley adjacent to the Pit when a scared-looking, young male ensign bursts in and says, "Sir, you need to come back, right away."

Cornelius leaves his coffee mug on the counter and follows the ensign up the slight ramp that goes up to the balcony level that holds his desk and others, and that overlooks the large video display screens and computer monitors.

He gets two steps into the darkened room before he freezes, looking at the displays, at the blinking and rapidly moving indicators, trying to keep it all in, trying to absorb what he's seeing.

His deputy, Marine Lieutenant Juanita Lopez, steps up to him, brown eyes worried. He says to her, "Lieutenant, please tell me that there's been a mistake, that we're watching a simulation, or a training exercise."

"No, sir," she says. "We've checked it twice. This is real time, this is happening."

Breathe, he thinks, looking at the flashing indicators marking the military forces of the People's Republic of China.

"Latest?" he asks.

"The PLA Navy is heading for open waters," she says. "Not a drill or exercise. Surface and submarine elements of the North Sea Fleet in Qingdao, the East Sea Fleet in Ningbo, and the South Sea Fleet in Zhanjiang are all heading out, at flank speed. Their naval air forces are also taking off."

"Taiwan?"

"Being ignored at the moment, it seems."

"What else?"

"Their strategic air force units are scrambling and are also departing their air bases."

"Their nuclear forces?"

"Still running that down."

His Marine deputy looks to his desk. "You might get additional information from your liaisons, sir."

"You're right," he says, going to his desk.

At his desk he picks up the phone linking him to the Pentagon's National Military Command Center, the command and communications center for the Department of Defense and the National Command Authority, i.e., President Keegan Barrett.

The phone rings once. A woman's voice states, "Major Juarez, NMCC Duty Officer."

"This is Lieutenant Commander Johnson, Joint Intelligence Center Pacific."

"Acknowledged."

"I have a Flash message. Ready?"

Her voice remains cool and steady. "Roger that."

"Our surveillance assets are reporting a major deployment of Chinese naval and air forces. The air forces seem to be dispersing to alternate landing fields. The naval forces are leaving port, heading to the open sea."

Cornelius looks up at the colored moving indicators up there, spreading out like a flower blossoming, each deadly petal heading for safety. Even in their most challenging test drills, he's never seen a deployment like this.

"Copy that," she says.

"We'll have a detailed report on numbers of air force and naval assets being deployed within a half hour."

"Copy that," the major says, voice still cool and composed, and Cornelius feels a bit of anger. *No wonder you're so cool, Major,* he thinks, *you're way over on the other side of the globe, far away from the Chinese strategic weapons force. Here, on the other hand, we're at ground zero for an upcoming second Pearl Harbor.*

"That's all for now," Cornelius says. "Signing off."

He hangs up the phone, feels like he's missing something, and he remembers that cup of coffee back in the kitchen area.

Screw that, he thinks. *With everything that's going on, I'm not about to send a junior officer back there, and I'm not about to move.*

He has a feeling he's not leaving his desk for a day or two.

He sits down, goes to the old-fashioned logbook, notes the time, and writes, "Alerted Major Juarez, NMCC, of current status."

The phone from the NSA rings and he instantly picks it up.

"Hey Corny, it's Tina," the familiar, kind voice from the NSA says. "Bet things are hopping over in your neck of the ocean. Give me a quick brief, will you?"

He gives her a bit more detailed report than the one given to the NMCC, for in the past minute or two, messages have been placed on his desk, giving details of the naval and air force movements taking place in and around China.

Tina says, "Sure jibes with what we're hearing over here."

"Which is what?"

"Nothing good," she says. "Our SIGINT resources are showing massive army movements and mobilizations taking place in all urban centers in the country, and they're all calling up reserves, and members of the Chinese People's Armed Police Force."

"Heading anywhere interesting, like Tibet or India?" he asks.

"Hell, no, internal only. Like they're preparing for massive internal unrest or disorder."

"Shit," he says.

"Yeah, and one more thing 'cause I like you, Corny," she says. "Our friends down the way— the National Cybercommand—are busy swapping reports and warnings. Based on the chatter and what we can see through our online snoopers, our counterparts in Beijing are getting ready for a massive cyberattack on everything and anything that's hooked up to a computer."

"When?" he asks.

"Could be an hour, could be a day, but it's coming," she says.

Cornelius says, "But for fuck's sake, what's triggering this? This can't be a bolt-out-of-the-blue attack. With all their military deployments and battle prep in cyberspace, they're practically telling us what they're about to do."

"Maybe it's the biggest warning in the world, telling us to stop whatever it is we're doing. Question is, Corny, is who's out there on our side listening."

A pause and Tina says, "Well, got to get back to work. War's coming today . . . hope you're deep enough and have enough MREs to ride it out, Corny. Wish we had gotten the chance to meet face-to-face."

The phone clicks off. He should feel melancholy at Tina's last words but looking up at the screens and seeing the messages pile up on his desk, he has no time for that.

War is coming.

CHAPTER 116

CIA DIRECTOR HANNAH Abrams says, "Under attack in what way?"

Her security officer Ralph says, "All of our communications systems, from telephones to radios, are being jammed or have been disabled."

Jean Swantish says, "I thought that was impossible."

Hannah picks up one phone, and then another, and then a third.

Not even a dial tone.

"Improbable," she says, "but not impossible. All the secure phones are installed and maintained by the Agency's communications support group. Someone over in Langley got the word and multiple plugs were pulled. My guess, it was President Barrett to one of his loyalists."

Jean takes out her cell phone, starts sliding through the screen.

"Nothing," she says.

For years Hannah has loved this house of hers, with a small yard and stone walls and fences all around, in a safe and historic part of Georgetown. With her advancement to CIA director, she secretly welcomed the added security and protection. She felt like it was her little bubble of safety, in a world increasingly dangerous and disorganized.

Now the bubble of safety is broken.

To Ralph she says, "Anything else going on out there?"

"The street's practically unpassable with all of the double-parked police vehicles out there, including a white van that's probably the source of our phone blockage."

Hannah says, "No chance you'd go out there and blow it up?"

Ralph doesn't smile. "Beyond the scope of our duties, ma'am."

Jean says, "What now, Director? We're isolated, trapped, and we don't know what Liam might be doing in South Africa, if he's doing anything."

A short, dark-haired woman—Gina Stasio of the Agency's Technical Services Division, and Noa's friend—raps on the doorframe and steps in. "Sorry to bother you, Director, but Noa needs to see you, right away. Something's going on."

Upstairs in the spare bedroom, Noa is sitting up in one of the beds as Gina, Ralph, and Jean walk in.

Noa points to a low bureau on the other side of the room and says, "Director, you need to see this."

"This" is a portable television with an over-the-air antenna Hannah had gotten two years ago, when a sudden series of windstorms had knocked out power and utilities to this part of DC for nearly a week. She couldn't stand being out of touch for such a length of time, and the small TV was purchased and nearly instantly forgotten.

Until now.

Noa says, "Turn it up. It looks bad."

Jean goes over and NBC News is on live feed, split screen. A worried-looking male anchor is speaking as Jean turns up the volume.

"...what you're seeing here is a live shot of the Chinese embassy on International Place Northwest, where diplomats and staff are apparently burning their papers and files."

Two lines of smoke are rising from a fenced-in and concrete-walled compound with boxy and triangular-shaped concrete buildings.

"Attempts to contact the embassy for comments have been unsuccessful. There's also been no word from the White House or the State Department as to why the Chinese are taking such an extraordinary step. Hold on...please...we've just received word that the same thing is happening at the five other consulates that the Chinese maintain in the United States..."

Jean says, "Director, the last time something like this happened was back in 1962, during the Cuban Missile Crisis, when the Soviets did the same thing at their embassy. That means they're anticipating war breaking out, and soon."

Hannah checks her watch.

No more waiting.

"Ralph, I don't care if the DC National Guard is out there," she says. "We're leaving."

Noa speaks up, face still pale. "Director, before you leave . . . we need to talk."

"Is it important?"

Her friend Gina says, "Very important, Director. And helpful."

CHAPTER 117

TO LIN, LIAM Grey says, "You still have to honor your deal."

"How?" she says. "We can't contact your director. It's up to you, not me, to establish contact with someone."

From the couch Benjamin Lucas says, "Liam? How about the local station chief?"

He shakes his head. "Time. I contact the station chief, it takes a while to establish my bona fides. We pass along Lin's information. That gets kicked over to Langley. It's reviewed, evaluated, discussed at a committee. Then it gets run upstairs to the seventh floor, to the director. But where's the director?"

Liam stalks over to the narrow windows overlooking the yard. The dirt road leading out to the paved road and the service station, gnarled trees, red dirt, and broken-down fencing and rusting barbed wire.

Benjamin says, "Lin. It's up to you."

She folds her arms, seemingly in defiance. "Why?"

He coughs. "Because I'm asking you, Lin. Liam did his part. With your help, he got me freed. Please."

Liam stares at them both. *Is this how this op is going to be saved? Not because of planning or weapons or tradecraft, because of an old relationship, of affection and love?*

He is sure that any of his deceased instructors from the Farm are now whirling so fast in their graves that the US Geological Survey could detect them.

Benjamin says, "Please. For me."

Lin stands still and looks over to Liam.

Her still, brown eyes look into his.

"Can you do it?" Liam asks.

She says, "If I do, it's for Benjamin. Not you or your country."

"I don't care if you do it for your favorite aunt. Will you?"

Another heavy pause.

"I will," she says.

"How?" Liam asks.

"Does it make a difference?"

Liam says, "You bet it does. I want to know how and to whom you're passing along this information."

She says, "Someone I've been running since he

was at the Stanford School of Medicine. He's come up a long way since then."

"Where is he now?"

Lin takes a breath. "Walter Reed Hospital. In Bethesda. Maryland. I'm sure he can pass this information along to the team taking care of the vice president."

"Do it now," Liam says. "And do it in English. I want to listen in."

Lin takes out her phone. "Still not trusting?"

"It's my nature, and it's my training," Liam says. "I don't know if you're running something deep, some kind of wheels within wheels, or some complicated honey trap. I just don't know. But know this."

Benjamin is looking on, uncomfortable. Lin asks, "And what's that?"

"Make the call," Liam says. "But if you're not telling the truth, if this is some scam, and if what you pass along ends up making things worse for the vice president, I'll kill you."

Surprising Liam, the next sentence comes from his fellow CIA operator.

Benjamin says, "You'll have to kill me, too, Liam."

"I accept your terms," Liam says. "Lin, get to work."

CHAPTER 118

IT'S GOING TO be crowded this morning in the president's private office in the family quarters, and Keegan Barrett minds it not a whit. Right now it's just Carlton Pope and himself. Barrett says, "Are you certain that Abrams can't communicate from her home?"

Carlton smiles. "Not a chance. We've borrowed radio and cell phone–blocking devices from our friends at the FBI. The secure lines between her house and Langley have also been disabled. The DC police are waiting outside on her street, ready to arrest anyone stepping out."

"Noa Himel?"

"She's in the house, wounded. She won't be leaving anytime soon."

"Liam Grey?"

Carlton says, "Wandering around South Africa it seems, heading to Johannesburg. It seems he hopped a ride from the Air Force, some general who owed Abrams a favor."

"What the hell is he doing there?"

Carlton says, "Best guess is that he might be trying to retrieve Benjamin Lucas. From the Chinese. By himself."

Barrett laughs. "If he pulls that off, I'll appoint him director. There's going to be a vacancy by this time tomorrow."

A knock on the door.

"All right," Barrett says. "Let our guests in. We've no time to waste."

Carlton opens the door and a male Army four-star general walks in, along with a female Army colonel. They are dressed in the new Army green service uniforms, introduced a few years back in homage to similar uniforms worn by the Greatest Generation back in World War II. In Barrett's eyes, they've stepped out of a game of make-believe from 1944.

Barrett stands up, walks around his desk, buttons his light-blue jacket. "Thank you both for coming."

He shakes the hand of General Henry Peterson, head of the United States Cybercommand, then Colonel Karen Yankins, his deputy. He's tanned, with short black hair and brown eyes. Yankins is about a foot shorter, with closely trimmed blond hair, wearing plain black-rimmed glasses.

"Please," he says, pointing to the couch. "Have a seat. How was your flight up from Fort Meade?"

"Reasonable, Mr. President," Peterson says. "No complaints."

The colonel just nods.

Peterson's carrying a briefcase, and the colonel has two heavy-looking black satchels. As they sit down, the satchels and briefcase are placed on the floor next to them. Barrett takes the couch, pointing up to Carlton.

"This is Carlton Pope, my special assistant. He's at my side every day, morning to night. He has my ultimate trust, so I have no hesitation discussing what we're about to say in front of him. All right?"

The two Army officers nod.

"Good," Barrett says. "General Peterson, I'm aware that the Cybercommand has in its possession, a cyber-offense plan called Case Shanghai. Correct?"

"Yes, sir," Peterson says. "We ran a simulated war game with that same scenario in December."

"Was it a successful war game?"

Peterson says, "Mr. President, well, the means of declaring a success is a variable, meaning that there are certain outcomes we look for in such an exercise. If you'd like, I could prepare an overview of the war game's results."

Barrett says, "That won't be necessary."

"Sir?"

"At twelve hundred hours today, General Peterson, the United States Cybercommand will commence Case Shanghai against the People's Republic of China. That is a direct order. Do you understand?"

Peterson seems shocked, and so does Colonel Yankins.

"Sir?"

Barrett softly says, "I said, the United States Cybercommand will commence Case Shanghai against the People's Republic of China at twelve hundred hours today. That's in just under three hours. Do you understand my order?"

The general says, "Yes, sir."

Finally, it's all coming together, that voice inside of him says. The same voice that told him years back he was destined to greatness, to be chosen to save his country. What that voice said is being confirmed at this very moment.

"Good. Let's begin."

CHAPTER 119

IN HER ATTACHED garage, CIA Director Hannah Abrams takes a deep breath, and then steps into the rear of her armored Chevrolet Suburban, her leather briefcase in her right hand. She's not alone back there, and she pats the hand of her companion, Jean, as Ralph settles in on the other side.

Two other security officers—Alec and Walter—take their places up front.

The garage door opens, the Suburban starts up, and on the cobblestoned driveway, the second CIA Suburban—the blocking car—moves forward. The metal gate at the end of the driveway slides open.

In her years in the CIA, Hannah has driven hundreds of times to Langley or other government locations, but she knows this trip is going to be a memorable one, and she's not disappointed.

The lead Suburban—flashing red and blue

lights in the radiator grille and on the top of the windshield—goes to the left, and the Suburban she's in follows. As the gate behind her starts to close, DC police officers in tactical gear step out, hands up, in front of her Suburban.

"Ma'am?" comes the voice of Alec, the driver.

"As we discussed," she says.

"Very well."

Her Suburban stops.

The lead one ahead also stops.

One of the armed DC cops steps forward, gestures for the window to be lowered. Alec does so.

"Alec," Hannah says. "Lower *all* the windows. I don't want any misunderstandings."

"Yes, ma'am."

"And put your hands on the steering wheel."

He doesn't say anything but Hannah can tell from his tense neck and shoulders that he'd rather not do that.

But Alec follows her orders, and his large hands are now on the steering wheel.

Another armed DC cop approaches the Suburban, but he's dressed in black uniform pants, white dress shirt, and a uniform cap. A ballistic vest is over his torso, and Hannah thinks he's overreacting, but then recalling the firepower in this Suburban and the other, maybe he's being cautious.

He takes his time approaching, peering into the

open windows, and when he comes close enough, Hannah calls out, "Is there a problem, officer?"

He doesn't take the bait. He's wearing lieutenant bars on his collar and his name tag says BROOKS.

The police lieutenant says, "I'm looking for Noa Himel."

Hannah slowly pulls out her ID. "I'm Hannah Abrams, Director of the Central Intelligence Agency."

His face is drawn but red, like he's trying to control his temper. "I know who you are."

"Thanks," Hannah says. "I guess those Sunday morning talk shows have paid off for me. This is my deputy, Jean Swantish. Jean, show him your identification."

"Absolutely." She reaches into her soft leather case, pulls out her CIA identification, and passes it to Hannah, who in turn gives it to Lieutenant Brooks. He gives it a close look, passes it back, and then he peers again into the Suburban.

"Lieutenant, if you'd like, I have no objection to you looking into my two vehicles, but I promise you that Noa Himel is not with us."

Lieutenant Brooks says, "Noa Himel is wanted for questioning regarding a hit-and-run yesterday, leaving the scene of an accident, threatening a resident with a handgun, and about a half dozen other violations."

"As I said, feel free to look through the Suburbans,

but make it quick, if you can," Hannah says. "I need to get to Langley as soon as possible. I'm sure you've heard the news this morning, of the Chinese embassy burning their diplomatic papers?"

He says, "Yes, I'd like to take a quick look in your vehicles."

"Alec," Hannah says, "be a dear and help out Lieutenant Brooks, will you?"

Her driver gets out and walks up to the first Suburban, to talk to that driver, and the doors and the rear hatchback pop open. Alec returns and in a moment, Hannah's vehicle mirrors the first one.

The tactical-clad cops do make a quick search—one whistling in appreciation at the weapons mounted in racks at the rear—and when the searches are over and the doors and hatchbacks close, the police lieutenant comes back. A number of Hannah's neighbors are standing on the narrow sidewalks, looking on.

"We all set?" Hannah asks.

"No," he says. "Is Noa Himel still in your house? And if not, do you know where she is?"

Hannah smiles. "Feel free to call 703-482-0623 and ask for the CIA's general counsel's office. I'm sure they'd love to be of assistance. In the meantime, I have nothing to say, and nobody's entering the grounds of my home without a warrant."

Brooks says, "I can hold you as a material witness."

Hannah puts a hand on the window frame and gestures the police lieutenant to come closer, which he does.

She lowers her voice, "My dad was a cop for the Capitol Hill Police force, and my mom was a senior clerk for the DC Police. I have the greatest affection and respect for law enforcement, Lieutenant Brooks, but right now you and your officers are keeping me from doing my job. Things are slipping away out there and I need to stop them, and that means, if you and your men don't step away, right now, I'll instruct my security officers to drive right through you. And don't think they won't."

The lieutenant works his jaw. She adds, "Now, have I made myself clear?"

He doesn't say a word. Backs away, barks out a few words, and whirls a hand in the air. The armed police in tactical gear back away.

Hannah rolls up her window, lets out a breath.

The two Suburbans resume their drive.

She says, "For once there was a policeman around when you needed one. Alec, step on it. Not a minute to waste."

CHAPTER 120

IN HIS PRIVATE office, President Keegan Barrett keeps his focus on the two Army officers from the US Cybercommand who are sitting across from him, who are like cocked weapons, ready to be discharged at his imminent command.

He hasn't felt this good and focused since November, when the state of Wisconsin's electoral college votes had gotten him past that magic number of 270. Like that night, he feels like every sense he has is heightened, that he knows America has chosen him to settle accounts with its greatest emerging threat, and the voice inside of him that promised greatness is right once more.

General Peterson says, "Mr. President, with all due respect, this is a major offensive move. Has it been discussed with the National Security Council?"

"Of course it has," he says, easily lying.

"And have the leaders of both the Senate and House been informed?"

"An hour ago, of course."

"Secretary of Defense Williams?"

"I talked to him last night, just as he was getting up in Singapore and heading to Japan."

General Peterson pauses. "And General Wyman?"

"The Joint Chiefs Chairman was briefed about thirty minutes ago. He told me that our conventional forces are ready to respond if there's a force retaliation from China."

General Peterson pauses, and Barrett just knows what's going on within that four-star general's mind. The general is concerned about what his commander in chief is about to order, but POTUS has assured him that all the necessary notifications, briefings, and decisions have been made.

Peterson is in a position where he has to believe POTUS is acting under proper advice and authority.

He can't refuse to obey the orders, can't excuse himself for an hour or so to make the necessary phone calls to see if the president really has made the necessary phone calls.

Peterson just can't.

He has to trust the president of the United States. This president is under no media pressure from earlier actions or statements, is high up in the polls, and is not a defeated president looking to lash out at his enemies before departing the White House.

Plus Barrett knows this man. When Barrett was secretary of defense, he made sure that General Peterson—who shares his own concerns about the Chinese—was on a fast career track and would end up in charge of Cybercommand at this vital moment.

The vice president is in a coma, the secretary of state and secretary of defense are both overseas, and the last Barrett heard, the speaker of the House is on an aircraft, heading back to California, to drum up support before she's expelled from House leadership.

He is utterly and completely alone, and in command.

"Very well, Mr. President," he says. "Colonel Yankins, please prepare the communications system."

The colonel takes one of the black satchel-like carriers, unzips it open, and folds it out. There is a keyboard and switches and a small display screen in a rectangular instrument, nestled in gray foam, on the right side. She touches a switch and the keyboard and screen light up. In the other side of the satchel is an accordion-type folder.

This is a cousin of the famous "football," the communications system that can launch a nuclear strike. That nuclear football is a few yards away, in a hallway outside of this office, in possession of a Marine major. Little known to the news media and elsewhere, a second football was secretly developed two years ago, to address cybersecurity and cyberattacks.

Barrett intends to use that lack of knowledge to his benefit, and that of the country.

General Peterson says, "Case Shanghai, correct, Mr. President?"

"That's correct."

"Colonel?"

She opens up the folder, pulls out a letter-sized plastic-protected sheet. It has the logo of the United States Cybercommand at the top, with borders marked in red and black. Various stamps and signatures are at the bottom, along with the bold red words TOP SECRET / SENSITIVE COMPARTMENTED INFORMATION.

General Peterson takes the sheet. "Mr. President, per protocol, I need to confirm that you are cognizant of the cyberattack profile contained in Case Shanghai."

"Proceed," Barrett says.

General Peterson clears his throat. "Once we receive the appropriate activation code, Mr. President, our offensive capabilities will commence crippling the command-and-control systems of the People's Liberation Army, including its five service branches: the Ground Force, Navy, Air Force, Rocket Force, and the Strategic Support Force. Soon after their communications systems are offline, the next wave of offensive operations will attack their military's infrastructure from electricity to logistical support up to and including POL facilities. Any questions so far, Mr. President?" POL is petroleum, oil, lubricant.

"No," Barrett says, the excitement and knowledge of what he's about to unleash practically making his hands nearly quiver in anticipation.

"Following those actions, the third wave will go against the twenty-one government ministries, from the Ministry of Foreign Affairs to the Ministry of Culture and Tourism. The fourth wave will target the largest banks and financial institutions in China—including all overseas branches—and lastly, all foreign embassies and overseas consulates. Any questions, sir?"

"No," Barrett says.

Barrett looks over. Carlton Pope stands silently in the corner of the tiny office, arms folded, a pleased smile on his face.

"Sir...for my own confidence level, I just want to ensure that you realize the scope of this attack," the general says. "By this time tomorrow, the world's financial systems will be in free fall, there will be widespread panic and disturbances in Chinese urban centers, and the Chinese military and their cyber capabilities will be coming for our throat."

"I understand, General Peterson," Barrett says.

"Considering we spend about $750 billion on defense each year, including $2.6 billion for cyber defensive and offensive capabilities, I know we will hold our own. As to our adversaries, they are going to learn a quick lesson when they grow too fast, push too much, against us and the standard world order."

Silence for a few heavy seconds.

Barrett says, "What now?"

From the inside of his uniform jacket, General Peterson removes a piece of blue plastic, about twice the size of a credit card. "Sir, you're going to need your authorization card. Once the codes are matched and verified, then your orders will be enacted at twelve hundred hours today."

Barrett also pulls out his blue plastic card, known for some reason as "the biscuit."

"Any questions now, Mr. President?"

Barrett smiles in triumph. "No. Proceed."

CHAPTER 121

LIAM GREY IS sitting on a chair in the living room of the safe house, as Chin Lin sits next to Benjamin Lucas on the couch and tries again to reach her contact at Walter Reed Hospital.

Two earlier calls went to voicemail and as she makes the third call, Liam says, "You have a backup plan if you can't get through?"

Lin says, "Yeah, calling in a film crew from SABC and make a live broadcast from this place's dirt driveway. Shut up, will you?"

Benjamin says, "Please, Liam, let her work."

Work? Liam thinks. *Damn Chinese intelligence officer is playing dial-a-spy and for all we know, it's still part of a ploy, a setup.*

The phone starts to ring and Liam says, "And how did you happen to get in possession of this vital information, Lin?"

"Stole it from my father."

"Stolen or given?"

"Stolen," she says. "I hate him for what he's doing to my mother, not paying attention to her when she started feeling sick."

The phone rings again, and again, and is picked up. "Hello?" a male voice says. "Who's this?"

"Charlie!" Lin says, and Liam is impressed at how her voice rises in both pitch and excitement. "This is Sally Yoo."

"Um, hey, Sally, you know...I really don't feel comfortable talking to you on my regular cell. Is something wrong?"

She says, "Charlie, please, I have something important to tell you, something that must be passed on to someone in authority at Walter Reed. Can you do that?"

"Depends, I guess, Sally," he says. "What is it, and who do you want to get it?"

"It must be given to the most senior person in strict confidence, do you understand? It can't be traced back to me."

Liam thinks, *Right, traced back to one Sally Yoo, who probably only exists in a computer file somewhere in Beijing.*

"Gee, Sally, you're starting to scare me. It's nothing illegal, is it?"

"Oh, Charlie, it's so very important to you and your country," she says. "This information has to be given to whoever's in charge of the medical team taking care of Vice President Hernandez."

Charlie doesn't answer.

"C'mon, Charlie, I'll make it worth your while. Twice the monthly payment next week?"

A sigh. "Okay. That'd be great. I thought for sure that the Yankees would win yesterday and—"

Liam glares at Lin as she says, "You know I don't understand baseball. Are you ready to take notes?"

"Yeah."

"Great. I'll take it slow. Here we go . . ."

Liam listens in amazement as Lin describes in slow and steady detail how Vice President Laura Hernandez was poisoned, what she was poisoned with, and what steps need to be taken to free her from her coma.

When Lin appears to be finished, Liam mouths, *Make sure he's got it. And have him read it back to you.*

"Charlie, did you get that last bit? Can you read this back to me?"

The cell phone's little speaker hisses.

Benjamin slowly gets off the couch and mouths, *Need some water. Be right back.*

He limps off to the small kitchen.

Lin says, "Charlie, you still there?"

Nothing.

Lin examines the screen and says, "I've been

disconnected."

Liam's throat tightens. "Call him back. Now."

Her fingers work and she looks up at him, face worried. "I can't get a signal."

Liam pulls his own phone out.

No signal at all.

"Benjamin!"

"Yo!"

"Pick up the house phone. Tell me if you've got a signal."

A few seconds pass.

"Not a thing." Benjamin limps in, sipping from a glass of water.

He stops.

"Hey, Liam."

"What?"

"We got visitors."

Liam gets up and looks out the main window of the small farmhouse.

Three black Range Rovers are parked on the dirt driveway, just beyond the gate; armed men with helmets, black jumpsuits, and ballistic vests are jumping out, taking position.

Lin says, "Oh, no."

"Well?" Benjamin asks.

Liam says, "If you ever wondered what it felt like to be with Davy Crockett at the Alamo, you're about to find out."

CHAPTER 122

BUT BEFORE GENERAL Peterson can proceed as ordered, there's a knock on the door, and another, and the door swings open.

Barrett's chief of staff, Quinn Lawrence, steps in, looking concerned, his face pale.

"Mr. President, I'm sorry to interrupt you, but you've got an urgent message," he says.

"Quinn," Barrett says, "Can't you see I'm busy?"

"I know, sir, but Deputy Secretary of Defense Kim wants to talk to you. He says it's extremely important."

"It'll have to wait," Barrett says. "I'll reach out to him when I'm available."

"Mr. President, I really must insist," he says. "The deputy secretary is desperate to talk to you."

"And I'm telling you he'll have to wait."

Barrett watches and is stunned as his chief of staff apparently grows a pair.

He walks up to his desk, picks up the phone, and says, "With all due respect, Mr. President, you've got to take this call. The Chinese embassy and its consulates are burning their papers. Chinese military forces are on the move. The situation is precarious."

Barrett watches in amazement as his chief of staff actually puts his hand on one of the telephone handsets at his desk. Barrett gets up from the couch and slaps his hand over Quinn Lawrence's. It feels soft and flabby and he again wonders why he had placed such a cipher in a position of power.

Because of this day, he reminds himself. Where he had to make this important decision on his own, with no naysayers, no backbiters present.

Barrett says, "Quinn. Take your hand away or I'll break it. Got it?"

It seems like Quinn Lawrence is about to tear up. Barrett gently lifts his hand a few millimeters and Quinn's hand follows, and then his chief of staff steps back.

Barrett smiles with reassurance. "Quinn, it's all right. Go back and tell the deputy secretary of defense that I will get back to him in due course."

Quinn looks to the quiet Carlton Pope standing in the corner, and to the two silent and uncomfortable Army officers. Like he's looking for reassurance or support.

But he gets nothing.

"It's important," he says. "It's very, very important."

"I'm sure it is," Barrett says. "Now. Leave me be."

Quinn turns and leaves the office. Barrett sits back on the couch, across from General Peterson and Colonel Yankins.

"General," Barrett says. "Where were we?"

CHAPTER 123

WITH A FIRM and determined voice, General Peterson says, "Are you ready to proceed with the authorization?"

"Yes, General, I am."

"Sir, would you please activate your authorization card?"

"With pleasure," he says, picking up the blue plastic card. Another one in his possession is red, marking the one to be used for the nuclear football. He snaps it in half, revealing a stiff sheet of white paper. It has the correct month and year, and the dates running down in a column to the left. Each date has a row of letters and numbers to the right.

General Peterson does the same with his own blue plastic card.

Barrett says, "Today's date is the twelfth."

"Confirmed."

"Today's code is one niner alpha alpha eight six bravo yankee two."

General Peterson says, "Confirming, one niner alpha alpha eight six bravo yankee two."

"Confirmed."

"Mr. President, what is the challenge word?"

"General, the challenge word is *Potomac*."

"I confirm," he says. "Challenge word is *Potomac*."

General Peterson lowers the card.

"Sir, according to procedure, I now need you to officially issue your orders."

With his voice strong and unyielding, Barrett says, "General Peterson, at twelve hundred hours today, you will issue orders to execute Case Shanghai."

"Yes, sir," he says, no hesitation.

And in another surprise, Colonel Yankins speaks up. "Mr. President, I—"

"Colonel, that's enough," Peterson says.

"No, no," Barrett says. "Let her speak. Go ahead, Colonel Yankins."

Her eyes flicker right to her superior officer, and Barrett knows what she's thinking: she's about to commit career suicide, but she has to say something.

He knows what she's going to say, but feeling generous, he lets her say it anyway.

"Mr. President, I...excuse me for being so up front, but I want to make sure you've thought through the major impacts this decision will have not only on China and the world economy, but also on the United States," she says, voice nearly shaking. "It has the possibility of causing irreparable harm to our economy…and our way of life."

Barrett says, "I've thought it through. And have had in-depth discussions with the secretary of the treasury and my council of economic advisers, and I'm assured that we will be able to ride out the Chinese response with minimal impacts."

He waits a moment, then says, "I'm taking on this heavy responsibility, Colonel Yankins. The Chinese government takes the long view, planning ahead fifty years or a century. We act now, before they are in a position to cripple us, we can knock them down for a hundred years, letting those who succeed me have opportunities and chances to make sure they never threaten us again."

The colonel's voice is quiet. "I see, sir. But it seems the Chinese are already on the move."

Barrett says, "They are always on the move against our nation. In attacking the United States, they are attacking me, personally. And I won't let that stand. The American people elected me to keep them safe. I will do anything and everything to make that happen."

CHAPTER 124

CARLTON POPE IS walking back to his office, feeling tingly, excited, looking forward to the events later this day. For years he's been treated like crap, from reform school to the Army, until that day in Kosovo when he was in serious hack, and the former Army officer back there had saved him. From that moment Pope had worked tirelessly for Barrett Keegan, following his orders, following that man's dreams, and spilling lots of blood in the process.

One of his burner phones starts vibrating in his suit jacket pocket and as he goes into his office—usually the one closest to the Oval Office is reserved for the chief of staff, but not in this administration—he closes the door behind him and answers the phone.

"Pope."

It sounds like the caller is outside. "This is Morgan. Metro Police."

"Yeah?"

"Your target is mobile. Said she was heading to work."

Good, Pope thinks. If she's at Langley she can be ignored, allies of Barrett can screw up her communications, and she can be kept occupied with memos to be signed, reports to be read, meetings that need to be attended.

"Thanks for the heads-up."

Morgan says, "Do you want me to go on, or keep on cutting me off?"

"What?"

"She told my idiot lieutenant that she was going to Langley. She's not going to Langley, or any other place in Virginia. I'm following her right now."

Pope says, "Where is she headed?"

"Don't know," he says. "But I've got a guess."

"Tell me."

The Metro cop on his payroll says, "Pennsylvania Avenue. Looks like she's going to visit your boss."

Shit.

"Do what you can to stop her or delay her," Pope says.

He disconnects the call, pacing around his office twice, squeezing the burner phone hard.

That damn woman.

If only the bitch had waited her turn for her confirmation, this wouldn't be happening.

Instead, she had to bully Senate Majority Leader Cleveland Hogan and get her sneaky ass into Langley, where she started poking around in programs and people better left alone.

Now what?

Time to settle it.

He takes out another burner phone, scrolls through his contacts, until he finds another one of his unofficial supporters out here in the District of Columbia, stationed at various office buildings and hotels, kept on a monthly retainer for moments just like this.

And true believers like him and the president.

He makes the call.

It's answered before the second ring.

"Turner," the man says.

"It's Pope," he says. "I've got an emerging job that's urgent."

"How urgent?"

"Like the next ten minutes urgent."

"All right," Turner says. "If it helps you and the president, I'm in. Time, location, and target?"

"About ten minutes. The West Wing access gate to the White House, West Executive Avenue. Target is Hannah Abrams, CIA Director."

A low whistle. "Aiming pretty high, Carlton."

"You got a problem?"

"No, never did like the CIA," he says. "A pussy organization if I ever saw one. But you know she'll be driving up there in an armored vehicle. Sorry, I don't have a rocket launcher in my possession."

"That's all right," Pope says. "I'll be at the gate, making sure she gets out of her vehicle."

The assassin laughs. "It'll be a hell of a shot, but I can make it."

"Then do it."

"Consider it done."

CHAPTER 125

FROM A VAULT hidden in one of the bedroom's closets, Liam Grey comes out with a pair of binoculars. Goes to the near living room window and focuses in on the armed men emptying out of the three Range Rovers.

Benjamin says, "What have we got?"

"We got twelve apparent hostiles," Liam says, watching them spread out. "Well armed. Trained. But no IDs on the vehicles or the men."

Benjamin says, "Contract force."

"Yeah."

Lin says, "Who do you think?"

Liam lowers the binoculars. "Not to be rude, Lin, but I'm pretty sure their paycheck comes from your side of the world."

Benjamin says, "What are you thinking?"

"Time to arm up," he says.

To Lin he says, "And you? As one sad former president once said, are you with us or against us?"

Lin says, "With Benjamin."

"Close enough," Liam says.

Back to the vault, and in a number of minutes, the three of them are wearing ballistic vests and each is armed with an M4 automatic rifle, with six magazines apiece.

Liam goes back to the window.

"They're still there, stretched out in a skirmish line," he says. "Not moving. Lin, check out the kitchen, there's a window looking to the rear. Want to make sure we don't have another group coming up that way."

"All right," Lin says. She goes to the small kitchen, peers out the small rear window over the sink. "All clear back here."

Liam waits.

Benjamin walks up to him. "Well?"

"Still waiting. Is there such a thing as a South African standoff?"

"If there is, we're about to find out."

A black Mercedes-Benz sedan comes up the dirt road, parks behind the line of Range Rovers. The four doors open and three well-dressed men look out, and then a fourth man steps out. There's a brief conversation and the fourth man starts walking alone up the dirt road.

All four men are Chinese.

"Lin?" Liam asks. "Borrow you for a moment?"

Lin comes into the living room and Liam hands over the set of binoculars.

"Check out that man coming our way," Liam says. "Know him?"

She puts the binoculars up to her eyes, and then quickly lowers them.

"That's Han Yuanchao," she says. "The intelligence *rezident* at our embassy in Johannesburg. My boss."

Liam nods. "That's damn awkward."

CHAPTER 126

THE SECOND SCARIEST event in Tucker Wyman's life was when he was in the 82nd Airborne, and his main chute tangled up during a night drop over the Holland Drop Zone at Fort Bragg. He worked hard to get the lines free but it wasn't working, then the damn reserve chute was jammed some-how, and in the darkness all he knew was that he was approaching the unforgiving earth with just seconds to spare.

One more tug and the reserve popped open, late but still good enough to let him land and survive, with one broken foot and one broken ankle.

That had been some scary shit.

But that was fun and games compared to what he's seeing in the National Military Command Center at the Pentagon, now as General Tucker Wyman, Chairman of the Joint Chiefs of Staff.

The phones are ringing, the display boards are lit

up, and more support staff are streaming in as he and others on the Joint Chiefs of Staff are trying to figure out why in hell China is on the move this morning.

The NMCC is a labyrinth of rooms and conference centers deep into the basement of the Pentagon. General Wyman is in the Current Actions Center, where the latest information from the DoD's elaborate network of surveillance ships, aircraft, and satellites feed through in real time.

The information this morning is coming quick at him and the members of the J-3 (Operations) Directorate. A woman Navy commander comes up to him and says, "Sir, it looks like everything the Chinese can fly, float, and drive are heading out of port, bases, and airfields. I've never seen anything like it, even in simulations."

Wyman says, "Do we have contact with the SecDef?"

"No, sir," she says. "Communication problems in his aircraft over Japan. Might be electronic interference from the Northern Lights...there's a heavy solar storm screwing up transmissions. The deputy secretary is on his way here."

Wyman hears the low voices, the tapping of the keyboards, the ringing of the phones, but his experienced eyes are up on the screens, showing a massive Chinese exodus of military forces from their bases.

The vice chairman of the JCS, Marine General Wade Thompson, comes to him and says, "Never seen anything like it, sir."

"What in hell prompted this? Do we have any action reports? Aircraft encounters? Ship collisions? Inadvertent missile firing?"

"Nothing," he says.

"Any of our surveillance aircraft go off course?"

"No, sir," he says.

"And we don't have a Freedom of Navigation Drill going on near Taiwan or the disputed islands? That usually gets them wound up, but nothing like this."

"All quiet on that end for now," the vice chairman says.

Like all military officers of a certain age, Wyman knows his military history. He recalls how things quickly got out of hand during the early days leading up to the outbreak of World War I: panicked generals and leaders had to get their armies on the move first, afraid their enemies would strike first, and the Austrians, Serbians, Germans, Russians, Italians, French, and English soon fell into a maelstrom that killed millions.

If only someone could have nipped that chain of events in the bud before it got out of hand.

Like now.

To the vice chairman, Wyman says, "I'm going to duck into the Comm Room. See if I can chat with my counterpart. Hold down the fort here until I come back."

"Yes, sir," the vice chairman says.

A few minutes later, accompanied by his assistant, Colonel Doug Leonard, Wyman enters a cool, slightly darkened room, subdivided into two offices. The one on the right maintains the original hotline between the United States and Russia, begun in 1963, which evolved from teletype to faxes to secure emails.

The room on the left holds the latest hotline, set up in 2008, maintaining communications between Washington and Beijing. But this hotline isn't as robust as its older brother. It's a voice-only system, which can lead to awkward moments and silences.

He opens the door and he and his aide go in. Two female and one male Air Force NCO stand up when they spot him, and he motions them back to their seats. Before them is a communication console with computer screens and three telephones.

"I need to reach Beijing," he says. "Now. Make the call."

"Yes, sir," the male NCO says, handing over a headset, which Wyman puts on. The older female picks up the phone and through the headset, Wyman hears the ringing of the phone.

The other noncommissioned officer serves as a

translator, as the line is picked up, nearly seven thousand miles away.

"Zhongnanhai," the NCO says, repeating what he's hearing, and Wyman knows it's the Zhongnanhai telecommunications directorate in Beijing.

"This is the United States Department of Defense, General Tucker Wyman calling."

A slow sentence in Chinese, which is nearly instantly translated by the NCO to the room. "This call is in violation of Article 3, Section 2a of the Defense Telephone Link Treaty of 2008, indicating these calls should not be made without a forty-eight-hour notice to the other side."

Wyman says, "Tell him we're making the call under Article 3, Section 2c, allowing immediate communications in a crisis situation. We are in a crisis. We see a widespread movement of your military forces. I need to talk to either General Li Fenghe, minister of national defense, or General Wei Zuocheng, the chief of the staff. It's very urgent. We want to discuss what's occurring and how we can de-escalate the situation before shooting starts, before it all spins out of control."

No one on either side of the world speaks for a moment.

General Wyman feels a growing weight of responsibility and of history weighing down his shoulders.

A faint *click*.

The senior Air Force NCO turns to Wyman.

"I'm sorry, sir," he says. "The call's been disconnected. The Chinese don't want to talk to us."

CHAPTER 127

IN THE REAR seat of the armored Suburban, CIA Director Hannah Abrams keeps close view of the traffic and the pedestrians out there on the sidewalk, wishing for a moment that she was out there, just scurrying along, only worrying about one's bank balance or the grocery list or an upcoming visit with a school principal.

A minute ago they went through Washington Circle and now they're on the four-lane-wide Pennsylvania Avenue.

The driver, Alec, says, "Ma'am?"

"Yes?"

"We have two Metro DC police cruisers coming up behind us, lights flashing," he says.

Hannah turns in her seat, looks through the darkened windows.

Two white-and-blue cruisers are speeding through the traffic, and other traffic is moving aside to let them go by.

"Ma'am?" the driver asks again.

She turns around.

Just several more blocks to go.

"Ignore them," she says. "Keep on going."

"Yes, ma'am."

The air inside the Suburban is now thick with tension, with Hannah sensing growing fear and concern for what might happen next. Hannah checks the side street as they roll on by, 21st Street NW. Getting pretty close now.

Alec says, "Ma'am, there's a roadblock up ahead. Four cruisers parked across the road. They also have deployed spike strips."

Hannah shifts her position to look through the windshield. There's a mess up ahead, with four DC Metro Police cruisers parked front bumper to trunk, stretching across Pennsylvania Avenue, lights flashing, officers outside wearing ballistic vests, some carrying shotguns.

"Do we have comms with the lead vehicle, or are we still being jammed?" she asks.

"Hold one, ma'am," the driver says, and picks up a handheld Motorola radio and says, "Sparrow Two, Sparrow Two, this is Sparrow One. Do you copy? Over."

Quickly the loud reply comes through the radio.

"Sparrow One, this is Sparrow Two. Read you five by five."

Hannah says, "Good. Tell them not to stop. Tell them they're to open a path for us."

Not even a moment of hesitation from her driver. "Sparrow Two, Raptor advises you to clear a path. No stopping."

The answer comes back just as quickly. "Roger that, Sparrow One."

She sees two things happen at once: the lead Suburban speeds up and aims for a point where there's a gap between two police cruisers, and the three security officers in her Suburban take out their weapons.

"It'll be all right, Jean," she says.

No answer from her seatmate.

Alec says, "Make sure your seat belts and harnesses are tight."

It happens in a moment, the details coming hard at her, as the lead Suburban rams through the two cruisers, forcing them back and shattering metal, glass, and bits of bumper up in the air, sparks flying, the tires sending up black smoke as they are shoved across the pavement.

The Suburban wobbles some and keeps on going. Her own Suburban follows, the armored SUV shuddering as it drives over the spike strips, but each Suburban has special tires that remain inflated.

She turns in her seat, sees the chaos back there,

two of the cops raising shotguns but not firing. At least that's a bit of much needed luck this morning.

"Alec, check on the lead."

He picks up the portable Motorola, says, "Sparrow Two, this is Sparrow One. What's your status?"

"All fine," a voice replies.

"Good," Hannah says. In a minute or two, IDs displayed, they pass through the gate blocking Pennsylvania Avenue and turn right at the Northwest Gate, reserved for White House staff and credentialed visitors.

A gate is lifted and the lead Suburban goes in— Hannah can see its tires are partially shredded— and then her Suburban passes through, the gate is closed, and now they are on White House grounds.

But they could be a million miles away from the Oval Office for all the good it does her.

The Secret Service members out here are part of the Uniformed Division. Most now are wearing tactical gear, fatigue clothing, ballistic vests and helmets, and carrying automatic rifles.

Hannah lowers her window as a mustached officer approaches. She displays her identification.

"We have an emerging crisis on our hands, and I need to see the president, as soon as possible," she says.

The Secret Service agent carefully examines her identification and gives it back to her.

"I'm sorry, ma'am, but we're on lockdown," he says. "No one's getting in today."

Fool, she thinks, *I'm trying to stop a goddamn war and you're stuck on procedures!*

Hannah forces out a smile. "This is a national emergency, and I need to get in. Look, I know you have your orders. Understood. But contact Carlton Pope. Get him down here and we can sort everything out."

"Ma'am, I—"

"Please," she says, reaching out to touch his arm. "This is incredibly important."

He waits, and she waits, and if she lives through this day and tomorrow, a cynical part of her thinks this little showdown will rank at least a chapter in her memoirs.

The Secret Service agent nods.

"I'll give his office a call."

"Thank you so very much," she says. "You won't regret it."

He enters a guard station and next to her Jean says, "You think you can convince Pope to let you in?"

"I'd better," she says, "or I'll have to go to Plan B."

"Which is?"

"Shooting our way in."

But ten minutes later, there is no need for a Plan B, as a confident and smiling Carlton Pope comes down the paved driveway on the North

Lawn. To Hannah he looks like an over-muscled parolee, walking to freedom with a strut in his walk, already planning his next crime.

He stops in front of the open window and says, "Director Abrams."

"Mr. Pope."

"I understand you want to see the president."

"Urgently," she says.

"This is quite the surprise," he says, cocky smile still on his face. "Why didn't you phone ahead?"

Hannah thinks, *You bulky creep, you know exactly why I couldn't call you.*

"My cell phone battery died," she lies. "Just one of those things. Please, Mr. Pope, it's vital that I talk to the president. I know the White House is on lockdown, but it'll just be me and my deputy, Jean Swantish."

He leans down, looks over at Jean, stands up. Scratches the back of his head.

"Oh, I guess I could get you in," he says. "But do you mind stepping out so we can talk about it?"

CHAPTER 128

LIAM GREY STEPS to the door, with Lin and Benjamin following him. He's carrying one of the Agency's M4s slung over his shoulder when Lin says, "Be careful. He's smart, tough, and very tricky."

"I just want to hear what he has to say," Liam replies.

Benjamin says, "Suppose he shoots you on the spot?"

Liam puts his hand on the doorknob. "Why, Benjamin, I expect you to avenge me. I'll be back as soon as I can."

It's a late, cool afternoon and as Liam walks down the dirt driveway, he's filled with memories of old Westerns, when the good guy and bad guy met in the center of town to hash things out. Difference is, of course, that while this place does resemble the American West, the bad guy approaching him has about twelve other bad guys backing him up.

The Chinese *rezident* stops, nods.

Liam halts about a meter in front of him. "Good afternoon, Mr. Han."

He smiles, and looks like someone's grandfather who passes out sweets and money at family gatherings. "You have me at a disadvantage. Your name, sir?"

"Mr. Smith."

"Ah, how dull."

"But it'll work for now. How goes it?"

"Reasonably well," he says, pulling out a gold cigarette lighter and pack of cigarettes. As he lights one, he offers the package to Liam, who says, "No, thanks."

"Ah, good sense for you. Tell me, Mr. Smith, may I ask what part of America you are from?"

"Nebraska. How about you? Which part of China?"

"Guangdong province," Han says. "What a world we live in, that a child from Nebraska and a child from Guangdong should meet here, in South Africa."

Liam says, "Yeah, that's pretty strange. Tell you what, you leave now, and we'll go on our way. A year from now, we can have a reunion. Drinks on me."

Han's smile widens. "I'm afraid that's not a possibility."

"Figured as much. What do you want?"

"Chin Lin."

"Not going to happen," Liam says. "You see, that house and bit of property back there belong to the United States of America. She's asked for asylum. I'm duty-bound to give it to her."

He cocks his head a bit. "And I'm duty-bound to demand that she return to us."

"Well, we're at an impasse, aren't we?"

"There will be shooting, then, and deaths."

"Only if you and your folks come closer."

Han sighs and turns his head, still smoking. "All right, I'll sweeten the deal."

"Go right ahead."

"We take Chin Lin back with us, and you and Benjamin Lucas join her, and stay as our guests for as long as you want."

Liam can't help himself, and laughs. "That's something, that's for sure."

Han says, "I take it you haven't kept up with the news the last few hours, have you?"

His mouth suddenly feels dry. "Some news, not all."

Han nods. "Your president is a madman, and he is taking his nation to war with mine. Not with bombs or missiles, but through cyberspace. The war will start"—he checks his watch—"in less than two hours. In a day or so, most of the world will slip into chaos, with an economic collapse, riots, and other conflicts breaking out, and in days, most cities will start to starve."

Liam has a cold moment, thinking of what Han is saying, thinking about not being able to contact Director Abrams, not even knowing if the message to save the vice president even has made it to Walter Reed.

He says, "Guess I missed those headlines."

Han says, "That's my offer. We take Chin Lin, for obvious reasons, and you and Benjamin will be our guests, for as long as you want."

"Does that come with or without torture?"

"You'll be under my personal protection."

"Even with the death of Chang Wanquan? And the two guards at the gate?"

Han shrugs. "The guards...collateral damage, as we all know. As for Mr. Chang, he worked for me, an arrogant prick who was going to get himself killed, either by the Party or somebody else. Again, Mr. Smith, do consider my offer."

Liam says, "It's attractive, but there's one problem. I made a promise to Chin Lin that she would be protected by me, and not sent home."

The cheerful grandfather in front of him suddenly disappears and is replaced by a hard intelligence officer who no doubt has blood on his hands, up to his elbows.

"You fool, don't you understand what I'm saying? A week from now there will be no China, no America. None of us are ever going home, ever again. I have offered you and Benjamin safety during the upcoming chaos. And you would protect some...slut you barely know, to turn down such an offer?"

"Guess so," Liam says.

"Fine," Han says, looking at his watch once more. "In fifteen minutes, we are coming in, one way or another."

Liam says, "You'd better come in heavy or with your hands up. Either way, we'll be ready."

CHAPTER 129

CARLTON POPE CANNOT believe his luck, for the stupid bitch sitting just feet away from him is agreeing to get out of her armored Suburban, right out in the open. Five seconds after that, his contract shooter will remove that arrogant head from her shoulders.

That will cause one hell of a news headline and chaos, but at this time tomorrow, it will all be forgotten.

"Wonderful, Madam Director, just step out and—"

"Hold on, I want to show you something," and her hand comes out, holding a sheet of paper.

Up hidden on the roof of the Eisenhower Executive Office Building—formerly known as the Old Executive Office Building—the assassin called Turner is comfortably holding a .300 Winchester Magnum bolt-action rifle with a Schmidt & Bender telescopic sight, clearly seeing Carlton Pope talking to someone sitting in the rear of the black Chevy Suburban.

No doubt it's the CIA director, his target. If her vehicle was standard, he might have gambled and let loose two rounds right now, trusting the full metal jacket bullets to cut her down after passing through the thin metal.

But that's a gamble. Turner hasn't earned his record through gambling.

He waits.

His vision is such that he has a clear view of Carlton and the Suburban's left rear window, and—

Okay.

Movement.

His finger is on the trigger, just needing a steady squeeze to kill Hannah Abrams.

He sees her hand.

It's holding a piece of paper.

Step out, step out, he thinks. *Just give me two seconds and I'll get the job done.*

The hand goes back into the Suburban, a blur of action and—

Carlton Pope is slammed against the side of the Suburban.

Handcuffed.

Turner's not sure what's going on, only certain that his sweet job with Pope has just been terminated, and it's time to get moving.

He quickly unloads the rifle and starts breaking it down.

From the corner of Carlton Pope's right eye there's sudden movement, and he turns—

What?

Strong hands seize his shoulders and his arms, and he's slammed against the side of the armored Suburban.

From behind him comes a woman's voice. "Carlton Pope? Special Agent Paula Brewster, FBI. You're under arrest."

"What the hell?" he says, still unable to move. It seems there are two FBI agents holding him down against the cold metal of the vehicle. "Do you know who I am? Lady, you're in one hell of a mess. Let me go!"

"Mr. Pope," the voice continues. "You have the right to remain silent."

He struggles and his wrists are moved together.

"Anything you say can and will be used against you in a court of law."

The *click* and *snap* of handcuffs tight against his wrists.

"You have the right to speak to an attorney, and to have an attorney present during any questioning. If you cannot afford an attorney, one will be provided to you. Do you understand these rights?"

He's pulled away from the Suburban and turns and sees four FBI agents standing there, the one woman smiling, the three men looking satisfied.

Furious, Carlton says, "I'm special assistant to President Keegan Barrett. Release me now."

"Sorry, sir," the FBI agent says. "You're under arrest."

"For what?"

"Perhaps I can help," CIA Director Abrams says.

He turns his head and that bitch's face is filled with triumph. She has her phone to her ear and says, "Thanks, Deputy Director Hicks. And...oh? Really? Thanks for passing that along. Thank you very much."

The CIA director lowers her phone. "Pope, you're under arrest for violation of 18 U.S. Code Section 930: Possession of firearms and dangerous weapons in Federal facilities."

"What?"

Abrams holds up a previously folded piece of paper. A surveillance photo of some sort is in the center. Showing...

Him.

Running along the grounds of the National Ground Intelligence Center in Virginia, right after bailing out of the Town Car when Noa Himel and her crew arrived earlier than planned to take out the Iranian Quds force.

Pistol clearly in hand.

Carlton says, "It's a bullshit charge."

Abrams keeps on smiling. "Bullshit or not, it gets you out of the picture for the rest of the day. Thank God for that."

CHAPTER 130

GENERAL TUCKER WYMAN, chairman of the Joint Chiefs of Staff, returns to the National Military Command Center after his failed attempt to contact his counterpart in Beijing, to see not much has changed since he left. Lots of phones ringing, keyboards being tapped, and display screens being updated.

But it seems there's a cold spot in the center of the room, where Vice Chairman Marine General Wade Thompson is standing at his post, with Deputy Defense Director Clark Kim standing next to him, having come down from his office in the E Wing of the Pentagon.

From the looks on their faces, he knows the news is bad.

"What is it?" he asks.

The Marine general says, "We know what's behind the Chinese response. It's us."

"How in the world can that be possible?"

General Thompson says, "President Barrett had a meeting this morning with General Peterson, Cybercommand. He authorized a full-scale cyber-attack against China, commencing in"—he glances up at one of the digital clocks hanging from the ceiling—"in just over an hour. At twelve hundred hours our time."

General Wyman says, "How extensive?"

"He's throwing everything at them, including the kitchen sink. Attack profile is called Case Shanghai. Starting at the top with their military command and control, infrastructure, banking and finance systems, all the way down to their Ministry of Tourism and Culture."

For a brief moment General Wyman is speech-less. The vice chairman says, "I just got off the phone with General Peterson. He says POTUS had the necessary launch codes to start Case Shanghai."

Wyman explodes. "Of course he has the god-damn codes! He also has the launch codes to send nukes to take out Acapulco if he wanted to. Didn't Peterson find the situation unusual, something to make him stop and goddamn think?"

The vice chairman says, "Peterson says the president told him that he had buy-off from the National Security Council, congressional leadership, the secretary of defense, and you as well, General.

Peterson felt all of the necessary notifications had been made."

Wyman rubs at his forehead. "And everything the president told him was a lie."

Deputy Defense Director Clark Kim speaks up, voice high-pitched and squeaky. "But...General Wyman, can't you order the Cybercommand to stand down? To halt their planned attack?"

It feels like a ton of lead is now nestling in his chest. "No," he says softly. "Cybercommand has received lawful orders from the commander in chief. I can't countermand that. Like it or not, the president is in control. The only way this attack is halted is by another valid order from the commander in chief."

He looks up against the display boards. He thinks about all the training, scenarios, and classes he's gone through over the years, playing all types of scenarios from all kinds of attack.

But never has he faced a situation like this, a rogue president going out on his own to start a war.

And Wyman is under no illusions. Beijing is in the process of conducting a preemptive attack, to hit the United States before the full cyberattack begins, and he has to start issuing orders to get the conventional and nuclear forces prepared.

Escalation following escalation following escalation.

Until the spark, the mistake, the oversight, starts the war.

A war like none other, with cities going dark, fuel deliveries stopping, communications going silent, most of this entirely interconnected world being sent back to the nineteenth century.

He looks to his assistant. "Get me the White House Communications Office. Now."

"Yes, sir."

A few seconds pass.

"Here, sir." A phone receiver is passed to him. "It's Major Jewel."

"This is General Wyman, JCS," he says. "Major, I need to talk to the president. Now."

"Er, yes sir, straightaway. Hold on, sir."

He waits.

Looking again at the little symbols up on the status screens, each bit of light marking scores or hundreds of crew members, millions of dollars or yuans invested in submarines, surface ships, missile silos, and aircraft, all coming together.

"Sir?"

"Yes, go on."

Major Jewel sounds like he's about to cry. "I'm sorry, sir. The president is unavailable. He won't answer his secure line, the White House switchboard can't reach him, and I've sent a runner to the Oval Office. He refuses to answer the door. He... he's out of touch."

"Keep on trying," he says, then slams the receiver down.

Both the vice chairman and the deputy defense director look at him, like young boys, hoping Daddy can do something miraculous.

"Sorry, gentlemen," he says. "Our president has let loose the dogs of war, and we can't do a damn thing about it."

CHAPTER 131

LIAM GREY STEPS into the farmhouse, locks the door behind him, and checks the time. About thirteen unlucky minutes left.

Lin and Benjamin are staring at him. He says, "Benjamin, you up for a walk?"

Confused, Benjamin says, "Depends how lengthy."

He quickly strides past them both, heading to the small bathroom. "Long enough to get you and Lin out of here before the shooting starts."

Lin says, "What did Han have to say?"

"Nothing good," Liam says. "He wants you, and he's coming to get you in just over ten minutes. He also offered Benjamin and me asylum, and I hope you don't mind, Benjamin, I declined."

In the small bathroom, it's crowded. Liam kneels down, looks behind the toilet with its pipes, brings out a plunger. There's a porcelain sink and a stand-up shower, and two wooden shelves with folded and dusty yellow towels.

Lin says, "I'm staying here to help. I don't want to see Benjamin hurt."

"Gee, thanks," Liam says, tearing off the rubber end of the plunger. "But you're staying with Benjamin, and both of you are getting out of here."

At the end of the wooden stick is a small metal hook. Liam goes to the shower, pulls aside the mildewy curtain.

"And once you get out of here, Lin, you try your guy at Walter Reed, make sure he got your message." Liam gives his cell phone to Benjamin. "And you, pal, call the station chief, anybody at the station, or even the ambassador to rescue you and your girlfriend."

Checks his watch.

Ten minutes left.

He takes the plunger stick and metal hook, fastens the hook in the shower drain. He gives it a good tug and the floor of the shower comes out, revealing a wooden ladder going into the darkness. He reaches down, feels around, and throws a switch. Small lightbulbs flip on, illuminating smooth concrete.

Liam says, "Escape tunnel. Goes out a couple of hundred yards, emerges at a dry streambed. Go quick but be careful. Lord knows what snakes or scorpions have taken up residence there."

"But what about you?" Benjamin asks, face drawn, holding hands with Lin.

"Me? I'm going to play Beau Geste. I'm going to take your weapons and keep up the shooting from every possible window, door, or opening."

"Liam."

"Jesus, stop wasting time, all right? Look, Han told me that President Barrett is on his way to launch a cyberattack on China. You're both smart enough to realize what's going to happen...and when the computers are all fried and the cities empty out, they'll kick it up to traditional weapons. You've got to get out, and you've got to make sure the information about the vice president gets to the right people. The president needs to be stopped. Move."

Benjamin offers a hand. He gives it a brisk shake, and then helps him down the ladder. Lin follows, offers a hand, and he gives it a good shake as well.

"Take care of each other," he says. "And if this is still some kind of honey trap or intelligence op, my ghost will come back to haunt you."

Her eyes moisten, and there's a quick kiss to his cheek. "No trap. Just Benjamin and me. That's all."

"Good. Now get the hell out."

He waits until he can't see the top of her head anymore, replaces the shower bottom, tosses the plunger and hook behind the toilet.

Goes to the kitchen. Peers out the window.

Nothing yet.

He moves quickly, setting up an M4 with three spare magazines on the table.

Heads to the supply closet, retrieves more gear, and checks the time.

Two minutes.

He grabs a gas mask.

Liam goes to the front door, surprised at how calm he feels.

This is his territory, his turf, what he's trained for. As much as he loves intelligence work, being in open combat with no compromises, no falsity, just direct action, suits him.

He grabs the doorknob, opens the door a couple of inches. He quickly makes a barricade of a wooden coffee table and two chairs. He lays down, pulls up the M4 with its telescopic sight, sees the armed men out there are now moving toward the farmhouse.

Liam checks his watch.

"Han, you son of a bitch, you're a minute early."

He pulls the trigger of the M4 and starts shooting.

CHAPTER 132

WHEN THE SUBURBAN stops near the entrance to the West Wing, CIA Director Hannah Abrams gives a thick envelope to Ralph, her security officer. "Take this," she says. "If I don't come back in an hour, or you hear I've been arrested, or had a vase fall on my head, get this as quick as you can to the majority leader, Senator Hogan."

Ralph frowns, gives the envelope to Alec, the driver. "He'll take care of it. I'm coming in with you, Director."

She's struck at the flow of emotion that just rushes through her, knowing Ralph is doing this out of pure duty, even though death or the end of his career is likely before the day is out.

"Thank you," she says. "Jean, come along."

She gets out of the Suburban, gives the other battered Suburban a quick look, thinking, *Jesus, the paperwork that's going to have to be filled out on that.* A door opens at the West Wing and onto a Marine in full dress blues. Walking past him is Quinn Lawrence, President Barrett's chief of staff. His gray suit is wrinkled and flaps around him like it's two sizes too large, and he says, "Director Abrams, I'm still not sure the president will see you. He's…he's in a mood. Won't see anybody, won't take any phone calls."

Hannah says, "Quinn, I know you're having a rough day in a series of rough days. The chief of staff's job is to protect the president at all costs, and right now, if you want to protect him, you're going to let me in, along with my deputy director and my security officer."

The chief of staff's face is red and mottled. Hannah says, "A conflict is about to break out between China and the United States. I'm sure you've heard that their embassy and their consulates are burning their papers. That's one hell of a signal that war is near. Quinn, please, do the right thing."

He looks like he's about to sob, and then shrugs. "Fine. Come in."

Yes, Hannah thinks, *we just might make it.*

Might.

She follows him as they pass the Marine guard, who holds the door open. "Is he in his private office or the Oval Office?" she asks.

"Oval Office."

"Good," Hannah says. "Not so far to walk."

They enter the West Wing lobby reception area, Hannah nodding at the young female receptionist sitting there. They walk the familiar corridors past open office doors, antique oil paintings on the walls, and ceramics and glassware on display. She has taken this route many times over the years, yet senses something different this time from the staff members walking around these particular corridors of power. They seem to flatten themselves against the wall as she walks by. Their eyes are downcast, there are no cheerful smiles. She has a flashback to her childhood, growing up with an alcoholic father.

Dad never yelled, punched, or broke things, but when he was drunk, he would brood in long silences, or start long monologues telling stories of past fights or grudges, or just stare at you, like he couldn't quite figure out who you were and why you were in this house with him.

That's exactly the feeling she gets from the passing staffers.

The president is not right, and they know it.

They come to the closed door to the Oval Office, with a female Secret Service agent standing guard. Sitting nearby is a Marine officer, the familiar bulky nuclear football at his feet. There are two chairs flanking the closed door. Hannah says, "Ralph, Jean, have a seat."

Jean says, "Are you sure, ma'am?"

Hannah says, "If I need you, I'll call you. Same for you, Ralph."

They take the chairs and Quinn looks to her, a despairing look on his face. She says, "Quinn, thanks, you did the right thing."

He doesn't reply.

Hannah says, "One of my supervisors, back in the Directorate of Operations, had to make a tough decision that would end up in bloodshed. There were a lot of arguments back and forth, and finally, he said, 'It doesn't mean that it's the right thing to do. It means it's not the wrong thing to do.' That's what you've done."

Quinn says, "I'll announce you."

"Don't bother." She nods to the Secret Service agent, who unlocks the door and swings it open quietly.

Hannah remembers a prayer from her younger days, says it silently, takes a deep breath, and walks into the Oval Office.

CHAPTER 133

PRESIDENT KEEGAN BARRETT is sitting behind the old *Resolute* desk in the Oval Office and decides to hide his anger and aggravation as he stands up when CIA Director Hannah Abrams comes in, unannounced and uninvited.

He plasters a fake smile on his face—easy to do after years of practice—and comes around the desk, offers his hand.

"Hannah, good to see you, but still, this is quite a surprise," he says.

She gives his hand a quick shake, her hand firm and dry, and says, "Sir, there's a number of urgent emerging issues taking place that I need to discuss with you. Please, may I take a seat?"

"Absolutely," he says, pulling a chair free from the side of his desk, putting it in front, at an angle, so she has to twist her body to look at him. He resumes his seat, puts his folded hands on top of the *Resolute* desk, and says, "That sounds pretty ominous. Do go on but make it quick. My schedule is pretty full."

Hannah nods at him, looking like a schoolteacher about to issue a detention slip.

Go ahead, little lady, there's nothing you can do to touch me, or harm me.

She says, "Sir, I'll begin by saying that the American people—including myself—have admired the strong and decisive way you assumed the presidency this past January. There were no traditional bumps in the road or embarrassing incidents during the transition, you began your work that afternoon, even skipping most of the inaugural balls, and you set a tone of service that quickly became most admirable."

Barrett nods with satisfaction. This certainly isn't what he is expecting from this spook, and if he had his way, she would not be here. But Carlton Pope can't be reached, so he decided to give her just a few minutes, just to keep the situation calm.

Even though he was in charge of it a couple of years back, he's never trusted the CIA. He's sure the agency killed JFK, crippled LBJ's presidency with Vietnam, tried to take down Reagan via Iran–Contra, and for the past couple of administrations, illegally spied on candidates and subsequent presidents.

So he's watching this serious-looking older

woman and seeing a coiled rattlesnake sitting in front of him.

Hannah says, "Sir, you have had an admirable beginning to your term. But I'm in possession of key evidence that shows you have violated numerous federal statutes, as well as your oath to the Constitution, during the subsequent months. You had the background, experience, and passion to be elected president, sir, but you don't have the temperament to govern as one. Like Mark Zuckerberg of Facebook, your managing principle was to 'move fast and break things.'"

She shakes her head. "That principle may be admirable in business. But it's sheer poison and a disaster for a president."

Barrett frowns. "And you couldn't tell me this over a phone call, and save us both a lot of time?"

"No, sir."

"Why?"

Hannah says, "Because, sir, I needed to tell you to your face, that for the good of the nation and your legacy, you need to resign as president of the United States."

CHAPTER 134

THERE, HANNAH ABRAMS thinks, *I've tossed it out.*

All the fictional tales about presidents being forced out, compromised, blackmailed, from *Seven Days in May* and up to *House of Cards*, well, those disturbing fictions have now become a stone-cold reality this fine summer morning.

The director of the Central Intelligence Agency is trying to force a legitimately elected president from office.

She waits.

How will he react?

Barrett stares at her with focused eyes, and then smiles, leaning back in his chair.

"Hannah, that's one hell of a joke," he says.

Keeping her face set and impassive, she says, "This isn't a joking matter. I'm quite serious, sir."

He slowly brings his chair back to place in front of the *Resolute* desk. The air feels thick and heavy, like just before a severe thunderstorm, when killer lightning and high winds suddenly break out.

Barrett says, "You have some damn nerve to come here and say this to me. I'm the president of the United States, not one of your analysts or officers."

She keeps her voice steady. "To repeat, Mr. President, I have evidence that indicates numerous violations of federal statutes, as well as your oath of office. You need to resign."

He stops smiling, leans forward over his desk, voice cold. "The day before President Nixon resigned, three Republican members of Congress came to talk to him. House Leader John Jacob Rhodes, Senate Leader Hugh Scott, and Senator Barry Goldwater. The three of them told Nixon that his support in Congress was melting away, and that impeachment and conviction was guaranteed."

Barrett makes a point of looking over Hannah's shoulder. "Yet here you are. Alone. A spook. With no Senate or House leaders backing you up. Trying to destroy the will of the American people. To hell with you. Director Abrams, you're fired."

CHAPTER 135

LIAM GREY IS bleeding from his left wrist from some random bit of metal, either shrapnel or a ricochet from the attackers, but he's still keeping up the fight. All of the windows of the farmhouse are shattered, and there's a heavy haze of gun smoke and CS gas in the rooms, but so far, with his M40 gas mask, he's breathing reasonably well.

There are at least three bodies sprawled across the dirt lawn in front of the house. He's pretty sure there's one more at the rear. It's been a fast-moving battle on his end, rushing from the kitchen, bedroom, garage, and living room, then repeating, firing from previously positioned M4s.

In going back to the weapons storage locker ten minutes ago, he was delighted to find an M4 with an attached grenade launcher. It fired 40mm grenade rounds—too bad there were only four— but they had gone to good use, destroying two of the three Range Rovers, and putting a dent into the armored Mercedes-Benz.

Now it's just him and the other three M4s. He carefully shoots in three-round bursts, but he knows this is just a delaying action. Every minute that he holds Han and his mercenaries up, is sixty more seconds for Lin and Benjamin to get free to a place to start making phone calls.

He looks through the scope again, from the floor by the partially opened door, with furniture he moved to make a barricade, and sees quick movement.

Three men running out, taking shelter behind a crumpled Range Rover and—

Oh shit.

He instantly recognizes the weapon the middle man is about to use, an RPG-7 rocket-propelled grenade. Liam gets up and starts running to the rear as he hears a faint *whoosh* and an explosion and darkness as the farmhouse falls on him.

CHAPTER 136

CIA DIRECTOR HANNAH Abrams believes the president is hoping she will melt away, back down, or even worse, start sobbing. To hell with that. She's met with Sudanese militia leaders at night in remote campgrounds, with accused Serbian war criminals deep in their territory in a smoky café, and she's raised herself up the slippery and treacherous ladder to become the Agency director.

She hasn't—and won't—bend.

"I'm sorry, Mr. President, I no longer recognize your authority," she says.

Barrett sits cold and firm, like a stone sculpture.

She goes on.

"Mr. President, this is not your office," Hannah says. "It's the American people's office, and with your actions, you've shown you're not fit to carry out your duties."

"Such as?" he shoots back.

"Sir, more than two months ago, you authorized the illegal use of CIA assets to carry out missions in the domestic United States, including breaking and entering without a federal warrant, unlawful detention of foreign nationals, and spending funds to support same, without congressional knowledge or approval."

He smiles. "Says who?"

"I've made the necessary inquiries, sir."

Barrett shrugs. "A foul-up, then. Before your arrival I briefed Acting Director Milton Fenway on what I had planned, and he assured me that he would brief the Gang of Eight and other members of Congress. I guess he didn't do that in his hasty departure from Langley."

Hannah quietly and firmly goes on. "We also have evidence that you've personally directed your special assistant, Carlton Pope, to assist you in your illegal activities, including the purchase of various weapons and explosives for an Iranian terrorist cell operating in this country."

Barrett says, "If Carlton was here, he'd tell you you were lying, straight to your face."

She says, "Mr. Pope is currently in FBI custody, having been arrested for violating federal law concerning firearms possession near a military base."

Hannah's curious at how Barrett will respond to losing his right-hand thug.

He nods, seemingly without a concern in the

world. "Carlton. Always pushing the envelope, always taking my orders too literally. If you're expecting Carlton to turn on me, forget it. He's utterly loyal. You can waterboard him for a month or cut off his fingers, and he won't say a word, Ms. Abrams."

Hannah ignores the insult, him not using her title. "However that might be, a congressional investigation will reveal the truth behind the matter, and I have no doubt—despite your current popularity—you will be impeached and convicted."

"So says you. And your witnesses I suppose . . . let's see, Noa Himel and Liam Grey would be key. Last I heard, Noa was hiding out at your house, and a squad of FBI agents and federal marshals are about to break in to take her into custody. And Liam is somewhere out of touch in South Africa, for whatever that means. Ms. Abrams, if that's all you've got, then it's thinner than tissue. Now. You're to leave my office before I have the Secret Service come in and haul you out."

Hannah says, "Liam Grey is in South Africa, trying to rescue your son, Benjamin Lucas."

Barrett's face is impassive.

She says, "That goes against your impressive history and narrative, doesn't it, Keegan? How will your popularity survive among a certain section of the electorate, when they learn that you had a son out of wedlock, and that you didn't pay a dime of child support for him over the years?"

His eyes narrow, darken. "Inquisitive little bitch, aren't you? I'll tell you what will happen. Americans are a forgiving people. All I need is to give a maudlin speech about my past personal failings, the guilt I've carried all these years, a promise to do right, and, you know what, my popularity ratings will increase."

Hannah thinks, *Okay, time to go nuclear, strike deep behind that narcissism and raging self-confidence.*

"You mentioned past personal failings?" she asks. "How about your current personal failings, Keegan?"

"Me?" he answers. "You know what I'm called in the press and among the party. The warrior monk, only worried about his country and his people."

Hannah says, "Does being a warrior monk include threatening to sexually assault and murder a subordinate?"

CHAPTER 137

PRESIDENT KEEGAN BARRETT is aware of the time slipping away before the noon hour strikes— about fifty minutes away—but this damn coiled rattlesnake in front of him, who has the nerve to call him by his first name, is hissing and preparing to strike. He needs to kill it. He thinks back to his recent visit to Minnesota, how the thousands upon thousands of American citizens there showed their love and trust in him.

He will not let this professional creature, this inhabitant of the DC swamp, make him betray that trust and love.

"What the holy hell are you claiming, Ms. Abrams?"

"That on a certain date and time, in your private office in the family quarters in the White House, that you did threaten to assault and murder Noa Himel, an officer of the Central Intelligence Agency, your subordinate."

"That's a lie."

"I have proof," the woman says.

"What? Her notarized statement or something equally worthless?"

"No," she says. "This."

From her leather bag she takes out a small device that she places on the center of the *Resolute* desk. She presses a switch, a green light comes on, and two voices emerge, his and Noa Himel's.

"To make it even more clear, so even a woman like you can understand, I own your ass. You belong to me. All of you. You will continue to operate in the United States, and screw the laws, and screw Congress."

A pause in the recording.

"That's funny. You know why? Because you do have a cute ass, and I could take you now, toss you over my desk, and screw you six ways to Sunday, and you couldn't do a damn thing about it. Because I've got evidence that you're a stone-cold killer, Noa Himel, safely kept in my hands."

He hears his laugh.

"But that's beneath me, as you said. So think of this. You leave the White House and if I feel like doing it, within the hour, I'll come for you. You will no longer exist, your records will be wiped, you will become an un-person."

"Are…you threatening to kill me?" comes Noa's shaken voice.

"Worse. I'm threatening to make you disappear. Like you never existed. You think I can't do that?"

A faint hiss from the little recorder's speaker.

Barrett watches the bitch smile at him and switch off the recorder.

Don't let her see you blink, squirm, or sweat.

Don't do it.

He says, "A fake. Come on, Hannah, I know from experience the technical talent that is over at Langley. It'd probably take a day or so to mock up something with my voice and Noa's voice. You'll have to do better than that."

The woman suddenly stands up. "Challenge accepted."

Barrett reaches underneath the desk to press the button to summon the Secret Service, but Hannah is too quick and she opens the door to the Oval Office, says, "Jean?"

A second woman joins Hannah as she comes back to the desk. Hannah pulls out a chair for her, and she sits down.

Barrett recognizes her straightaway, dressed in a simple black jacket and slacks ensemble, with a plain white blouse.

Hannah says, "You remember Jean Swantish, my deputy director?"

"Of course," Barrett says, irritated and deciding enough is enough.

His fingers return to the Secret Service button,

as Jean shifts in her seat, brings up her hands as if in prayer, and he stops.

For the first time in a very long time, Barrett is afraid.

CHAPTER 138

NAVY CAPTAIN DAN Callaghan is walking to his office at Walter Reed National Medical Center in Bethesda, Maryland, dreading the rest of the day ahead for him, as the facility's commanding officer. The hospital's most famous patient, Vice President Laura Hernandez, is in a coma up in Ward 71, the medical suite reserved for the president and other high-ranking officials.

He yawns, opens the door to his office, nods greetings to the staff. A few minutes ago he was at the latest hospital-wide meeting to pinpoint the source of the vice president's illness, and how to reverse the effects so she'll come out of her coma.

The best working hypothesis is sometime before she collapsed at the Las Vegas dining room, she was either exposed to—or consumed—some sort of cholinesterase inhibitor, part of the family of nerve-gas weapons first developed more than a century ago.

Most recently, such chemical agents have been the poison of choice for the Russian FSB, the successor to the KGB, as its agents have traveled around the world to poison and kill dissidents currently protesting against the Motherland. But the standard treatment of atropine isn't working, and Captain Callaghan and other doctors here have received unofficial reassurances from counterparts in Moscow that they had nothing to do with the vice president's poisoning.

In his office he sits at his desk, stretches out his back. It's been a series of long and hellish days, with standard treatments not working, and rumors circulating that the Chinese were behind it, or the Iranians, or even Mexican cartels, still carrying a grudge against the vice president back from when she was a tough law-and-order governor in Texas. Pressure is coming at him from all places and circles, including a number of faith healers out in the parking lot, chanting and banging drums for the vice president's health.

He glances at his morning mail, thinking the drummers should go set themselves up over at 1600 Pennsylvania Avenue. Rumors have recently percolated along the corridors of Walter Reed about the president's current health, both physical and mental.

Another yawn. Christ, when was the last time he had gotten a solid night's sleep?

A crisp white envelope with his name and rank typed in the center catches his attention.

No postage, no return address.

Odd.

He opens it and a carefully printed sheet comes out.

He gives it a read, then reads it again, much more slowly.

It says:

Twenty-one days ago, VICE PRESIDENT LAURA HERNANDEZ was touring the Consumer Electronics Show in Las Vegas where she took part in a virtual reality demonstration, donning a V/R helmet. The helmet had a spray anesthetic device at its base, allowing a ceramic sphere holding a nerve agent to be injected into her skin, and a follow-up experimental healing agent left no wound visible.

This ceramic device is undetectable to standard imaging devices. It is designed to continually distribute the nerve agent over a sixty-day period. The only treatment for VICE PRESIDENT LAURA HERNANDEZ is to make an incision and remove the ceramic device, removing the continued distribution of the nerve agent. The device is approximately one centimeter above the first cervical vertebrae and can be removed via local anesthesia. Her recovery should be nearly instantaneous.

Captain Callaghan grabs the sheet of paper, steps up from his desk, and starts quickly walking out of his office. By the time he reaches the hallway, he's running.

CHAPTER 139

CIA DIRECTOR HANNAH Abrams watches with satisfaction as President Keegan Barrett stares at what's happening in front of him. Next to her there's a slow and steady process, as a well-fitted wig is removed and dropped to the floor, and fingers work under and around the face. There's nothing like the heavy latex masks one sees in the *Mission: Impossible* movies, just a gentle tug and slip as Agency-only materials are pulled away, thinner than a sheet of wax paper. Implants are taken out of the mouth. The woman sits up straighter and stares across at the man staring right back at her.

"Sir, I believe you know Noa Himel," she says.

There's a few seconds where no one speaks, and from her open bag, a light starts flashing. Hannah doesn't quickly respond, just casually drops her hand into the bag and rotates her Agency-issued cell phone—thank all the Heavens they're getting coverage here at the White House—and looks at the screen. No one else in the room can see the bright flashing light coming from her phone. Her specially made contact lenses, besides correcting her vision, allow only her to see the warning light and this urgent notification.

FLASH FLASH FLASH. PENTAGON CONFIRMS POTUS ISSUED ORDER TO CYBERCOMMAND TO ATTACK PRC AT 1200 HOURS TODAY. SWANTISH.

Hannah calmly looks up at Barrett.

"You see, sir, we now have a witness," she says. "A witness to back up this recording."

"But…" His shocked voice dribbles out.

"How? Noa, please demonstrate."

Noa opens her mouth wide, inserts two fingers, winces and then tugs an object free. It's placed on the *Resolute* desk. It looks like a silver cap for a molar.

Hannah says, "A recording device. Not too much range, the quality isn't that great, but it does its job well, don't you think?"

And now Hannah is thinking of two things: the war warning she's received from her deputy, and the need to get Barrett to resign. Now. So that somehow, she and others can stop what's about to break out.

There is no other option.

She waits.

No, there is a third option.

She doesn't want to even consider it.

"Keegan, please, this is where we've come to," she says. "There is evidence available and to be found concerning your illegal and unconstitutional activities."

Including starting a war, but Hannah won't touch that, not now. *Keep your eye on the prize.*

"There are two paths forward, sir," she says. "One that will involve your resignation, today, for health reasons. You will be seen as one willing to sacrifice his position for the good of the country. You will leave the White House as a hero. The other path...congressional hearings lasting months, daily humiliations and embarrassments, this tape of you threatening Noa Himel being aired over and over again, and your eventual impeachment and removal from office. With the possibility of prison time as well."

More silence.

"I will also guarantee you, sir, that everything I've revealed and mentioned here will remain in the Oval Office after your resignation. You have my word."

Barrett says, "You bitch."

"No argument from me, sir. But I need your answer. And I need it now. Your resignation, for the good of the nation, and the American people."

Hannah feels like her entire life has led up to these next few seconds, as she and Noa wait.

All the travels, all the sacrifices, all the devotion to duty and the Constitution and the United States of America.

Preparing to give up her life if necessary.

Barrett's hands start to move.

Her hand slips into her bag. In a concealed sheath is an Agency-issued hard plastic knife, invisible to scanners and magnetometers.

The third option.

If Barrett doesn't resign in the next minute, he will shortly be the fifth American president assassinated in office.

Her hand finds the knife.

CHAPTER 140

AT THE NATIONAL Military Command Center at the Pentagon, General Tucker Wyman, chairman of the Joint Chiefs of Staff, drops the phone after once again trying to speak to the president, and says, "Bullshit!"

Vice Chairman Marine General Wade Thompson looks up from his busy desk. "Sir?"

He starts heading to the door, followed by Colonel Leonard, his assistant. To the vice chairman he says, "You're in charge here, Wade, until you hear from me. Follow the plans and procedures. Do what must be done. I'm off to the White House."

The vice chairman says, "Good luck."

"Thanks," he says. "Should have done it an hour ago."

As he leaves the NMCC he says, "Doug, I need transport and escort fastest to the White House."

"Yes, sir," his assistant says.

Six minutes later he's in the rear seat of an armored black Chevrolet Tahoe, with two Pentagon police cruisers ahead of him, lights and sirens blaring, wondering just what in hell is he going to do when he gets to the White House.

His assistant is sitting next to him, a communications satchel at his booted feet.

"Doug?"

"Sir?"

"You were on the wrestling team at West Point, correct?"

Doug says, "The Wrestling Club, yes, sir."

"You were pretty good, right?"

"Twice was named Wrestler of the Year from the EIWA, sir," his aide replies. "The Eastern Intercollegiate Wrestling Association."

They travel for another thirty seconds, over the 14th Street Bridge, close to the District of Columbia.

The chairman of the Joint Chiefs of Staff says, "I need to convince the president to rescind his attack order. I might need your help."

"Certainly, sir," Doug says. A quick pause. "How, sir?"

General Tucker Wyman says, "If the president refuses my request, I might ask you to hold him down while I break his fingers. Are you all right with that, Doug?"

Not a moment of hesitation.

"Yes, sir," Doug says.

CHAPTER 141

PRESIDENT KEEGAN BARRETT stares with loathing at these two women who have outwitted and outplayed him. He's waiting for a thought, a whisper, some sort of inspiration to get him free.

Both Hannah Abrams and Noa Himel are looking at him with strong expressions of strength and fortitude, and also...

Hate.

Why hate?

All his life he's worked toward one goal, and one goal only.

To preserve and protect the United States of America.

That's all.

A personal mission that's driven him for years of hard work and sacrifice, guided by the inner voice that tells him he's been chosen for greatness, and this is the thanks he gets?

He looks to the clock.

Thirty-five minutes left.

He listens hard but nothing comes to him.

His resignation…a piece of theater, that's all. Even if it's signed and acknowledged, who will take over? The vice president, in a coma? The disgraced speaker of the House, stuck on an aircraft heading to California? The president pro tempore of the Senate, who, he knows, wears adult diapers and forgets his name after lunch? The secretary of state, in Davos at this moment, heavily drunk and consorting with high-priced escorts?

No, it'll be a temporary theater.

Sign the damn paper, get these bitches out of his office, and return to work.

Who will be believed?

The president of the United States?

Or the CIA director, whom he just fired?

He opens the center desk drawer of the *Resolute* desk, finds a piece of plain stationery with THE WHITE HOUSE centered at the top of the page, along with a drawing of it.

Taking a pen, he makes a short series of phrases addressing it to his secretary of state, after scrawling in today's date:

Dear Secretary Bray,

I hereby resign the office of the President of the United States.

Sincerely,
Keegan Barrett

He starts to say, "I'll have this couriered over to the deputy secretary of state at his office——"

And is shocked when Hannah Abrams takes it from his hand.

She scrawls something at the bottom, stands up.

"No offense, sir," she says. "I'll take care of it. Noa?"

Noa Himel gets up and shoots one more disgusted look at Barrett, but he keeps quiet, knowing that no matter what these two are up to, the clock is running out.

The Oval Office door swings open, but Hannah turns.

"This was for the best, sir. You have my deep appreciation, and that of the people of the United States."

He clears his throat. "Get out of my sight."

CHAPTER 142

OUTSIDE OF THE Oval Office, her security officer Ralph stands up. She's surprised to see chief of staff Quinn Lawrence standing there as well, like a battered son waiting to see how mom and dad's latest fight will shake out. There's even a huddle of White House staffers down the corridor, looking at them, not sure what they're looking at, only knowing that something historic is going on.

Hannah hands the resignation letter—with her initials and the time scrawled on the bottom—to Ralph. "Get the hell over to the State Department as fast as you can, and if you have to run people down, do it. Make sure it's hand delivered to the deputy secretary of state."

"Yes, ma'am," he says, glancing at the letter and breaking into a run.

Her bag is flashing again.

She takes out the Agency-issued cell phone, sees

the second FLASH message of the day, feels like collapsing in relief.

"Quinn...you've been a hero today. Honest to God. President Barrett resigned a moment ago. Best as you can, keep an eye on him, ignore any orders and directives he might issue."

"But...but...who's in charge?"

"I'm working on that," she says. "I've got to leave. Right now. Noa, come along."

Hannah starts briskly walking and looks back.

Noa is moving slowly, pain shadowing her face, and Hannah thinks, *God, what she did to grind on through back there, pretending to be Jean Swantish. And what her friend Gina managed to do, to successfully disguise her...*

"Go ahead," Noa says. "I'll catch up."

"The hell you will," Hannah says.

She goes back, grabs an arm and puts it around her shoulder, and half runs, half drags her way out of the Oval Office area, past the offices and reception. Out in the parking lot the lead Suburban is still there, all four tires flattened, with two security officers standing outside, Grant and Lenny.

"Help me get Noa in," she says. In a minute, the two of them are buckled in the rear seat, the two officers in front, Grant behind the wheel.

"Grant," Hannah says, "this thing mobile?"

"Yes, ma'am," he says, starting the engine.

"How long to Walter Reed?" she asks.

He backs out of the parking space.

"About thirty minutes, ma'am."

"We don't have thirty minutes," she says. "You'll have to do it in fifteen."

"You've got it, ma'am," he says. Sirens and lights are flipped on as they exit the White House grounds, heading north to Bethesda.

CHAPTER **143**

PRESIDENT KEEGAN BARRETT—and despite all that happened a few minutes ago, he still considers himself the President—gets up and walks around the *Resolute* desk, thinking he might return to his office up in the family quarters, but according to Hannah Abrams, Carlton Pope isn't in his White House anymore.

Damn.

Which means?

His chief of staff, Quinn Lawrence.

A pathetic man, no backbone, easy to manipulate, and a perfect choice to be his chief of staff.

He's not sure if Carlton Pope had scheduled helicopter transportation to Mount Weather, as he requested, but he's sure he can get Quinn to make the necessary arrangements.

Once at Mount Weather, when chaos sweeps across the nation in the hours ahead, who will the nation listen to? Him, the legitimately elected president of the United States, or some Cabinet member broadcasting via Zoom, playing pretend?

He opens the curved door to the Oval Office and a female Secret Service agent is there. He nods to her as she speaks into her wrist microphone, whispering, "Sierra on the move," using his code name.

Passes the empty office of Carlton Pope, feels a pang of concern, recalling Hannah Abrams's news of his arrest, and then he thinks, *Well, we can fix it.* Whip up a presidential pardon in the next couple of hours and Carlton will be where he needs to be, right at Barrett's side, performing the hard duties that must be done in the hours and days ahead.

He stops.

Speaking of hard duties, where in hell is the Marine major carrying the nuclear football? He's always within sight, and Barrett has never not seen him or his equal since Inauguration Day.

He resumes walking along the familiar hallways, nodding and smiling at the staffers he encounters, but something odd is going on. Most of them turn away or lower their heads, like they're embarrassed or ashamed.

Or not wanting to look at him straight in his face.

At Quinn Lawrence's office, he walks by Quinn's surprised secretarial staff and opens the door, and then he's surprised as well.

The office is crowded with senior White House

staffers and two Army colonels and the Marine major with the football. Quinn is on his phone and everyone save him looks at him, then looks away.

And in a second, bigger shock, Quinn remains on the phone.

Does not disconnect the call.

Doesn't even give notice to Barrett.

Intolerable.

Quinn finally hangs up the phone and says, "Yes? May I help you, sir?"

There is something seriously wrong with Quinn's voice, and it takes a moment for Barrett to realize what's going on.

The voice is even, calm, not weak or servile.

"Yes," Barrett says. "I want you to confirm that Marine One will be taking me to Mount Weather sometime after noon."

Heavy and uneasy silence in the room. Another phone starts ringing.

"I'm sorry, sir," Quinn says. "That's not happening."

"The hell it isn't," Barrett snaps back. "I ordered it this morning."

"Yes, you may have, sir, but Marine One is reserved for the president's use only."

Barrett feels heat rising along his face and hands. Quinn adds, "I saw your personally signed resignation letter a few minutes ago. Sir, you're no longer president. You can't take Marine One anywhere."

Barrett says, "Quinn, you'd better get off your ass and call—"

Quinn picks up his ringing phone, and with a stronger voice, says, "Sir, with all due respect, I have a lot of work to do. Please leave."

Barrett feels a wave of humiliation break over him. Voice firm and hard, he says, "Quinn, whatever you might have seen was a fake, a piece of theater, something to get Hannah Abrams out of my office. She was deranged, I fired her, and to make her leave, I wrote that note. I hereby disavow it. I'm still the president of the United States, Quinn, and you will treat me as such."

Quinn shakes his head.

Barrett says, "Quinn Lawrence, I am ordering you, as my chief of staff, to follow my orders and to ensure that Marine One is ready to transport me to Mount Weather within the hour."

Another phone starts to ring.

His chief of staff picks it up, and in a low and steady voice says, "Events are moving rapidly. Decisions need to be made. And you need to leave, sir."

Barrett starts to speak but Quinn cuts him off.

"Now, sir."

CHAPTER 144

CIA DIRECTOR HANNAH Abrams unbuckles her seat harness even before the battered Suburban arrives at the main entrance to Walter Reed National Military Medical Center, and when it screeches to a halt, she grabs Noa's hand and steps out.

Less than twenty minutes to noon.

The exterior of Heaton Pavilion is made of exposed concrete and brick. She walks briskly to the lobby, holding Noa's hand, and scans the interior, finds the lobby desk, where a male Army sergeant and two privates are manning the desk.

She flashes her ID to the sergeant. "Hannah Abrams, CIA director. I need to see the vice president, Suite 71, immediately."

The Army sergeant seems stunned.

"Ah, may I see your ID again?"

She practically shoves it under his nose.

Voice tight, Hannah says, "Sergeant, I need to get

to Suite 71. It's a national emergency. Please don't hold me up."

The sergeant waits, and Hannah says, "Please."

He picks up a phone, drops it, says, "Crap. Hey, Tomas! Over here."

A uniformed security officer comes from his station, and the sergeant says, "Something's up. Take these two women up to Suite 71."

The officer looks suspicious. "Has this been cleared?"

Hannah says, "Yes, cleared all the way."

"All right," the officer says. "Follow me."

Ninety seconds later, off at the seventh floor after taking a private elevator. A guard station is right outside the doors and she barrels right up, shows her ID, and says, "I need to see the vice president. Immediately. This is a national emergency."

One of the two female security officers picks up a phone, speaks low into it, and in a minute an older male physician in a white coat strides down the luxurious hallway, with wood paneling and antique paintings.

"Captain Callaghan, Walter Reed commander," he says. "What's going on here?"

Minute by minute, slipping by.

Once more, she shows her ID. "Captain, is the vice president conscious? Able to hear and talk?"

He frowns. "Well, in a manner of speaking. She's still quite weak. We just removed an implant—"

Hannah holds up her hand. "Captain, I've just come from the White House. Keegan Barrett has resigned his office. The vice president needs to be sworn in."

Callaghan says, "Wait, how come I haven't heard of this?"

"Damn it, Captain, it just happened less than a half hour ago," she yells. "And the damn fool has ordered a cyberattack against China that will knock us back to the nineteenth century! We've got to swear in Vice President Hernandez and stop this war. Now, take me there, or I'll find someone who will."

Captain Callaghan seems to grit his teeth.

"All right, this way."

Hannah follows him, going by one door, and another, Noa right beside her, the poor woman's face pale. They enter a suite that looks like it belongs to a high-end hotel in Manhattan. Two female Secret Service agents stand and seem to recognize both her and the Navy captain.

Vice President Laura Hernandez is sitting up in her bed, face drawn and pale, sipping through a straw from a plastic cup. Three nurses in brightly colored scrubs are hovering around her bed when Hannah barges right in.

"Madam Vice President," Hannah says. "How are you feeling?"

Her voice is a whisper. "Like . . . I got run over . . . by a truck . . . wait, I know. . . . you."

"I'm CIA Director Hannah Abrams, ma'am, and we're in the middle of an emerging national emergency," she says. "President Keegan Barrett has resigned. We need to swear you in."

"What...how...how did that happen...?"

From a large clock in the room, she can see that it's now 11:51 a.m.

"Reasons of ill health, ma'am," she says. "And he's issued a command to commence war against China at twelve hundred hours. We've got to get you sworn in, have you countermand those orders."

She blinks and says, "Not dreaming...am I?"

Hannah shakes her head. "No, Madam Vice President, not a dream. More like a nightmare."

Hernandez coughs and coughs. "Okay...if we have to...I...hope this isn't some...damn joke..."

Hannah feels the weight of history upon her, knowing that this has to go right, no matter the emergency, the lack of time, and she says, "A Bible! We need a Bible!"

More than a century ago, upon the death of President Warren G. Harding, his vice president Calvin Coolidge took the oath of office by kerosene lamp in a Vermont farmhouse, administered by his father, a notary public and justice of the peace. As a cabinet member, Hannah is confident this oath-taking will hold up as well.

One of the nurses ducks out, comes back with

a purse, pulls out a small yet thick leather-bound book. With a slight accent, she says, "It's Spanish, is that okay?"

"It'll work," Hannah says, stepping forward. She hands her phone to Noa and says, "Noa, record this, will you?"

Noa says, weakly, "Director, I'm hurting something bad. I think I'm gonna faint."

Hannah says, "Noa Himel, I'm ordering you not to faint within the next thirty seconds."

She takes the vice president's left hand, with IV tubes running out, and places it on the soft leather cover.

"Madam Vice President, please lift up your right hand, and repeat after me."

A nod.

"I, Laura Hernandez..."

"I...Laura...Hernandez..."

"...solemnly swear that I will faithfully execute the Office of President of the United States..."

The words are low, halting, and slow, but they gain strength with each word. Hannah fights to keep her voice under control as tears come to her eyes.

"...and will to the best of my ability, preserve, protect, and defend the Constitution of the United States. So help me God."

The words are repeated, and at the "So help me God," one of the nurses and one of the Secret

Service agents give the sign of the cross. Hannah says, "Congratulations, Madam President."

"Thank you . . . but this war you say is coming . . . how can I stop it?"

Hannah is stunned.

She looks around the suite.

According to procedure, a backup football with a military officer should be at the vice president's side, containing the important codes that authorize her to issue orders as president.

But they aren't here.

CHAPTER 145

IN THE REAR of his armored Tahoe, General Tucker Wyman, Chairman of the Joint Chiefs of Staff, is running through his mind what he's going to say and how he's going to say it to the president when he roars up to the White House.

In front of him his driver and security officer are murmuring back and forth, even radioing ahead to the lead police cars. Tucker ignores them.

What will he do?

Suppose President Barrett won't see him?

Can he break into his upstairs office? Or the Oval Office, if he's there? And will the Secret Service put up resistance? They are sworn to protect the president, but damn it, he's got to see him, convince him to reverse the order that will set off a chain of worldwide disasters.

There's a sudden braking, a swerve to the left, and the police cruisers up ahead have made a similar turn. Tucker slaps the driver on his right shoulder.

"What the hell is going on? You're going the wrong way! This isn't the way to the White House!"

His security officer turns to him. "Yes, sir, we know. But you want to see the president. The president isn't at the White House. The president is at Walter Reed."

"Is he—"

"No, sir," the security officer replies. "It's she. President Barrett has resigned. Vice President Hernandez has been sworn in."

Tucker sits back, relief coming to him, but checking his watch, he wonders if he'll get there in time.

Like they were sensing his mood, the police cruisers and Tahoe increase their speed, heading north to avert global disaster.

CHAPTER 146

NOA HIMEL KNOWS she should be paying close attention to what's happening in front of her in the Presidential Suite, because in future histories to be written, this room and its participants will be remembered as much as the crowded cabin on Air Force One in Dallas on November 22, 1963, and in the East Wing of the White House on August 9, 1974.

But she hurts too much to care about history.

Her wrist and side are throbbing something awful, and she feels faint and like throwing up on this nice clean floor.

Noa looks to the clock.

It's 11:54 a.m.

Just six minutes left.

In her haze she hears her boss yell, "Where in hell is the goddamn officer with the football?"

One of the nurses says something about how

since the vice president was in a coma, orders from the White House came to remove the football and the accompanying officer.

Noa has a sense of who was behind that move.

What now?

No football.

No communications.

War will break out shortly.

Her fault. If she hadn't been so wound up in getting revenge for her dead cousin, blown to pieces in Beirut, with only bits of bloody clothing, bone, and flesh remaining.

Clothing.

Shouts from outside the room and an Army general and his assistant rush in, the assistant carrying a heavy black satchel, the older general she now recognizes as Tucker Wyman, chairman of the Joint Chiefs of Staff.

"Doug, get the comm set up, get a link to Cybercommand in Fort Meade," he says. "Madam President, we don't have much time."

In her weak voice, she says, "I know...war... about to break out..."

The general says, "Your authorization card? Where is it?"

President Hernandez coughs. "I just woke up an hour ago. How in hell should I know?"

More loud words, the assistant saying, "General Wyman, I've got a secure line."

Her boss says, "But that's worth shit without the biscuit."

It comes to her.

Noa calls out, "Clothing."

The president says, "Can't...we...stop... without it?"

"No," General Wyman says. "We need the codes. We can't do anything without them. Cybercommand has received a duly authorized order from the National Command Authority. They won't step down without the proper codes."

Noa yells, "Clothing, people!"

The room is silent. Everyone swivels to her.

Noa coughs again, her eyesight graying out. "When Reagan was shot in 1981, his authorization code card was missing...it was found in his clothing after they stripped him in the ER and took him to surgery..."

She closes her eyes.

More yells.

A nurse's voice says, "I know where they are!"

Movement, voices, someone uttering a prayer.

Noa forces her eyes open, weakened hands clutching the side of her chair.

A nurse comes back with a large white plastic bag. Her boss and the chairman of the Joint Chiefs of Staff work to tear it open, piling up shoes, slacks, underwear, blouse —

"Here," Hannah says, holding up something.

"No," says General Wyman. "The red one is for the nuclear launch codes. We need the blue one."

Noa spares a glance to the clock.

The black hour and minute hands are too close together.

"Here it is!" someone yells out, and Noa starts to slip.

She hears bits and pieces of what is said next.

"This is General Tucker Wyman, my authorization code is charlie lima five one..."

Another voice, and he says, "Shut the fuck up. The next voice you hear is the National Command Authority, President Hernandez, canceling the offensive cyberattack scheduled for twelve hundred hours."

The new president starts talking into the phone handset that the general is holding. Hannah is holding the sheet of cardboard in front of her.

The woman's voice is stronger and again, Noa just hears bits of her words.

"This is the president. Authorization delta yankee foxtrot three niner..."

Noa's eyes flutter shut.

She's so thirsty, so damn cold.

A bullet wound and practically a knife wound to her wrist.

Just another glamorous day in the CIA.

"That is correct," President Hernandez says.

"Cancel the attack order at once. What? You heard me. At once."

Noa looks to the clock again.

It's five minutes past twelve o'clock.

Too late.

Noa closes her eyes and slips into darkness.

CHAPTER 147

AIR FORCE GENERAL Yvonne Knight of the US Cybercommand is at her desk in the command's operations center at Fort Meade, Maryland, not liking what she's seeing and hearing. She's the duty officer today and with the command staff out in DC or in Las Vegas or San Jose, she is it, she's the one in charge, and that's the problem.

For the past couple of hours she and her staff, grouped around workstations and desks clustered together in this secure basement bunker, have been seeing China deploy both physical and cyber assets this morning, prepping for war.

Sitting next to her is Army Colonel Patrick Coulson, the deputy duty officer today. He's staring at her with anticipation. Less than an hour ago she had received a verified order from the National Command Authority to launch a cyberattack on the People's Republic of China—Case Shanghai—

and now it's two minutes away from 1200 hours, the time she is ordered to issue the go code.

Her fingers trace across the keyboard.

The planned commands and dialogue boxes are up on her computer screen.

Just a few taps of the keyboard and the lawful orders from the National Command Authority—President Barrett Keegan—will be issued.

She waits.

"Ma'am," Colonel Coulson says. "We're one minute away."

"Got it."

For her past year at Cybercommand, she's been working low-level operations that didn't require presidential approval, called "persistent engagement." Poking in and around adversarial computer systems, installing surveillance and malware software where possible, and occasionally kicking a cyber opponent in the balls to let them know the United States isn't a passive victim.

Thirty seconds left.

But this . . . this is an incredible escalation.

Like going from a little border incident involving one or two rifle shots to a full nuclear conflict.

"Ma'am," Colonel Coulson says. "It's twelve hundred hours."

She waits, looking at all the display screens and terminals, and, one by one, the staff here turn their heads to her, to see what's going on.

"Ma'am, we have a lawful order to follow."

Yvonne recalls a time as a child when she took apart the family's laptop and installed extra memory, and Dad's anger was quickly dispersed when he saw how fast and efficient their old computer now was.

That's what Yvonne loves about computers and associated systems.

Enhancing, not destroying.

"General Knight, is there a problem?" her deputy asks. "It's one minute past the go time."

She says, "Get on the horn. I want confirmation."

"Ma'am, you know that's not allowed. That's not procedure. You have to—"

Yvonne snaps, "Screw procedure. I'm not about to incinerate most of the world's internet without additional confirmation. Make the call, Colonel. It's on me. You're just following orders."

His jaw is set and he's about to pick up the phone when it suddenly starts ringing.

"It's coming in for you, General," he says.

Career over, court martial coming, jail time in her future, but so what.

At least she would sleep tonight.

"Answer it," she says.

CHAPTER 148

CIA DIRECTOR HANNAH Abrams is sitting at a round wooden table, covered by a crisp white tablecloth, her hand shaking as she brings up a tumbler of ice water to her mouth.

Across from her is General Tucker Wyman. They are both in the dining room adjacent to President Hernandez's bed. She is back asleep, and Hannah wishes her well, for the press is gathering like a flash mob outside of Walter Reed. It's only going to get worse as the news spreads wider.

The general looks like he's just run a marathon. He's slumped back against his chair, uniform tie undone, face sweaty. Over the years Hannah has had some classified dealings with Tucker, and she's found him to be a rarity, a military officer who hadn't forgotten his roots in the mud and the field with bullets whistling overhead.

"Close," she says. "Very, very close."

Tucker picks up his drink, also a glass of ice water, and says, "That's what Wellington said, right after Waterloo. 'The nearest-run thing you ever saw in your life.' Yeah, the duke knew what he was talking about. Makes you think what he would feel about something like this, a worldwide collapse barely avoided."

"How much time to spare?"

"Maybe seventy, ninety seconds."

"But the clock in the room—"

Tucker sips again. "The duty general in Cyber-command wanted a confirmation before pushing the buttons that would turn the world black. Thank God. Something like that happened back in 1995. Russian military saw an incoming missile that looked like it was heading to Moscow for a decapitation strike. Yeltsin had his nuclear football up and running and was about to issue orders for a nuclear retaliation before the Russians realized the missile was a Norwegian weather rocket. Jesus."

Hannah just sits and refuses to think for a bit, but Tucker interrupts her silence and says, "How's your officer? Himel?"

"Somewhere in here being treated. A tough young lady indeed. She was with me for the past hour, not complaining, with a torn-up wrist and bullet wound in her side."

Tucker says, "Those are the kind of people who save us, aren't they? The ones who go above and beyond. Or ask questions, like that Cybercommand general."

Hannah nods. "You got any news to report?"

He says, "The word of our stand-down got to the right people. Chinese naval and aviation units are returning to port or their bases. But there will be a reckoning, you know. Here and there."

"I'm sure there will be."

Tucker says, "One thing that needs changing is how the president has the authority to commit this nation to a cyber offensive. There are checks and balances on the nuclear side of the table. But not in cyberspace. That will have to be fixed, and soon."

Hannah says, "Funny thing, I just got an email message from their *rezident* here, wanting to know if we could have a face-to-face. Reduce tensions even further. Beyond that, the two of us will be busy the next couple of weeks, talking to the Gang of Eight and others."

"You're right," he says, "but the basic problem remains. An outlaw regime on the other side of the world that keeps on pushing and violating boundaries, treaties, and agreements. We were lucky today. Don't know if we can be that lucky again, down the road."

He raises his glass and she does the same, and with a smile, they clink. "But we won't solve that today, will we."

"You know it."

CHAPTER 149

LIAM GREY IS slipping in and out of consciousness, sometimes forgetting where he is. He sometimes feels like he's having one of those nightmares where you're barely awake and can't move, and other times, like now, he knows exactly where he is.

Trapped under the wreckage of the South African farmhouse and CIA safe house, blown apart earlier—how long, he has no idea—from that RPG-7 round.

Seems like Han Yuanchao grew impatient and wanted to settle things.

Fair enough.

It's night and his lower legs are pinned by beams of wood. There're chunks of brick overhead, allowing him breathing space, and not much else. Both arms are free but so far, all they've been useful for is scratching at an occasional itch.

A couple of times he's heard voices but is pretty sure he's hallucinating.

He's hoping that some neighbor heard the ruckus over here and called the police, but he knows that in some rural parts of South Africa, good citizens retreat to their farms, lock their doors, set their alarms, and ignore what's happening out in the dark night.

Getting thirsty.

Hungry.

Speaking of hungry, what animals out there in the night might be circling this wreckage right now, smelling his blood, deciding it was the right time for a meal? Hyenas? Foxes? Some type of wildcat?

Whatever.

He'll do his best to fight them off as the night drags on.

He's hurting but he's content. He did the best he could, he held off the Chinese and the mercenaries, got Benjamin and Lin out safely, and if it ends tonight, well, at least it won't be in an assisted living facility, eating oatmeal and crapping in his jammies.

Damn, the voices are coming back.

Just like those long nights at the Farm and—

Wait a sec.

They're getting louder.

"Hey!" he yells. "Down here! Hello!"

More voices.

Things up there are being moved.

Voices louder.

The whine of a power tool.

He closes his eyes in relief.

He's getting out.

He'll have to come up with some story to bullshit his way out of here, but that's okay. He'll be free and alive, and that's all that counts.

More voices.

He can feel bits of wood and brick shifting up there. He closes his eyes as flashlight beams illuminate his surroundings, and then a familiar voice comes down to him.

"Mr. Smith," says Han Yuanchao, the Chinese intelligence officer. "So you are alive, after all."

He blinks his eyes. "Sorry to disappoint you."

A shrug. "One gets used to disappointments in our respective careers."

"What now? The traditional bullet to the back of the head?"

The Chinese intelligence officer looks both surprised and insulted. "Why would I do that? The war our current nations were about to commence has been postponed. Your death will serve no purpose."

"Good to hear," Liam says. With his pain and thirst, that news is welcome indeed.

"To continue this hopefully new era of good

feelings, my people will free you, apply necessary medical care, and return you to your consulate," Han says. "Are my terms acceptable?"

"Quite acceptable," Liam says.

CHAPTER 150

TWO WEEKS LATER

CIA DIRECTOR HANNAH Abrams can't help herself from smiling every time she goes back to her office, for that damn government-issued foldout bed is still gone. It was highly improper, but she passed word on to Jean Swantish, her skilled and dedicated deputy director, that the bed should be incinerated in some GSA facility so there's no chance she'll ever see it again.

Waiting for her in her office are Noa Himel and Liam Grey, dressed casually, sitting in chairs in front of her desk, coffee mugs in their hands. Noa looks a lot better than the last time Hannah saw her, while Liam still looks worn down.

Both look nervous, like their careers are ending and jail time is waiting for them.

She says, "How are you both feeling today?"

Noa says, "Much better, ma'am."

Liam says, "Same here."

Hannah says, "Kay Darcy from the *Washington Post* is being released from the hospital today. I'm sure both of you will be happy to hear that."

Nods from her two officers.

Hannah says, "I still don't know how—from her hospital room—she became the first reporter to break news that Keegan Barrett had resigned. Almost like someone had tipped her off."

Liam says, "Don't blame me. I was buried under a South African farmhouse."

Noa says, "Someone fulfilling a promise, I suppose."

Hannah smiles. "I suppose." She takes a breath. "Just so you know, Benjamin Lucas and Chin Lin are still safe in an undisclosed location, with new identifications and legends."

Noa says, "Does he know that Keegan Barrett is his father?"

Hannah shakes her head. "He won't learn that from me. Or either of you. There are a lot more important things going on, like the Department of Defense revising their procedures on how future presidents can order a cyberattack. On this side of the Potomac, I've been working—when she's up for it—with President Hernandez and select members of Congress to make changes to the CIA's charter. The time for it being a private army for the president is over. Now, how about you two?"

Liam says, "You'll have my resignation today."

Noa says, "Mine as well."

"No," Hannah says. "Don't even consider it. Going forward, the Agency is going to need leaders like you—who've been through the fire—to be in a position to make sure what happened here never happens again. I'm ordering you not to resign. Understood?"

Liam, "Yes, Madam Director."

Noa, "Yes, Madam Director."

Hannah stands up. "Good. I'll also make sure your respective teams are left alone. Now, let's get moving. We don't want to be late."

Liam asks, "Late for what?"

She says, "Your comrade in arms, Boyd Morris. He's getting his Memorial Star dedicated in the lobby. At least that's something that can be easily made right."

They both get up from their chairs. She says, "Once I'm convinced that this whole affair is buried where it will never be discovered by future directors or historians, and that both of you will be safe, then I'll have one more thing to do."

"What's that, Director?" Liam asks.

Hannah says, "Isn't it obvious? I need to leave, so you two and the Agency can have a fresh start."

Shocked, Noa says, "You're resigning?"

"At the right time, yes," she says, smiling. "I've already done enough here, don't you think?"

CHAPTER **151**

FOR THE PAST two weeks, Benjamin Lucas has made it a point never to let Chin Lin leave his sight, and except for a medical visit or two, he's been successful. Now they're sitting on a wide farmer's porch at a home on the shore of a nearly deserted lake near the million-plus-acre Boundary Waters Canoe Area Wilderness in Minnesota.

The two of them have spent their time here checking out the three small towns, turning on the utilities, and getting used to their new lives and new names.

But here, in this remote house, it will always be Benjamin and Lin.

Lin looks out over the waters and says, "So quiet. So empty."

"Is that okay?"

Lin squeezes his hand. "It's perfect. I've grown up in cities, have gone to school in cities, and have worked in cities. I will enjoy years of peace and quiet with you, Benjamin."

"Me, too. But your parents?"

A sigh. "My mother will soon pass. And Father . . . he's already gone to me, Benjamin."

He enjoys holding Lin's hand and seeing the lake view with its distant woods and peaks and hearing the loons out there. A long way away from the consulate annex basement. He's doing his best to forget his time in South Africa.

Lin says, "My former employer has a long reach and a longer memory. I'm sure they're looking for me. When that time comes—"

Benjamin quickly says, "I'll protect you."

"You interrupted me," she says. "I was going to say that I will protect you."

He waits for a moment. "How about we agree to protect each other?"

"Deal," Lin says.

CHAPTER 152

IN HIS SMALL guest suite at the Blair House—within walking distance of his previous home—former President Keegan Barrett is listening to his lawyer, Hiram Gloucester, a defense expert from an old-fashioned white shoe law firm in Boston. He's his third lawyer in as many weeks, since he fired the previous two for not showing the proper enthusiasm in defending him.

Hiram's a large man, with a tailored gray pinstripe suit, crisp white shirt with French cuffs, and a Harvard necktie. His hair is snowy white and his skin is deeply tanned. He shakes his head as he gathers his latest notes together and places them in his briefcase.

"Mr. President, I can't—and won't—sugarcoat the legal difficulties you are facing," he says, in a fluid voice that's familiar to millions of viewers on CNN and MSNBC. "The FBI investigation into the alleged financial improprieties against Speaker Washington has revealed a number of criminal forgeries connected to your administration. Speaker Washington has been cleared of these accusations. Your former special assistant, Carlton Pope, has had his fingers into many areas of malfeasance, including hiring private contractors, or mercenaries, to perform illegal acts. Possibly even murder. He is currently in custody of US Marshals, pending his arraignment."

Hiram snaps his briefcase closed. "There is also evidence of you misusing government funds and agencies for your personal use, and I expect hearings on this matter to start in Congress later this summer. Trust me, they will be bipartisan and they will be thorough."

Barrett thinks, *Is this how the gods punish one who rises above the mundane, to protect the country and people he loves?*

"I expect that," he says.

"Well, prepare yourself for more bad news."

"What's that?"

"The FBI investigation into the VR headset that poisoned the vice president," he says. "The company that makes those headsets...not only do they get secret financing from a Chinese company, two members of its board of directors were campaign bundlers who worked very hard to get you elected."

Barrett just stares at the high-priced lawyer sitting before him. He is a guest in the Blair House for as long as he wants, but he knows if he decides to move somewhere else, the FBI will ask him not to leave. It's a very gentlemanly form of house arrest before any charges get formally filed.

Hiram looks embarrassed at what comes next. "As incredible as it might sound, I'm hearing whispers that the FBI and CIA are looking into whether those two board members worked with Chinese intelligence to set up that VR helmet. And whether you had, um, previous knowledge of same. Or involvement."

Barrett closes his eyes for a moment. So close, so very very close he had come to winning his dreams, fulfilling his destiny.

"Now what?" he asks.

Hiram stands up. "We have to look at a temporary insanity defense, Mr. President. That because of your lifestyle as one dedicated to the United States, who worked every day in challenging circumstances, from the military to defense to the CIA, Congress, and the White House...that you eventually snapped. I'm sure I can get a fair number of prominent psychiatrists to testify on your behalf. That your mental abilities weren't at full capacity during your term as president."

Barrett's voice is just above a disbelieved whisper. "Temporary insanity?"

A firm nod. "Mr. President, I don't see any other avenue available to us. I know it sounds distressing, but as your attorney, I advise you that an insanity defense will be our least worst option."

He heads out of the suite. "I'll be back tomorrow, sir. Nine a.m."

Barrett doesn't say a word as the door closes.

Alone, he thinks over what his attorney has just said.

Insane?

He gets up, stumbles into his desk as he goes to the other suite. It has stacks of cardboard boxes of his personal belongings and clothing that left with him that horrid day, when he realized that not only had the presidency slipped from his grasp, but his yearslong plan to take on America's most prominent enemy and secure freedom and safety for his people was gone as well.

Insane.

The newspaper stories, the cable broadcasts, the books upon books written in the future, about him, all saying the same thing, that he was unstable, a paranoid, delusional.

A sickening thought comes to him.

Suppose all the upcoming trials reach the same conclusion, *not guilty by reason of insanity*?

He could spend the rest of his life at Saint Elizabeth's in DC, past home to such luminaries as Charles Guiteau, the assassin of President James

Garfield, the mad poet Ezra Pound, and John Hinckley Jr. There will be sanity hearings in his future, more stories, more coverage, until his name becomes a national and worldwide joke.

No.

He will not allow that to happen.

He starts going through the cardboard boxes of his personal belongings and after fifteen minutes of frantic searching, he finally finds what he's looking for.

Grandfather's Colt .45 pistol, which he managed to smuggle out of the White House.

Keegan Barrett, former president of the United States of America, quickly realizes how cold and oily the muzzle of the pistol is as he puts it into his mouth.

CHAPTER 153

HE PULLS THE trigger, closing his eyes, steeling himself for what comes next.

Nothing.

The trigger won't budge.

The door slams open and the room quickly fills with strong men and women in suits who crowd around him, tough hands taking the pistol away from his weak grip.

He stands there, not saying a word, until a familiar-looking woman strides in, wearing black slacks, jacket, and light-blue blouse.

"Mr. President?" she asks. "Edie Hicks, Deputy Director, FBI. Sorry for this reaction, but we're under orders from President Hernandez to ensure your safety at all times. Both us and the Secret Service."

"My pistol..."

"Disabled, of course. We couldn't have a function-
ing weapon in your presence. But we also realize
it's a valued family heirloom and decided it would
be best to leave it in your possession for now. Without the firing pin and other necessary parts."

Barrett says, "But you've bugged my rooms..."

"Active only when your lawyer isn't present," she
says, smiling. "This may be a concept you haven't
quite understood over the years, but laws are to
be followed. And in your case, we intend to follow
them to a T."

Barrett snaps back. "Laws be damned. I was
acting in the best interests of my country as president of the United States."

She says, "With all due respect, sir, you *were*
the president of the United States. You're now a
former president. And soon, you'll be a criminal
defendant. You should keep that in mind in the
weeks and months ahead, as you prepare your
defense, as you reflect as to how far you came, and
how far you've fallen."

The woman pauses, like she's trying to choose
the right words. She says, "Lucky for all of us, you
fell at the right time. As for now, we'll leave you
alone, sir."

The FBI deputy director leaves the suite, followed
by FBI and Secret Service agents. The door closes
and former president Keegan Barrett is finally and
utterly alone, for the first time in his life.

He slumps down in a chair. The lifelong voice inside telling him that he was special, that his enemies would be defeated, that all of his dreams and desires would come true—that voice has fallen silent.

ABOUT THE AUTHORS

James Patterson is the world's bestselling author. His enduring fictional characters and series include Alex Cross, the Women's Murder Club, Michael Bennett, Maximum Ride, Middle School, and Ali Cross, along with such acclaimed works of narrative nonfiction as *Walk in My Combat Boots*, *E.R. Nurses*, and his autobiography, *James Patterson by James Patterson*. Bill Clinton (*The President Is Missing*) and Dolly Parton (*Run, Rose, Run*) are among his notable literary collaborators. For his prodigious imagination and championship of literacy in America, Patterson was awarded the 2019 National Humanities Medal. The National Book Foundation presented him with the Literarian Award for Outstanding Service to the American Literary Community, and he is also the recipient of an Edgar Award and nine Emmy Awards. He lives in Florida with his family.

*   *   *

Brendan DuBois is the award-winning author of twenty-two novels and more than one hundred seventy short stories, garnering him three Shamus Awards from the Private Eye Writers of America. He is also a *Jeopardy!* game show champion.